the Philadelphian

Philadelphian
the

50th Anniversary Edition

Richard Powell

Plexus Publishing, Inc.
Medford, New Jersey

First printing, 2006

Published by:
Plexus Publishing Inc.
143 Old Marlton Pike
Medford, NJ 08055

Originally published in 1956 by Charles Scribner's Sons, New York

Library of Congress Cataloging-in-Publication Data

Powell, Richard, 1908-1999
  The Philadelphian / Richard Powell.
    p. cm.
  ISBN-13: 978-0-937548-62-2 ISBN-10: 0-937548-62-6 (hard)
  ISBN-13: 978-0-937548-64-6 ISBN-10: 0-937548-64-2 (soft)
  1. Philadelphia (Pa.)--Fiction. I. Title.
  PS3531.O966P45 2006
  813'.52--dc22

                                                              2006030133

Printed and bound in the United States of America.

President and CEO: Thomas H. Hogan, Sr.
Editor-in-Chief and Publisher: John B. Bryans
Managing Editor: Amy M. Reeve
VP Graphics and Production: M. Heide Dengler
Book and Cover Designer: Lisa Boccadutre
Proofreader: Lisa Schaad
Sales Manager: Pat Palatucci
Marketing Coordinator: Rob Colding

The publisher wishes to express its deepest appreciation to Blaine Novak for support and encouragement beyond what was asked or expected.

FOR MARIAN

Who didn't understand

PHILADELPHIA

THE PEOPLE AND events in this story are imaginary. I have, however, used some names which have been well-known in Philadelphia history for a few of my characters. The names given to my characters are in no way intended to, and to the best of my knowledge, after investigation, do not identify any living person as being involved or a participant in any actual or supposed event or series of events similar to those described in this book. If there is any resemblance between my characters and actual people it is entirely coincidental and unintended. A check of many types of directories, including local telephone directories, the Social Register, Who's Who and Poor's Register of Directors and Executives indicates that the full names of these imaginary people do not match any of the names listed therein.

On the other hand, any resemblance between the Philadelphia way of life, and the way of life depicted in this book, is intentional.

—R.P.

Foreword to the
50th Anniversary Edition

IT WAS 1958 and I was an eager, brash twenty-five-year-old actor. Fresh from a stint as a drill instructor in the military and a rash of B movies, I was offered the part of Chet Gwynne in Warner Bros.'s "The Young Philadelphians." Based on Richard Powell's novel, *The Philadelphian,* the film gave me the opportunity to work with Paul Newman in a studio picture and was the breakthrough I had been waiting for. In the book I discovered a powerful and timeless story, one that I related to personally.

The role of Chet Gwynne led me on a journey to seek out what was at the root of this tragic character. Returning from war an injured veteran, Chet plummets from millionaire's mile to skid row: a ravaged alcoholic standing trial for murder. To understand this depth of despair, I spent a night on skid row in Los Angeles, experiencing a taste of rock bottom firsthand. In the studio, when the director yelled action, all the fear and pain and loss that I felt from the men and women of skid row poured out of me and into Chet Gwynne. Apparently audiences responded, because critical acclaim followed from the motion picture academy and the Hollywood foreign press, with best supporting actor nominations for the Oscar and the Golden Globe. It was a time I'll never forget.

The Philadelphian helped to launch my career in film and television, and I have reflected on it many times over the years. At long last, the book is back in print.

—Robert Vaughn
(with appreciation
to Caitlin Vaughn)

A Daughter's Reflections on Richard Powell and The Philadelphian

by Dorothy Powell Quigley
with Dorothea Allen O'Shea

ON JANUARY 7, 1957, *The Philadelphian* by Richard Powell hit the bookstores with a bang and exploded like fireworks to the top of the national bestseller lists. Philadelphia was abuzz and aglow with its very own story, while in New York, publisher Charles Scribner's Sons was in happy fits trying to get out sufficient copies to meet demand.

I was 17 years old at the time, and this suddenly famous author was "Dad" who went off to work during the day and typed all night. My 19-year-old brother Steve and I had to be very, very quiet whenever he was in his den, and thanks to our good behavior he'd already succeeded in having 11 books published. Neither Steve nor I had read a one of them. He was our father: What could he possibly have written that would interest us?

I've always thought my parents were a handsome couple. He was 6'3", lanky, and imposing, while Mother was statuesque and serene. They matched each other in humor and wit and, together, gave our young lives a sense of security and quiet comfort. The only thing noisy in our house was me; at least, that's what the neighbors said.

Mother and Dad met while at college, he at Princeton, she at Vassar. Dad was dating another Vassar girl at the time. Eventually he proposed to the nicer of the two (in writing, no less!) and, in 1932, Marian Carleton Roberts of Cleveland, Ohio, moved to Philadelphia.

Dad was a reporter for the *Philadelphia Evening Ledger* in those years, and in his off hours he wrote fiction. This allowed little time for socializing but Mother rarely complained.

Out of the blue in 1936, three of my father's stories were bought by three different magazines, each paying $400. The $20-a-week-newsman had become an author! Many years later when women oohed and aahed and said how wonderful for Mother to be married to a man like my dad, she wrote to a friend, "I haven't wrung any of their necks yet, and mostly, in fact, it really *is* wonderful."

The idea for a story about Philadelphia took root in those early days of the marriage. Mother questioned and sometimes scoffed at what she considered the odd traditions and customs of the city. Her "discussions" with Dad on the subject led him to evaluate ideas and attitudes that as a seventh-generation Philadelphian he had always taken for granted. He began to notice the often-subtle ways that Philadelphians were different from, say, Bostonians or New Yorkers, and the "why" of this piqued his curiosity.

In the 1950s Dad became a vice president of the prestigious advertising agency N. W. Ayer. He no longer depended on writing to pay the bills and, thus, he began at long last to write the novel that had been in his head for 25 years. It took him two years to complete his manuscript. "When I finished it," he wrote, "I felt I had already received a very large reward for my work because I had done the best job I could, even if nobody ever bought it."

***

THE PHILADELPHIAN WAS dedicated to my mother. Dad originally wrote, "For Marian, who doesn't like Philadelphia." Mother asked for a minor revision "to make it easier for me to go on living in the city." The resulting dedication—as it is reproduced in this edition—was, "For Marian, who didn't understand Philadelphia."

Mother, by the way, had proved several years earlier that she knew something about putting one word in front of another: In 1950 she entered a *Cosmopolitan* contest that required contestants to explain why they liked the magazine in 25 words or less. She won the Grand Prize—a 1951 Cadillac convertible. Mother and Dad drove this car across the country, and the many stops between Philadelphia and Los Angeles provided inspiration for Dad's 1953 mystery, *Say It with Bullets,* which has recently been reprinted. But that's another story.

The Philadelphian was adapted as the 1959 movie "The Young Philadelphians," starring Paul Newman, Barbara Rush, and Robert Vaughn. When the film premiered in Philadelphia that May, I was away at college with senior exams coming up and Dad chose not to bring me home a week early. I was chagrined at the time, but I understood that his priority was for me to graduate. We were at our summer home in Brant Beach, New Jersey, one week after graduation when Dad folded up his newspaper and said, "Dorothy, we're going to the movies." The local theater was showing the film! As we stood in line (me wondering why we couldn't go right to the front) it struck me for the first time that Dad was "famous." I wanted to shout that my Dad had written the book, but I held my tongue for his sake. Later, when we left the theater, Dad put his arm around me and confided that this was the first time he'd really seen the movie—he'd been too busy and distracted to enjoy it at the premiere.

The Philadelphian was the first of four of my father's books that made it to the big screen in one form or another. His next novel was *Pioneer, Go Home!* in 1959, and this time there were several movie offers even before the book went to press. Dad said this was "beyond my wildest dreams" and, ironically, the motion picture was released as "Follow that Dream." While the films did not always meet with his approval ("The Young Philadelphians" did), he got a kick out of seeing them made.

In 1959, Mother and Dad "retired" to Fort Myers, Florida, where Mother's dream house was built on the Caloosahatchee River, and Dad fished, played bridge, and wrote several more novels. Among these were *The Soldier, I Take This Land, Daily and Sunday, Don Quixote USA, Tickets to the Devil,* and *Whom the Gods Would Destroy.*

Mother died in 1979. Dad wrote no more books after that.

Dad was remarried to Margaret Cooper and led an active and happy life for 20 years more. On December 8, 1999, two days after being top scorer at the local Life Master bridge game, he died at the age of 91. He is survived by his wife, Margaret, two children, and 10 grandchildren.

Over the years, when people commented to Dad about his success as a best-selling author, he would often respond, "I just like to write." Certainly his life as a writer was a successful one, but for those of us who knew him, humility, kindness, and compassion stand as equal parts of his legacy.

In the novel *I Take This Land,* Dad wrote of one of his characters, "His life was a story of people being magnificently human, wise and foolish, humble and proud, gentle and violent, triumphant and tragic." Those words ring true in respect to my father, and I used the quote to eulogize him in 1999. If Dad were alive today he would be thrilled to see this 50th anniversary edition of *The Philadelphian*—his personal favorite among his 19 novels—and to know that it continues to be read and enjoyed.

Preface to the 50th Anniversary Edition: "The Personality of Philadelphia"

by Richard Powell

AN AUTHOR IS on relatively safe ground when he uses a setting which is either vague, or invented, or foreign. In such cases, although a few experts may charge him with errors or poor craftsmanship in developing the setting, his neighbors will not know the difference. But when the author picks his hometown as the setting for his book each and every one of his neighbors automatically and rightly becomes an expert critic. So if the author does a bad job in describing his hometown, he had better be prepared to leave quickly in the dark of night, unless of course he has done such a dull job that nobody is interested in reading it. However, fools and authors rush in where angels fear to tread, and so from time to time some of us write about our hometowns.

My knowledge of Philadelphia comes from being born here, getting most of my education here, and doing most of my work here. On one side I'm a seventh generation Philadelphian or maybe even worse ... I haven't tried to check back any further.

This Philadelphia background, however, only gave me part of the knowledge which I needed in order to write *The Philadelphian*. Left to myself, I would have accepted the city's traditions and beliefs and customs without question. They would have seemed so normal and natural to me that I would not have thought of them as material for a novel. But I was not left to myself. In 1932 I married a girl from Cleveland who proceeded to question each and every one of my accepted ideas about Philadelphia.

The book is dedicated to her with these words: "For Marian, who didn't understand Philadelphia." I might just as honestly have dedicated it to the author, who originally didn't understand Philadelphia either. In order to defend my beloved city against my wife's unprincipled attack, I had to learn how to look at the city objectively. This book is the result of many years of hot and heavy family argument. And, for once at least, a husband manages to get in the last word in an argument with his wife. In this book, in fact, I get in 150,000 last words.

As an author, I feel fortunate in having been born and raised in Philadelphia. My city has a personality. It is a strong one, and it is out of strong personalities that authors dig up the material for novels.

Most American cities are merely oversized housing developments with no personalities of their own. The result is that these cities produce almost nothing in the way of literature. Every important book grows out of the author's reaction to his environment. If it has no personality, the writer has nothing to react with or against.

Of the major cities of the United States, only nine have distinct and individual personalities. These are New York, Chicago, Philadelphia, Boston, Los Angeles, San Francisco, New Orleans, Charleston, and Savannah. The rest may be nice housing developments, but as far as the stimulation of writers is concerned, all you can say is thank heaven for the American small town. Our small towns and small cities often have very strong personalities. For example, we are in debt to Sauk Center, Minnesota, for Sinclair Lewis's *Main Street,* and to Asheville, North Carolina, for Thomas Wolfe's *Look Homeward, Angel.*

In order to stimulate writers, the personality of a city or town need not be lovable. In fact, of the nine major cities which have personalities, only San Francisco has a really nice one. The other eight cities often annoy people who have not had the good fortune of being born there. I hope I am not revealing anything top secret when I say that, to many outsiders, Philadelphia and Boston have highly irritating personalities. To many outsiders, these two cities are rather like a pair of sheltered maiden ladies who have become crotchety and eccentric but who happen to be awfully well-heeled.

New York, of course, has a very strong personality. Naturally, as a good Philadelphian, I dislike the place. But one must admit that, like Shakespeare's Cleopatra, "Age cannot wither her, nor custom stale her infinite variety."

Here is a quick review of the personality or lack of personality of other major American cities:

Chicago—Yes, it has personality. It's the neighborhood big shot of the Midwest.

Detroit—No personality. It's just the hot-rod kid of American cities.

Los Angeles—Lots of personality, but of kinds that delight a psychiatrist.

Baltimore—No more personality than one of its own Chincoteague oysters, and just about as retiring.

Cleveland, St. Louis, Cincinnati, Kansas City, Columbus, and Indianapolis—These are the great faceless cities of the Midwest, representing nothing more than the lowest common denominator of many rather interesting small towns.

Pittsburgh—It has no personality. It's merely a pro football player who struck it rich.

Washington—It's not really a city at all. It's just a big international motel whose guests only sign in for overnight.

Milwaukee—A freckle-faced kid peering wistfully through a knothole at the Milwaukee Braves.

Seattle, Rochester (New York), Portland (Oregon), Buffalo, and Minneapolis—All you can say about these is that the name is familiar but you can't place the face.

San Francisco—The most delightful personality of any American city: cultured without being snobbish, cosmopolitan without seeming foreign.

New Orleans—Like Paris, it is one of the few cities with sex appeal. It's a sort of Creole Marilyn Monroe.

Newark and Jersey City—These are nothing but a couple of dead-end kids.

Houston, Dallas, and Fort Worth—They merely pretend to have strong personalities, in the manner of cowboys whooping it up on Saturday night.

Charleston and Savannah—These are lovely old ladies, who sometimes get a bit tiresome in talking about the men who courted them when they were young.

Miami—Just a chromium-plated diner at a crossroads.

Atlanta—It has a split personality, because it can't decide whether to play the role of Scarlett O'Hara or that of Perle Mesta.

The fact that a city has a strong personality does not necessarily mean that it will produce many authors and many books. As we have noted, Philadelphia has a strong personality. Nonetheless it is a fact that Philadelphia, while producing many writers over the years since Ben Franklin wrote his *Poor Richard's Almanac* and his autobiography, has been the subject of very few books. A good illustration of this is the classic novel *The Virginian,* by Owen Wister, which laid the groundwork for the western novel. Owen Wister was a Philadelphian. So what did he write about? He wrote about a Virginian in Wyoming. In modern days such Philadelphia authors as Christopher Morley and Alexander Woollcott moved to New York to carry on their writing careers. The late Joseph Hergesheimer, who was born and educated in Philadelphia, wrote about Java and Palm Beach, while Philadelphia-educated James Michener writes about the South Pacific, the Orient, and Hungary.

Why is it that, in the past, Philadelphia authors seldom found anything worth writing about in their native city? For one thing, they failed to see anything remarkable in the traditions and beliefs and the social structure here. If I may paraphrase the old saying about not being able to see the forest for the trees, I think that, in the past, authors have not been able to see Philadelphia for the Philadelphians.

An even more important reason is that, in the past, Philadelphians were quite contented with their city. Complacency of this type had a bad effect on Philadelphia writers. Either they moved elsewhere and picked more interesting subjects than Philadelphia to write about, or else they stayed here and in their turn became contented and complacent. Where you have upheaval and discontent, you have authors writing books. Often, in the past, the Philadelphia author became so contented that he stopped being an author.

In recent years, however, there has been a great change in Philadelphia. Many people became discontented with what we used to regard as our

Promised Land. They realized that a lot of the promises had never been kept, and they set out to make some of those promises come true. Anybody who looks around Philadelphia and sees Penn Center, the Mall projects, the new airport, the Schuylkill Expressway, the new City Charter, the start of work on the $100,000,000 Food Distribution Center, the plans to save and develop the old Society Hill section, and the memorial to the Unknown Soldiers of the Revolution in Washington Square, can hardly fail to realize that there have been great changes. I have been fortunate, as an author, in being able to see some of these changes first-hand in working with Harry Batten and the Greater Philadelphia Movement, the moving force behind many of these projects.

This is no longer the city of the tattered old joke about rolling up the sidewalks at nine o'clock every night. And these physical changes have been matched by changes in thought and feeling. A very exciting Renaissance is taking place here. And, as a natural result, Philadelphia has become an exciting subject to write about.

It has made me very happy to have been able, in my book, to contribute in some small way to this revived interest in our city. Everybody knows that Philadelphia has a great past. There is now no doubt at all that Philadelphia will also have a great future.

From a talk given by Richard Powell on May 15, 1957 at the
Annual Dinner of the Twenty-Five Year Club of N. W. Ayer & Son
(Previously unpublished and special to this 50th Anniversary Edition)

1

HE CAME SLOWLY downstairs from the bedroom, with the pulse of blood hammering inside his skull like a rivet gun. He had always trained himself, however, not to let things that hurt him show on the outside. So he kept a smile clamped on his face as he went into the library of his home. He lowered himself into the desk chair with a sigh of relief. A man felt better at his own desk. It was like a fort protecting you from a strange and sometimes hostile world. If you were fighting another man, it was always a mistake to carry the attack into his office. Get him into yours, in front of your desk, where he wouldn't feel sure of himself.

But this time his opponent was not a man. It was a woman, and women felt just as much at home fighting a man across a desk as across a bed.

The pounding in his head made him dizzy, and for a moment his thoughts whirled in every direction like autumn leaves in a gale. He had to work hard to sweep them back into neat piles. He started slowly, one leaf at a time. His name was Anthony Judson Lawrence and he was forty-two years old. He had come into the library to make a decision. He had made a number of important decisions in his life, and judging by the results he had made them carefully and well. But this one would be the most important of all.

When you were a lawyer, as he was, you did not make snap decisions. You looked up the law and the precedents that bore on the case. He would do that now before trying his case and reaching a decision. There were ninety-nine years of precedents, from 1857 to 1956, which had to be studied. He had been building his whole life on these precedents, and adding new ones to the record. He unlocked a drawer of the desk and took out a photograph in an old German silver frame.

There they were, the three wonderful and rather frightening women who had created many of those precedents. His great-grandmother and grandmother were standing like sentries behind a chair. His mother was seated on it with a baby on her lap. For a family picture it was unusual because no one was looking at the camera. The three women were staring at the baby, who was looking up with wide eyes as if asking what they wanted of him. The baby's name was Anthony Judson Lawrence.

As he studied the photograph now he could feel the blood of the three women pulsing through his body and their ideas marching through his head. It was queer to feel all that so vividly and yet to know so little about the women in the picture. He knew what their hopes and beliefs had been. But he didn't know why they had clung to certain hopes and followed certain beliefs. It was like reading a judge's decision, and knowing you ought to abide by it, without having a chance to look at the testimony that came before the decision. He wished he could have read the testimony of their lives, because it would have helped him now ...

MARGARET

1857–1860

2

MARGARET O'DONNELL came to Philadelphia from Ireland in the spring of 1857. She was a quiet girl, waiting for life with soft parted lips and eyes full of dreams. She did not stay up on deck with the other steerage passengers when the morning mist lifted, and the brig *Evelyn* trimmed her yards to the southerly breeze and caught the flood tide up the Delaware. Instead, she got an empty bucket and carried it to one of the deckhands.

She smiled and said, "Could you now be getting me some water?"

"What's the matter with the water in the cask?" he said.

"It's not for drinking that I want it. It's to wash meself."

"I don't hold with a lot of washing," the deckhand said. "It saps a man, I figger. But maybe women are different." He tied a line around the handle of the bucket and lowered it overside and brought it up filled. He paused a moment to let his glance move slowly down her body. "Are you washing all over?" he asked softly.

She grabbed the bucket angrily from him and hurried down the companionway. Below decks, the steerage was partitioned into two big cabins, one for men and one for women and small children. She caught her breath at the smell when she entered the women's cabin, with its long tiers of bunks along each side. The brig had made a good passage from Liverpool, twenty days, and there had been no storms or sickness. But even so, when you crammed fifty women and small children into steerage for twenty days, with the portholes clamped shut, you brewed a smell that made the bogs of Ireland seem like French perfume.

No one was in the cabin, for which she was thankful. Twice during the voyage she had tried to clean herself properly, using a bucket of sea water, but she had had to give up. The other girls giggled, and peered at her as if they didn't have bodies of their own, and the older women made loud comments about how you could always tell a hussy. She unbuttoned the high-necked wool dress and stepped out of it, and took off the layers of cotton shift and petticoats and bloomers, and stood bare as a peeled potato. Beams of light striking in through the opened portholes polished the curves of her body: the strong square shoulders, the forward thrust of young breasts, the small waist and rounded hips, the sturdy legs and good solid ankles. She poked thoughtfully at her stomach and wished she could do something about it. Her stomach curved in so you could see the pointed hip bones jutting against the tight skin. It would be much better to have a nice plump stomach, but of course few people in Ireland could boast of plump stomachs since the potato blight began back in '45.

She got out a cotton petticoat, ragged but clean, which she had been saving for this, and tore it into pieces and dampened one of them in the bucket and began scrubbing herself. For once she didn't mind the sting of the lye in the cake of yellow soap. The water itself, from the big river, felt soft as a caress. Finally she sat on the edge of the bunk and worked at cleaning her feet and in between the toes. Probably she could never hope to get the bottoms of her feet white, after a lifetime of padding around on the hard packed dirt floor of the cottage, but they looked fairly good.

When she had dried herself, she untied the old shawl that held all her belongings. A few of the girls in steerage had those fine bags made from carpeting, and it was even rumored that some of the older women had real trunks in one of the cargo holds, but a shawl did well if that was what you had to use. She took out her one set of clean linen undergarments and slipped into them, taking time to enjoy the sleek feel as they slid over her body. Her older sister, back in Ireland, had jabbered endlessly about how it was putting on airs to waste good shillings on linen cloth to make into things to wear under your dress, where nobody would ever see them ... she hoped nobody ever would, her sister said grimly. But Margaret O'Donnell had gone stubbornly ahead and bought the material and made it into undergarments, using the neatest, smallest stitches of anybody in County Clare. Over the linen she put on the clean cotton dress, with its dark blue color that went nicely with the blue of her eyes. She put the wool shawl over her shoulders and pinned the ends together in front with the pewter buckle. Then she bundled everything else into the old shawl and tied it and climbed back up on deck. No matter how long it took to reach Philadelphia, she was never going below again.

They had entered the river the day before and were far upstream now. To port and starboard the low green shores were still far apart, though. She wouldn't doubt you could put all the rivers in Ireland into the Delaware and still have room to spare. She tilted her head back and watched the square sails high on the masts dig through the sky like big white plows.

"Here's a girl who's looking mighty pert today," a voice said.

She looked down and smiled at the man who had spoken. He was a very important man who was part of the ship's company and was called a supercargo, whatever that might be. "It's a fine thing to be young and sailing up to Philadelphia," she said. "How soon would we be getting there?"

He squinted up at the topsails. "An hour, if the wind holds. Whoever's meeting you won't have long to wait."

"Oh, there's nobody to meet me."

"But you've got a place to go?"

"Why, of course," she said, laughing. "I'm going to Philadelphia."

"It's a big city, girl. More than half a million people."

"Would that be bigger than Dublin?"

"You could drop Dublin in Philadelphia and it would be lost."

"Oh no, not Dublin. The people in Dublin are so loud and full of quarrels you could never make them stay lost anywhere."

He chuckled. "You may be right. But if you have no friends here and nobody sent for you, where's your family?"

"There isn't much left of the O'Donnells," she said. "Last fall when the crop failed again me father just lay down and died. Have you ever seen the potatoes when they go bad in the field? Instead of lovely plump things in their brown skins you dig up chunks like coals from the devil's own furnace. Me mother passed on three years back. So that just left me sister Sheila and me. It's a bad thing, the famine. Twelve years of it, now, and the trouble it's brought Ireland."

"Your sister didn't come?"

"She's older than me. And there was a man down the lane thought he could do something with our field, if Sheila had a mind to bring it as a dowry and get wed to him. So we sold the cottage, and little enough it brought, and I took the money from that and here I am."

"You and a hundred thousand others," he said. "It beats me how you can chance it. All of you fresh as daisies from the field and just about as dumb. What will you do, girl? Work in the weaving mills?"

"Not me," she said proudly. "I'm going to work in a fine house for the best people."

"You'll just walk into a big house and say here I am, will you? The streets are full of girls like you looking for housework. They—" He stopped and took a careful look at her, at the smoky black hair with lights in it like a peat fire, at the dark blue eyes and at the skin as clear as new cream. "Maybe not just like you," he said finally. "Not as pretty. But you may find that's not a help. Why did you pick Philadelphia and not New York?"

"It was a lucky thing. It was in Liverpool and I had not made up me mind, and this man in the office showed me a picture of Philadelphia. And there were all those straight streets and fine houses and church steeples everywhere—"

"Most of the steeples," he said sharply, "are Protestant."

"We have Protestants in the Old Country too."

"He didn't tell you about the riots against the Irish, did he? Or about the Native American Party? Or about the notices in the papers that say—here, let me read you some." He pulled a folded newspaper from his pocket and opened it. "Listen to this," he said. "Respectable girl for chambermaid. Protestant only ... Girl for housework. Must have city references and be Protestant. How does that sound to you?"

She reached out and stroked the newspaper. "Would it really be a paper from the city itself?" she asked.

"Didn't listen to a word I said, did you? Yes, it's the *Public Ledger*. The pilot brought it aboard when he met us down in Delaware Bay. It's only four days old. Like to read it?"

She said wistfully, "There would be too many big words for me."

"Sure, I forgot. None of you can read. How will you go about finding work when you land?"

"I will ask where to go."

"Pretty girls who wander around a port asking questions don't always get the right answers. Look, there are a couple of employment agencies listed here. One isn't far from where we dock. I'll ask the pilot to take you there. He's got a couple of girls your own age. Mind now, don't wander off alone."

She promised, and thanked him. The talk gave her a warm glow inside, like the comfort of strong black tea on a winter morning. She had known all along, no matter what anybody said, that wonderful things were going to happen to her in this new city. Now right at the start a pilot, a very great man in a bowler hat and with a gold chain across his vest, was going to lead her into the city just as carefully as he would take a ship upriver with its precious cargo.

The breeze was so gentle that the ship seemed to be anchored with the land floating downstream past them. She watched breathlessly as the city came to them: first a few scattered farms, then little clumps of houses, and finally the mass of slate roofs and brick chimneys and steeples sweeping past on the shore like a marching army under its banners of white smoke. Mind you that: white smoke! In Ireland and over Liverpool smoke from chimneys was nearly always black. A man nearby was explaining the smoke to friends and saying it was because of the hard coal in Pennsylvania. Margaret O'Donnell wished she had not heard him. For some reason people insisted on explaining away magic things, like white smoke from chimneys. And, now that she thought about it, the smoke was not really white but more a pale blue. She would rather have thought it white and not understood the reason for it.

Upstream an important little boat came bustling out from between the land and an island, puffing steam like a fat man hurrying on a cold morning, and came down to them and made a great thing of taking them in tow. It swung them toward docks where tall masts almost fenced away the city. She could hear the city now, the noise of iron wheels over cobblestones, the cries of people on shore, the soft liquid note of a bell marking the hour. Thick ropes whirled from the ship to dock and men snubbed them on pilings and pulled them tight, and to Margaret O'Donnell it was as if every rope had been tied to her and was linking her forever with this shining new place.

3

THERE WERE SO MANY things to see that she kept lagging behind the pilot and having to run a little to catch up. Take the horses, now. She had not thought there were so many in the world. They were everywhere, hauling carts and drays, pulling carriages and omnibuses. Their droppings lay neglected in the streets, and that proved how rich the people must be. In Ireland people would have come out to collect the droppings and put them on fields to help the crops.

"Well, miss," the pilot said, "here you are. This is Third Street. That there is Spruce. Looks like this is the place you want. Good luck to you." He hurried off quickly, as if he liked to be rid of all responsibility once he had steered a ship or person to the right dock.

She paused a moment, before going into the employment office, to admire a carriage and pair waiting at the curb. The horses were matched chestnuts, and their coats glowed like polished wood in the May sunshine. The carriage had black leather seats and yellow-spoked wheels and brass lamps shined enough to make you blink. A solemn looking young coachman was standing by the heads of the horses, pretending not to notice her, but she saw him peeking from the corners of his eyes. She gave him a smile that turned his face red, and went into the employment agency.

One side of the big bare room held a bench crowded with girls. They looked her up and down hunting for things they didn't like, and had no trouble finding them. Across the room was a desk, and a woman with a face you could have used to split firewood.

Margaret O'Donnell went up to her and said, "Please, ma'am, it's looking for housework I am."

"Another one," the woman said tonelessly. "Name?"

"Margaret O'Donnell."

"Age and address?"

"Sixteen. I have no address yet because I only landed this morning and—"

One of the girls on the bench behind her said, "Just off the boat," and the whole lot of them began giggling.

"Quiet, please," the woman snapped. "We have a customer in the master's office. Well now, Maggie—"

"Please, ma'am, it's Margaret, not Maggie."

"You'll be Maggie and like it."

"Yes, ma'am," she said, although she did not like it and did not intend to be called by any such ugly name.

"I suppose you're like all the rest. Can't cook, can't sew, can't clean."

"But I can, ma'am."

"That's as may be. Let's see how different from the others you are. There's a situation in the country, a very nice place, only twenty miles out. Do you want it? Three dollars a month, and found."

"I would rather be in the city."

"We won't even charge you the usual fee. How about that?"

"Please, I would rather stay in the city."

The woman sniffed angrily. "You're no different from the rest. Very well. You can wait or not, as you please. Find yourself a place on the bench if they'll make room for you."

As Margaret turned toward the bench, she saw that the other girls were not going to make room for her. There was a quick spreading of skirts, and whatever space there had been on the bench vanished. They faced her in a cold hostile row.

That was the moment when the door of the inner office opened and a soft clear voice said, "I'm sorry, but none of them will do. So I will have to try elsewhere."

Margaret looked at the lady who had spoken, and knew at once that the lady and the carriage outside belonged together. Just as the carriage and pair were spotless and perfect, so was the lady, from her black bonnet down to the hem of the black silk dress which she held up daintily from the floor. She was likely in her forties, but she had either kept her figure wonderfully well or was wearing one of those things they called corsets. Without pausing to think, Margaret dropped her bundle and hurried forward and said breathlessly, "Please, ma'am, I can cook and sew and clean and—"

The man who had been in the office said sharply, "Here, girl, don't run up to Mrs. Clayton that way without being invited."

"Let her alone," the lady said, tilting her head on one side and studying Margaret. "You didn't show me this one, did you?"

The woman at the desk said, "She just came in. And Mrs. Clayton, *she's just off the boat!*"

"And what would be wrong with being just off the boat?" Margaret said. "Sure and how else would anybody get here?"

"Looking for a situation, are you?" Mrs. Clayton asked.

"Please, ma'am, I don't know what a situation is. I just want to work for you."

Mrs. Clayton smiled. "Everybody has become so high-toned nowadays that they don't talk about work any more. They talk about situations, and hope they can get one that doesn't involve work."

"I don't mind work," Margaret said.

Mrs. Clayton said to the man, "I'd like to talk to her alone in your office, if I may."

Anything Mrs. Clayton wanted was all right, and presently Margaret was alone with her in the office, answering questions. Anybody else might have flustered her with so many questions about where she came from and why, but Mrs. Clayton had a nice easy manner that put her at ease. Mrs. Clayton looked at her hands and teeth, and had her walk back and forth across the room and said pleasantly that it was nice to see a girl who didn't trip over her own feet.

"Now about the sewing," Mrs. Clayton said. "Is it really true that you can sew?"

"Oh yes, ma'am," Margaret said. "Let me show you." Again without thinking, she lifted her skirt to show the fine stitches she had put into the linen petticoat.

Mrs. Clayton laughed gently.

Margaret's face stung to a surge of blood and she gasped, "I shouldn't have done that, should I? I beg your pardon, ma'am."

"That's all right. But remember that in Philadelphia skirts are kept in place. I think you'll do, Maggie."

Even if it cost her the chance, she had to say this. "Please, ma'am, could you call me Margaret?"

For the length of a heartbeat Mrs. Clayton seemed to hesitate, studying her. "Very well, Margaret," she said at last. "You will get the usual three dollars a month, and uniforms. From time to time there may be some clothes of mine you may have. Although," she added, with a light sigh, "I don't doubt but that you'll have to take them in. Now you will have to pay the people here a dollar and a half for their services, little as they were. Do you have some money?"

"One pound, eleven shillings and tuppence. Would that be enough?"

"More than enough. Give the man six shillings, and meet me outside at my carriage."

Margaret paid her fee, and swept out grandly past the bench full of bitter-faced girls. Mrs. Clayton was in the carriage and the young coachman was already upon his box.

"Margaret," Mrs. Clayton said, "this is our coachman, George Symes. George, this is our new maid, Margaret O'Donnell."

The solemn young man touched a finger to his top hat, and looked at her as if he wouldn't mind another of her smiles. Margaret nodded to him coolly. If they were going to know each other, he could start working for those smiles.

So that was how Margaret came to the home of the Logan Claytons in Philadelphia, riding in a carriage like a princess and with the pattern of her future already taking form. And even if she had known what the pattern was to be, it was doubtful that she would have jumped from the carriage to run away from that future.

4

THE CLAYTONS LIVED in a three-story brick house on Fourth Street near Locust. Never for one moment did Margaret doubt that it was the finest house in the city. Of course you could find envious people who would try to make you dissatisfied with the house, but Margaret quickly learned how to handle them. She picked up that knowledge one afternoon when Mrs. Clayton was giving a tea for friends, and Margaret was carefully handing around the delicate cups and saucers.

One of the friends said to Mrs. Clayton, "My dear, don't you ever find yourself longing for a new house? One of those lovely brownstone mansions with gas lighting built right into it?"

"The Claytons," Mrs. Clayton said, "have lived here for three generations."

"I'm not sure you answered my question," the other lady said.

"Logan always says," Mrs. Clayton said quietly, "that we will consider these new things after they have proved themselves."

"But the neighborhood, my dear. While Fourth and Locust was the place to live forty or fifty years ago, you must admit that everybody's moving way out Walnut Street, even as far as Eighteenth. Don't you think that this section has slipped just a bit?"

"How can it slip," Mrs. Clayton asked, "while we're living here?"

Margaret was very pleased at the way Mrs. Clayton had handled the questions. After Mass that Sunday, when she was talking to several of the other girls who worked in fine houses, one of them began teasing her about working in a house where she had to collect and empty the chamberpots every morning.

"My Mister and Missus," the other girl said loftily, "has a bathroom where you do the necessary."

Margaret gave her head a scornful toss. "We'll consider bathrooms," she said, "after they've proved themselves."

There were six people, counting Margaret and Mrs. Clayton, in the household. Mr. Logan Clayton was a big good-looking man with full bushy whiskers all around his face. Ordinary men often had crumbs and tobacco stains in their whiskers, but Mr. Clayton's whiskers were white and clean. He was head of one of the banks on Chestnut Street near Fourth. Long ago, before the Revolution, his grandfather had been Mayor of Philadelphia, and every once in a while visitors talked about how Mr. Clayton ought to let them put him up for Mayor. But he wouldn't agree.

"I don't think it's a sound thing for a man to get into nowadays," he would say. "Back in Grandfather's time a gentleman could go into politics and stay clean, because there wasn't all this money and graft in it. But things have changed. Take the City Gas Works. Take these franchises for horse car lines that everybody's grabbing for nowadays. Politics has become a dirty business, and I don't care to be in it. I'd rather stay behind the scenes, making sure that these political fellows don't get too far out of hand."

The third member of the family was a son, Mr. Glendenning Clayton. He was a tall young man, quick and active and spirited as a blooded race horse, with curly black hair that kept flopping down over his high forehead and which he would impatiently brush back into place. Most of the time he was away, studying law at a place called Harvard. Of course he could have studied law at the University of Pennsylvania, only a few squares away at Ninth and Market Streets. But the University of Pennsylvania had only started giving law courses a half-dozen years earlier, after not teaching law for a long time.

"Can't tell how a new school like that will prove out," young Mr. Glendenning Clayton said. "You can rely on Harvard. Might send my son to Penn Law School if it holds up properly."

Not that young Mr. Clayton had a son or even a wife, but the Claytons were great ones for looking ahead. Or maybe for looking into the past, Margaret wasn't quite sure which.

There were two other servants. Mrs. Muller, a German woman whose husband had died of the yellow fever, was the cook. From the beginning she and Margaret didn't get along, and it was easy to find out why. Mrs. Muller had a niece, a heavy girl with a face like dough starting to rise, and Mrs. Muller had wanted her niece to get the situation as maid. Then there was George Symes, the coachman, who had come over from England with his parents as a baby. He was a serious young man who handled pennies like a cat counting her kittens. He was going to start a livery stable when he had saved enough. She liked George, but he wasn't much fun and if you teased him he went into the sulks. He lived above the stable behind the house. She and Mrs. Muller had rooms in the back of the third floor wing, big enough not only for a bed but even for a chair.

Margaret knew she had a wonderful situation and ought to be completely happy, but there was something wrong. At first she thought the trouble grew out of the fact that she was so ignorant. There were many things she didn't know. Like keeping your thumb out of dishes when you served people, and like knowing what a drawing room was. It really wasn't a room where people drew pictures. It was, Mrs. Clayton explained, a *with*drawing room. The ladies withdrew to it after dinner while the gentlemen had segars and brandy or port at the dining room table.

Margaret put her mind to learning such things, and Mrs. Clayton was very kind and patient teaching her. By the end of her first year she even overhead Mrs. Clayton telling some friends what a fine maid Margaret was getting to be. Then there was the matter of not knowing how to read and write, but she was working on that, too. She bought Mr. McGuffey's First Reader and studied it nights at the kitchen table. She also bought a slate and practiced her letters. Sometimes George Symes sat by her to guide her hand, while Mrs. Muller glowered at her knitting and mumbled that some girls were getting above themselves.

Learning things, however, didn't seem to be the answer, and gradually she saw what the trouble really was. She wanted more than anything in life to feel that she belonged in the fine house among the best people, but she was actually further from belonging than a piece of furniture. Take the walnut highboy in the north drawing room, for example. That was just wood, lovely as it was, but sometimes Mrs. Clayton would stroke it and tell friends how it had been in the family for almost a hundred years. Margaret wondered if she would have to live to be a hundred before a Clayton would say proudly that she had been in the family most of that time.

She could no more enter their lives now than she could climb into the big pier glass in the front hall and become part of the brilliant scenes that were often reflected in it. From a certain angle in the back hall, the pier glass showed most of what was happening in the north drawing room. She often watched from there, hidden in the shadows, when the Claytons were having a party at night. If she left her place in the shadows, the reflection of the drawing room vanished, and if she actually went into the drawing room she was only the maid coming to see if the Claytons wanted anything. No matter what she did, there was always a cool shiny barrier between her and the Claytons, like the one between a person outside a mirror and the scene reflected in it.

For a time Margaret thought that maybe religion might be the main cause of the barrier, because of course the Claytons were Protestants and she was Catholic. So one Sunday she followed secretly when they went to church. It was an Episcopalian church, and Margaret went in holding her breath, half afraid that the first smell she would get might be brimstone. Nothing went wrong, however. A pleasant man took her down a side aisle to a pew which he said was owned by people who wouldn't be coming today. She sat in it and watched the Claytons, who were on the center aisle in the first row. She didn't learn much by watching them. Mr. Logan Clayton gave the service his respectful attention, but you got the feeling that God was not a frightening and majestic figure to him. More like, say, a rather large depositor in Mr. Clayton's bank.

The next time Margaret went to confession she had to tell the priest what she had done. He laid a penance on her and gave her to understand she was only two steps away from hell. She didn't go back to the Claytons' church again. It wasn't because of what the priest had said. It was because she had seen, in the back pews of the Episcopalian church, several girls who looked as if they were housemaids too. And they seemed to be very far away from the best people up in the front of the church.

One night early in August, 1859, all her vague feelings of wanting something, and not quite knowing what it was, came to a head. She was walking out with George Symes these days, and they were strolling down Walnut Street. Rain had washed the air, and the city was cool and quiet. Now and then she peered up at George as his face floated through the pool of light from a gas lamp. He looked even more solemn than usual, which meant he was probably thinking about money.

"You're a good girl, Margaret," he said finally. "The last few months we must have walked by the Walnut Street Theatre a dozen times, and you've never begged to be taken there to a play."

"Sure and the prices are out of reason," she said. "Twenty-five cents for the cheapest ticket."

"Plenty of girls wouldn't think of that. They think a man ought to spend money on them all the time."

"I wouldn't be thinking a thing like that. Wasn't it two weeks ago you took me on a picnic to Windmill Island in the Delaware, with the ride on the little steamer costing money and all? And manys the time you took me on a ride in the horse cars to see the city."

"It's been a pleasure, Margaret. And like I say, you're a fine girl. Not many would have stuck to the reading and writing lessons like you have. You're doing well on your sums, too."

"George," she said, with a sudden ache in her body, "I want awful to better myself."

"So do I, Margaret. Won't be long before I can start that livery stable. I have an eye on just the spot. Horses, that's where the money is, horses. City as big as this, and growing, people have to depend more and more on horses. One of these days I'll have half a dozen rigs for hire. That'll be something, won't it?"

"Indeed and it will that," she said, although it wasn't precisely what she had in mind in regard to bettering herself. On the other hand, she didn't seem to have anything precisely in mind.

They walked on back to the house, and as they reached the kitchen door he said, "I'll come in for a bite of something, but first I'll see if my beauties are all right. Want to give them their lumps of sugar?"

Margaret said she'd like to, and followed him to the stable. He unlocked the big padlock and swung open the door. Inside it was very dark and warm and full of heavy sweet odors. There were thudding and creaking noises as the two horses moved up to the bars of their stalls. George's hand touched hers and pressed two lumps of sugar into it. She felt her way to the stalls, unable to see clearly. Out of the dark two soft muzzles came thrusting at her, seeking the hand with the sugar. She put a lump of sugar in each closed hand, and let the horses nibble gently down her arms and try to burrow into her fingers. It sent pleasant light shivers through her body. She opened her hands and let them take the sugar.

"The pair of them are the sweet things," she said.

"You're a sweet thing," George said in a queer thick voice, close behind her. His arms moved around her in the darkness.

She gasped and did not move, because a new feeling swept her body. Not a pleasant light shiver, like when the horses nuzzled her, but a deep tremble that was half ache and half delight. He turned her around in his arms and began kissing her. His lips were dry and almost hot, and seemed to be stealing her breath. Her body began going limp as an old dust rag. Then George had her up in his arms and was carrying her somewhere and was letting her float down onto a pile of hay, and his hands turned into busy things that worked on the cloth above her breasts and crept up beneath her skirt. She made fluttering motions to stop him but he seemed to have a dozen nimble hands. Suddenly the weakness fell away from her almost as if he had stripped it off, and she twisted violently and slapped hard at the pale blur above her face.

"Ow!" George cried.

She slapped again, and he tumbled back away from her. "Well," he said, "there was no call to slap me twice."

"It's a leather strap I should be taking to you, George Symes," she said indignantly. "Coaxing me in here with that sugar story and then taking advantage of a girl."

"I'll have a black eye by morning," George said, "but it was worth it."

"Was it, now? Then I'd better be giving you another to keep it company! I don't come as cheap as a black eye."

"You don't understand, Margaret. I don't mean having a little fun with you was worth a black eye. I mean it was worth it to find out you're not the girl to let a man make free with you."

"I could have told you that for nothing."

"Yes, but a man don't believe it when he's told. Anyways," he said, with a solemn pause, "not a man who might be thinking of asking a girl to marry him, if she's the right sort."

That left her a little dizzy, although of course she had known that a man doesn't start walking out with a girl unless he has the idea of maybe speaking for her. She got up and tried to brush off her dress. "Don't go beating around the bush with all this talk of a man this and a girl that," she said. "If this is us you're talking about, say it straight out."

"You're kind of rushing me, Margaret."

"It wasn't pushing me away you were, a few moments ago."

"What I had in mind was maybe asking you to marry me. Not right away, but maybe next summer, when I'll be all set to start that livery stable and you'll have your reading and writing and sums learned. You could be a big help, keeping accounts and all. And meanwhile we could have an understanding."

She felt a shocking urge to giggle, but she held it back because it would hurt his feelings awful. George had been trying her out like he might try out a horse for his livery, checking her gait and soundness of wind and giving her a test for skittishness. Now he had decided she would work all right in harness. "I don't know about all this," she said.

"I guess," he said, lamely and with an effort, "I ought to say I'm in love with you."

"I hear folks sometimes get around to that."

"I don't know much about how a man in love is supposed to feel, Margaret. I'd like it awful well for us to get married next summer. Would ... would that sound like being in love?"

"George, it's something I've got to think about. You know I like you. But I'm not used to this other idea."

"Sure, sure," he said, almost in relief. "Of course you've got to think about it. Only don't forget, Margaret, you're past eighteen. It's time for you to be picking a man before you get in your twenties and find you're on the shelf."

"I won't leave you dangling. But for now, let's go in and have that bite to eat."

She tried to brush herself off properly before going into the kitchen, but she must have missed a few wisps of hay. When they got inside, Mrs. Muller's sharp little angry eyes looked her over and Mrs. Muller said "Hah!" in a triumphant tone, as if she had been waiting many nights for this. Mrs. Muller got up and made a great thing of rolling up her knitting.

"Don't expect me to stay," Mrs. Muller said. "No decent woman could be expected to."

George scowled at her. "We won't miss you," he said.

"No, I don't believe you will," Mrs. Muller snapped, sitting down again. "So maybe it's all for the best if I stay. At least I can make sure nothing disgraceful happens in my kitchen."

They had something to eat, and then George said good night and left, and Mrs. Muller clumped heavily up the back stairs to her bedroom. Margaret stayed at the table and tried to sort out her ideas. She knew that many girls would have jumped at the chance of marrying George Symes. It was queer that she couldn't make up her mind. She got up, restlessly, and walked into the north drawing room. A couple of night candles were burning, and the light glowed on curves of mahogany and the crystal of the chandelier. She saw a dim, faraway image of herself in the pier glass in the hall. It was easy to imagine that the girl in the mirror had black ringlets tumbling down over bare shoulders, that diamonds from one of the family necklaces were glinting on her bosom, and that she was waiting there poised and gracious to receive her guests. She walked up close to force the reflection to become plain Margaret O'Donnell. It was time she learned some sense. It was bad enough to have silly fancies, but it was frightening to feel them set a gnawing hunger to work deep in her body.

She turned to walk to the back stairs, then was stopped by a sound outside. Somebody wearing boots was coming down the street, moving as if he were learning how to walk on stilts. The boots teetered up to the front door and a key danced a jig around the keyhole.

Outside the door, young Mr. Glendenning Clayton's voice said cheerfully, "I could get the key in, if the damned house would stop wiggling."

Margaret fled down the hallway, her heart fluttering like a lid on a boiling kettle. She mustn't stay and let him catch her snooping around after his parents had gone to bed. On the other hand, it didn't sound as if he could get in. If he kept on trying he might wake his parents, and they would be very upset that he had been drunk in public. She crept slowly back to the front door and reached for the latch. She planned to unlock it quietly, open the door just a crack and then slip away before Master Glendenning saw her. He would think the door had been partly open all the time. But just as she opened the door, the man outside gave it a shove and came tumbling in against her.

He gripped her shoulders to keep from falling, and peered foggily at her. "A vision!" he said. "A vision, and on the loose in Philadelphia. Was this the face that launched a thousand ships, and burnt the topless towers of Ilium? Sweet Helen, make me immortal with a—"

"Please sir, this is Margaret," she said. "There isn't a soul here named Helen."

"My God," he said, "I'm glad you spoke up. I hope you don't know the rest of that line."

"What line would that be?"

"I was quoting poetry. Funny thing, Margaret. Poetry never seems to pop into my head when I'm sober."

"It's not often you have one too many, sir. That was fine-sounding poetry."

"Marlowe. Christopher Marlowe. He wrote those lines in a play called *Faustus*. In a way," he said, smiling faintly, "I'm sorry you identified yourself. Well, many thanks for unlocking the door. I'll head upstairs." He walked to the stairway, his boots sending dull echoes through the hall. He stopped, sat on the steps. "Got to get these off," he said. "I'll wake Father and Mother. They won't be happy to find me drunk, even if it was the dinner of the First City Troop." He began tugging at the boots, but without budging them.

"Let me help," Margaret said.

"You couldn't get them off. I need a boot jack, and I'm too fuzzy to remember where mine is."

"Manys the time I took off me father's boots. I'll show you how." She lifted his right leg, straddled it with her back to him, gripped the heel with both hands, and said, "Put your left foot against me bottom, and push." The moment she said that, she realized that what she was doing was vulgar and not proper. But it was too late to stop now.

"It seems a shame," he said in a thoughtful voice. "However ..." He put his left foot against her rear, and pushed.

The right boot came off without any trouble. "Now the other," she said, keeping her hot face turned away from him.

She gripped the other boot, and felt his stockinged foot start to brace against her bottom. His toes wriggled a little, sending a shiver up her spine. For a moment she didn't pay attention to what she was doing. And so, when he shoved and the boot came off, she went stumbling forward with it and hit her head against the door and went down in a heap.

The next thing she knew, she was floating through the air, and Master Glendenning's anxious face was close to hers. "Are you all right?" he said. "Are you hurt?"

He had picked her up and was cradling her in his arms. That was an odd thing. Twice in one night men had lifted her in their arms, and twice a delicious weak feeling had crept like a robber through her body, stealing its strength. But this time she didn't think she could get back the strength by any effort of will. The candlelight glinted on the locks of dark hair that tumbled over Master Glendenning's forehead, and turned his eyes into pools of mystery.

"I think I'm all right," she said faintly. His face was so close that her breath stirred his curls of hair.

For a moment his arms tightened on her, and sweat dripped like candlewax down his forehead. She felt a hard swallow go down his throat. "That's good," he said in a harsh tight voice. He lowered her carefully to her feet. "Sure you're all right?"

"I'm all right," she said, still in a dream.

"Many thanks," he said. "I'll get along, then." He grabbed his boots and almost ran up the stairs, without looking back.

She went into the north drawing room and sat on the couch until her head cleared. Across from her, the light shone on long rows of leather-bound volumes with their titles stamped in gold. She got up, and took a candle and looked along the rows. There it was. *Faustus.* Christopher Marlowe. She carried it back to the sofa and began leafing slowly through it. Much later, when her eyes were beginning to see all the print on a page as a horde of busy ants, the lines marched slowly into focus.

"... And burnt the topless towers of Ilium? Sweet Helen, make me immortal with a kiss ..."

She closed the book and managed to replace it, and crept slowly toward her bedroom. Her head felt dizzier now than when it had crashed into the door.

5

SHE LAY ON HER BED on the third floor of the Clayton house, pressing her hot face into the pillow and listening to the sullen thud of her heart. Nearly a month had passed since the night Master Glendenning had come home with the drink on him and had wanted to kiss her. Ever since that night a fever had been burning in her.

It was September now. He was going back to Harvard tomorrow, and she was glad. Those had been shameful weeks just past. Whenever he had been out at night, and the others in the house abed, she had found a queer sort of force pulling her to the front door, so that she could listen for his steps coming down the street and open the door for him. The first few times she had done that, he had smiled pleasantly and thanked her and gone upstairs without more ado.

Then the next time he said, almost sharply, "You don't have to wait up this way, Margaret."

After that she hadn't dared open the door for him, but she would wait in the shadows in the rear of the hallway and let him catch a glimpse of her. It seemed to bother him more and more each time. The last time, two nights ago, he had peered down the hallway at her and then had gone upstairs like the devil himself was on his heels. She was terribly ashamed of her actions but she couldn't seem to stop. It was like taking a drug, except that after taking it there was no relief. There was just one more night, though, and then she could recover. And tonight she would not creep down through the quiet house when his footsteps sounded along the brick sidewalk.

Her heart was making an awful clatter. Much more than it should. She lifted her head, and the sound broke into two parts. One was her heartbeat. The other came from boots that wove a drunken pattern of sound through the night. He was coming home, and with the drink on him again. There was something defiant about the sound of the boots. She would not go down. She would not. But even as she told herself that, she was springing up from the bed and throwing a robe over the cotton nightgown and jamming her feet into slippers and hurrying down the back stairs. As she reached the first floor hall, his key was jabbing angrily at the lock. This time she did not wait back in the shadows. It was as if somebody else had borrowed her body and forced it to glide to the door and to open it.

He stood in the doorway, staring at her, his face all jagged angles of light and shadow. "I hoped you wouldn't," he said harshly.

She couldn't find any words in her. A tingle started upward from her toes, shaking every bit of her body into a queer kind of wakefulness.

He closed the door behind him. "I've been drinking," he said. "This time you'd better do the running."

His face was close and she smelled the drink on his breath, sharp and pungent. She couldn't have run if this had been damnation reaching out for her.

His hands came up and touched her shoulders, parting the robe and pulling it aside so that it peeled slowly down her body of its own weight. "You're very lovely," he said hoarsely. "How much of this night-after-night teasing do you think a man can take?"

Somebody borrowed her voice and used it to say, "It's a man you are, is it? I wouldn't have guessed."

That was like throwing a match into black powder. His face twisted, and his hands clawed at the cotton nightgown and hooked in the fabric and ripped it from her. He pulled her body close. His clothes felt harsh against her skin and the big buttons of his coat pressed into her like smooth chunks of ice. His stubble of beard left a delicious rasping track over her face and throat and shoulders. He carried her into the north drawing room and threw cushions onto the floor and stretched her out on them.

She did not own this body of hers at all. She was merely a lodger in it, with a wee small room up in her mind that she could call hers. From that room she watched as her body turned into a limp boneless thing that the man could spread out and fold and pat into whatever shape he wished. She tried to get back her senses by telling herself who she was and what was happening.

She was Margaret O'Donnell of County Clare, and this was the Claytons' fine house in Philadelphia. The gleam over there was from the highboy that had come down through three generations of Claytons. The solemn tick-tock tick-tock was from the clock that stood higher than herself and had been made in London more than a hundred years ago. Up on one wall hung an oil painting of a Clayton who had lived long before her time. He seemed to be watching calmly, as if reserving judgment, while a younger Clayton took a little Irish girl on the floor. *I do not know as yet,* he must be telling himself, *what this means to the Claytons, if indeed it means anything. So for now I will just watch.* He did not seem curious over whether or not it meant anything to the little Irish girl.

A warm tide was rising higher and higher in her head. It was lapping into the small room to which she had retreated. She tried once more to tell herself about Margaret O'Donnell and what was happening to her, but the tide was flooding too strongly now. She gave a small sigh and let herself sink into it.

"Margaret," he was saying. "Margaret!"

She opened her drowsy eyes and saw him bending over her. She was still lying on the cushions on the floor, but he had brought her robe and covered her. "I'm here," she whispered. It was a daft thing to say, but there seemed to be nothing else to tell him.

His face looked thin and white, with the skin stretched tightly over it. "I'm so terribly sorry," he said. "I don't know what came over me."

She knew, exactly, by instinct, what she must do. She must clutch the robe close about her, and weep softly, and tell him that she had loved him for ever so long and that he had been too strong for her. It called for a bit of play-acting, but any girl could do that without half trying. And then, because he was a nice and normal young man, he would feel strong and ashamed and would want to protect her. The trouble was, she didn't want to play-act. She did not feel like weeping. She had not been weak and fragile. She had been strong, and she had used the man's strength against him, and she felt warm and happy and triumphant.

"And what is there," she said, "to be sorry about?"

He stammered, "Why ... why, about this!"

"I wanted you," she said, "and I made you take me."

He jumped up. "You didn't!" he cried. "You couldn't have done that! It was my fault and—"

"I ought to be blubbering and wailing, shouldn't I? Would you like that better, Master Glendenning?"

"How can you take it this way? It makes you seem like ... like a ... no, I won't say it! Margaret, you're not yourself right now. You've been through a terrible thing and your thoughts are disordered."

She whispered, "I've been through a wonderful fine thing, and I'm proud of it."

He let out a choked sound, and turned away and walked to the hall. Then he swung around again. "Margaret," he said, almost pleadingly.

She stretched lazily and smiled at him.

He whirled around and ran stumbling up the stairs. Tomorrow he would be gone, perhaps without more words to her, but if she had to do it again she would not have changed a thing. This way she had a proud memory. The other way, what had happened would have been a sneaking, shameful thing. She looked up at the oil painting of the Clayton who had lived long before her time. His eyes seemed hooded now, and had no inter-est in her. Perhaps he had decided that, as it turned out, this would mean nothing to the Claytons, whatever it might mean to Margaret O'Donnell.

6

THE HOUSE SEEMED to be waiting for something to happen this morning. Margaret had finished her upstairs work an hour ago, but Mrs. Clayton had not yet called her to talk about what needed mending. Mrs. Clayton had not told Mrs. Muller, the cook, what she wanted for dinner that evening, and Mrs. Muller was grumbling about it. On the street outside the house, George Symes waited to take Mrs. Clayton to the market. He was not liking the wait, either. It was cold this January morning of 1860, and his horses stamped and filled the air with plumes of frosty breath.

Margaret was not impatient. She sat quietly on a chair in a second floor bedroom, holding herself erect so as to give the small thing growing inside her plenty of room. You wouldn't think a baby could grow so fast in only four months. Perhaps she ought to be worrying about the future, but she had not been able to fix her mind on it. All she wanted to do these days was close her eyes and drift on quietly, as if a big gentle river were carrying her downstream. Perhaps somewhere ahead there was a waterfall, or rapids, or a place of jagged currents where the river met the sea, but she could not bring herself to care. Not even Mrs. Muller had been able to jolt her out of her dream, two weeks ago, when Mrs. Muller's sharp and angry eyes noted the swelling of her stomach.

"Getting big around the middle, I'd say," Mrs. Muller had said.

"It's eating too much I am," Margaret said.

"Hah. Eating for two, maybe? You'd better get that George Symes to make you an honest woman. You didn't fool me, that night you came in all frowsy with hay from the stable."

"There's nothing between George and me."

"There couldn't have been much space between you that night. Wait till the mistress spots this."

"Don't go telling her anything," Margaret said in a cold even voice, getting up and moving toward Mrs. Muller.

The woman backed away. "Don't threaten me," she said. "I don't have to say anything. She's got eyes. I'll give you a month until she can't miss it."

That had been two weeks ago. If Mrs. Muller's guess was right, that gave Margaret two weeks more to go drifting along.

From downstairs a voice called, "Margaret. Oh Margaret." That was Mrs. Clayton, ready at last to get the work of the house under way.

"Yes ma'am," Margaret called back, and went downstairs.

The moment she saw Mrs. Clayton she knew there would not be two weeks more for drifting. Mrs. Clayton stared at her, with that tapemeasure look that women often had in their eyes when they wondered if another woman was growing a baby. "Margaret," she said, "please call out the door to George that I will not want the carriage this morning. But after he puts up the horses I'd like him to stay within call."

Margaret went to the door and relayed the message.

"Now," Mrs. Clayton said, "I'd like to talk to you." She led the way into the north drawing room and sat down and motioned Margaret to sit on the couch. "I may not," Mrs. Clayton said carefully, "have done the right thing by you, Margaret. You're very young and inexperienced. Perhaps I should have looked after you more closely."

The dream-like trance in which Margaret had moved, these last four months, was gone. She was wide awake now, nerves strung tight, like a cat backed into a corner by a dog. "In what way, ma'am?"

"You know what I mean," Mrs. Clayton said, with an edge to her voice. "I'm talking about men."

This was like the dog barking and making little lunges, trying to get the cat off balance. "I don't know much about men," she said.

"Don't sit there with that closed look on your face! You know more than you should about one man. Has George Symes asked you to marry him?"

"Yes, ma'am."

"I'm glad to hear that. Have you set a date?"

"He wants it to be this summer."

"This summer!" Mrs. Clayton cried. "Is the man crazy? Doesn't he know that you ... that you're going ... well—"

"That I'm going to have a baby? No ma'am, he doesn't know."

"It's going to be in June, isn't it, Margaret? The baby?"

"Mrs. Muller's been talking, has she?"

"That has nothing to do with it. So you haven't told George. Afraid, I suppose. Well, I'll see that that's taken care of. When Mr. Clayton comes home for lunch, I'll have him speak to George. There won't be any trouble, Margaret. The wedding will be next week, and you'll have a nice present. Nice enough to make George step lively to marry you. I know that young man. If there are any doubts in his mind, money will take care of them."

There was more to this than you might have thought, just hearing the cool tones of Mrs. Clayton's voice. She had slurred over that word "doubts" a shade too quickly. It was as if Mrs. Clayton thought the subject of doubts had to be brought up but shouldn't be kept around long. "What sort of doubts would you be meaning?" Margaret asked.

"Well, men have a tendency to put off getting married. But we'll see that George doesn't."

"Nobody can make George do anything."

"You don't know Mr. Clayton, Margaret."

"Begging your pardon, ma'am, *you* don't know something. George didn't give me this baby. I never let him make free with me. So nobody can scare George into marrying me."

There. It was out now. You couldn't see the words she had spoken but they hung in the air between her and Mrs. Clayton like sharp edgy things that you wouldn't want to grab at fast. Mrs. Clayton got up and walked to the front window. Her face had gone white as the cameo pinned to her plum-colored dress.

"You haven't been walking out with any other man," Mrs. Clayton said, talking to the window.

"No ma'am."

"Do I have to ask who else it could be?"

"I haven't thought whether you ought to know, ma'am."

"You haven't thought!" Mrs. Clayton cried, whirling back toward her. "You don't need to tell me that. If you'd had an ounce of brains you'd have made sure George Symes couldn't find an excuse to back out." She took a shuddering breath, and walked to the mantel and picked up something from it. "A letter came for you this morning," she said, and dropped it in Margaret's lap.

Margaret's trembling fingers turned it over and over. She had never had a letter before. Her name and address were written in block lettering, and the stamp had been cancelled in New York City. "I—I'll just go up to me room and read this," Margaret said.

"You'll do no such thing," Mrs. Clayton said, low and fierce. "I know my own son's writing even if he did print your name. I've been sitting here for an hour with that thing burning in my hand."

"It couldn't be from him, ma'am! He stayed up in Boston for the holidays. This came from New York."

"The postmark means nothing. Somebody mailed it for him. Open it!"

For a moment Margaret had been frightened. Now she wasn't. They could only do one thing to her, and that was try to take the baby away. If they tried, they would learn what a fight was. She looked at the flap of the envelope. "You didn't open it, ma'am," she said. "I take that kindly of you."

"It was a struggle," Mrs. Clayton said grimly.

Margaret opened the envelope and began reading the letter.

"Dear Margaret," it said, "I trust that this finds you in the best of health. I have been endeavoring for some weeks to write this letter, which I will give to a friend to mail from New York City. You have no doubt had your own ideas as to why I did not return home for the holidays, and perhaps you surmised that it did not seem wise that we should meet again. It would be different if we had discovered within ourselves a tender and sincere feeling toward each other. But indeed such a feeling appears to be lacking, as you yourself gave me to understand the night before I departed for the college.

"I have hoped and prayed that there would be no consequences as a result of our thoughtless act, and I have been emboldened to conclude that this is the case, due to the absence of word from you to the contrary. Had there been such consequences, I should have endeavored to accept them as any man of honor ought to do.

"But since this problem has not arisen, I trust that you will help me solve the remaining problem, in regard to our not meeting again. Obviously I cannot remain away from home indefinitely, so it would seem advisable for you to seek another situation. My personal funds are limited, but they are entirely at your disposal to help you maintain yourself while you seek a suitable place with another family. Yr. obdt.-svt, Glendenning Clayton."

Margaret finished reading the letter, and smiled faintly. He seemed very far away, and a stranger. But then he had almost always seemed like a stranger, although a fine one who took her breath away.

Mrs. Clayton said, "Do you dare let me read it?"

Margaret gave it to her. As Mrs. Clayton read it, the tight lines around her mouth softened, and her head lifted and spots of pink glowed in her cheeks like banners.

"You made your grab too fast," Mrs. Clayton said. "You forgot there had to be love, or a pretence of it. He'd never marry you now."

"I wasn't thinking of all that, ma'am."

"Of course you weren't. Just a little Irish biddy, grabbing at the best thing in reach. I should have known, from the quick way you lifted your skirt that day I hired you. And the way you insisted on being called Margaret, not Maggie. I thought then: is this girl going to act above herself? Will she know her station? I gave myself the wrong answer."

"I'm sorry I've hurt you, ma'am. I never intended to."

Mrs. Clayton walked up and down the room twice. Each time that she passed the fireplace she hesitated, and then moved on as if it took an effort to do so.

"Would you like to burn the letter, ma'am?" Margaret asked.

Mrs. Clayton's head jerked around, and she stared at Margaret. She gave a short laugh. "You're a sharp little piece, Maggie."

"It's Margaret, ma'am, if you want me to say you can burn it."

"Pish, girl. I could drop it on the coals before you could say a word."

"But then you wouldn't feel good about it."

"You're a strange creature. I wouldn't have expected you to sense that. May I burn the letter, Margaret?"

"Yes, ma'am."

A yellow flame licked up from the coals, and a ragged black line ate slowly across the letter.

"There," Mrs. Clayton said in relief. "Now let's consider what should be done. I'm glad that you're being sensible. Obviously you couldn't hold another situation for very long. I suggest that you return to Ireland. We will provide you with money for the passage. The sum of two thousand dollars will be payable to you through a bank in Dublin, at the rate of five hundred dollars a year for four years. You should have no difficulty finding a husband in Ireland, with that money to help. You will have done very well for yourself."

"It's thanking you I am," Margaret said. "But you may keep the money. I am not going back to Ireland."

"What are your plans? To stay here and try to ruin his life? You can try, and perhaps you can do it. But it won't get you a penny. Think carefully, Margaret."

Margaret clenched her hands together, as if she hoped to wring some thoughts from them. It was hard to put ideas into words, especially when she was not sure of the ideas. How could she tell Mrs. Clayton it was a proud thing she had done, a thing not to be soiled by money and by sneaking back to Ireland, when Mrs. Clayton thought it was a dreadful thing?

"You don't understand, ma'am," she said earnestly. "The last thing I would want to do is harm the Claytons. I will leave and not bother a soul."

"But what will you do? How will you live?"

"I have me plans," she said. It was a lie, but it was a good stiff-necked lie, and it let an O'Donnell look a Clayton square in the eye with no nonsense about being humble. "So I'll say goodby, ma'am."

She went upstairs to her room, and packed quickly. She owned a carpetbag now, although she had never used it, and fine clothes to put into it. The clothes had belonged to Mrs. Clayton once, and for a moment she thought of leaving them. She put that thought out of her head. She might give up two thousand dollars out of pride, but she would not give up clothes that had been part of her pay. She had earned them. As for money, she had saved nearly fifty dollars in the two and a half years with the Claytons. She would find something to work at, before that was gone.

She went down the front stairway of the house, carrying her carpetbag. A servant should use the back stairs, but she was no longer one, and besides she did not want to trade ugly words with Mrs. Muller in the kitchen. Mrs. Muller would know a great many things, and guess at others, if she saw the carpetbag. Margaret passed through the front hall and caught a glimpse of herself in the pier glass. She remembered the fine scenes she had watched in that glass, nights when there had been parties in the drawing room and when she had stationed herself at just the right place to catch the reflection. She remembered how she used to wish that she could walk into the pier glass and become part of those scenes. Well, she had tried, and the mirror had shattered in her face and the scenes were vanishing.

The door knob turned in her hand. Back in the kitchen a voice was calling her name. It was Mrs. Clayton, calling up the back stairs. Margaret could not think of anything they needed to be talking about now, so she stepped outside and closed the door behind her for the last time.

She walked down the street, hearing the snow squeak underfoot and feeling the January cold bite into her. She was beginning to feel cold inside, too. It was a creeping cold that had nothing to do with the weather. Now that she had finished carrying things off with such a high hand, she was frightened. There was no one she could turn to in the city. There was trouble ahead, and she was not sure she had the courage to face it.

Behind her, somebody was running down the street, calling after her. She stopped and turned. It was George Symes, without coat or hat, leaving a fog of breath in the air as he ran.

"A fine thing!" he gasped, catching up to her. "Afraid to stay and face it out with me?"

Her legs started to tremble. George was a good reliable man. If he would be kind and understanding, he could have her now and for the rest of her days, and she would worship him. "I wasn't sure you'd want to see me," she said faintly. "I suppose you know. Things like this get around fast, with Mrs. Muller to help them along."

"Who was he?" George said. "You held me off, right enough. Who was the one you didn't hold off? Why was he so much better?"

"I don't want to talk about it."

"Well, I do, you little Irish bitch. Leading me on about us getting married."

"Was it to tell me you wouldn't marry me that you ran all this way, George? Sure and the way I walked off, you might have guessed I already knew that."

"Don't put words in my mouth! I don't know what I've decided. I'm not a man who makes plans and gives them up easy. I've got to think about this. Maybe if you showed how sorry you are, I might come around to talk things over. But I'm not promising anything, mind you."

He wanted her to weep, and maybe grovel a bit and beg for his forgiveness. In his mind, he was the one who needed kindness and understanding. And in a way, he had a right to feel like that. But he would have to feel that way alone. "I'm sorry, George," she said, "but we won't be seeing each other again."

She turned and walked away. There was trouble ahead, and perhaps she couldn't handle it. But at least she knew now that she had the courage to try.

7

THE PANES OF GLASS in the window were old and wavy, and in the June sunlight they looked as if they were about to melt. Margaret's room was under the eaves of the house on Market Street near Third. The ceiling was low, and the roof kept in the heat like the lid of a bubbling kettle. She rolled on the bed and felt sweat cut fiery itches over her body. The pains were coming full and steady now, like a giant hand squeezing her, and it would not be long until the restless creature inside her came plunging into life.

Now and then she had to fight off an urge to call out for Mrs. Cooperman, the landlady. But she didn't trust the woman. For the last few weeks Mrs. Cooperman had made it very plain that she did not want a bastard born in her respectable house. Only the fact that Mrs. Cooperman did not know that the baby was coming this month had saved her from being ordered out of the house. Her rent was paid until next week, and she had promised to leave then. Her money would be gone by that time, too, so Mrs. Cooperman would have a double reason for making her go.

After she left the Claytons in January she had worked two weeks in a weaving mill and one week in a shop. Each time, people had seen she was making a baby and had told her, kindly enough, that she would have to leave. Her money would have lasted longer if she had not spent so much on food. But she had been determined to give the baby a good start, no matter what it cost for food.

If she called Mrs. Cooperman now, the best she could hope for was that the woman would send her to the Poor House or someplace like that. And they might take the baby away from her.

She writhed on the bed and tried to separate the sounds coming into the room from those in her head. There was a shrieking of steel on steel. That might be her teeth grinding, or the wheels of a freight car on the railroad tracks outside, making the turn toward the wharf at Dock Street with the horses straining to get it around the corner. There was also a solid clanging noise. That might be her heart, or the big bell at the State House sending out a fire alarm in its echoing code. There were cries and calls and bellows, and she did not know if they came from the street or from noises stifled in her own throat.

A few hours ago she had scrawled a note to Mrs. Clayton, asking for help. She had crawled to the window and dropped it to a neighbor's boy, with a five-cent piece wrapped in it, and got his promise to run with it straight to the Clayton home. But you couldn't depend on boys, and there was no reason why she could count on Mrs. Clayton. It had cost her something in pride to write the note, but pride meant nothing right now.

The sun swung more to the west and sent a blaze into her eyes. She tried to get up and pull the curtain, but her body was far out of balance and she fell back onto the bed. Some people said sunlight was good for you. It looked as if she would find out for sure.

Something let out a small shriek, and this time it happened to be the hinges of the door. She rolled her head over to look. A lady in a black silk bonnet was easing her hoop skirt through the doorway. Behind her, Mrs. Cooperman was peering into the room like a cat at a mousehole.

"Hello, Margaret," the lady said.

Margaret tried to rub the sweat from her eyes so that the lady's face wouldn't blur and go wavy. It was Mrs. Clayton. "Oh, ma'am," she said, "I didn't mean for you to come."

"It's good that I did. How soon will it be?"

"I—I think any moment, ma'am."

Mrs. Cooperman cried, "She swore it wasn't due till next month! I'd have put her out long ago if I'd known. A good respectable house like this, and she sneaks into it to have her brat."

"Be quiet," Mrs. Clayton said coldly. "Get me some clean sheets. I want some boiling water, and a pair of scissors and some clean waxed thread. And do you know where Doctor Blakeslee lives on Spruce near Fourth?"

"Well, yes, I do, but—"

"Don't argue, please. Send somebody for him. He won't get here in time. They never do when you want them. But I might as well try."

"Who might you be," Mrs. Cooperman said, "to give me orders?"

"I am Mrs. Logan Clayton, and my husband is president of the Merchants and Mariners Bank. It might be helpful for you to know me, if you ever need a favor from a bank."

"Oh, I dearly beg your pardon, Mrs. Clayton. I never thought this girl would have somebody like you to turn to."

"She was my maid, and got herself in trouble, and I dismissed her. Would you start on all those things now?"

"I will that, Mrs. Clayton. There's just one thing. Kindly don't ask me to help with the birthing. I never could stand it."

"I never could either," Mrs. Clayton said, grimly. "But I'm about to learn how."

She watched Mrs. Cooperman start downstairs, then went to the window and fixed the curtain to block the sunlight. "That's better, isn't it?" she said. "Now all I know about having a baby is what I remember of my own, and that's mighty little. When you feel the pains coming one right after another, get your legs up and bear down with your stomach muscles. I'll try to help all I can."

"I hate for you to see me like this, ma'am," Margaret gasped. "I hated to write that note. But I didn't know where to turn."

"If it hadn't been for your silly pride, you could have saved yourself a lot of trouble. I've been trying to find you all over the city, ever since you left."

"You're too good to me, ma'am."

"I'm not doing this for you. I'm paying a debt my son owes to the baby."

A pain wrenched at her body, and Margaret cried, "It's my baby, do you understand? You're not going to take him away from me!"

"Mighty sure it will be a boy, aren't you?"

The pains were coming faster, now. "Sure and he'll be a boy," she said. "And he'll grow up and be one of the best people. He'll have a fine house and the Claytons will be glad to shake his hand." She knew she was starting to rave and rant, but she couldn't help it. For months she had been thinking about what had happened to her, and why it had happened, and she had found the answer. It had all been piled up in her head, boiling around and trying to get spoken, but she hadn't had anybody to tell it to. "You tried to chase me back to the Old Country," she gasped. "Well, I'll never go back. There are going to be O'Donnells around here just as proud as any Claytons, and don't you forget it." She paused, and jerked up her legs and tried to make the baby come.

Mrs. Clayton yanked back the damp sheet, and helped brace Margaret's legs. Her face turned very pale. "You're doing fine," she said. "Get on with it, now."

"You don't think I mean all this, do you, ma'am?"

"You're a little Irish bog trotter who thought you could come over here and be a queen. Only it's not that easy."

Her body was tight as a drum, now. Waves of blackness kept foaming up over her eyes and washing back as she fought to keep her head above them. "Sure and I don't blame you for hating me," she moaned. "But I never meant to harm the Claytons. It was only that you were all so fine and cocky and high above everything, and all I wanted was just a wee bit of that for meself that would never be missed."

"You Irish girls with your hot young bodies. As if all you had to do was wave them at a man to get anything you want."

"I haven't got all I want yet. But I'll get it, and not from asking you for it. My boy will be somebody in this city. He'll marry a girl with money and a big house and a fine name. Do you hear me? Do you hear?"

She could see that Mrs. Clayton was almost as done in as she herself was. Mrs. Clayton looked sick and ready to faint, as she wrestled for the baby. Her hair was flying around her face and her dress was stained and her eyes were wild.

Mrs. Clayton glared at her and said, "You aimed too high once and look what happened. You're mad to aim so high again. You think it's easy. You think it's just a matter of money. It takes a lot more than that. It takes breeding, and you wouldn't know what that is."

"My boy will have the breeding. Good warm O'Donnell blood and your cold Clayton blood."

"A plow horse and a race horse. You don't know what you'll get from breeding them. You never heard of blood lines, did you? You never heard of breeding true to type, so you can be sure generation after generation of what you'll get. In this city we want to be sure what we get. And nobody can be sure until the breeding has run true from father to son to grandson. If your O'Donnell blood makes it in three generations you'll be lucky. The chances are a million to one against it."

"A Clayton woman talking, with the Clayton money back of her."

"Do you think only the Irish know what it is to be poor? The first Claytons were so poor you'd have looked down on them. They came over in Penn's first ship. For their first winter they dug caves in the riverbank at the foot of Market Street and lived in them. And there was nobody rich that any of them could marry. It took the Claytons a hundred years to get anywhere, and it took my people eighty, and now that we've got things we know enough to hang onto them, whether it's money or position or breeding. If you think you could have married my son and won all that, you're mad. None of my friends would have given you or him so much as a look. They'd have let you both slide back into the mob, and I couldn't have stopped it. So all your talk of not wanting to harm the Claytons is silly. You wouldn't have harmed the Claytons. You'd have stopped my son from being a Clayton."

"Keep an eye on my son," Margaret gasped. "He'll show you."

Her body bent like a bow and the pain fell suddenly away from her and left her strong and ready to bring him into the world. Her strength rippled slowly down her body, and she felt him come out in a long straight plunge. She gave a small glad cry and closed her eyes and let herself drift away into warm blackness.

When she awoke the room was full of bustle. A man who might be the doctor was doing things, and Mrs. Cooperman was carrying off a bundle, and Mrs. Clayton, cool and poised again, was sitting quietly in a chair as if ready to pour tea for her friends.

The doctor stood up and wiped his hands and said to Mrs. Clayton, "She'll be fine. These Irish girls come from sturdy stock. I'll keep dropping in."

"Thank you," Mrs. Clayton said. "Please send the bill to me."

He left the room, and Margaret and Mrs. Clayton were alone once more.

"I have arranged everything with Mrs. Cooperman," Mrs. Clayton said. "She will make sure you have the best of care. And I have written a note and put it under your pillow. It will introduce you to a gentleman at my husband's bank. He will be instructed to give you, either in one sum or over a period of time, the sum of two thousand dollars. I am taking a chance, but I believe I can trust you. And I hope this time you will be sensible and accept the money. It's not really for you but for the child."

"Where is he?" Margaret whispered. "I want my boy."

Mrs. Clayton went to a crib in the corner, and lifted out the child and brought it to her. "A fine baby," Mrs. Clayton said.

Margaret peered at the patch of pink face. "He'll show you," she whispered.

"I don't really think so," Mrs. Clayton said, coolly and without much interest. "Your baby is a girl." She turned and left the room.

MARY

1889–1894

8

UNTIL SHE WAS well into her twenties, Mary O'Donnell never looked at other girls her own age without a feeling of scorn. They were so very silly. They got together in noisy chirping groups, like the English sparrows that were starting to swarm all over Philadelphia, and talked about nothing but clothes and men. Each of them claimed she was waiting for Mr. Right, but somehow he was always the first man who passed by.

There was a Mr. Right for her, of course, but he was very special. He belonged to one of the best families in Philadelphia, and when she was in her teens she often wondered which one it would be. Naturally it would not be easy to get him. So, while she was growing up, she prepared herself very carefully to make the capture. Every night she brushed her long black hair one hundred times. She kept her skin as clear as porcelain, and carried a parasol whenever the sun was hot. Before she went to bed she put on gloves dusted inside with oatmeal so that her hands would always be white and smooth. Her mother taught her how to walk gracefully across a room, and to sit with feet together and hands folded lightly across each other, the way the ladies in the Clayton house had done.

She learned how to sing to her own piano accompaniment, because that was a good way to catch the attention of men at parties without seeming to try. Often, when she sang "Listen to the Mocking Bird" or "Ben Bolt," young men looked at her in a slightly dazed way, and gulped until their Adam's apples became quite red from scraping past their stiff collars. It would have been ridiculously easy to marry one of them. If she had picked one and given him a few smiles, the way you might give the huckster's horse lumps of sugar, he would have started to plod solemnly after her. But of course not one of these young men was even faintly suitable.

As far back as she could remember, she had known what her mother hoped for her in the line of marriage. One of her earliest memories was of perching on her mother's lap and listening to the story of Margaret O'Donnell and Philadelphia and the Claytons. In her mother's soft Irish brogue the story came out as a lovely fairy story. It was rather like the story of Cinderella, except that Prince Charming never came back and the Fairy Godmother limited her gifts to the sum of two thousand dollars. It was up to her, Mary O'Donnell, to finish the story the way it was meant to end.

Of course, as a girl, her mother had been completely silly and romantic. Her mother had had a chance for a sensational marriage right in her hands and had let it slip away. Oh, the Claytons would have raged and ranted, and for a time everybody would have snubbed the young couple, but such marriages often worked out all right in twenty years or so, just in time to benefit the children. It would have been much better to be a Clayton whom people snubbed than an O'Donnell whom they did not notice. She, Mary O'Donnell, would never make any mistakes like that.

Fortunately her mother had put aside the worst of her romantic notions while she could still get two thousand dollars. With the money, her mother set herself up in a little dressmaking shop off Market Street on Tenth. The awkward matter of having an illegitimate child had been neatly taken care of by Mrs. Clayton. In the letter Mrs. Clayton wrote to the bank, in regard to the two thousand dollars, she referred to "Mrs. Margaret O'Donnell." The bank had helped Mrs. Margaret O'Donnell rent the dressmaking shop, and from then on everyone assumed that her mother had been married and that Mr. O'Donnell had died.

So Mary had been brought up in the rooms above the shop, and had brushed her hair and tended her skin and learned to be a lady. She had also become an excellent student at school, because she had a good brain and was not distracted by the trivial things which affected most girls. She graduated at the head of her grammar school class, and was accepted by Girls Normal School and headed the class there too. Then, just to fill the time until the chance for the right marriage came along, she began teaching school. It turned out that there was a very great deal of time to be filled.

On a Saturday in April, 1889, she sat in the back room behind the shop, watching her mother basting the seams of a dress. Her mother was showing her age these days, Mary thought. Her hair was very gray, and her face was as deeply cut with wrinkles as the chunk of beeswax she used on her thread. Her mother made no attempt to hold off age, the way many women did; she wore nothing but black, without frills on the high collar and tight cuffs.

Of course, speaking of age ... Mary glanced at the big fitting mirror, and studied her reflection. You might say that she had never looked better. But how long could she hope to look that way?

"Mother," she said, "do you realize that in June I'll be twenty-nine?"

The needle whipped in and out, in and out. "That I do," her mother said.

"Do you think that's old, mother?"

The blue eyes flicked a glance at her, above the steel-rimmed spectacles. "It's a fine-looking woman you are, if that's what you're coaxing at me to say."

"A fine-looking woman, and here I sit on a Saturday morning wondering what to do with myself. Mother, what would you say if I told you I'm scared?"

"Scared, is it? You've never been scared in your life. Maybe if you had been, you'd have done something more about getting the right man for yourself."

"What chance have I had?" Mary said angrily. "How do I find the man I want in a dressmaker's shop? How do I find him at school? You were luckier. You may have been a servant, but at least you met the best people. I never get near people who matter."

"If I'd had your advantages, I'd have found ways."

"You had an advantage I don't have. You didn't know how far you were from the top, so you made a leap and almost got there. I know I'm miles away, and how hard it is to jump that distance. You probably think I should go out driving and make the horse run away and let myself be rescued by an eligible young man."

"It's been done," her mother said drily. "That, or things like it."

"Only in books."

"That's the trouble with all this learning. It's taught you what can't be done, not what can. You've got looks and brains. But you'd be better off with less of them, and more heart."

Mary closed her right hand until the nails cut into her palm. "I'd be better off with a man," she said.

"I never made you promise me anything," her mother said. "Would you be liking to pick a husband from the men you know? I'd never say a word against it, not if it would make you happy."

"Well, it wouldn't! I'd never draw an easy breath. Maybe you don't know what it is, to have our history bottled up in me. I lie awake at night and get hot all over thinking how those Claytons trampled on you, and how I've got to show them that the O'Donnells can be as good as anybody. It's like a fever. I'm going to marry well and be somebody, do you hear me?"

"All I hear at the moment," her mother said, putting down her sewing, "is the bell at the shop door. And you can be sure it's not your fine young man come to claim you. So if you'll excuse me ..."

Her mother went into the shop. For a few moments Mary paced up and down in the back room, moving like a cat instead of with the ladylike little steps she had learned so carefully. At times her mother made her want to scream. Her mother had as much as accused her of wanting to give up.

"You're the one who gave up, mother," she whispered to the empty room. "You could have married Glendenning Clayton, but you played the princess instead of the servant girl. And you've played the princess ever since. Have you ever acted curious about what happened to my father? Have you ever wondered what happened to that coachman of the Claytons who wanted to marry you? No. But I could tell you the name of every child my father has by the fine lady he married, and the details of every big Clayton party that the newspapers have ever written about. I could tell you that your coachman married that niece of the cook who hated you, and started his livery stable and is doing well at it. If either of them had ever come around, you would have smiled graciously at them and maybe let them court you. Yes, you can play the princess. But me, I'm supposed to go out and drag in a man by his hair."

The rumble of a man's voice drifted into the back room just then. The door into the shop was partly open, and Mary glanced through the opening, curious as to the kind of man who would come to a dressmaker's. He was tall, and he stooped a bit to get down to the level of other people. His face was rather long and thin, and he had light brown hair parted in the exact center and mashed down on each side of his head. He moved around the shop like an enormous lanky puppy trying to be dignified. He had the kind of shy smile that probably made girls want to muss his hair. His voice was deep and full of vibrations, like a church organ muttering away in the bass pipes.

Mixed with the rumble of his voice was a bright chirping from a girl who was hidden by the door. "Don't you think it's just lovely, Harry?" she was saying. "Oh, it will look so nice at the party. Don't you think?" She seemed to run out of breath, from ecstasy, every few words.

Mary frowned. It was amazing what a girl could do to a man when she had him hooked. She could even drag him to a dressmaker's on a Saturday morning so that she could swirl and pirouette before him, and show off her figure and prove to anyone watching how completely she owned him. Mary pushed the door open and stepped forward to see what the girl looked like. She was a pretty thing, you had to give her that. She was swishing around trying on a new cape. She had a plump young face and yellow curls. Her family had probably called her "Kitten" most of her life, and she worked hard to live up to that name.

The girl was saying, "Oh, I just love it, Harry! Don't you? Now come on, like a good boy, and say some nice poetry for Clarissa to prove how much you like it."

There was a hint of baby talk in the way she spoke. The man's face got red, and he wriggled like a boy called on to recite before strangers.

"Right at the moment," he stammered, "I—I can't think of any."

"Oh yes you can," the girl cooed. She turned to Mrs. O'Donnell and said, "Harry is most dreadfully smart. He's assistant headmaster at Franklin Academy and he's going to be the next headmaster. And he quotes poetry just so wonderfully! I want you to hear him. Come on now, Harry, say some poetry about how I look in my new cape." Her tone was playful but quite firm, as if she did not intend to let him get away with any small revolts.

"There's a stanza by Byron," he said rather desperately. "It's something about beauty and night, but I can't quite get it."

Nobody had noticed Mary standing in the doorway. On an impulse she walked into the shop and said, "Would this be it? 'She walks in beauty, like the night of cloudless climes and starry skies; and all that's best of dark and bright, meet in her aspect and her eyes.' "

There was a pause, and the echoes of her low soft voice seemed to go on murmuring around the room. The man looked at her with wide stunned eyes. The girl stared at her as if they had just met at a party, wearing dresses from exactly the same pattern. Across the room, her mother peered curiously at her above the top of the steel spectacles.

"Well," the girl said finally. "Well! Thank you very much, I'm sure."

"That was something!" the man said, somewhat breathlessly. "What a voice you have. And what a memory."

Mrs. O'Donnell said, in a tone that seemed to hide a gurgle of laughter, "This is my daughter Mary. And Mary, this is Miss Clarissa Gomery, and Mr. Harry Judson."

"So glad to meet you," the Gomery girl said. "I suppose you help your mother in the shop."

Mary smiled at her, trying to put as much dislike as possible into the smile. "I teach English at Girls Normal," she said.

"Why, we're both teachers!" the man said. "No wonder you know Byron. I say, you must be awfully good to teach at Girls Normal. That," he told Clarissa Gomery, "is the top teaching job a woman can hold in the city."

"Remarkable," Clarissa said. "Well, we must be going. Mrs. O'Donnell, I'll take the cape with me and you can send the bill around. Thank you for the poetry, too. Come, Harry."

She tucked her arm through his and led him to the door. She did not quite manage a grand exit. All the way to the door, Mr. Judson's head was turned back over his shoulder as he tried to say something proper in the line of a farewell. He bumped into the doorway. Miss Gomery gave his arm an angry jerk, and pulled him out to the carriage waiting at the curb.

"What a frightful idiot she is," Mary said.

"I wouldn't be saying that," her mother murmured. "The girl is young, and a bit drunk with the power she has over an older man. She has to show it off."

"How old do you think he is?"

"The man might be thirty. And next you'll be asking me if they're pledged."

"It's of no interest to me at all."

"Then I might as well keep it to meself."

"Well, are they?"

"I think it's to be announced in June."

"Did you hear her?" Mary said furiously. " *'I'll take the cape and you can send the bill around. Thank you for the poetry, too.'* She would have loved to tell me to send around a bill for the poetry."

"It's not too gentle you were with the girl. There she was, making the poor man jump through hoops, and you come in and spoil it. You stood in the doorway talking poetry and looking like a Holy Saint, and with nothing but the devil in you."

"Do you suppose it's true that he'll be the next headmaster of Franklin Academy?"

"You know who the Gomerys are," her mother said. "Sure and he'll be running the school if they want it. I don't like what's in your mind, Mary."

"Oh, don't you? Who was at me, only a half hour ago, about not getting the right man for myself?"

Her mother said sharply, "He wouldn't be the right one for you. In one way you're reaching too high, and in another too low."

Mary was not really listening. "So that girl wanted to tell me to send a bill for the poetry, did she? Well, I'll see that she gets one."

9

LATE ON THE FOLLOWING Monday afternoon, Mary O'Donnell sat in a hansom cab watching the buildings of Franklin Academy, west of her on Locust Street near Juniper. Hiring a cab just to sit in it was a slight extravagance, but after all she couldn't pace up and down the street in plain sight. The closed body of the cab provided a discreet place in which to wait and watch. For the past hour there had been a steady straggle of boys in their blue and gold caps and blue blazers coming from the school. And at least fifteen minutes ago the noise of the shinny game, going on behind the wall of the school yard, had died away. He ought to be coming out soon.

She smoothed her coat and made sure she was not sitting any wrinkles into it, and fluffed out the lace that filled in the neckline of her plain gray jacket. The lace was a bit too dressy, but it relieved the straight lines of the suit and called attention to her smooth white throat. Planning like this for a man's benefit was new to her. It put a dancing beat into her blood. Of course she was not sure she wanted Harry Judson. It would not be the brilliant marriage she had once pictured. But if he came from a good family, and really was in line to be headmaster, it would definitely be a big step upward. A headmaster of Franklin Academy would move in the best circles, even though he might only be a courtesy member of them.

Up the street, a tall figure came through the gateway of the Academy, a green cloth bag tucked under his arm, and moved toward her cab with a loping stride. Mary leaned forward and called to the driver through the open hatch.

"Turn around and drive to Twelfth," she said. "And please hurry."

The driver shook the reins, and the cab swung about and rattled down Locust. Mary watched through the rear window. The man she was watching reached Thirteenth and came straight on, which meant that she did not need to have the cab circle the block. She told the driver to turn into Twelfth and to stop right after making the turn. She paid him and got out and walked to the corner and peeked up Locust. He was coming down the pavement a hundred feet away, head tilted forward and coat tails flapping. She timed herself carefully, and walked into his path just as he reached the corner. They bumped into each other, and the book she had been carrying fell to the sidewalk.

"I do beg your pardon," he gasped. "I was steaming along without looking and ... and ..." He gave her a startled look, and said, "Aren't you the young lady I met last Saturday? I don't suppose you remember me, but—"

She laughed and said, "Indeed I do, Mr. Judson. The way you bump into things is unmistakable. Wasn't it our doorway, last time?"

"What you must think of me," he said mournfully. "I'm not always that blind, really. Oh, I say, I knocked your book out of your hands." He picked it up. "Byron!" he exclaimed. "A copy of *Childe Harold!* That is a coincidence, isn't it!"

She said, with just a hint of fluster in her voice, "That incident on Saturday reminded me I'd been wanting a copy of *Childe Harold* for my own, so I've just been getting one from the bookstore." If he wished, he could decide that Harry Judson as well as Byron had been on her mind since Saturday.

"You have a magnificent voice for poetry, Miss O'Donnell. It was such a treat to hear lines spoken that way. The boys in my classes mangle poetry so badly."

"Do you teach English?"

"Just one class. I have two Latin classes, and the rest of my time goes into administration."

"Latin," she said. "How wonderful. I loved it, but I didn't do well in Latin when I was a student. I never had a teacher who could make it come alive. They all seemed apologetic about teaching what they considered a dead language."

"Dead, indeed!" he said angrily. "It's the rock on which the English language is built. It's the international language of science, and of the Roman Catholic Church."

"Mr. Judson, you owe me a couple of lines of poetry, in payment for my Byron. I've never heard anyone who loved Latin recite any Latin poetry. Would you say a few lines for me?"

"It would be a real privilege," he said. He tilted back his head and stared upward for a moment, and then intoned, "Arma virumque cano, Troiae qui primus ab oris ..." He went on through the whole first stanza of the *Aeneid*.

The deep organ tones of his voice made the words throb, and she did not have to pretend that it affected her. She felt a tingle rippling up and down her spine, and said dreamily, " 'I sing of Arms and the man, driven by Fate from the shores of Troy ...' oh, they're such tremendous lines!"

"I ought to apologize for picking out schoolboy stuff," he said. "But it's rather hard for a Latin teacher to keep the first book of Vergil's *Aeneid* from popping into his head. Probably you'd have preferred something less hackneyed. Catullus, perhaps. But it's not always easy to choose a proper line from Catullus. Proper, that is, for mixed company."

"Oh no, I loved it. There's a wonderful beat in those lines. Like the tramp of an armed sentry, or the pounding of surf on a beach. But no one ever got it across to me before."

"I'm awfully glad you like it," he said.

For a few moments they stood looking at each other, groping for something more to say. This, Mary knew, was the critical moment. He was not a boy who could be led around by a few smiles. He was a man, settled and responsible, and almost engaged to Clarissa Gomery. He would not carry on this acquaintanceship unless he found an honorable reason for being with one girl while almost engaged to another. The slightest hint that physical attraction was involved might send him flying. She had to give him that honorable reason within a few seconds, before the pause became awkward and they were forced into the stumbling phrases that would lead into goodbys.

"What a shame that we're both teachers," she said. "If I were a student, I could ask you to read a few pages of the *Aeneid* to me. That would give me the rhythm and feeling of Vergil so I'd never lose it."

"Well now," he said, and stopped.

He was about to make a decision. And, although he didn't know it, the decision might be the most important one of his life. She felt that it was going to be a close thing. She hadn't dared make the invitation too clear, because that might have frightened him. So he might not be sure that an invitation really existed. Or he might have recognized the invitation and thought it too bold. Her next remark had to take care of both those possibilities.

"Oh dear," she said in a faintly shocked tone. "I've just realized what I did. Why, I almost came right out and asked you to spend an hour reading to me. I didn't really mean it that way. You're a busy man and after all—" she threw in a light laugh "—I'm sure the private schools don't want to be bothered with the problems of the public schools."

Was that keeping it on the proper intellectual level? Had the pretended retreat seemed real to him? Had the reference to private and public schools appealed to his sense of duty? She took one step away from him, as if about to leave.

"Now just one moment," he said quickly. "You can't rush off like that, with a bad impression of private schools. I'd be delighted to read some Vergil for you. My copy of the *Aeneid* is in my room down the street and I'd have to pick it up and then we could, well, let's see ..."

"It's too much trouble for you. And we can't sit in a park, because it's getting cool and it will be dark soon. I'm afraid I've been a bad teacher and given you an impossible bit of homework."

"Not at all. Is there anything wrong with us having dinner together? There's a nice place down a few squares, off Walnut Street. The planked shad is very good. I hope you won't think I'm too forward."

As a matter of fact he was delightful at the moment, with his big honest brown eyes looking pleadingly at her. He had the charm of a puppy diving into deep water to bring back a stick.

After he picked up his *Aeneid* from his rooms they walked to the restaurant and got a table in a quiet corner, where the reading

would not disturb anyone. It was a pleasant meal and they sat at
the table a long time afterward, and Mary was careful not to let all
the time be wasted on the reading of Vergil. Bit by bit she learned
quite a lot about him. The Judson family lived in Moorestown,
across the river in Jersey. There had been Judsons in that section
for two hundred years: farmers, shopkeepers, lawyers. None of
them had done anything very good or very bad. Harry's father
was a judge of the county court. Harry had been graduated from
Princeton and had taken his degree of Master of Arts at the
University of Pennsylvania. Then he had taught in New Jersey
public schools for two years, and joined the faculty of Franklin
Academy five years ago.

"And you're already assistant headmaster!" Mary exclaimed.
"That's remarkable in such a short time."

"It happened six months ago," he said, chuckling. "I don't mind
telling you it startled me. Most of the time I'd been helping out
in one department or another, without a real spot I could call my
own. What I was hoping for was a permanent place in the Latin
Department, because that's my favorite subject. Then one day old
Doctor Quimby—he's the head—called me into his office. For all
I knew, he was going to give me a dressing down about something, or even sack me. Instead of that, he said, 'Harry, I've been
watching you carefully and hearing good reports of you. I'm getting along in years, you know. I could use some help. I'd like you
to drop all but three of your classes and take the office next to
mine and help out on the administration. You'll be assistant headmaster. How does that strike you?' Well, as you can imagine, it
struck me dumb."

It would be interesting, Mary thought, to know where the
"good reports" came from. "I'm sure you're much too modest," she
said. "Probably everybody else on the faculty saw it coming for a
long time."

"No, as a matter of fact, I think the others were rather surprised. One of them even dropped a remark that bothered me. The
chaplain, that was. He's a pushing sort of fellow, I must say, even
if he does wear the cloth. And of course we're a Church school and
perhaps he felt that as chaplain he might have an inside track to
be assistant head. What he said was, 'Doesn't hurt to know the
Gomerys, does it, old boy?' It really made me quite angry!"

"The Gomerys?" Mary said, as if she couldn't exactly make the
connection. "Now let's see, the girl you were with Saturday was
named Clarissa Gomery, I believe. But—"

"You see," he said, flushing. "Clarry and I are, well, we have an
understanding. Did you know that?"

"Yes. Mother mentioned it. And of course I know who the Gomerys are. I suppose they're very important in the Episcopal Diocese here, but do they have a direct connection with the Academy?"

"Mr. Gomery is a graduate, but he isn't on the Board of Trustees. So I thought the chaplain's remark was quite uncalled for."

"How did you happen to meet the Gomerys, Mr. Judson?"

"Mother and Mrs. Gomery knew each other at school. They were rather good friends. So when I came here to teach, Mother dropped a note to Mrs. Gomery and they had me to dinner and one thing led to another. I came in handy as an extra man for parties and dances and such."

Mary nodded. Probably there wasn't a hostess in the city who couldn't have used an extra man like Harry Judson: good family, pleasant, available. Of course he wasn't really eligible, as the Gomerys would rate eligibility, but he wasn't ambitious either, and so he wouldn't have seemed dangerous to have around girls of the best families. It must have shocked the Gomerys when Clarissa set her heart on Harry. And it must have been the girl's doing. Mary couldn't imagine him sweeping a girl ten years younger off her feet. Or any girl, for that matter.

She said, probing gently, "Clarissa Gomery must have been quite young when you first met her."

"Oh, she was, of course. Fifteen. I thought of her only as a sort of younger sister. I taught her how to ice skate, and took her sailing when I visited the Gomerys at Cape May in the summer, and things like that, so we were together from time to time. I never suspected that our feelings would ripen into anything beyond friendship. But, well, that's how the world goes. Mr. and Mrs. Gomery were a trifle upset about it at first. All I could do was assure them my only wish was for Clarissa's happiness, and that I would even stop seeing her if that seemed best. Perhaps it's indelicate of me to tell you all this?"

"Oh, I wouldn't say so. Somehow I feel that we're already friends, and have a right to confide in each other."

"Do you really?" he said eagerly. "That's just what I was thinking. Remarkable, isn't it?"

"Yes indeed. So Mr. and Mrs. Gomery withdrew their opposition?"

"I can't remember them taking any positive step to do so. But things worked themselves out."

She smiled at him. He was such a nice man and so very dense about certain things. It was all quite clear to her. With girls like Clarissa Gomery, where there's a whim, there's a way. Perhaps at first she merely had a girlish crush on him, but her family may have teased her until she decided to teach them not to take her ideas lightly. The Gomerys would have backed away from the tears and pouting, hoping that Clarissa would find some more suitable man before a serious decision had to be made. But when the time came to be serious, somehow the decision had already been made.

The only course for Mr. and Mrs. Gomery was to improve Harry Judson's eligibility, while still hoping that the affair would end. It would not have been difficult to arrange for the assistant headmastership. Mr. Gomery undoubtedly knew all the trustees of Franklin Academy. A few words here and there—"Remarkably able chap you fellows have on the faculty, that Harry Judson. What are his prospects?"—would have started things moving. Some of the trustees would start mentioning Harry Judson to Doctor Quimby, and the headmaster would realize he had a man on his staff of whom the best people thought quite highly. That was all there was to it.

If events moved in their proper course, Harry Judson and Clarissa would become engaged in June, and perhaps married the following June. In another year or so Doctor Quimby might find the trustees urging him to take things easier and become Headmaster Emeritus. Then Harry Judson would step into the position, still a bit dazed and never really understanding how he reached it. The question was: could he make it without the Gomery backing? By himself, no. But with the help of an ambitious wife, it ought to be possible. Of course she had to make sure that, in taking him away from Clarissa, she did not make enemies of Mr. and Mrs. Gomery. That shouldn't be hard to avoid. If she did the job smoothly, the Gomerys might even be grateful.

She walked home with Harry through the cool April night, and it took very little hinting to get him to suggest a walk the next Sunday afternoon, during which they could do a few more pages of the *Aeneid.*

He said goodby at the door, and then said, "Do you know, I don't believe I'll ever forget those lines of Byron I heard you say on Saturday."

"Let's hear them," she said. "Let's see if you've learned your homework properly."

He said the lines slowly: " 'She walks in beauty, like the night of cloudless climes and starry skies; and all that's best of dark and bright, meet in her aspect and her eyes.' " He cleared his throat, and added, "They don't really fit Clarissa. They sound as if they were written for you." He cleared his throat again, and tipped his hat and left as if fleeing from something.

Mary smiled. He might find it was too late to start running away now.

10

As the horse car trundled east on Girard Avenue, Mary talked busily and brightly about the things they had seen and done that June day in Fairmount Park. The rowing races on the Schuylkill ... hadn't they been exciting? The diorama of the destruction of Pompeii by Vesuvius, in Memorial Hall ... very educational, wasn't it? The new bear at the Zoo ... hadn't he been funny?

But all the time, beside her, Harry Judson sat as stiff and silent as a marionette waiting for somebody to pull the strings. She hadn't been able to find the right strings. He had acted like this the whole day, and of course she knew what the trouble was. He had to decide very soon between her and Clarissa. She was sure that he wanted her, Mary O'Donnell, but that he felt duty-bound to the other girl. He had a very emotional way of looking at things although, being a man, he probably called it being honorable.

During the past two months she had given him many chances to let his affair with Clarissa fade away. She had tried to lead him into being late for appointments with Clarissa and into breaking dates with the girl. But Harry was not the type to be late or undependable. He trotted faithfully to Clarissa whenever he felt it was his duty. So now it was June, and Harry and Clarissa would be engaged in two more weeks, and then his sense of duty would prevent him from going out with any other girl. It was maddening.

When they arrived back at her mother's shop, he paused at the door and said heavily, "Well, it's getting close on five-thirty."

It had taken him several hours to think up that remark. If she could coax him to stay another two hours, he might be able to inform her that it was getting close on seven thirty. "We'd love to have you stay for dinner," she said.

"Thank you. But I, well, have something to go to tonight."

That had been obvious all afternoon. Of course he was taking Clarissa somewhere. She wanted to say angrily that he could do as he pleased, and go flouncing into the shop, but she couldn't afford to do things like that. Besides, there was a slight satisfaction in keeping him around even a few minutes longer. It was a way of punishing him, because his sense of duty was nagging at him for being with her so close to the time of a date with Clarissa. "You haven't seen Mother for a week," she said. "At least come in and say hello to her."

She led him into the shop, where he greeted her mother and mumbled a few comments about the weather being pleasant. Then he cleared his throat again, getting ready to leave.

"Oh, I just remembered," Mary said. "I have a book of yours I want to return. Just a moment and I'll get it."

She went upstairs and found the book and turned to come down again. It startled her to find her mother at the head of the stairs, waiting for her. Sometimes her mother could drift around like a witch.

"Was it a nice afternoon?" her mother asked.

"It was awful."

"I don't think you're doing so well with the man."

"It's maddening," Mary said. "Trying to do something with him is like squeezing a toy balloon. As soon as he's out of my hands he pops right back the way he was."

"You'd better not coax him to stay too long right now. Early this afternoon Clarissa Gomery brought a dress around to be let out a wee bit. She's wearing it to a party tonight, and she'll be back any moment to pick it up."

"Putting on weight, is she?"

"A pound here, a pound there. I'll give you a few moments alone with the man, for all the good it'll do you. But don't forget that his girl will be here any time."

Mary went slowly down the steps and back into the shop. Harry was sitting on the edge of a chair, balancing his straw boater on his knees. He looked as tense as if waiting for a photographer to set off flash powder and take his picture.

He got up and said, "Good of you to return the book. Well, I must be saying—"

"Harry," she said softly, "what was wrong today?"

He stared at her like a boy caught cribbing in a test. "Wrong?"

"You've hardly spoken a word all afternoon. Have I done anything wrong?"

He walked up and down a couple of times, as if he hoped to find a little courage lying around the shop that he could borrow and nobody would miss. "Anything wrong that's been done," he said finally, "is all my doing."

"You couldn't do anything wrong. You're the finest person I've ever known."

"No, I'm not. I've been unfair to you, Mary. I've had no right to take up your time the way I have, these last two months. And I know I've been unfair to Clarissa."

"Why, Harry. You've danced attendance on her every time she beckoned."

"That isn't the point. The point is that at times I've almost had to force myself to do it. I'm going to be engaged to her! I ought to be eager to see her, every possible moment! My mind shouldn't be pulling me back."

"Pulling you back to what?"

"Do you have to ask me that? Back to you, of course. We've had so much fun together that I didn't realize what it was coming to mean to me. Mary, it can't go on like this."

She took a deep breath. Was he really going to decide, right now? "It has come to mean a great deal to me, too," she said. "What do you want to do about it, Harry?"

Yes, he had finally decided. She could see it in every ridged muscle of his jaw. He said, speaking a memorized piece, "We mustn't see each other again."

There was a long silence, with nothing to break it but the clop of hooves and rattle of wheels on cobblestones outside the shop. A carriage was halting at the curb. Mary had been waiting for this, and so she was in position to see the carriage and watch the flurry of skirts and petticoats as Clarissa got out. Harry was facing away from the shop windows, staring miserably at her.

"Whatever you say," she murmured. "I'm sure you know what's best. Harry, do you realize that you've never kissed me?"

"Yes," he said hoarsely. "I realize that."

"I want you to kiss me goodby."

Before he could debate what that meant in terms of duty and honor, she slid her arms up around his neck and kissed him. For a moment it felt like embracing a hitching post, then his arms swooped around her. It was only for a few seconds. He wrenched himself away, breathing heavily. But those few seconds had been enough. Over his shoulder, Mary saw something pressed against the shop window that looked like a mud pie a child had made. The mud pie jerked back, and became Clarissa's round furious face.

"I will remember that," Harry said, "all my life."

The shop door crashed open. "What a fool I've been!" Clarissa cried. "I should have known something like this was going on. Don't bother coming around, Harry Judson. I don't want to see you any more." Her face twisted like that of a child about to have a tantrum, and she turned and rushed back to the carriage.

"Clarissa!" Harry gasped. "Please wait. I must—"

As he ran out of the shop the carriage was already rolling away. He tried to run beside it, calling up to the girl who sat stonily in it, but the carriage moved faster and faster and at last he stopped and let it go. Mary stood in the doorway and watched him. After a minute he scrubbed a hand over his face, and moved away down the street at a shambling pace.

"Well," a voice behind Mary said, "that was quick and nasty."

Mary swung around and glared at her mother. "Nasty, was it? Who told me that the girl was coming any moment?"

"I wouldn't be denying that."

"You knew what I'd do. If you don't like it, why did you tell me?"

The blue eyes in their lace of wrinkles peered curiously at her. "I wasn't sure what you'd do, Mary. But I thought you ought to have a chance to make your choice, just as I did, once. I had a chance to play that same kind of game, mind you."

"And you played it differently. Do you think you chose right in letting your man go?"

Her mother stared into the distance. "I've never been able to decide. But what I did was from the heart, not from the head. So it's never rested heavy on me."

"You needn't worry about my heart. It won't give me any trouble. And I've beaten her, do you understand? She'll never take him back. And he'll be coming to me before a week is up."

"You've got him, I wouldn't doubt."

"I told you I'd send her a bill she wouldn't like."

"That you did. Now you and the man himself may have to pay one. I hope it won't be steeper than you think."

11

MARY O'DONNELL JUDSON sat in the parlor of her house on Spruce Street, her fingers making quick neat stitches in the cloth on her embroidery hoop. The pattern was coming along nicely. Four blocks away, on Locust Street near Juniper, another pattern on which she had worked ought to be coming along nicely, too. On this April day of 1894, the Board of Trustees of Franklin Academy was meeting to choose a new headmaster. Naturally they would choose Harry Judson, B.A., M.A., Ph.D. With old Doctor Quimby retiring, there was no one on the faculty as well qualified as Harry.

It was five years since she first met him. She had broken up his affair with Clarissa two months after they met, and had married him two months later. For four years and eight months, therefore, she had been arranging the pattern of his life as carefully as if it had been stretched out before her on an embroidery hoop. The pattern had been designed to make sure he became headmaster. There had been so many tiny stitches to take. The house they lived in, for example. It was on Spruce Street near Sixteenth; a three-story row house in that substantial neighborhood was just right for a man who expected to be the next headmaster. It was of brick, with white marble steps which the maid scrubbed every other day. Actually it was too big for them, but some day her mother would be living there with them and then the extra space would come in handy.

The parlor was solidly furnished, and there was no trace of that frivolous Oriental style so many people were taking up. The chairs and sofa and tables were heavy walnut. The pictures of Roman and Grecian ruins, and of Galahad in his armor, were in the best possible taste. The velvet drapes at the windows and doorways hung in deep lustrous folds without any tassels to disturb their classical effect. It was a room that said: you can trust the man who lives here. You can trust him with the running of Franklin Academy and with the education of its pupils.

She had furnished Harry's life just as solidly as the house. Of course she had known, all along, that the Gomerys could have wrecked Harry's career to punish him for the break with Clarissa. But she had counted on them merely to ignore him. After all, the proposed marriage of Harry and Clarissa had been unsuitable, and the breakup had been private, with no damage to the Gomery prestige. She had been right in her figuring. As far as she knew, the Gomerys had done nothing more than withdraw their support from Harry. That, however, had been a serious enough matter. It had been very clear to her, right from the start of their married life, that something had to be done to make up for the loss of Gomery backing.

Well, it had been done. She had coaxed and bullied Harry into completing his work for a degree of Doctor of Philosophy in Latin. It had been hard for him, because he had to do it in his spare time and because he was not a brilliant student. Night after night he had asked plaintively if they couldn't give it up. She hadn't let him; that might have meant giving up the chance to be headmaster, too. Fortunately she had been able to help him over some of the rough spots. Harry might not realize it, but she had written at least half of his thesis. The struggle was over now. His thesis had been accepted and he had passed the Doctor's Oral. And now, in the closet upstairs, hung the hood of his degree, lined with the red and blue silk of the University of Pennsylvania and trimmed with the blue velvet of a Doctor of Philosophy. Owning it was like having the right to wear a crown.

She had given up her own teaching job as soon as they were married. The money would have come in handy, but an assistant headmaster could not have a wife who taught in public schools. It was bad enough for him to have a mother-in-law who was a dressmaker. She had devoted her time to helping Harry work for the doctorate, and to the very difficult job of trying to make allies of the faculty, trustees, leading alumni and, most important of all, the wives. In some cases she had done fairly well, in others not so well. She had failed completely with old Doctor Quimby. She could not put her finger on anything in particular, but she was sure he did not like her.

Her needle flicked in and out of the embroidery, and she tried not to think of her other failure. She and Harry had no children. If she thought about that too much it made her feel ill. Nothing would have any value if there were no children to take advantage of it. The first O'Donnell in Philadelphia had climbed a little way toward the top. She herself had made probably a bigger jump than she had a right to expect. But it would take another generation to go all the way. So far there was no third generation. Some women would say it was because she was cold and did not really love her husband. She didn't believe that. Plenty of wives merely tolerated their husbands, and yet year after year went dragging around with another baby in them.

A key clicked in the front door, and her nerves twitched as if it had been a firecracker. That was Harry. He had hung around the school hoping to learn the results of the trustees' meeting. There was a rustle as he hung up his hat, and changed his coat for a smoking jacket. She forced herself to wait, without calling to him. He came into the parlor and kissed her cheek and carried his newspaper to his favorite chair, just as if it were an ordinary afternoon.

"Did you learn anything, dear?" she said.

He opened the newspaper, and slouched in the Morris chair so that most of his face was hidden. "Oh, nothing official," he said.

All she could see above the paper was his brown hair, parted in the exact middle. His hair was starting to thin, and he ought to stop slicking it down so firmly. Nothing official, he said. It wouldn't be like Harry to tease her by holding back good news.

"If you have any word at all, no matter how unofficial it is, please tell me, Harry."

"I managed to talk to Miss Eddington after the meeting, when all of them had left. But she wasn't there during the discussion. They called her at the end to take down the resolutions."

"But there must have been something in the resolutions about the new headmaster."

"Oh, naturally. But anything official will have to come from Doctor Quimby. I dare say he'll call me in tomorrow."

"Harry! What did she tell you?"

The voice that came from behind the newspaper was flat and toneless, like sounds you might get from tapping two pieces of wood together. "They are going to bring in Doctor Luther Hay Whitney, rector of St. Stephen's Church, as headmaster. The title of assistant headmaster is being dropped."

Because his tone was so empty of feeling it took her a few moments to realize what he had said. She got up unsteadily, and crossed the room to him. His newspaper lifted and continued to hide his face. "Harry," she said, "do you really mean that?"

"Yes," the flat voice said.

She reached out and pulled the newspaper away from his face. For a moment she almost thought a stranger was sitting there. His face was writhing as if every muscle in it was separately alive and in pain. The bright calm mask which he usually wore had come apart like wet cardboard. For the first time she noticed what the strain and study of the last few years had done to him. There were deep hollows in his cheeks and at his temples. His skin had a tight, unhealthy shine. He stared up at her, almost like a frightened child waiting for punishment, and then lowered his face into his hands. His shoulders quivered with the force of hard dry sobbing.

"Oh God," he moaned. "I tried so hard. I knew it meant so much to you. But I just wasn't good enough."

"Was it something the Gomerys did?"

"No, no, Mary. It was just me. They knew I didn't have the stuff to be headmaster. I let you down."

He slid forward until he was on his knees, with his face pressed against her skirt. She stared down at him and tried to realize that the shaking body kneeling before her meant the end of her hopes and plans. He could never come back from this defeat. She waited, almost not breathing, for the numbness of shock to drain from her body and let her think and feel again. Perhaps she was going to hate him when the numbness passed. She hoped not. He looked so lost and alone. There was such a sad little bald spot at the top of his head. She reached down and touched it gently.

"Mary," he said, his voice muffled in the folds of her skirt, "do you think you will want to leave me?"

The numbness was going away now, leaving nothing but a queer ache in her throat. "You mustn't say that, Harry."

"But the headmastership is the only thing you ever really wanted from me. And I can't get it for you."

She moved around him and sat down in his chair. "Come sit on my lap," she said.

He lifted a wet, shocked face. "On your lap? Would that be proper? Would—"

"Come on. Like a good boy, now."

He looked horribly ashamed, but he got up from his knees and lowered himself onto her lap and sat there stiffly. "It seems very high up," he said in a choked voice.

She pulled his head down onto her shoulder, and suddenly he curled up against her and wept. It was no longer the hard dry sobbing that had shaken him so terribly. His long angular body seemed to be relaxing every moment. When the sounds faded away, she said softly, "You may be right that the headmastership was the only thing I used to want from you. But I want something else, now. Do you think you could love me?"

"I've always loved you," he mumbled. "From that first day I saw you in the shop."

"Please keep on, then. And everything will be all right."

"Of course I shall resign," he said in a calmer tone. "I won't have the wives of everybody on the faculty snickering at you behind your back."

"Forget me for a moment, Harry. Do you want to resign?"

"You'll think I'm weak and a fool, if I tell you the truth."

"No I won't. And I'd like to hear it."

"Funny thing about that school. It's grown on me. I hate the idea of going anywhere else. But I really don't think I should stay there, under the circumstances. I might even have trouble controlling my classes, once the boys realize how poorly I rate."

"Can we talk about that later? Why don't you go upstairs and rest? We can have a late dinner."

"A nap might do me good, at that." He got up and smiled shyly at her. "That was a very astonishing thing, having you hold me on your lap."

"An astonishing thing happened to me, too. You run along upstairs, and I'll call you around eight for dinner."

After he went upstairs she looked at the clock. It was not quite six. Doctor Quimby, the retiring headmaster, lived a few squares away on Delancey Street, and would not be having dinner until seven. This might be as good a time as any to talk to him. She studied herself carefully in the hall mirror, before putting on hat and coat. It was bad enough to have to visit him at all, under the circumstances, but at least she could make sure she didn't look haggard. The shadows under her eyes were a shade too dark, and there was a tight line at each corner of her mouth, but otherwise she looked passable. This was going to be very different from the way she had planned to act toward Doctor Quimby after Harry had been named headmaster. She had intended to be friendly but a bit patronizing. That would have brought home to Doctor Quimby the fact that he had been put on the shelf and was no longer important. It would have helped pay him back for never having liked her.

She walked quickly to his house on Delancey, and tugged at the bell-pull beside the door. Doctor Quimby was a widower. His housekeeper came to the door and admitted her reluctantly, with a look that said no respectable woman would visit a widower's home unchaperoned. She went into the library on the first floor, and presently Doctor Quimby came in. He was plump and bald, and in these later years of his life was obviously looking more and more the way he must have looked as a baby. There was nothing babyish, however, about the alert look in his eyes.

"So good of you to call, Mrs. Judson," he said. "I was just thinking the other day, it's been too long since we've seen each other."

"It's nice of you to say that," she said, permitting herself a tiny smile. "And I only wish you meant it."

"Why, my dear Mrs. Judson, I—" He paused, peered again at her. "I see you have something on your mind."

"Can we talk freely, Doctor Quimby? There's something very important I have to find out, and I can't do it if we merely trade small talk."

He settled in his deep leather chair like an old bear backing cautiously into its den. "Talk as freely as you wish, Mrs. Judson."

"This afternoon the trustees picked Doctor Whitney as the next headmaster, and dropped the job of assistant headmaster."

He sighed heavily. "Well, I suspected that was why you came. But I didn't really expect you to learn about it so quickly. Your information is correct."

"Why wasn't Harry chosen as headmaster?"

"My dear Mrs. Judson, these are very difficult things for the trustees to decide, and Harry is rather young for the position, and … wait a minute, you don't want me to feed you that sort of stuff, I can see."

"I want to hear the truth. Would it be easier if I said that I know you don't like me, and if I admitted that in return I don't like you? I respect you, but there's no liking in it. Does that clear the decks so we can talk frankly?"

A rumbling chuckle came from the depths of the chair. "For clearing decks," he said, "your words are at least as effective as shrapnel. You're quite a woman, Mrs. Judson. I will be frank with you, and hope that I will get out of it alive."

"Harry wasn't considered too young when he became assistant headmaster, more than five years ago. So obviously he couldn't be too young now. Am I right that marrying me cost him the chance to be headmaster?"

"That question has many angles. Could we chop it into smaller pieces?"

"The Gomery influence played a big part in making him assistant headmaster, didn't it?"

"I've often wondered about that," he said. "If there were pressures, they must have been quite subtle, and I really thought at one time that it was all my own idea. But you may be right. At the same time and in my own defense, I must say that I looked on Harry as an excellent prospect and thought he would turn out nicely."

"So," she said bitterly, "if he had married a spoiled, empty-headed creature like Clarissa Gomery, he would have turned out nicely."

"Mrs. Judson, you shouldn't simplify it so much. If he had married the Gomery girl and let her run his life, he would not have remained a good prospect for headmaster. But if he had controlled her moderately well, he'd have been all right. Need I point out that part of a headmaster's job is to raise money? The Gomery connection would have been very useful. We have to be practical about these things."

"Scholarship is also important. That's why I encouraged Harry to go after his doctorate. Doesn't that balance the money-raising angle?"

"Luther Hay Whitney is a Doctor of Divinity and a noted scholar."

"He has no better financial connections than Harry does."

"Let me try to explain something rather complicated," he said. "Franklin Academy exists because it serves the upper classes rather well. But in serving it cannot be servile, if you know what I mean. We take young squirts who are rebellious and full of life, and break them to the saddle just as you would train a thoroughbred horse. And we have to do this without breaking their spirit. We turn out young men who are at least slightly educated in formal courses and highly educated in the things society will expect from them. Our ideal is a graduate who will respond in a planned and predictable way when he meets problems involving honor, duty, and all the rest of it. We seldom reach the ideal, but in general our graduates have a passing grade. Do you follow me?"

"I don't see what this has to do with Harry."

"Many of the boys resist our training. Some of their parents put pressure on us to go easier on them. A headmaster has to be able to stand up to the boys and their parents. If he doesn't, the school goes to pot. It is no job, Mrs. Judson, for a social climber. And, since we're being honest with each other, I have to point out that you're a social climber. Your influence would weaken Harry in dealing with parents of high position."

"What makes you think I could influence him so greatly?"

"Because you always have," he said gently. "I don't know the details of his break with the Gomery girl, but I'm sure you arranged it. Since your marriage, I have watched you make every major decision for Harry. He isn't the man he was, five years ago."

She looked down at her white-gloved hands and watched them tremble. She hadn't realized it had been like that. Of course she had made decisions, but only because the decisions were obvious and Harry had seemed to fumble about making them. It had been like watching a nice but slow child try to parse a sentence when she was teaching school, and reaching out impatiently to show how it ought to be done.

She said slowly, "What of his future?"

"I feel quite sure that Episcopal Academy or Penn Charter or Germantown Academy or Haverford School would find a place for him. The University might offer him an assistant professorship. None of these positions would be very grand, of course, but at least they would be good openings."

"Do you really believe that, Doctor Quimby? That his prospects would be good?"

"Perhaps I spoke too quickly. Harry is what, thirty-six? A bit late to start a career. And getting that doctorate took a lot out of him. You drove him hard, Mrs. Judson. So his prospects might not be glowing."

She tensed her muscles, and said, "He loves Latin. Ever since Mr. Case retired, no one has headed the Academy's Latin Department. You've been supervising it, but you will be gone, and Doctor Luther Hay Whitney is not a Latin scholar. Would you consider naming Harry the head of the Latin Department?"

There was a long silence. "That took my breath away," he said finally.

"I'm serious about it."

"That's why you came, isn't it? To propose that?"

"Yes and no. First I had to find out what you thought of Harry and of me. It might not have been worthwhile to suggest it."

"And why do you think it's worthwhile now?"

"Because you're sorry for Harry. Because you'd do a lot to help him, if it wouldn't hurt the school. You would have done some polite lying to help him get another job. I'm asking you to do something that will help the school. And you won't have any polite lies on your conscience."

He levered himself out of the chair and began clumping up and down the room, pausing now and then to kick at furniture. "If I may say so with all due respect," he growled, "confound you, Mrs. Judson!"

She said grimly, "I know just how you feel."

"It must have cost you a lot, to come here with this idea in mind."

"I'd rather have my teeth pulled."

"Mrs. Judson, as head of the Latin Department, Harry would be absolutely in a blind alley. That would be the extent of his career."

"He wouldn't look on it as a blind alley. It would be heaven to him, surrounded by a lot of saints named Cicero and Vergil and Tacitus and all the rest."

"What would it be to you, Mrs. Judson?"

"Yesterday," she said softly, "it would have been hell. Today the answer is that more than anything I want him to be happy. I hope I haven't been too late in realizing that."

He walked to the doorway and bellowed suddenly, "Emma! Emma! Where'd you hide my coat and hat?" He turned back to Mary, and grumbled, "She hates me to go anywhere at night, for fear I'll take a chill. So she hides my things."

Mary got up. Doctor Quimby could be rather frightening. "Where are you going?" she said faintly.

"Where? Where? Good heavens, Mrs. Judson, where do you think? To your house, of course. I want to talk to the new head of our Latin Department. Emma! Ah, there you are. With the winter coat, I see. Well, this time I'll let it pass. But from now on please remember this is April and I wear my light coat."

12

ALL THROUGH DINNER HARRY had been like a small boy at a picnic. Now, as Mary sat in the parlor pouring their after-dinner coffee, he was pacing up and down still talking about how wonderful it was to be made head of the Latin Department.

"And the grandest thing about it," he said, "is that you're not disappointed. Queer. I would have thought that—"

"Your coffee is ready, dear."

"Thanks." He came to the table and stretched out his hand for the cup and saucer. "What's this?" he said. "A big cup? Did the maid break my demi-tasse cup?"

"You'd rather have a full-sized cup."

"But you always said a demi-tasse was correct."

"We just made a new rule. A big cup is correct if you want it."

"Well, that's very fine." He sat down and took several happy swallows from the cup. "Ah-h. I can taste that. Sipping from a demi-tasse never seemed like drinking coffee. Wasn't it wonderful of Doctor Quimby to come here, all on his own, to explain about the trustees' meeting and to offer me that job? You certainly must have been startled when he came to the door."

Harry had been upstairs resting, and had not known of her visit to Doctor Quimby. Now he would never know. "Yes, I was very startled. But of course all along I thought that he must have something very important in mind for you."

"You were smarter than I was. All I could think of was that I was being dropped. I didn't realize that obviously Doctor Luther Hay Whitney wouldn't need an assistant headmaster, since he's just in his forties. He'll be a good head, Mary. He's got a knack of making people do things and liking it. You know, come to think of it, I never had a big urge to be headmaster. But I thought it meant everything to you."

"Isn't it odd," she said, "that people can live together for years and not quite know what's in the other person's mind? I thought you would never be happy unless you became headmaster. So naturally I wanted it for you."

She watched him carefully as she spoke, but there was not the slightest wrinkle of doubt or suspicion on his face. He seemed to have forgotten the talk they had after he returned from school, when she had admitted that the headmastership was all that she had once wanted from him. He had wiped that from his memory. Now he accepted everything she said with the wide-eyed happiness of a boy listening to a story about Indians. In many ways he would always be a boy, and perhaps that was a very good trait in a man who would spend the rest of his life teaching boys. She must make sure that he never lost it.

He said, "I couldn't ask anything better than to head up the Latin Department. My, that coffee was good."

He brought his cup over and put it on the tray and leaned down to kiss her cheek. She turned her head so that their lips met, and curled an arm around his neck.

"Mary!" he gasped. "What's got into you?"

She got up from her chair. The surge of her blood was toasting every inch of her skin. She put an arm through his. "Let's go upstairs," she said.

"Upstairs? It's only nine o'clock. Not time for bed."

She felt that her face must be glowing like a Japanese lantern. "I wasn't thinking of sleep."

He stared at her almost in horror. "You mean ... oh, Mary! It doesn't seem proper just to go to bed for that. And what will the maid think?"

"Do I have to drag you up, Harry?"

"Well, no, but—"

As a matter of fact she did almost have to drag him. She took his hand and kept tugging at him all the way up the stairs. Usually they undressed in a normal, proper way: one of them in the bathroom and the other in the bedroom. Harry offered to take the bathroom, and when she said that shouldn't be necessary, he didn't seem to know what to do. He sat on a chair, facing away from her, and worked on his shoelaces as if they were padlocked. Mary went to the closet and began taking off her clothes. Tonight she did not put on her nightgown before slipping out of her undergarments. She undressed completely, and peeked out at Harry. He had only managed to get off one shoe. She tiptoed to the gas mantle and turned off the light.

"Now I can't see," Harry said in a shaky voice.

"I don't want to shock you," she said, and felt her way to him.

"Mary! You haven't any clothes on!"

"Do I have to take yours off?"

"Look here, young lady, I—"

He got up and fumbled for her in the darkness. Usually when they had each other it was a furtive act, carried on under bedclothes and with sleeping garments getting in the way. This was something new for Harry, and obviously he was ashamed. The touch of his hands was soft and uncertain. She bit his ear slightly and broke away from him and found herself giggling.

"Why, you devil!" he gasped.

There were quick rustling noises as he yanked off his clothes. He came hunting for her in the darkness. She slid out of his grasp several times, laughing, and then suddenly he caught her and the shock of their naked bodies coming together took her breath away. It was the first time that their bodies had ever touched without clothes being somehow in the way. He was startlingly strong, and a bit frightening and quite wonderful. It was strange to have been married to a man like this for almost five years without ever having known it.

Afterward, she lay on the bed without the slightest desire to move, and listened to the strong happy throb of her blood. It was ridiculous to be so sure of anything, but this time she knew she was going to have her baby.

KATE

1913–1914

13

On a June day in 1913, Katherine Judson was dancing around her bedroom getting ready for an outing at Willow Grove Park with a young man. It would be warm in the afternoon, but now there was a tang of coolness in the air that made her deliriously aware of her bare arms and shoulders. Her mother would not approve of the way she was running around half-dressed.

"Modesty is one of the best traits a girl can have," her mother would say. "It is a trait you should practice all the time, even in the privacy of your bedroom. If you are to marry well, Kate, your actions must always be correct."

That, Kate thought, would be very dull. It was fun to be wrong some of the time. For example, this afternoon she was going to do a very wrong thing, from her mother's point of view. She was going to Willow Grove Park with a young man who was not eligible. Her mother thought she was going with two of the girls from her graduating class at Miss Rogers' Select School. The young man was the son of the caretaker at her father's school, Franklin Academy, and he was much older—oh, eight years, at least—than she was. His name was Mike Callahan and he had hair so red it almost seemed you could cook over it. She had known him for years and years, ever since she had been a little girl waiting outside the Academy for her father, and once when she was eight she had announced that she was going to marry Mike when she grew up. Her mother had never forgotten that remark. From then on, Mike had not been welcome at the Judson house, and whenever Kate wanted to see him she had to do it secretly.

Of course, now that she was eighteen years old and quite grown up, she was not at all sure that she still wanted to marry Mike. But, before she could make a final decision, she needed the answer to a very important question: did Mike want to marry her? He had never said anything about marriage, one way or another. She hoped that he would get around to it today, so that she could make up her mind.

She went to her bureau and leaned close to try to get a full-length view of herself in the mirror. The mirror was not very satisfactory. It showed the lace and ribbons of her chemise and the faint upper swell of her breasts, but it ignored her waist and merely gave a glimpse of the sheer black hosiery below her bloomers. Worse than that, it made her legs look short and fat, although any sensible mirror would know they were long and sleek and slim. Her mother did not approve of full-length mirrors for girls. They were not modest. She stepped back and spread her fingers around her waist until they almost met. It was a very nice waist, mirror or no mirror, and today she was going to give it a treat by not wearing a corset waist.

She decided to wear a dress of handkerchief linen and dotted swiss, with lace insertions and hand embroidery. With it she would wear a guimpe, which would keep the dress fresh and clean longer than if she wore a dress with attached collar and sleeves. She tried two hats on her pompadour of dark brown hair. The sailor would be best, she thought, with her regular features.

She finished dressing and came whirling out of her room and saw Grandmother O'Donnell in the hall. Kate was a bit afraid of her. Grandmother O'Donnell was always flitting around the house like a small fierce bird looking for something to peck.

She peered at Kate and said, "That's a fine color you have to your face. Not all of it is a rub with wet red flannel, I'm thinking."

"You know I wouldn't put on rouge, Grandmother."

"Indeed and I know that. It's a nice honest color you have. But don't try to tell me you're that flushed up just for an outing with some girls. What man would it be, now?"

"Suppose it was a man. Would you run and tell Mother?"

"I've never been one to bleat anything I know. Is it that Mike Callahan? You've been sneaking out to see him for years."

"What's wrong with him?"

"Pah," the old woman said. "Bog Irish. Are you going to give up everything your mother's worked for, to marry a Callahan?"

"I don't know," Kate said angrily. "But I'm going to decide for myself, do you understand that?"

"You wouldn't be a crazy O'Donnell if you didn't. There's only one thing I ask." She put a hand on Kate's arm. Her fingers were like dried sticks, but they had a grip that hurt. "Give me a boy in the family. That's all I live for. A boy, do you hear?"

"Yes," Kate said, feeling a bit faint. "Yes, I hear."

The hand relaxed. "And hurry up about it," the old voice said. "I can't wait forever. Even a brat with the name of Callahan to him would be better than nothing." She turned and walked away.

Kate took several deep breaths to steady herself. She had an idea that Grandmother O'Donnell sympathized with her, and understood what it meant to want to grab a little happiness when it came along. Her mother wouldn't have understood; to her, happiness was something you examined suspiciously. You didn't accept it until you could prove it wasn't trying to coax you away from the path of duty.

She walked quietly downstairs and looked into the parlor. Nothing in it had changed for as long as she could remember. There were still the heavy pieces of walnut furniture, and the pictures of Roman and Grecian ruins and of Galahad in his armor. The velvet drapes at windows and doorways hung in the same folds as always, as though no breeze or careless person were permitted to disturb them. There must have been wear and tear on the furnishings of the room over the years, but somehow her mother managed to hide it.

Her father was reading in a chair near the front bay window, and her mother was doing embroidery. Neither of them had noticed her yet, and she paused in the doorway to study them for a moment. Ordinarily she didn't really see her parents. Today, however, she had an odd feeling that some great change was coming into her life, and that she would never again see the room and her parents exactly the way they were today.

Her father was tall and gaunt and bald. Every year he looked more like the bust of Caesar which stood on the table beside him. As far back as she could remember, her father had lived in a pleasant dream world peopled only by the students and faculty of Franklin Academy, by ancient Romans, and by her mother. Kate always felt like a stranger whenever she wandered into his world, a stranger who was welcome but who was not expected to stay.

Her mother was still a lovely woman, tall and slender, with beautiful silver hair. Kate had never quite understood her. At times her mother seemed like two different women. One was grimly intent on making a place in society for her daughter. The other woman was interested only in her husband, and in keeping the sharp edges of life from cutting him.

Her mother looked up suddenly, and said, "I didn't hear you come downstairs, dear. You look very nice. Your picnic lunch is all packed and waiting in the kitchen. You won't stay late and get too tired, will you? I wouldn't want Mrs. Lawrence to make a decision and stop around to see us, and find you all bedraggled."

"Mrs. Lawrence?" her father said. "A decision? Is this something important? Who is Mrs. Lawrence?" He sounded a bit lost, finding himself back in Philadelphia instead of ancient Rome.

"You've met her a few times, Harry. She's very wealthy and has a lovely brownstone house on Rittenhouse Square. She has taken quite an interest in Kate."

"Ah yes. But what is this decision you mention?"

"She has no daughters, Harry, and her husband died some years ago. She has a son of about twenty-seven who is rather an invalid.

At least he is away much of the time, travelling for his health. Every year she picks one girl to sponsor socially—girls from good families who can't afford a debut. I have been very friendly with her for years, and I've been hoping she would give our Kate a debut."

Harry Judson tilted his head back, and frowned thoughtfully. "Debut," he said. "Debut. Let's see now. I'm afraid that word doesn't have a good Latin root. One of those French words. It used to mean starting to throw something at a mark."

"Now it means a girl's first big party, dear. The one at which she is introduced to society."

"That's it, is it?" he said. "Ah well, words lose their force, especially when they don't have a good Latin root."

Kate caught her mother's glance, and smiled faintly. To have a debut still meant starting to throw something at a mark. Yourself, for example.

Her mother had made the whole thing sound very casual, but it was far from that. For years, her mother had devoted much of her thought and energy to trying to win Mrs. Lawrence's sponsorship for her. Her mother had spent years listening to Mrs. Lawrence, slaving on Mrs. Lawrence's many committees, and flattering Mrs. Lawrence. Other women had been doing the same thing, although perhaps not on such a scale, in the hope that their daughters would be chosen. If you were picked, it meant making your debut in the brownstone mansion of Mrs. Lawrence's, wearing clothes paid for by Lawrence money, and meeting people invited by Mrs. Lawrence. The chosen girl was expected to show her gratitude in various ways, such as acting as Mrs. Lawrence's aide at bazaars, flower shows, charity affairs and other events during her debutante season.

It was tremendously exciting to think about, but Kate felt she had little chance. All the girls who had been chosen in the past had been ones who rated a debut but couldn't afford one. There was no use fooling herself; as the daughter of the Harry Judsons she didn't rate a debut. Mrs. Lawrence usually made her decision late in June, and took the chosen girl to the seashore for the summer to prepare for an October debut. There had been no hint yet of what Mrs. Lawrence proposed to do this year.

"I'll be home early, Mother," she said. Then she added lightly, "If there's any news while I'm gone, put that bust of Caesar in the front window, looking out at the street. Then I'll know that Mrs. Lawrence has crossed her Rubicon."

"A good classical phrase," her father said. "To cross the Rubicon, that is, to make a fateful decision. By George, the girl learned a little at that school of hers."

Her mother gave her a small twisted smile, as if it was hard to accept even a tiny joke about something which meant so much.

Kate picked up her lunch box and left the house. Outside a faint breeze stirred the leaves of the buttonwood trees until they rustled like a ballroom gown. She tried to imagine herself whirling around a dance floor at her own debut, gliding from the arms of one handsome man to those of another. The thought stirred a faint, sick excitement in her body. And yet it wasn't just the idea of being the center of attraction at a big dance. What was exciting was the thought of finally being somebody, of belonging, of being accepted. She walked slowly down Spruce Street toward Thirteenth, where she was to meet Mike Callahan, dreaming of the day when she would be a leader of Philadelphia society. She would be very kind and gracious to others, because when you were at the top in Philadelphia you were so secure that you could afford to be. It was only people on the way up who felt they had to snub people below them. She would set everyone a good example by doing charity work. And finally, of course, her son would marry the daughter of an old Philadelphia family, and—

Beside her a voice said, "Should I wake her up or let her go on sleeping?"

"Oh, Mike!" she gasped. "You startled me."

"Good somebody did. You'd have walked right on down to the Delaware and plopped in. How are you, Kate?"

She pushed the dream out of her mind, and smiled at him. In most ways Mike was better than any dream. He was certainly too big to fit into any normal-size dream. He had big feet and big hands, and shoulders that probably had to turn sideways to go through some doorways. He had a chin like half of a red brick, and a snub nose and blue eyes. His bowler hat was set squarely on his head, instead of shoved back the way he liked to wear it. He wore a new brown suit, fashionably tight at ankles and cuffs, and he looked as if he might split open the seams at any moment. His stiff white collar had already cut a red line into his neck.

"Oh Mike," she said, giggling, "you look just miserable, all dressed up that way."

"I'm not miserable," he said. "I've licked other things in my life. I can lick this suit and collar. You look fine. Any trouble getting out?"

"Grandmother guessed I was going to meet you."

"She's a lulu. Nobody puts anything over on her. Well, let's grab this trolley and get started."

During the long trolley ride to the Willow Grove amusement park, Mike spent a lot of time telling her about a new type of work he was about to start. For the last few years he had operated a little hauling business, working for building contractors. Now he was going to branch out into the wrecking business and had a contract to tear down two old buildings at Twelfth and Chestnut. He wasn't going to try to make money out of salvage, the way most wreckers did. He was going to gamble for bigger stakes; the contract offered a bonus for each day by which he beat the deadline for wrecking the buildings and clearing the site, and he was going to try to beat the deadline by months. There was a new thing you could use in wrecking—a huge iron ball that swung from a crane and battered down walls—and it was many times faster than the old way of picking places apart with little crowbars. If he could make a lot of bonus money, Mike wanted to start his own contracting business.

He went into great detail about all this, and Kate wondered if he might be hinting that, provided the wrecking job worked out nicely, he would be in a position to get married. He didn't say anything definite, though. Perhaps he needed encouragement. She was quite ready to consider a proposal of marriage, even though she didn't know what she was going to do about it. But she couldn't consider it properly until Mike made it.

When they reached Willow Grove she began trying to encourage Mike. She gasped in awe when he rang the bells on the strength machines. She shivered against him in the darkness of the Coal Mine. They went on the Chase Above the Clouds, and Pike's Peak, and she was careful to scream every time the cars started down a big drop, even though roller coasters didn't frighten her at all. Mike began showing more and more confidence. Finally he suggested, with great casualness, that they take a ride through Venice. Every girl who had been to Willow Grove at least once with a young man knew what to expect in Venice. It was a big building that covered winding channels of slowly moving water, and you rode in gondolas past lighted balconies and through deliriously dark tunnels. Kate lowered her eyelashes modestly, and nodded agreement.

The first time around, Mike put his arm along the back of the seat and slowly inched it down over her shoulders. She snuggled into the curve of his arm. Mike suggested that they stay on for the next ride. As soon as the gondola drifted away from the landing, Kate unpinned her flat-brimmed sailor hat. She didn't want Mike bumping into it in the dark after he worked up enough courage to kiss her. It only took Mike until the second dark tunnel to get around to the kiss. He had kissed her during other dates, of course, but only briefly when they said good night. This time she let the kiss go on for quite a while.

As they glided through the next lighted space Mike was very restless, and if he had had a paddle they would have reached the next tunnel much sooner. He kissed her again, immediately, as soon as they were in the dark. Kate let her head droop back against the top of the seat. She felt his free hand slip down from her shoulder and move tremblingly onto her breast. Ordinarily she would not have permitted this sort of spooning at all, but she wanted to know how she would react. The warmth of his hand came through the handkerchief linen of her dress and the thin linen chemise underneath. It was really quite exciting, and her nipple became an electric little thing, lifting into a taut point. She put a hand over his to keep him from doing anything more. Her breath mixed with his in warm waves. There was no question about it; Mike could stir her very deeply if she ever decided to let him.

The light at the end of the tunnel crept toward them, and Mike sat up, breathing like a steam engine on a long upgrade. "Kate," he said, "you know I'm crazy about you. I've been in love with you since the day you put your hair up and all of a sudden weren't a little girl any longer. You know what I was leading up to on the trolley. If things go right, in four months I can offer you a decent sort of home and all that. Would you marry me then, Kate?"

It would be pleasant to shut her eyes and say yes and just go drifting off into life with him, the way they were drifting now through Venice. She would never have to worry or struggle. She would settle into Mike's level like a person putting on a pair of comfortable old shoes. The trouble was, sometimes you wanted to wear new shoes even if they pinched.

She sighed and said, "I don't know, Mike."

"I'm not in your class, Kate. But I can better myself."

"You're a sweet thing, and there's nothing that needs to be improved about you. But ..."

"Another man?"

"It's not a man. It's an idea, and it's been hanging around our family a long time. Mike, do you know what a debut is?"

"Is it something you buy, Kate?"

"It's a formal dance at which a girl is introduced to men she might want to marry."

"Give me enough time and I'll buy you all the formal dances you want. But I'd break the neck of any man who came with the idea he might want to marry you."

"Mike, most people could give all the dances they wanted and none of them would rate as a debut. What makes it a debut is who comes to it. It's one of those society things."

"I don't get this society stuff," he grumbled. "I know some people set themselves up as better than others, but they don't sell me on it."

"Well anyway, Mike, there's a chance I might get a debut. Not that we can afford it, or that anybody in society would come to a debut we gave. But a friend of Mother's who has a lot of money and is in society might give me one. Next fall."

"What would happen if you had one of those debuts?"

This was very hard to say, but it was only fair to tell him. "I might meet a man from a very fine family and want to marry him."

"I don't follow it," he complained. "How am I supposed to fight something like this? You might meet a man you might want to marry. Sure, you might meet one next week or next month or next year or when you're fifty. Does that mean nobody ought to marry until they meet everybody they might want to marry? Look, this is a big world, Kate. You have to draw the line somewhere."

She would never get the idea across to him. She would merely hurt him more with each attempt to explain. "Could we leave it this way?" she said. "I'll give you an answer, yes or no, before next October."

"I guess that's as much as I have a right to expect," he muttered.

Somehow, after that talk, the magic had gone out of the trip through Venice. It became a rather silly place in which you noticed that the water wasn't very clean and that the paint was peeling from the balconies and that a ridiculous lot of giggling went on among the other couples in the gondola. They climbed out at the exit platform and, without even talking it over, found themselves walking back to the trolley terminal. On the return trip to the city they dragged out empty ideas and tried to make conversation from them. It was like trying to get fresh lemonade from lemon halves that had already been well squeezed.

It was only seven o'clock, and still quite light, when they walked up Spruce Street and approached Kate's house. "I'd better leave you here," Mike said. "Your mother might be looking out the window."

"I had a lovely time, Mike."

"I think I made a mistake," he muttered. "I don't know what it was, though. If I had done or said exactly the right thing back in Willow Grove, you might have said yes. Now I have a hunch you never will."

"I hope you're wrong."

"I hope so too, Kate. But I don't want to bet on it."

He turned away, and for a moment she watched him stride off down the street, big and solid and dependable. Then she walked slowly to her home. The house sat primly in the neat row with its neighbors, its three white marble steps shining from the morning scrubbing, looking as if this was a day like all other days. Something had changed about it, though. The lace curtains of one window had been pulled back and there, unbelievably, sat the bust of Caesar, looking out at her with hooded eyes.

An odd thrill, blended of fear and joy, lanced through her body. There might be glory or defeat waiting for her in the future, but she would not turn away from it. And somehow Mike had sensed what was coming. The moment had passed, if it had ever really existed, when he might have said or done exactly the right thing.

14

As she went about the last of her packing, Kate could not help stopping every minute to peek out the window to take another look at the car waiting in front of the house. It was a big black Stearns-Knight that must have cost more than six thousand dollars. Not a spot on it needed cleaning but the chauffeur was polishing the brass of the electric headlamps. Of course she had seen Mrs. DeWitt Lawrence's auto before, but this was the first time it had been sent around for her.

It seemed incredible that only twenty-four hours had passed since she returned from Willow Grove Park. She had found her family running around like ants in an overturned nest. Yesterday afternoon Mrs. Lawrence had swept grandly into the house, announced that she had decided to sponsor Kate as a debutante and that she wished to take Kate to the seashore for the summer on Monday morning. They would start early on Monday and therefore Kate was to stay at the Lawrence house the night before.

As Kate closed the last hat box she saw her grandmother in the doorway, watching her with bright eyes.

"It put me in mind of meself, fifty some years ago," her grandmother said softly. "Not that I had so much as a carpet bag. But sure I felt like a princess, with me things in an old shawl, going to work in a fine house for the best people."

It was like Grandmother O'Donnell to pick such a moment to talk about her past. Ordinarily you couldn't get a word out of her on that subject. But now, when Kate had no time to listen, her grandmother was ready to talk. "Things have changed for our family, haven't they?" Kate said, almost irritably.

"Don't be too sure it's a change, girl. Guest or not, you'll be working for what you get, just as I did. If you've a head on your shoulders you'll keep that in mind. And don't be thinking your Mrs. Lawrence is so fine. Herself couldn't hold a candle to the Logan Claytons."

In spite of her need to hurry, Kate had to explore this. "Who were the Logan Claytons, Grandmother?"

"I worked for them when I first came here. You may meet some Claytons one of these days, but I have me doubts that they'd call on your Mrs. Lawrence. Fifty years ago the Lawrences didn't have a penny to their name. They got rich out of the horse car lines and their money still has the newness on it. Grand as she thinks she is, Mrs. Lawrence knows it's not her but her son's children, if he ever gets well enough to marry, who might have a chance to reach the top."

"I wish I could talk longer, Grandmother, but I've got to rush."

"Indeed and we mustn't keep your fine lady waiting in her fine house. But I want you to remember one thing, girl. Keep your pride hot and bright. They'll respect you better for it." She started to leave, and then stopped and said, "Will you be doing me a favor? Ask that coachman waiting for you if his name is Symes?"

"Do you mean the chauffeur, Grandmother?"

"That's what they call them nowadays, is it?"

"Yes. Does he look familiar to you?"

"It's not the looks of him, it's the idea of him that's familiar. When you're writing to your mother, you might let me know." She went off slowly down the hall, feeling her way as if remembering the doors and stairs and turns of a house from the past, and finding this one new and strange.

Fifteen minutes later Kate was in the Stearns-Knight with the chauffeur tucking a robe carefully around her. You might think they were making an enormous journey of a hundred miles instead of the four blocks to the Lawrence mansion on Rittenhouse Square.

Her mother leaned over the side of the car, and said in a low voice, "Now that it has all started, have I done right, Kate?"

She felt closer to her mother in that moment than she had for years. "Of course you have," she said. "It's what we both wanted. I won't do anything to shame you. Goodby. Take care of Daddy. I'll see you after Labor Day."

Up front, the chauffeur used the electric starter and the motor began coughing. Kate waved to her parents and the car moved off down the street.

The chauffeur turned his head slightly, and said, "I neglected to ask, Miss, if you would rather have had the top up. But it is such a fine evening I thought perhaps you would prefer it down."

"This is very nice," Kate said. Then, remembering her grandmother's request, she asked, "By any chance is your name Symes? One of my family thought it might be."

"No, Miss. My name is Bledsoe. Rather odd name, Symes, if I may say so. There is a small garage out near Twentieth Street which carries that name. George Symes and Son. I believe the original proprietor has been dead for some years, and that the son and grandson are carrying on. At one time it was a livery stable. That is the only Symes I can call to mind."

"Thank you, Mr. Bledsoe."

"Just Bledsoe, Miss. The mistress prefers it that way. Am I talking too much, Miss?"

"Not at all. It's nice having someone to talk to."

"Thank you, Miss. You will find, however, that I talk very little when the mistress is in the car. She prefers to do the talking. Here we are, Miss, safe and sound."

He braked the car to a halt at the curb, and jumped out to open the door. Kate walked slowly up the steps of the big brownstone mansion. Mr. DeWitt Lawrence had built it at the turn of the century, and two years later had died in the house of a heart attack. According to rumor, the attack had come on when he backed the losers in a city election, and as a result failed to get the franchise to build and operate the Market Street subway-elevated. A maid opened the door and ushered Kate into a drawing room to the right of the entrance. It was an enormous room with panelling of golden oak and great square pieces of fumed oak furniture. In one wall was a fireplace of smoothly-dressed stone, curving up in a Gothic arch. It was big enough to walk into. Above the fireplace glinted two crossed swords and a battered shield. Mrs. Lawrence, who looked capable of having put the dents in the shield, got up from a chair to welcome her. She was a large woman, with a figure like a tightly-rolled mattress. It was rumored that not even her personal maid had ever seen her in any state other than fully and carefully dressed. Tonight she was wearing pale blue voile, embellished back and front with lace and raised embroidery. The dress had a round neck of Irish lace, and three-quarter length sleeves of embroidery and lace.

"You're in good time, my dear," Mrs. Lawrence said. "It isn't quite eight o'clock. It's good to know you're prompt."

"I can't thank you enough," Kate said, not knowing how to begin.

"Please don't mention it. I trust this will be a lovely experience for both of us. I'm sure you are the prettiest of the girls I have sponsored. Let me see, there have been seven. No, eight. No, I will call it seven, because I won't count that girl I had to send home. Do you know, she never showed the slightest bit of gratitude. She accepted everything as if it were her due. I am sure you are far more sensible."

"It's a wonderful chance for me, Mrs. Lawrence. I hope I can prove how much I appreciate it."

"That's nice, my dear," Mrs. Lawrence said, this time without urging Kate not to mention it. "You know, of course, that this is

75

somewhat of a pioneering venture in your case. It would have been so much easier to have taken on a girl whose family is already in society. However, if I have a position in this city, and I would like to see anyone deny it, this will show people how strong it is. I suppose you have brought all kinds of clothes."

"Heaps of them, Mrs. Lawrence. I hope you won't be shocked at how many they are."

"Probably they will be quite unsuitable. When we are settled in the cottage at Beach Haven, I will have a dressmaker come down and fit you out. That tailored suit you are wearing with the plain white collar and cuffs is not right for you at all. You must learn the softening values to the complexion of filmy lace neckwear, in white or delicate cream tones. The Mechlin laces, and fine Brussels net, should be exactly right for you."

"I can see I'll be a terrible trouble."

"Not at all. I will enjoy it, my dear. Nothing pleases me more than to start a nice girl off properly in life. Of my eight girls, no, we agreed to call it seven, four made very good marriages and three made passable ones. The latter could have done better if they had followed my advice more closely. Now I am going to show you your room, Kate, and then I will ask you to excuse me so that I can retire early. We will leave at nine o'clock in the morning for the shore."

She led the way up a wide golden oak staircase to a room on the second floor. The bedspread was pink satin, and there were pink draperies on the windows, and the wallpaper and even the lamp shades were pink.

"We call it the Pink Room," Mrs. Lawrence said. "Now tomorrow, my dear, you will only be able to take one suitcase and one hat box in the car. The rest will follow by van, arriving I trust a day later. So you may wish to do some repacking. I will leave you to it. Of course feel free to go downstairs to read if you wish." She started to leave the room, and then hesitated. "There's just one thing, my dear ..."

"Yes, Mrs. Lawrence?"

"I don't believe we have mentioned my son. I hope he will eventually join us at the seashore, but I cannot count on it. His health is not good, and he insists on riding horseback and doing active things that harm his health further. Personally I feel that the sea air would be excellent for him, but the doctors always seem to think that the air in other places is better in his case. It is very difficult to argue with doctors. They take refuge in long medical terms which even they, I suspect, do not fully understand. His present doctor has recommended a trip to northern Maine for Billy this summer, and I suppose he will go there as soon as I am out of the way and unable to oppose it. He has only been back a month from Africa, of all places. He was away almost a year and did a lot of hunting and claimed that it did him a great deal of good, although I must say that I saw no improvement when he returned. I believe he would have stayed there indefinitely, wrecking his health completely, if I had not insisted that he return. Well, it is unlikely that you will see him before we are settled at the shore, if then, but I thought I had better mention it. Good night, my dear. The maid will call you at seven in the morning."

Kate repacked a suitcase and hat box with things for the first day at the shore. Then, because it was too early to start to bed, she went downstairs, her feet seeming to float over the thick carpeting. The drawing room looked big and desolate, like a department store furniture sale which was not quite ready to open, and she crossed the hall to the library. There was a bare patch of floor between the hall carpeting and the rugs in the library, and her heels clicked sharply on it. Somebody in the library made a quick rustling movement. She paused, frozen, and found herself staring across the room into the eyes of a young man. His face had rather a baby plumpness and he was almost pouting, as if someone had threatened to take away a toy. His hair looked like small curled shavings from the golden oak. He was poised beside a bookcase, one hand behind a row of books, and his blue eyes seemed to be staring at her fearfully.

Then the fear, if it was fear, left his eyes. He scowled and said thickly, "Who the hell are you?"

"I'm sorry," she said. "I didn't mean to startle you. You must be Mrs. Lawrence's son."

"Thanks for telling me who I am. As it happens, I already know. I wanted to know who you are."

"I'm Katherine Judson," she said. "I just arrived tonight and I'm going to the shore with your mother tomorrow. I'm sorry I disturbed you."

"Oh. You're next season's project, are you?" He walked toward her, lurching a bit, and she saw he was carrying a glass partly filled with a brown liquid. "Don't run away yet," he said. "This is a good time to get a couple of things straight. If you've got any idea you'll see much of me, forget it."

He was so close now that she could smell his breath, which was thick and musky with liquor fumes. "I had no ideas about you at all," she said. "I'd rather talk to you some other time when you haven't been drinking."

He glared at her and flourished the glass. "Medicine," he said loudly. "Have to take it for my health."

"It's liquor. I even saw you shove the bottle back of that row of books."

He gave her a smile full of cunning and said, "We had a maid two years ago who went to Mother and said I was sneaking drinks. Mother said she was a spy and a liar, and fired her."

"I'm not a housemaid or a spy or a liar, Mr. Lawrence."

"You're a girl," he said, and somehow he managed to make that sound worse than spy or liar. "You're a girl and you'll be buzzing around trying to hook a man. Just cross me off the list, do you understand?"

If she had to leave the house for it, she was going to give him something to remember. She brought up her right hand and slapped him. "Run and tell your Mother that," she said.

For a moment he stood there, weaving, with the white print of her fingers slowly fading from his cheek. He shot out a hand suddenly, grabbed her wrist. "I ought to teach you a lesson," he cried. "I ought to take hold of you and—and—"

He was acting like a small boy who was about to throw himself on the floor and kick and scream. He couldn't find any more words to fling at her because obviously he didn't know what to do after grabbing her wrist. She had met many small boys and seldom had trouble handling them. "We're both being silly, aren't we?" she said in a calm voice. "I'm sorry I slapped you but you really did ask for it. That's quite a grip you have. You're very strong, aren't you?"

He looked down at the hand which still held her wrist. His fingers relaxed. "Yes," he said, with a pleased note in his voice. "I am strong. I can lift two hundred pounds over my head."

This was strictly small-boy talk, and she felt more and more confident. "That's a lot. I don't suppose the average man can lift half that much."

He took a drink from his glass, and wiped his lips on his sleeve. "A lot of people are strong but don't have any endurance," he said. "I can ride horseback all day and not get tired. In Africa last winter I hiked miles and miles every day while we were on safari. I had one of the white hunters who guided Teddy Roosevelt. He started off thinking I was one of these weak greenhorns. Before we were done I showed him. Maybe you don't believe me?"

"Of course I believe you. What sort of things did you hunt?"

"Oh, lions, rhinos and all that. I got a Cape buffalo with a record pair of horns. Wounded him with the first shot and had to go into deep brush to get him. My white hunter had a fit. The Cape buffalo thinks almost like a person, and tries to figure out how to get you."

Kate looked at him curiously. "I thought you were supposed to be sick all the time. You don't look it."

She saw at once that it hadn't been wise to bring up that subject. His eyelids drooped and he peeked out from under them watchfully, like an animal from a cave. "It comes on me from time to time," he said. "The only thing that does me good is to get away."

"You're going up to northern Maine this summer, I hear."

"Mother told you that, did she? Good camping up there. Good fishing. The air in Maine does me good."

"I hope you enjoy it. Catch a fish for me, will you? I've always wanted to go fishing."

He drained the last swallow from the glass. "I'd have expected you to urge me to come to Beach Haven."

"Why should I? You have a right to lead your own life."

"Tell that to Mother," he said. "She wants to lead everybody's life for them." He swayed a little, and leaned close. "Tell you a secret," he whispered. "She wants to be the founder of a goddam dynasty in Philadelphia. But you know what? To keep a dynasty going you got to have a crown prince. He's got to have a crown princess. You know what? All she's got is a crown prince, and that's all she's going to have." He started to chuckle, and turned away from her as if she were no longer there and walked out of the room. She could not hear his footsteps on the carpeting but she heard the ghostly chuckle drifting away through the hall and up the stairs.

15

By mid-morning of the next day the Stearns-Knight had crossed the Delaware to Camden on one of the Pennsylvania Railroad ferries and was miles down the White Horse Pike. It was a pleasant day and the top was down. Mrs. Lawrence and Kate sat in the back seat, wearing big loose dust coats and veils tied around the tops of their hats and down under their chins. It had been a strangely silent ride. Mrs. Lawrence had hardly spoken except to ask Bledsoe, every five minutes, if he was sure of the route. The rest of the time she sat looking grim.

"We are coming to another town, Bledsoe," she said. "Do you know which one it is?"

"Yes, Madam. The Blue Book says that at twenty-five and four-tenths miles we turn sharp left onto a gravel road past a white frame house, while the Pike bears right beside a lake."

"There's a lake and a white house, Bledsoe."

"Yes, Madam. This should be our turn."

The Stearns-Knight made a sweeping left turn onto the gravel road, and the smoothness of the Pike gave way to a steady vibration mixed with jolts. Behind them, dust lifted in a long tan-colored veil.

Mrs. Lawrence rode in silence for a few minutes, then said in a low voice, "I cannot help feeling deeply disappointed, Kate."

"About the road?" Kate asked timidly. "I suppose it is a little bumpy but it's so exciting to drive along like this."

"Not the road. I'm disappointed in you."

"Oh but Mrs. Lawrence, what have I done!"

"My son told me that he met you last night."

"But Mrs. Lawrence, it was an accidental meeting in the library, and while we weren't chaperoned everything was quite proper." She was taking a chance in saying that, but she could not believe that young Mr. Lawrence would have mentioned the slap.

"Proper!" Mrs. Lawrence snorted. "Don't you have any gumption, Kate? Here you're alone for minutes on end with a young man who is too shy to spend seconds with most girls, and all you thought about was being proper! Oh, if I had ever suspected you might meet him I would have arranged things differently. He's terribly backward about girls. At best, I hoped to have you meet him after Labor Day, by which time you would have known something about grooming and clothes. There you were in that plain little tailored suit with almost mannish collars and cuffs. Perhaps he wasn't even sure you were a girl. Now he'll come back from Maine and have another relapse and take to his bed and then some idiotic doctor will suggest another trip for his health. What did you talk to him about?"

"I'm awfully sorry. You see, I didn't know he was shy. He told me some fascinating things about hunting in Africa."

"Oh good heavens! Hunting! Africa! Haven't you had any experience at all with men? With using womanly charm?"

"Actually, Mrs. Lawrence, I kept thinking of him as a small boy who wanted to talk about a game he had just played. You see, what with Daddy being head of the Latin Department at Franklin Academy, I've met dozens and dozens of small boys, and they're all very much alike. They sneak off into corners, unless you can find what they're interested in and talk to them about it."

"You have an extremely childish outlook, Kate. My son is not a small boy. He is twenty-seven years old and it is high time he married. While nothing of the sort has been in my mind in connection with any of the girls I have sponsored, I did hope that at least one of them would bring him out of his shell so that he would start taking an interest in the gentler sex. Oh, I am so disappointed."

Kate said meekly, "I will try to do better next time."

"There will never be a next time. There—"

The car lurched, and began bumping heavily on one of its wheels. Bledsoe steered it to the side of the road and stopped. "I beg your pardon, Madam," he said, "but we have our first puncture."

"I wish," Mrs. Lawrence said irritably, "that you would take a different attitude toward it. By talking about our first puncture you give the impression that you are looking forward cheerfully to more. Now I suppose you will insist that we get out of the car."

"When a person is in the car, Madam, a sudden motion might send the car off the jack."

"Oh, very well, very well," Mrs. Lawrence grumbled, starting to climb out.

Bledsoe removed the spare wheel from the back, and jacked up the left rear axle and began to remove its wheel. There was a nail in the tire, and Mrs. Lawrence said she was sure that farmers went about scattering nails on roads in order to get back at motorists for causing dust and killing chickens. She walked up and down the road a short way, looking for a farmhouse whose farmer could be blamed. However, they were already in the pine woods, with the gravel road stretching emptily in front and back of the car, and she was disappointed in her search.

Bledsoe almost had the spare wheel in place when there was the first sign of another car on the road. There was a steadily rising hum from behind them, and a car swung around the curve of the road a mile back. Rolling waves of dust surged up behind it. The hum thickened to a low roar.

Mrs. Lawrence glared down the road. "It is drivers like this madman who give all of us a bad name with farmers," she said. There was an almost pleased note in her voice, now that she had found someone to blame for their puncture. "Get out your handkerchief, Kate, to cover your nose. The dust will be terrible."

"I do believe he's slowing down," Kate said.

"Nonsense. Drivers like that never slow down. They—good heavens, Bledsoe, isn't that a gray Marmon? A two-seater?"

Bledsoe peered at the car, which had definitely cut its speed. "I believe you are right, Madam."

"It's quite impossible. And yet ... and yet ..."

Kate had no idea what they were talking about. The car was close, now, and obviously was going to stop. It was a racer with a long gray hood and no top. The driver wore a visored cap and dust jacket and heavy goggles. A hand in a leather gauntlet reached outside the body of the car and tugged back on a long-shafted brake. The car stopped beside them with its motor growling.

"Good heavens, Billy!" Mrs. Lawrence cried. "Has there been a fire at home? What on earth are you doing here?"

Young Mr. Lawrence opened a low door and got out, pushing the goggles up on his forehead. He seemed startlingly different to Kate than the person she had met last night. There was something crisp and positive about every move he made. Hard white lines fanned out from his eyes through the film of dust, and his mouth was set in a firm line instead of a babylike pout.

"Hello, Mother," he said. "Good morning, Miss Judson. Hi there, Bledsoe, need some help with that tire?"

"Thank you, sir, all I have to do is tighten the lugs."

"I'll put the old wheel back," he said, lifting it casually with one hand and setting it into place on the rear of the car.

"You didn't answer me, Billy," she complained. "I asked if there was a fire at home or some other trouble."

"There's nothing wrong, Mother."

"But Billy, you were coming at a terrific rate. You can't deny it."

"Just letting the engine warm up for a minute or two, Mother. I've been crawling the rest of the time. Do you like my car, Miss Judson?"

"It's beautiful," she said, touching it almost reverently. "How fast can it go?"

"It can do eighty. Not that—" he glanced at his mother "—I've ever had it anywhere near that speed."

His mother said, "Tell me honestly, how long did it take you to get here, Billy?"

"Let's see. I left home about a half-hour after you did. That makes it two hours on the road."

Kate said in a low voice, so that Mrs. Lawrence couldn't hear, "I'll bet you did it from Camden to here in forty minutes."

"Yes, at least two hours," young Mr. Lawrence said loudly. Out of the corner of his mouth he muttered to Kate, "Thirty-one minutes."

"It must be such a thrill to hold the wheel of a car like this," Kate said. "I don't know why people think that a girl shouldn't drive."

"No reason at all why you couldn't learn to drive," he said. "I might even teach you. That is, if I stay at the shore more than a couple of days."

"You're coming to the shore?" his mother gasped. "But I thought—then there was what the doctor said—and about Maine—"

"I thought I'd at least see you settled in the cottage before taking off. Well, if you're all set, I'll be on my way. Goodby, Mother. Take it easy on the punctures, Bledsoe. I'll see you at the cottage, Miss Judson."

He snapped his goggles down into place, and climbed back into the big racer. A gauntleted hand waved at them and the growl of the motor deepened and the car moved away. They watched it roll sedately down the gravel road, hardly stirring a wisp of dust. It swung around the next bend a few hundred yards away and suddenly the exhaust thundered and dust smoked up through the tops of the pines.

Bledsoe tightened the last lug and walked toward the tool box on the running board. As he passed Kate he whispered, "Personally I think he can do at least ninety."

"I will never get over it," Mrs. Lawrence said. "He is actually coming to the shore." She looked at Kate, with her glance taking in everything from the tips of Kate's dusty shoes and the shapeless dust coat up to the ends of hair straggling from under her hat. "I must admit," she said, "that I am no longer disappointed in you, my dear. Perhaps womanly charm was never the answer."

16

IT WAS A SUMMER like all summers on the coast. There were hot blue days. There were days like champagne fizzing from a bottle. There were days that reeled drunkenly to thunder and squalls and quick bright blasts of sunlight. There were days when northeasters swept in clean and hard, and scrubbed the sea and beach as if nature were doing its wash. It was a summer like all summers but it was new to Kate. Back in Philadelphia, nature did not force itself on you this way. It came around politely to the back door like a tradesman, hat in hand.

And also in Philadelphia, Kate thought, your emotions were expected to use the servants' entrance. Down here they did not. For the first time she found herself drawn slowly and painfully deep into the lives and problems of two other people. The storms and calms and sun and shadow that moved across this meeting place of sea and land found echoes in the pattern of her own life.

Young Mr. Lawrence did not go to Maine. At first he was only going to stay at the shore a few days. Then he decided to round out the time to a week. Next he planned to spend July at Beach Haven and August in Maine. But long before July ended there was no more talk of Maine, and he had settled for the summer into the big Victorian house which Mrs. Lawrence called her cottage.

Kate soon became aware that somehow she had created a new and delicate balance in the relationship between young Mr. Lawrence and his mother. Without her, the balance would have swung violently one way or another, and young Mr. Lawrence would have had one of his strange illnesses or would have broken away to travel for his health. The balance was not perfect even now. There were days when he sat huddled under blankets on the porch, saying nothing and with his eyes as blank as bits of old clam shell. There were other days when he charged furiously out of the house and climbed into the Marmon racer and vanished for hours. On one frightening day of a northeaster he ran to the beach and plunged into surf so heavy that it shook the house.

He returned from these bursts of action pale and tired but in an oddly elated mood, as if the action had been a stimulating drug. Then in a day or so the drugged effect disappeared, and what happened next depended on how evenly the new balance in the Lawrence family was adjusted.

Of course Kate knew what was wrong. For Mrs. Lawrence there were two classes of things in the world: those she wished to own and those she did not wish to own. She looked on people in the same way. And when she wished to own something she wanted absolute possession. Young Mr. Lawrence had grown up fighting against such ownership, and giving in to it, and fighting again, and retreating into the truce of illness. But it was much easier to see what was wrong than to know what to do about it.

At first her emotions had not been involved. She had been flattered that he had come to the shore for a few days, obviously to see her, and it had been an interesting game to try to make him stay. But gradually it became more serious than a game. She learned that she could head off many of his depressed or violent moods by coaxing him to talk about the hunting or fishing or riding or driving he had done. He boasted about such things like a small boy but he was telling the truth. You couldn't ride with him in the big Marmon and watch him take the curves of gravel roads at high speed without realizing that. He could swim for hours in the surf, his golden head and smooth brown shoulders sliding in and out of the waves like a seal. Once, sailing far out on Barnegat Bay, they were caught in a squall that struck the water like a giant fist. He did not drop the sail and try to anchor. Instead, he turned downwind and made the little sloop skim like a gull under the coaxing of his hands. At times like those, when he was doing something well and she was watching, his happiness made her throat tighten and she would want to reach out and touch his hair or skin. Not that she gave way to such urges. If their bodies brushed casually, when he was teaching her to drive or swim or sail, he did not seem to mind. But any deliberate contact made him withdraw, as a friendly wild animal might jump back if you reached out a hand to pet it.

So the storms and calms and sun and shadow of the summer went by, and the Labor Day weekend arrived. Kate hardly knew where the summer had gone, but she knew that with it had vanished the rather calm and practical girl who had once gone to Willow Grove Park and experimented carefully to see how deeply she cared for a man. Now, with another man, she was afraid to test her feelings.

On the Monday night of the Labor Day weekend she was sitting on the porch of the cottage. She had been in the living room, reading, but the lines in the magazine had started to run together and she had come outside to rest her eyes. Across the road and beyond a curve of sand dune, the black ocean wore a tinsel scarf of moonlight. She breathed deeply, trying to get air to a spot in her lungs that seemed to be starved for it. She could not force the air quite that far. Tomorrow they would return to Philadelphia and begin the serious preparations for her debut. Once it had been an exciting prospect. Now it was something that she would do because she had been told it would be good for her, like holding her shoulders back or taking Latin.

The door from the house opened and someone came across the porch to her. "There you are, my dear," Mrs. Lawrence said, lowering herself into a rocker beside Kate. "Lovely night. Are you sorry the summer is over, Kate?"

"I don't know," Kate said. "I feel sort of mixed up about it."

"At your age, girls often feel mixed up. I wanted to have a little talk with you. Tell me honestly, Kate, would you feel cheated if you did not have a debut?"

In the darkness Mrs. Lawrence's face was a solid block of shadow, and Kate could not see her expression. Six weeks ago such a question would have thrown her into a panic, for fear she might have displeased Mrs. Lawrence. Now, when a debut no longer meant much to her, the question merely made her alert and wary. Usually Mrs. Lawrence spoke directly to the point. But when Mrs. Lawrence began sidling toward whatever subject she planned to discuss, it was a good idea for the listener to remember how fishermen circled a school of fish before closing their net. Kate said carefully, "I couldn't feel cheated, Mrs. Lawrence, because nobody owes me a debut."

"A very sensible answer, my dear, but not exactly what I was after. Perhaps I'd better say at once that I am not in the least disappointed in you. Quite the contrary. You know the basic purpose of a debut, do you not?"

"To meet eligible men, of course. And then to marry one of them. The parties and dances are just the trimming."

"Exactly. You are a very practical girl. Now then, if the basic purpose of the debut can be carried out without all the trimmings, it would be sensible to discard them and not have the debut, would it not?"

There really was a net closing, and Kate's thoughts were darting around like frightened minnows. "I'm sure you're right," she said, "but I can't imagine what it has to do with me. I—"

"Now think, my dear," Mrs. Lawrence said kindly, and patted her arm.

"I—I'm really afraid to."

"Your modesty is most becoming to you, Kate. Who would have thought, when you came in so timidly last June in that drab little suit with the mannish collar and cuffs, that in less than three months you would almost be a member of the family."

There was not enough air on the porch now to fill her lungs. "It's been so kind of you to treat me as a member of the family," she said faintly.

"Come now, Kate," Mrs. Lawrence said with a touch of annoyance. "You're fencing with me, and I don't like to be fenced with. I use the term, almost a member of the family, in its most practical and legal sense, not as a term of courtesy. You understand what I mean."

There was no use darting and twisting any more. The net had closed tightly. "You want me," she said, forcing the words out, "to marry Bill."

"Really, my dear! It's not a matter of my wanting such a thing, although naturally I would expect my wishes to be considered. It is a matter of you wanting to marry Billy, and of Billy wanting to marry you. Happily, all three of us feel the same way."

"But I don't know how I feel!" Kate cried. "I've thought of Bill that way, but I don't know him well enough yet. I like him tremendously. I enjoy being with him. But there's so much of him that's still strange and remote and that I can't get close to. If things aren't rushed, if we can go on this way a year, or even six months, I—"

"Many girls feel like that at one time or another about the man they're going to marry."

"But how can I marry a man who is still partly a stranger?"

"Pish and tush. I hardly knew DeWitt when we were married. My father was a minister, and came from a fine old family but one which had never received the recognition due it. We were poor as church mice. DeWitt was a member of our parish and always placed twenty dollars in the collection plate and wanted everyone to know it. He was in his thirties, but he was already putting together some of the small horse car lines into a larger company. I thought him a rather loud and pushing creature, and as a matter of fact he was. He came courting me as if I were a horse car line, to be snapped up with as little fuss and delay as possible. It took an effort of will on my part to go through with the marriage, and even more effort of will afterward to make him over. But it worked out very well. So you see, my dear, you have great advantages over me. You are already very fond of Billy."

The rush of words had tumbled over Kate like waves breaking. She felt dizzy, and said, "I just don't know. I just don't know. What has Bill said? Or haven't you talked to him?"

"I mentioned it to him just now."

"What did he say, Mrs. Lawrence? Don't you see, that's the important thing! What did he say?"

"You know Billy. He gulped and stammered something and buried himself in a book."

"He didn't rush out? He isn't in his car?"

"No. He didn't really do anything. You know how shy he is. I said that I planned to talk to you about it at once, and he was probably relieved to have me offer to, shall we say, break the ice. I think we should plan the wedding for early October, which will give us a month to prepare."

Kate tensed herself and shut her eyes, the way she always had to do before she could jump off a diving board. "I can't be ready in a month," she said. "I can't be ready in six months, or a year or five years. Not unless Bill convinces me that he's ready."

"Well!" Mrs. Lawrence gasped. Then she paused, and breathed heavily for a few moments. Finally she said, "I suppose, after all, your point of view is reasonable. If you will remain here, Kate, I will send Billy out."

She got up and marched into the house, managing to leave the impression that Kate had almost carried reasonableness too far. Kate closed her hands into fists and pushed them against her temples. Her head felt like a boiling tea kettle, and her thoughts kept escaping from it like steam.

Another set of footstepts tramped across the porch, and a queer flat voice said, "I understand that you have agreed to marry me."

She shook her head, without being able to speak.

"You might do me the courtesy of giving me the same information you gave Mother."

He was standing a little distance away, and was not looking at her. His profile looked as cold and remote as one of those plaster statues of Greek athletes, with closed blank eyes, that she used to sketch in art class. "I did not agree to marry you," she whispered. "I said I didn't know."

"What don't you know?" he said sharply.

"Bill, your Mother threw this at us without warning. We only half know each other. I'm terribly fond of the part of you that I know, but it isn't enough. I like being with you. I like doing things with you, driving, swimming, sailing, dancing. I wish we could go on this way for a while and see if ... if ... I guess I'm not explaining very well."

The cold profile turned toward her. "This is not exactly what Mother told me."

"Don't stand there looking so cold and scornful," she cried. "I'll make it stronger if you want. I'll go in and tell her that never, under any circumstances, would I marry you. Does that make you feel better?"

"I believe you would tell her that," he said, with awe in his voice. "You have a lot of courage."

"I don't at all. I'm scared to death."

"It's a hell of a thing," he muttered, "when a man's mother takes over a thing like this. Of course there may be some question that I'm a man."

"You can't say that! I've seen you do all kinds of things that take courage."

"Yes, I try very hard to prove I'm a man, don't I? Fast driving, hunting, anything in the active sports line. I can prove it in all the ways that don't matter. Everything but standing up to her. I don't know what's wrong with me."

"You don't have to worry about standing up to her in this case. I can do that."

He was silent for a moment, and then said, "The funny thing is, I'm not sure I want you to."

"Bill, you can't do this to me," she said in a choked voice. "You've got to make up your mind."

"Why should I? You haven't made up yours. I wish we could go on the way things were, just as you do."

"All right. Then why don't we? All we have to do is tell her we're not ready to decide."

"Kate, you don't know Mother. You haven't tried fighting her. If you fought her, she'd send you home in a minute. If I fought her, she'd insist on giving you a debut and she'd throw at you every good-looking man she could get her hands on. Then she'd sit back and watch me squirm."

"Do you mean that would bother you?"

He dropped to his knees and put his head on her lap. "It would drive me crazy," he mumbled, "and she knows it. I used to hate girls. I had no time for any of them until you came along. I can't lose you, do you understand?"

She touched his hair, and felt him tremble. But he did not draw away. "Why would you lose me?" she asked. "If I went home, you could still come and see me."

"She'd close the house and insist on taking me away on a trip. I don't think I could get away with saying no to her. I'd probably end up sick. You know that habit of mine. It may have started as a trick when I was a kid but now I can't control it."

"Bill, suppose you fought her and I went along with her plans for a debut. What would be wrong with that? We could still see each other, no matter how many men she brought around for me."

He said huskily: "I'd never be able to compete for you. I'd see a lot of men around you and I'd want to go off somewhere alone. Then after a while your feelings would be hurt, and you'd start pushing me out of your life."

"I'm not thinking very clearly now, Bill. But haven't you blocked off every possible choice? What do we do about it?"

His hands dug into her legs and made them hurt. "Thanks for asking me," he said. "I think that gives me just enough courage. Kate, will you marry me in October?"

"No! I won't have it this way. I—"

He jumped up suddenly, and grabbed her hands and jerked her upright. "You've got to have it this way," he said violently. "You've got to take a chance on me. If I'm ever going to be a man, it's got to be with you. Do you hear me? Do you hear me?"

He shook her roughly. It made her feel oddly limp, like a rag doll, and she began to cry. His arms clamped around her and pulled her body close to his. There were wild quivers going through him. His head bent and he kissed her. It was unlike any other kiss she had ever received. He was handling her like a racing car he had to control, or a wild animal he had to kill or a boat he had to drive through a storm.

His head lifted and he said, "You're going to marry me, aren't you?" It was less a question than an order.

"Yes," she whispered.

He released her and stepped back. "I'll go tell Mother."

She sank back into the chair and gave way to hard dry sobs that seemed to be twisting her ribs out of place. It was terrible not knowing whether there had been love in his kiss, or hate.

17

SHE CAME DOWN the aisle of the church on her father's arm, timing her steps to the relentless beat of the Wedding March. It had not been difficult in rehearsal but now it felt like walking a tight rope.

Among the people in the crowded pews were some who represented bits and pieces of her past life. There was a boy who had once pulled her braids when she was eight years old. Here were a couple of rows of her classmates from Miss Rogers' Select School; the ones who had dropped her from party lists, back when boys first became interesting, were eager now to be friends. She took two more steps and walked into last June and Willow Grove Park, because there was Mike Callahan.

He had come around to see her soon after the announcement appeared in the papers. "I won't come in, Kate," he had said. "It wouldn't look right. I just wanted to wish you happiness."

They talked for a few minutes, rummaging through important thoughts on a search for casual topics. Mike told her that his job of wrecking the buildings at Twelfth and Chestnut was coming along fine, just fine, and that he was sleeping in a little shack right on the property so that he could keep an eye on everything. It seemed funny to be sort of camping out, he said, right in the center of the city.

Finally he scuffed his big feet on the front stoop and said, "Would you do me a favor, Kate? Send me a bid to the wedding. I'd like to see a big one."

So here was Mike at a big wedding, watching her tight-rope walk down the aisle toward a tiny distant figure. But of course in a real tight-rope act the person waiting at the far end would represent the finish of the test. Here it was only the beginning.

For a moment she felt slightly faint, and her father's right hand swung over and patted hers where it lay on his left arm. He approved of formal weddings. "They represent," he had explained, "a bow to centuries of tradition. The bride takes her father's left arm, for example, in order to leave his right hand free to draw his sword if it becomes necessary to defend her." Dear Daddy, she thought. You would probably cut yourself if you had to draw a sword. Once he had started telling her that the throwing of rice or the use of other seeds was an old custom even in the time of the ancient Romans, and that it was a fertility rite. Then he had stopped himself and become embarrassed, realizing that fertility was not a proper subject to discuss with a bride.

She saw her mother in the front pew on the left. Her mother was holding herself rigid against the urge to turn and make sure that Kate was not tripping over the long princess satin gown or walking with a slouch or getting out of step with the organ. Next to her was Grandmother O'Donnell, peering around to make sure of not missing a thing. There was a dissatisfied look on her sharp old face, as if she were looking for flaws in the arrangements and not finding as many as she hoped. Grandmother O'Donnell did not approve of Mrs. Lawrence. "New rich," she would say. "No more breeding than a pig in a wallow. As for the lad you're marrying, it's doubtful I am that you can untie him from the apron strings." Grandmother O'Donnell had talked that way from the moment when her ideas for a wedding gown had been rejected by Mrs. Lawrence, who insisted on having it made by her dressmaker.

A few more steps brought Kate to the end of the tight rope, and suddenly her father was no longer beside her and a stranger named William DeWitt Lawrence was stepping into his place. What with all the parties and fittings and preparations of recent weeks she had seen very little of him. Perhaps that had been just as well. On the few occasions when they were alone they had tried to talk about the summer and found it a subject that had dried up and blown away like autumn leaves. It was impossible to talk about the future, because neither of them had become used to the idea that they were going to live together. It was as if a man and a woman had reached a pleasant stage of friendship and suddenly found themselves penned up together in a room, naked.

And, of course, that was actually going to happen within a very short time.

She forced the thought out of her head, and managed to keep it out while the wedding and the reception and the wedding supper went by in a jangle of talk and music and laughter. Then finally she and Bill were running out of the Lawrence house and climbing into the Marmon while rice pattered down on them. At that moment the thought began to creep back. She wished they had been starting a long drive through the cool October night, because that would have given her time to relax. But they were only driving four blocks, and stopping for the night at the Bellevue Stratford Hotel. It was a let-down to pull up meekly to the hotel entrance, two minutes after leaving on their honeymoon, but Mrs. Lawrence had arranged it that way.

They would be tired, Mrs. Lawrence had pointed out, and ought to stop at the first convenient place. Tomorrow they were taking the train for New York, where Mrs. Lawrence was going to see them off on a trip to Europe. They would visit all the places in Europe which Mrs. Lawrence said were worth seeing.

They rode upstairs in the gilded cage of the hotel elevator, trying not to look at the bright new luggage which marked them so plainly as bride and groom. When the elevator stopped, they followed the bellboy down a red-carpeted hall to the suite which Mrs. Lawrence had reserved for them.

"I instructed the manager," Mrs. Lawrence had told Kate, "to make sure to provide a double bed. I do not approve of the modern trend to twin beds, which I am sure is contributing to the divorce rate."

After the bellboy left, Bill took off his coat and shook grains of rice onto the carpet. "Why do they throw rice at weddings?" he said.

"It's one of those very old customs," Kate said. "They even did it back in ancient Rome. It's a sort of fertility rite."

As soon as that popped out she wished she hadn't said it. "Very interesting," he said, in a tone like the rattle of a stick on a picket fence. "Let's get on with it, shall we?"

"Get on with what, Bill?"

"The fertility rite."

It sounded terribly crude but of course he didn't mean it that way. His face looked tense and white, as if he had been driving himself hard and was almost at a breaking point. "There's no reason why it has to be tonight," she said in a low embarrassed voice. "You're awfully tired. And maybe we ought to start making friends with each other again, now that we finally have a chance."

"You're my wife," he said hoarsely. "Get in there and take off your clothes."

She walked slowly into the bedroom, her legs feeling as if they were walking uphill, and closed the door. Her hand seemed icy when she rubbed it over her face. Ordinarily she liked releasing her body from its husk of clothes but tonight it was something to be done quickly and almost furtively. She turned out the light and climbed into bed and waited. Her heart measured out the time loudly and solemnly, like the big clock on the landing of the Lawrence stairway, and it seemed to tick away half a lifetime before her husband finally came in.

18

SHE RODE DOWNSTAIRS in the Bellevue Stratford with the same elevator operator who had taken her and Bill and the new luggage upstairs only two hours earlier. No doubt he was wondering about her but nothing showed on his face. You might think that a neat starched expression was part of the uniform he put on every day. When she reached the lobby, the bellboy who had taken them upstairs gave her a pleasant smile, as if it were the most natural thing in the world first for a bridegroom to rush out of the hotel and then for the bride to go for a midnight stroll.

Kate was not really interested in what the hotel staff thought or did not think, but it kept her from being forced to think about herself. Sometime later she would put her mind to work, but not now.

Not when her nerves were being scraped like out-of-tune violin strings and when her body felt as if she had forgotten to put on her skin when she dressed. She walked out to Broad Street. The clock on City Hall tower hung above the street like a small yellow moon and told her it was a quarter to twelve. According to the Cinderella stories she had not received good measure; the golden coach should not have turned into a pumpkin until the stroke of midnight.

One block south and half a block east was Franklin Academy, where her father taught. Two blocks south and two west was the house where she had lived all her life. Four blocks west was the DeWitt Lawrence mansion on Rittenhouse Square. It was odd; she was close to all the places she knew best and still didn't know where to go. She began walking, choosing a route that would keep her away from the landmarks of her past life. It was a quiet night and her footsteps echoed in the caves of the streets. A trolley floated over a crossing two blocks away, a lighted ship on an empty black ocean. Far off, the Klaxon of an auto cleared its hoarse throat. She shivered. Somewhere farther off the gray Marmon was howling through the night, with her husband at the wheel trying to prove he was a man.

She glanced up and saw that she was walking past a solid wooden fence that blocked off some kind of construction. It was painted green and carried big white letters: Michael Callahan, Wrecker. Apparently, no matter which way she turned, it was not going to be easy to walk away from her past life. She was at Twelfth and Chestnut Streets, where Mike was taking his big gamble to get ahead. Perhaps she had not been walking as aimlessly as she had thought, because now that she was here she felt no urge to hurry away. A door had been cut in the fence. There was a staple for a padlock but the door was slightly ajar. She pushed it open. The buildings had already been leveled except for part of a wall back toward Sansom Street, and most of the ground was a jackstraw mess of bricks and broken timbers. To the left, against the inside of the fence and at the street corner, was a shack hardly big enough to take two steps in. There was a light in the single window. She picked her way across the jumble of bricks and peered in. The shack contained a small wooden table on which a lantern glowed, a box to sit on, and a bunk. Mike wasn't there. She went back to the door in the fence and then halted, trembling.

A man coming up Twelfth Street from Market was singing "When Irish Eyes Are Smiling" in a tomcat yowl. Two other voices, a woman's and a man's, were arguing with the singer.

"Now look, Mike," a man complained, "it wouldn't be for me to stop a little quiet fun, but this would wake the dead."

The singer stopped, and said in a cheerful slurred voice, "Which dead do you mean, O'Toole? The ones that are buried or the ones who are still walking around Philadelphia?"

The woman said, "Ah, Mike, don't go arguing with a cop."

"And on top of that," the sober man said, "why do you have to bring a chippie like her into the center of town on my beat? What if Mr. Wanamaker was driving by and saw this going on just a block from his fine store?"

"That's a solemn thought about Mr. Wanamaker," Mike said. "It's enough to make a man take the pledge. But now wait a minute. The pledge is only for drinking, isn't it? The human race has never, thanks be to God, taken a pledge against the other thing. So—"

"All I'm asking for is a bit of quiet, Mike."

The three people came into the sizzling blue glare of the arc light on the corner. Mike was walking between the policeman and a woman, his bowler hat pushed far back on his red hair and his arms linked through those of his companions. The woman wore a hobble skirt, a tailored jacket and a shirtwaist that spouted a fountain of dirty ruffles. She had a feather boa around her neck and kept stroking it nervously with her free hand.

"When I meet a nice cop," she said, "and that's not often, I like to be nice to him. Be quiet for the nice cop, will you, Mike?"

"All right," Mike said. "I'm outvoted. Just stand there and watch, O'Toole, and you'll be proud of how quiet I am." He dropped the policeman's arm, gripped the woman firmly and tiptoed across the street. "How's that?" he bellowed.

The policeman shuddered, and walked quickly away.

Kate edged along the inside of the fence and pressed close against it. Her heartbeat thudded on the boards like a hammer driving nails. The light from the lantern did not reach far, and if Mike and the woman came through the doorway and turned directly toward the shack they would not see her. Their footsteps scraped on the pavement and Mike flung open the door through the fence and stepped in.

"Here we are," he said. "Maybe I ought to carry you across the doorway."

"What's this you're showing me?" the woman said, with a sharp high note of anger. "The city dump? Where's the house you was talking about?"

"There it is," Mike said. "The palace of the Callahans. None of the inconveniences of home. No leaky faucets to fix. No cooking odors from the kitchen. No coal to shovel into the furance. No—"

"You're crazy if you think I'm going in there," the woman cried. "Here I thought you was a real gent and you waste my whole night and drag me in this hole."

"Give me a chance," Mike said. "You wait right there, and I'll go in and turn up the lantern and you'll see how nice it is. Don't go away. I'll be right back."

He stumbled to the shack, leaving the woman outside on the pavement. He tried to open the door and complained that somebody had moved the knob and then stood back and kicked the door in. His big shadow flickered across the window and suddenly the shack went dark. "Aah, I turned the damned thing the wrong way," he announced loudly. "Now where are the matches?"

Kate left her hiding place against the fence and moved quickly to the doorway and stepped out onto the pavement. The woman waiting there let out a tiny scream.

"Shut up," Kate said. "Shut up and leave."

The woman got over her fright and moved closer, looking Kate up and down. "Isn't this a nice thing?" she said. "A lady comes back to a gent's place with him and finds somebody else waiting to nab him. What's your game, dearie?"

"I want you to leave," Kate said tensely.

"Well now just wait a minute, dearie. I don't waste my time sitting around half the night with a big loud Irish slob for nothing. I got my living to make just like you."

Kate dug into her purse and found a bill and handed it to her. "All right," she said. "Now get out."

The woman peered at her craftily. "That's only a dollar, dearie. Where's the other one?"

"That was ten dollars and you know it."

"Well, well, so it was. I'm beginning to think this gent must be a gold mine, and here I thought he was only a fellah trying to forget some floozie who gave him the air for some rich fellah. Maybe I ought to stay."

"Get out," Kate whispered. Her right hand went to her hat and drew out the long steel hairpin. "Get out or I'm coming for you with this." She took a step forward, violence trembling in her like a dog straining to get at a throat.

"All right, all right," the woman said, backing away. "I'm going." She hurried off, almost running by the time she turned the corner.

Kate took a deep breath and looked at the hatpin in horror and threw it into the street. She had not known there was a dark alley in her mind where murderous thoughts waited in the shadows. She stepped back through the opening in the fence and closed the door. Her fingers touched a block of wood which swivelled on a nail, and she turned it until it held the door securely closed. There was still no light in the shack, and Mike was grumbling loudly and feeling his way toward her along the fence. She waited, her legs weak as old broomstraws, as he came nearer. His hand touched her body.

"You're not the door," he said. "You feel soft." His hand patted her in a questioning sort of way, and then he said, "Oh, yes. I remember you now. You're that woman. I can't find the damned matches. Come on anyway. A little darkness won't matter. Might help, huh? I guess neither of us is a bargain."

He caught her hand and fumbled his way back into the shack, pulling her after him. He tried to kick the door shut but it was broken now and finally he dragged something against it. His hands came back to her in the darkness and he began to take off her clothes, working with slow concentration.

"The boys tell me no nice whore likes to take off all her clothes," he said. "But maybe you're not a nice one, huh?"

She couldn't answer him. She was standing there with her eyes closed, although that was silly because it was pitch dark, letting a warm soft feeling creep through her body and thaw the icy lump in her stomach. He was down on his knees now yanking at her shoes, and peeling off her stockings. He pulled himself up with his hands gripping her bare waist and drew her close against him.

"You're so soft," he said hoarsely. "You smell so clean. I didn't think you would be like this. I could almost pretend you were ... that you were ... the hell with that, Callahan. Take what you can get and forget her."

He lifted her onto the bunk. Her breath mixed with his in warm waves. As she had thought once long ago at Willow Grove Park, Mike could stir her very deeply if she ever decided to let him. Tonight she wanted to let him. It was bad and wrong and everything you could say against it, but it was making her into a woman again.

When she dressed and left the shack, he was sleeping. She opened the door of the fence and slipped outside and tried to see if she looked presentable. Not to a woman's eyes, perhaps, but with luck she would not see any this time of night. She walked back to the Bellevue Stratford, and watched her return jolt the doorman and desk clerk and lone bellboy and the elevator operator wide awake. After a few blinks, though, they got their starched expressions in place. She went into the empty bridal suite and hung up her clothes carefully and put on a nightgown that no bridegroom would ever see and went to bed.

She slept long and dreamlessly, because this was a pause between two parts of her life, and there was no use regretting the part that was past or rushing into the one ahead. It was almost noon when the heavy knocking on the outer door roused her. She threw on a robe and went into the living room.

"Yes?" she called. "What is it?"

"Mrs. Lawrence," a man said, "this is the manager. I am terribly sorry. I'm afraid I must break tragic news to you."

She paused for a moment. It had been shocking to hear herself called Mrs. Lawrence. She never really had been. She unlocked the door and opened it slightly. "What is it?" she asked.

The man gulped and wet his lips and said, "We tried to locate your mother-in-law, but she has left for New York City, so I thought it best to tell you without further delay. Mrs. Lawrence, there has been an accident. Your husband. Last night on the Lancaster Pike. The car turned over several times. Your husband never knew what happened. Mrs. Lawrence, the hotel physician is with me. Would you like him to come in and … and—"

"Thank you very much," she said. "You have been very kind. I do not need a doctor. I would just like to be alone for a while."

She closed the door softly. *Your husband never knew what happened.* That wasn't true. He had known what would happen before he left her. And perhaps she had known, too, but had not been quite ready to face the thought.

19

SHE SAT IN the Pink Room of the Lawrence house, watching her son nurse with a sort of quiet fury at her breast. His lips mumbled and his firm gums chewed and his hands, spread like pink starfish, pushed and prodded. It was a warm day in late August, and the work brought a film of sweat out on his head. A month ago, when he was born, his head had been covered with thin black hair that sometimes caught a red gleam when light struck it, but it had rubbed away and now there was only a slight fuzz. Anthony Judson Lawrence was not one of those babies who became thin and fretful in the summer heat of Philadelphia. Six times in every twenty-four hours he let out a single angry howl, and if fed at once had nothing more to say to the world. He wanted what was due him, no more, no less.

Having Anthony had made a great difference in her life. A year ago, in Beach Haven, she had been trying anxiously to fit herself into the lives of two other people. Now everything was complete within the limits of the chair in which she sat. The chatter and bustle of other people was a remote thing, like the buzzing of flies outside a screen. Far away a war had started in Europe but she hardly knew who was fighting. Ever since the baby first stirred in her body she had lived in a closed and magic circle.

There was a sharp knock at the door and someone came in without waiting for a reply. It was Mrs. Lawrence—that is, the senior Mrs. Lawrence—come to buzz around her magic circle. It seemed to Kate that Mrs. Lawrence had been slowly shrivelling since her son's death. The change might be partly in her own mind, of course. Still and all, Mrs. Lawrence's bristling shako of white hair looked too heavy for the face beneath it, and her grenadier manner had become nervous and hasty.

"How are you, Kate?" she said. "I don't know why you admit so much sunlight into the room. It is likely to give my grandson a rash."

"I think a little of it is good for him," Kate said. "I let him play fifteen minutes a day in the sun with nothing on but diapers."

"It is not healthy. He should be kept dressed. I have bought piles of undershirts and dresses for him and you haven't even looked at most of them. And another thing, Kate. I have been talking to the doctor about breast feeding. He agrees with me in disapproving of it. So I have obtained a formula which we can start using at once."

This was a new kind of buzzing, and it was breaking into her magic circle. Her muscles tightened and a tingle of anger rippled through her body. At her breast, the baby let out a small choked howl, as if something had cut off the flow of milk. He began pushing and kneading with more force than ever. Kate smiled down at him and felt herself relax. Nothing could really break in unless she gave it permission.

"Have you any other ideas, Mrs. Lawrence?" she asked.

"I certainly have. Really, Kate, you have become quite spoiled in recent months, and it is time you realized your obligations. Not only to me, but also to my grandson. I have had the back room on this floor done over into a nursery, and have engaged an excellent nurse. We will move Anthony into the nursery. I did not look forward at my age to taking on such a problem but I see it is necessary."

"The problem," Kate said, "is that of bringing up Anthony?"

"Yes, of course. It means starting all over again with a task I once thought had been accomplished."

It was interesting, Kate thought, how calm she felt. She had considered this problem a long time ago and knew exactly what she must do. "I appreciate your offer," she said, "but it is not necessary."

"Offer? Offer? I'm not offering anything, Kate. I'm explaining what I am going to do."

"I hoped it wouldn't come to this, Mrs. Lawrence. But I suppose it had to. Let me explain what I'm going to do. I'm going to bring up my baby as I see fit. I am going to nurse him and keep him with me."

"You're talking wildly, Kate. You're not well."

"I feel well enough to make my own decisions and to lead my own life."

"Lead your own life, indeed! You're not leading it now. Whose house are you living in? Whose clothes are you wearing? Who is paying for everything? How ridiculous of you!"

Kate said softly, "You're confusing things you can buy with things you can't buy, Mrs. Lawrence. There are only two ways you can pay for a baby. The first is by giving birth to him. The second is by raising him. I've paid the first price and I intend to pay the second."

"Well!" Mrs. Lawrence gasped. "I almost believe you're trying to lecture me. I know all about the price a mother pays for a baby. I paid it many times for my son. I—"

"But you never let him get out of debt to you. That's not going to happen with Anthony."

A red stain seeped over Mrs. Lawrence's face. "I've been waiting for that!" she cried. "Ever since my son was killed I've been waiting to see how soon you would try to throw the blame on me. You first came into this house as meek as if butter wouldn't melt in your mouth. Yes, Mrs. Lawrence, no, Mrs. Lawrence, whatever you say, Mrs. Lawrence. I should have known that back of it you were scheming how to get your own way and turn my son against me. And then the night you were married you shocked him in some horrible fashion and drove him out into the night and—do you dare confess what happened between you two that night? Do you? Do you?"

"Don't push me too far," Kate said in a whisper. "I might tell you. Do you really want to know?"

"Of course not! Keep it on your own conscience, don't try to put it on mine. All I have to say is this. While you are under my roof, you will do as I say. Do you understand that?"

"I understand it perfectly, Mrs. Lawrence." She hesitated a moment, and then said clearly, "I will leave in one hour."

Her mother-in-law halted in front of her, staring down in shocked silence. "You can't mean it," she said at last.

"I have another home to go to."

"Don't bluff me, Kate. It won't work. I take back not a thing that I said."

"I'm quite sure of that, Mrs. Lawrence."

"Don't think that you can eat your cake and have it too. You will not get a penny from me. Nor will your son get a penny, now or ever, if you disobey me."

"That's odd," Kate said. "I believe that's the first time you have called him my son. Always before he's been your grandson."

"If he leaves here he won't be my grandson. Don't think you can get yourself a lawyer or do anything, either. I know more than I've ever let on. Do you think I accepted what happened that night without looking under the surface? Within twenty-four hours I had investigators working. They talked to the elevator operators at the hotel, to the bellboys and the doorman. You left the hotel at a quarter to twelve, twenty-five minutes after my son left. You were seen going north on Broad and turning east on Chestnut. Unfortunately your trail gets dim at that point. But the mere fact that no one else saw you, before you returned almost two hours later, proves you could not have stayed in the open walking. A policeman was at the corner of Twelfth and Chestnut very soon after you would have passed. He saw no one crossing Twelfth Street on Chestnut as he came from Market. He saw no one up or down Chestnut Street when he reached that corner. He remembers it very well because he was trying to keep a friend quiet, and was worried about other people hearing the noise the friend made. Shall I tell you the rest?"

"I wish you would," Kate said. "I didn't suspect you had been so thorough."

"The friend's name was Mike Callahan. Does it sound familiar?"

Kate said coolly. "I've known him most of my life."

"Yes, I'm aware of that. Your friend Mike had a woman of the streets in tow. The policeman left. Your friend Mike, who was of course drunk, tried to coax the woman into a shack on a lot he was clearing, at the corner of Twelfth and Chestnut. She hung back. He went into the shack. Another woman stepped out of the shadows and paid the street-walker to go away. The street-walker cannot quite identify the woman who paid her because the shadows were so heavy. But if she were paid enough, she would remember. I regret to say that nothing could be learned from your friend Mike Callahan."

"There was nothing to be learned."

"Your friend Mike Callahan is apparently a real brute. He hit my investigator a number of times."

"Good for Mike."

"You're taking this very calmly."

"You've been taking it calmly for how long, ten months? All that time you've been wondering whether Anthony was your grandson or not."

"I have not been wondering at all. While he stays here, under my control, he is my grandson. If he leaves, he is not. I don't plan to use my information unless you take Anthony away and then try to make some legal claim on me. What is your decision?"

Kate did not answer at once. She knew what her own answer was, but she had to consider what this meant to her son. If she took him away, he would lose any chance of inheriting the Lawrence millions; Mrs. Lawrence was no more likely to change her mind than to change her character. On the other hand, how much good had it done Bill Lawrence to be the prospective heir to that fortune? "Yes, I've made my decision," Kate said. "I'm leaving with Anthony."

"You understand that my son had no money of his own? That you can expect very little from his estate? That I will fight you in every court in the land if you claim any money from me?"

"It would be a real scandal, wouldn't it?"

"I would face it," Mrs. Lawrence said.

"I don't plan to make any claims, Mrs. Lawrence. I'm sorry it had to end like this."

"Well," Mrs. Lawrence said, in a tone that sounded oddly puzzled. "Well, that's that. I suppose I should be angry. Quite suddenly I find that I don't care." She stood there for a moment, and there was no doubt now that Mrs. Lawrence had shrivelled and grown old. The fire in her had gone out. She walked heavily from the room.

Kate looked down at her baby. Anthony had just finished. His heavy head dropped onto her arm and he sighed once and went to sleep. He was a single-minded baby, going about his business with no concern for the storm which had broken over his head. That was good. He would need to go about the business of life in the same way.

20

IT WAS A DECEMBER day with a sky like old pewter and a feel of wet snow in the air. Kate walked briskly across Rittenhouse Square, glancing only once at the boarded-up windows of the Lawrence mansion. It seemed incredible that she had been living there four months ago. Mrs. Lawrence had gone to a place in Florida called Palm Beach, which was becoming popular with wealthy Philadelphians, and there were reports that she would not open her house on Rittenhouse Square again. Kate was not very interested. All that was past, and she had started to build a new life for herself. She swung along, on her Sunday afternoon walk, almost wishing for a gale so that she could test her strength against it.

She cut over to Spruce Street, returning home, and saw a big man walking toward her. He wore a Chesterfield and derby, and looked as out of place in them as a pile of bricks under velvet. It could only be Mike Callahan. Her cheeks stung suddenly, and her heart seemed to wobble around in her chest. It was the first time she had seen him since … since … she set her jaw firmly and told herself it was the first time since she had walked down the aisle at her wedding.

"Well, if it isn't Kate," he said. "I didn't think I'd have luck like this on such a bad day. How are you, anyway?"

She thought it might be planning rather than luck that brought Mike on a Sunday walk past her house. "It's ever so nice to see you," she said. "And look at the Chesterfield and derby! Mike, you're coming up in the world."

"I'm doing all right. Can I walk you home, Kate?"

"Of course. Have you won some new contracts, Mike?"

"Two more wrecking jobs, and a couple of small but nice construction jobs. I'm on my way, Kate. Do you know what I made from that first wrecking job I had, at Twelfth and Chestnut more than a year ago? Better than seven thousand dollars."

"Oh, Mike! That was a small fortune!"

"Nobody expected me to beat that deadline by six months, with a bonus for every doggone day. I won't ever get any deals as good as that again, because now they know what I can do. But I'm getting bigger jobs. Speaking of jobs, didn't I hear you had one in a store?"

"Where did you hear that?"

"I bumped into somebody on the street. Can't quite remember who it was."

"Could it," Kate said, peering at him suspiciously, "have been my grandmother?"

"I'd remember if it was her, wouldn't I?"

"I was just curious. She happened to mention your name several times lately."

"And besides, she doesn't go out of the house at all, does she?"

"I don't think so. You didn't happen to bump into her at our house, did you?"

"I sure ought to remember that, shouldn't I?" He cleared his throat, with a noise like a steam shovel picking up rocks, and said, "What's the idea of you working in a store when there's all that money in the Lawrence family?"

They had reached the front steps of her home, and she remembered how they had stood there, hunting for casual things to say, before her wedding. Mike didn't seem to be hunting very hard for casual remarks this time. "Mrs. Lawrence and I don't see eye to eye on how to raise a child, Mike. So she's not offering any help and I'm not asking for any. My husband had no money of his own."

"Well, maybe it's for the best. Kate, I'd kinda like to see that kid of yours. Can I?"

She studied his big red face, and saw nothing in it that you couldn't have seen by studying a brick. "Yes, of course," she said. "It will have to be a short visit, though. A photographer is coming to take a family picture, and I'll have to get ready for it."

As she led Mike upstairs to the bedroom, her heart was working harder than the climb warranted, and it was not easy to keep insisting to herself that she had last seen Mike at the wedding. Anthony was lying on his back trying to get a big toe up to his mouth. That was much more interesting to him than a visitor. His eyes with their big dark blue irises looked briefly at the man bending over the crib, then looked back at the toe that was resisting him.

"Quite a kid," Mike said in a husky voice.

"He's very healthy," Kate said. It was a shock to look at the two faces so close together. Even with the baby fat, Anthony's chin jutted out like Mike's. The width and set of their shoulders, and the way their hands clenched, was very much the same.

"Hasn't got much hair," Mike said.

"Babies seldom have much. Even if they're born with hair, it usually rubs off. Anthony had a lot of black hair when he was born. You can see how dark the fuzz on his head is now."

"Where's the red hair in your family?"

"What do you mean? There isn't any red hair."

"There's a touch of red in that fuzz of his."

"His grandmother had black hair," Kate said, a bit breathlessly. "My grandmother O'Donnell, I mean. Sometimes with Irish girls you find red tones in black hair. Then of course I don't know about Bill's side of the family. They—"

Mike swung away from the crib, grabbed her wrist. "Don't give me that side of the family," he said.

"I don't know what you mean. Please let go my wrist!"

He pulled her close so that he could stare down into her face. "All right," he growled, "so I was pretty drunk that night. It was dark. There wasn't any light in the shack. Even at that I knew something was a lot different from what I expected. Maybe I'd have passed it off as a dream, one of those dreams where a guy who's crazy for a girl kids himself that he's found her. Only now I don't think it was a dream. What have you got to say to that?"

"Mike, you're talking wildly! I don't understand you at all."

"Some snooper came around asking me questions October a year ago. I let him ask questions until I found out a lot. Then I smacked him a little and threw him in the street. You know what I'm talking about. That mother-in-law of yours must have thrown it in your face."

She yanked her wrist from his grip. There were white bands on it where his fingers had tightened. "I will have to ask you to leave," she said in an unsteady voice.

"This is my kid," he said, throwing each word at her as if it were a rock.

He stood there, big, grim, red-faced, hands clenched to fight anybody who stood up against him. But now that he had brought the subject out into the open she was no longer unsure of herself. "No, Mike," she said. "You're wrong."

He hadn't been ready for a calm denial. He blinked, and slammed his right fist a few times into the palm of his left hand. He wanted to reduce the problem to something that could be solved by muscles and anger, but there was nothing for him to strike at. "Goddam it," he said. "Goddam it. I don't know how to go at this, Kate. I always did want you. Now I want you more than ever. I want this kid of mine, too. It's not wrong for me to want that, is it?"

"Mike," she said softly, "I think you're wonderful. It's not wrong for you to want anything in the world. If I didn't have a baby I think I'd marry you in a moment. But I'm never going to, do you understand?"

"No, I don't. What's the reason?"

"He's right there in the crib, Mike. You think he's yours. Nobody will ever get me to admit it. Suppose we married, and he grew up with a chin and eyes and shoulders and hands like yours, and with red lights in his black hair. You wouldn't be the only person claiming he was yours. A lot of people would say it. He'd have to drag that with him all through life."

"I'd beat that idea out of anybody! I'd—"

"Women would do the talking. You couldn't stop them."

"What if I took you away somewhere? I could start over again. Nobody would have to know the date we were married or anything."

"I won't go anywhere else," Kate said. "Maybe you'll think it's silly. But three generations of us have been living here and trying to get ahead. Perhaps a city can get into your blood, I don't know. Maybe it's the idea of not giving up a fight that's been going on for so many years. Maybe it's just being used to things here, so you feel nothing can satisfy you anywhere else."

"It's just a town that's set in its ways, like you."

"I don't think you can change it or me."

"All right," he said. "All right. Don't think I'm not going to try. I found out how to knock down its walls. I'll be around pounding at you."

He walked out of the room without another word, and she heard the old tired stairway creak under his heavy steps. She felt sorry for Mike. He was only a second-generation Philadelphian. He didn't realize, yet, that the city's ways were much stronger than anything built of brick and mortar.

She changed her clothes to get ready for the family photograph, and then began dressing Anthony. While she was doing that, her grandmother came in and watched with bright unblinking eyes, like a robin studying a lawn in the morning.

"He doesn't grow very fast," her grandmother said.

"Anthony? Why, he's put on weight beautifully."

"There's not a tooth in his mouth yet."

"But he's only five months old. Six to nine months is about average for first teeth."

"It's not an average baby that one ought to be. He won't even sit up."

Kate said patiently, "He's perfectly normal and he probably won't sit up for a month or two."

"Well, I'll take me time with him. I don't doubt he'll come along." She perched on the edge of the bed and stared into distance and muttered. "There's good blood in you, lad, that's a sure thing. First there's hot blood from the bog Irish, and ..."

Kate was busy dressing Anthony, and her grandmother's voice had dropped to a mumble and Kate wasn't paying much attention. Her mind merely picked up her grandmother's words and filed them away in case they should be wanted later. She put long white stockings on Anthony's legs and eased a frilly white dress over his head. She reached for his soft white shoes, and suddenly realized that her grandmother had been saying something quite important. She riffled through the words her mind had filed, and brought them out and studied them. It was a startling collection.

"First there's hot blood from the bog Irish," her grandmother had said. "And that's a good solid start if I do say so meself. Then there's the Clayton blood. A wee bit cool, maybe, but the sort of thing that breeds true to type. You'll get brains and good looks and a feeling for what's right and wrong from the Claytons. It's not so keen I am for the Judson blood, which you might say is no more than Clayton blood watered down, but I'll tell you, lad, the Judsons are a human kind of people you can sometimes look up to and sometimes feel sorry for, and it's not so bad to have a touch of that in you. The Lawrence blood, now, that's a pot on another fire. There's bad blood in that family somewhere and it can't help coming out and it's lucky you are that you didn't get it. You'll have to push and shove to get ahead, and another line of hot new Irish blood could be just what a lad like you will need, so it's never from me you'll hear a word against the Callahan in you."

Kate whirled around to face her grandmother. "Stop it!" she cried.

Her grandmother looked up, and her eyes came slowly into focus. "What's that, Katie dear?"

"Grandmother, you don't know what you've been saying!"

"It was just an old woman mumbling to herself about things past."

"Things like the Clayton blood in our family."

"Did I, then? Me tongue must have twisted some words out of the right shape."

"You twisted some other words," Kate said grimly. "They had to do with the name Callahan."

The bright old eyes peeked up at her. "Meself it is that's so mixed up today you can't trust a word that's in me."

"I hope you won't twist those words again."

"I'll watch meself. I haven't been mumbling before any of the others, Katie. It's just that all at once I took to thinking of the pair of us like one person, living through the same story twice but having it come out a bit strange and different here and there." "Grandmother, I'll be glad to forget what you said."

"Well, and it was never said at all, at all."

"There's just one thing more. You've been seeing Mike, haven't you? And maybe encouraging him to come around?"

"It was just coming to the back door he was and asking how you were and passing the time of day. Sure and the man deserved his chance at you, and from the way he left in a black Irish rage it's little enough chance that was. I used to fear the man would get you and hold you back, but now I see he'll do some climbing, and you've got your son and a name on him that's not so bad and you might do worse than take Mike Callahan."

Kate said deliberately, "You haven't seen Mike's face close to Anthony's or you wouldn't say that."

Her grandmother peered into the crib. "Well now," she muttered, "and that would be a troublesome thing, wouldn't it, now? And it's meself that never saw it before. But if they were together it would be hard to miss. All right, Katie, I'll not give the man another kind word."

"Good," Kate said. "Because he'll be back, trying to get some. Now I'd better finish dressing Anthony for that photograph ..."

They took their positions, a half hour later, for the photograph. First Kate, sitting on a chair holding Anthony, and then her mother and grandmother hovering behind her shoulders. The photographer had set up a big box camera on a tripod, and had drawn a black cloth over the camera and his head so that he could get the focus right. His head popped out and he picked up a T-shaped piece of metal and scattered gray powder along the top of it.

"All looking at the camera and smiling, please," he called gaily.

Kate remembered, suddenly, that her father was not in the group. They would have to get him in the next one, or people in later years would think that men had not played much of a part in the lives of Margaret O'Donnell and Mary O'Donnell Judson and Katherine Judson Lawrence. Just then the photographer pressed a trigger, and the gray powder threw a blast of light at them.

"No, no, no," the photographer complained. "At the last moment you all looked down at the baby, and no one was smiling. Well, we'll get a better one. Good baby you have there. Most of them scream at the flash powder." He put a new glass plate in the camera and picked up his flash powder holder.

A scream of rage knifed through the room. It was Anthony, with only a small red rind of face showing around his open shrieking mouth. Kate soothed him and they tried again. It was no use. As soon as the photographer lifted the holder of flash powder, Anthony screamed. So, after all, only one photograph was taken. It seemed that you could take advantage of Anthony once but not twice.

ANTHONY

1921–1956

1

ANTHONY HAD VERY few personal memories of his great-grandmother, Margaret O'Donnell. She had died during the flu epidemic after the First World War. But he could remember being taken, when he was five, into the bedroom where she lay propped against a pillow, looking like the thin transparent shell of a human which had been outgrown and left behind by the owner.

She stared at him from faded blue eyes and said, "I hope you know what you have to do, Anthony. You're the boy we've been waiting for, the three of us, with the years going by like time when you lie awake in the night." The words were slivers of glass, cutting through the soft Irish brogue she had never managed to lose.

His mother's hand gripped his arm and he said, "Oh yes, I know," just as his mother had told him to say. He had no idea why she wanted him to say it, or what he was supposed to know and to do. Great-grandmother Margaret O'Donnell nodded and closed her eyes. Not long afterward she died quietly, as if she had only been clinging to life until she could hear that assurance from his own lips.

Two years later, for the first time, he found out one of the things he was expected to do. It was not a happy discovery. Before it came along he had lived in a typical child's world, peopled by three kinds of creatures. First there were boys his own age; at one moment they might be nice to play with and at the next they might run screaming home or else try to hit you. Next there were older boys; mostly they acted as if you weren't there, and if you tried to insist that you were there, they brushed you aside roughly. Finally there were large, all-knowing creatures called grown-ups. The reason grown-ups were in the world was to give you candy and make you wear your rubbers, to take you on wonderful trips and force you to study your lessons, to love you and to spank you. It was good that there were grown-ups, even though they were bothersome at times. They had no problems of their own so they were always able to take on your problems.

It was a terrifying moment when you discovered that grown-ups had problems, and that you had to help them. You could never go back to your child's world after that.

The moment came for him in 1921. Although he didn't know it at the time, there was a postwar depression. All he knew about it was that his mother was staying home, instead of going every day to a place called The Office, and that the nice fat colored woman wasn't cooking and cleaning for them any more. He was in his first year at Franklin Academy, in "A" Form. He didn't like it very much. The masters thought that because his grandfather taught there he should do better work. The boys in "A" Form kept pushing him out of their games because his grandfather taught at the school and that made Anthony a teacher's pet. He was supposed to stay on the school grounds and play games after classes ended, but by springtime he had found he could climb over the back gate and go home early. If he crept in the back door he could get up to his room on the third floor, and read *The Green Fairy Book* or *Tanglewood Tales*, without his mother knowing that he was back.

On this particular day, as he skipped out Spruce Street, making sure not to step on any cracks in the pavement, he saw the Buick standing in front of the house. He made a long joyful skip that covered two squares of pavement. The Buick meant that Uncle Mike was visiting them. He wasn't a real uncle but he was nice. He liked to rumple Anthony's hair and sometimes wrestled with him, and had given him a hockey stick and a real baseball, not one of the nickel rockets that lost their covers in a very short time. This Saturday he was going to take Anthony on a pirate trip in a canoe in Fairmount Park if it didn't rain. If it rained, Anthony was going to leave God out of his prayers for a week to teach God a lesson. Probably Uncle Mike was as strong as God was, anyway, and Uncle Mike said he was not going to let it rain.

He thought about going in the front door and throwing himself without warning right at Uncle Mike, but it might be better not to, because his mother would want to know why he was home so early. He went down the side alley and in the back door and crept through the kitchen. There was a door from the kitchen to the hall, and he was going to use that way to get to the stairs. But as he crossed the kitchen he heard his mother's voice. It sounded very queer, and he pushed the swinging door of the dining room open a crack and peered through.

His mother and Uncle Mike were standing close together, and Uncle Mike had his arms around her. He was kissing her. He wasn't doing it just once, the way people sometimes did when you came into a room, but lots and lots of times. That was a strange thing for anybody to do. Anthony couldn't decide whether his mother liked it or not.

She was saying, in a voice that sounded as if she had a bad cold, "No, Mike, no. You must stop. I won't have it. Do you hear?" She wasn't making him stop, though. Maybe it was a kind of game that grown-ups played.

"I should have done this long ago," Uncle Mike said. "You've been living in your mind so much you've forgotten you have a body."

"It's not fair," his mother cried, and finally pushed Uncle Mike away. Her hand made little dabs at her hair but couldn't get it back into place. "I shouldn't have let you come around. You've just been waiting for a moment like this when I'd be feeling weak and discouraged."

"Damn right I have," Uncle Mike said, and poked his jaw out at her. "You've always thought you could do everything by yourself. You've been scraping and scrimping and pretending to be doing fine. You're killing yourself, do you hear? Now with this slump we're in you haven't got a job. It's about time I took over."

"A job will come along any moment," his mother said breathlessly. "Just the other day the woman at the Junior League said she might need an assistant. I—"

"You're going to marry me, Kate."

If they got married, Anthony thought, that would make Uncle Mike his father. That would be all right. He would go on calling him Uncle Mike, though.

"You know I can't," his mother said. "Things haven't changed a bit since the first time we talked about it."

"Tell you what," Uncle Mike said. "We'll let that ride for a while. But only if you'll let me help you out. Damn it, who's got a better right to help you out?"

"It wouldn't work," his mother said. "I know you too well. I'd start depending on you, and getting weaker and softer all the time."

"Stop thinking about yourself so much, will you?" Uncle Mike said. "What about Anthony? The kid needs a father. Look how he takes to me."

"You keep bribing him with presents and things," his mother said angrily. "You're coaxing him to depend on you."

"Is anything wrong with that? He's a swell kid. I dare you to ask him what he thinks of us getting married."

"It doesn't matter what he thinks."

"It doesn't, huh? What time does he get out of school? I'll pick him up and bring him home and ask him about it, right in front of you. Then we'll see if it matters to you what he thinks."

"You mustn't!" his mother cried. "Mike, you know I couldn't stand that! I—"

"Good," Uncle Mike said. "I'll be back with him." He hurried out the front doorway.

Anthony's mother stood there making sounds as if she had swallowed the wrong way. Then she walked to the couch and sat down and began crying. It was frightening to see a grown-up cry, especially his mother. It made him feel hot and prickly. He wondered what he could give her to make her stop crying. There was his hockey stick, and the baseball, and some sourball candy in his room, but mothers didn't play games like hockey and baseball, and the candy wasn't very clean. The bag had broken and let the sourballs drop while he was carrying it home.

He pushed the door open and walked up to her and said, rather helplessly, "Don't cry, Mother."

She jumped, and looked up at him. "Anthony!" she gasped. "What are you doing home now? How long have you been here?"

He picked the easier question to answer. "Just a few minutes. Do you want some candy, Mother? I've got some upstairs. It's not very clean but I can wash it off."

"Oh, Anthony," she said in a weak little voice. "Oh, Anthony."

"Are you mad at Uncle Mike?" he asked.

"Anthony, did you hear everything we said?"

"I heard everything you said after I got here. He said you were going to marry him and you said you weren't, and then there were some things I didn't understand and he's gone to school to get me. He's going to ask me what I think of it and I think it's all right but I'd rather keep calling him Uncle Mike because I think of him as Uncle Mike."

"Anthony, did we say anything about … about … no, I remember now, we didn't. So that's all right. It's very sweet of you to offer me your candy. Was that to make me stop crying?"

"I don't like to hear you cry. It makes me feel kind of sick."

"Come here," she said, taking his hand and pulling him onto the couch beside her. "I'll stop crying now." She put her arm over his shoulder, and let him burrow close against her into the warmth and nice clean smell. "Anthony," she murmured, "Uncle Mike does want to marry me. But I'm not going to."

"He can't make you if you don't like him."

"It's not that at all," she said. "I like him very much. But we can't get married."

"Oh, well, I wasn't really counting on it, Mother. I didn't think about it until just now, anyway."

"The thing is, Anthony, I like Uncle Mike so much that if he keeps on being nice to us it's going to get harder and harder to say no."

"Well," he said comfortably, "then you'd just have to marry him."

She started to cry again. "I mustn't, I mustn't," she said. "You don't understand you can't realize—I can't even try to explain it to you. It's—now wait. Maybe this will do it. We're Episcopalians, you know that."

"Oh, yes," he said. He did not really like being Episcopalians. They made him put a nickel from his allowance in the collection at Sunday School. He wished there was something else to be that did not cost a nickel every Sunday.

"Anthony," she said, "Uncle Mike is a Catholic!"

From her tone he could see that was very bad. "Maybe it isn't his fault," he said.

"It simply won't work for an Episcopalian and a Catholic to get married. But if Uncle Mike keeps on being nice to us I'm afraid I'll lose my head and say I'll marry him. I'm just not strong enough by myself. Will you help me be strong, Anthony?"

He stirred restlessly in the curve of her arm. He often played games by himself in which he was very strong and did things other boys couldn't do, but he knew they were only games. Other boys were stronger. "If I can," he said doubtfully.

She turned so she could look straight at him. "I want you to run back to school and find Uncle Mike and pretend you've been there all afternoon. Don't say anything about having been home and hearing us talk and talking to me. Uncle Mike will bring you home in his car. I want you to pretend that you don't like him at all, and that you don't want to go on that trip with him Saturday or anything. Do you understand all this?"

While she talked a big heavy lump had started bouncing in his stomach. It was trying to make him sick. "But I do like him," he said in a choking voice. "And it wasn't going to rain Saturday and—"

"Anthony, it's terrible to ask you to do this for me. It isn't fair to you. I'm being a coward. But if you can do it you will help me a great deal. Do you think you can?"

There was a hot wet mist in front of his eyes. He had felt like this a couple of times before, when other boys at school had pushed him and dared him to fight. Those other times he had run away. He could run away now, too. But that would leave his mother alone and scared. He hadn't thought that anybody else in the world was a coward. If his mother was one, he knew how she felt. It wasn't much fun. "All right," he whispered. "I'll go back to school and pretend the way you said."

She wanted to kiss him, but his body was going to hurt if anyone touched it, and he ran quickly out of the house and back the few blocks to school. He climbed over the rear gate and went through the main building. The schoolyard was filled with boys playing shinny and movings-up baseball, with several of the masters keeping order. Uncle Mike was talking to a master and looking around for him. Anthony wandered out into the schoolyard as if he had been there all the time.

Uncle Mike waved, and called, "Hello there, Tony."

At any other time he would have gone running to Uncle Mike, and would have been caught and swung around in a breathtaking circle. Today he did not move. "Hello," he mumbled.

"Going to high-hat me today, are you?" Uncle Mike said, and strode up and gave him the swing anyway.

"Put me down, put me down," Anthony whined. "I don't like that any more." He did not have to pretend the whine, because he tasted something rising hot and bitter in his throat, and he didn't want to be sick in front of everybody.

"Sure," Uncle Mike said, lowering him to his feet. "Aren't you feeling good today?"

"I feel all right."

"How about a ride home with me, Tony?"

"Do I have to?" he asked sullenly. "I was having fun here."

"Sure, I can see that. I wanted to talk over something important with you, though."

It was tempting to refuse to go with Uncle Mike. Then he wouldn't have to pretend any more. But that wouldn't be helping his mother. "I guess I can go if you ask Mr. Ansley," he said. "He's the one by the front gate."

Mr. Ansley said it was all right, and Anthony went with Uncle Mike to the big Buick touring car at the curb and climbed in. They drove slowly out Locust Street.

"Well," Uncle Mike said happily, "I have that sunny day all ordered for Saturday. You know what? There's a little island in the Schuylkill where we can land and have lunch. They tell me that a pirate, Captain Kidd, maybe, buried some treasure there. Of course people have been digging for it for years. But I got a feeling if we looked hard we might dig up a jar with a few silver quarters in it."

There was a hard lump in Anthony's throat, like the time he swallowed a sourball whole and it stuck halfway down. "I don't want to go Saturday," he said faintly.

"Not want to go! What's the matter, Tony?"

"I just don't think I'd like it."

"Maybe you'd rather go to a movie? There's a swell Douglas Fairbanks picture at the Stanton. You ought to see him jump over things and fight off dozens of people with his sword. Hey, and we could have chocolate ice cream sodas afterward."

Anthony hated it when his eyes started squinching up all by themselves, and stinging. "I don't want to," he said shrilly.

The car had swung right onto Sixteenth Street and was now turning out Spruce. Uncle Mike halted it in front of their house, and said, "Something's wrong, isn't it, Tony? Come on. Tell me straight out."

The only way he could keep going was to shout and get mad. "You don't want to take me on a canoe trip or to the movies!" he cried. "You just do things like that so you can get around my mother. You—"

A big hand gripped his arm. Uncle Mike stared down at him with his jaw struck out, and shook him a bit. "Listen to me," he said hoarsely. "I couldn't like you better if you were my own kid."

"I'm not your own kid! I'm not your own kid!"

That seemed to hurt Uncle Mike. "Maybe you're going to be," he said. "I want to marry your Mother. That would make you my kid. That—"

All of a sudden Anthony found himself pounding as hard as he could with his free hand at Uncle Mike's chest. "I don't want you to marry her," he screamed. "I don't want to be your kid. I don't like you any more. Let me go!"

The big hand went slack and Uncle Mike's face got as blank and empty-looking as a house when all the shades were pulled down and the curtains gone. Anthony squirmed around and wrenched open the car door and raced up the steps of his house. His mother had just come hurrying to the doorway and Anthony threw himself against her, sobbing.

Behind him he heard Uncle Mike say in a flat voice, "Something went wrong. It turns out I never got to him at all. Goodby, Kate." The car moved off quietly down the street.

His mother whispered, "I'll never forgive myself for doing this to you, Anthony. I should have been brave enough to say all those things to him myself. Now I've hurt you both instead of just hurting Mike."

He lifted his head and screamed, "I didn't do anything! I just told him I don't like him any more and that's true. I don't like him! I don't like him!"

He broke away from his mother and ran up the stairs to his room. The baseball Uncle Mike had given him was on the bureau, waiting for the time when the other boys would let him play and he could bring it proudly to the game. He grabbed it and threw it as far as he could through the open window. The hockey stick was in the corner. He held one end of it and jumped on the middle until it broke. Then he flung himself down on the bed.

His mother must have known that he needed to be alone, because it was dark when she finally came up, bringing a supper tray. He wasn't hungry, though. The bag of sourball candy had been under his pillow and somehow he had stuffed them into his mouth one right after another during the afternoon, and had eaten them all without knowing it.

2

ALL DURING THE Nineteen-twenties, he realized later, his mother tried hard to make a living and to keep some kind of standing in Philadelphia society. She might have done one of those things successfully. In trying to do both, she did not do well at either. She held modestly-paid jobs with the Junior League and the Acorn Club and the Matinee Musical. She worked earnestly as a volunteer on charity committees, but she was never asked to be chairman, and the committees to which she was named were always the ones that did the greatest amount of work and had the least amount of prestige. Probably she would have slipped back out of sight into the middle class but for the fact that she was moderately useful. In the family of Philadelphia society she was like a rather dull maiden aunt who sometimes came in handy to look after the children. You might let her have one of your seats at the Academy of Music from time to time, but you would never take her there for the opening of the opera season.

Fortunately, as far as money was concerned, she did not have to pay for Anthony's tuition at Franklin Academy. Because his grandfather was on the faculty, Anthony was given a scholarship.

There was one flurry of excitement early in 1928. A woman named Mrs. DeWitt Lawrence died in France, where she had been living for many years. The cabled news stories identified her as a former Philadelphian, and rewrite men on the *Bulletin* and *Inquirer* and *Record* and the two *Ledgers* dug through brittle clippings to learn that she had been the widow of a traction millionaire and was survived by a daughter-in-law, Mrs. William DeWitt Lawrence, of Spruce Street near Sixteenth (no longer an address with any social pretensions) and by a grandson, Anthony Judson Lawrence. For two days, Anthony was a center of interest at school, and in some quarters there was talk that Mrs. William DeWitt Lawrence ought to be asked to take the chairmanship of one of the Devon Horse Show and County Fair committees.

But then the cables from France carried the terms of Mrs. DeWitt Lawrence's will, and Anthony was no longer a center of interest and nothing more was said about the chairmanship. The will mentioned the daughter-in-law and grandson merely in passing, as a precaution against legal claims that there had been an oversight, and then left seventeen million dollars for a DeWitt Lawrence wing of a Philadelphia museum and a DeWitt Lawrence School of Engineering at a Philadelphia college. There were also minor bequests to servants, including one of two thousand five hundred dollars to a chauffeur named Bledsoe. The will drew a great deal of favorable comment around the city, proving as it did that people remained Philadelphians at heart even when they had long been absent.

The episode had one important by-product. It reminded people that Mrs. William DeWitt Lawrence, nee Judson, had once really had her feet on the lower rungs of the social ladder. Among the people who noted this fact was a Mrs. Hoyt Phelps. She was the widow of a doctor and had two small children. She had been trying to support herself and her children by doing the same kind of work that Anthony's mother had been doing. Unlike Anthony's mother, however, she had no desire to be considered a member of society. She merely wanted to make a good living from it. She had been studying the structure of Philadelphia society closely. In the lower ranks of society, she saw, there were many people scrambling to get higher. In the upper middle class there were more people trying to get into society. From her point of view both these groups had two delightful things in common: they were not sure how to go about climbing higher, and they had money. Mrs. Phelps wanted to develop a procedure that would leave these people with more social standing and slightly less money.

In later years, of course, she became famous as a social counselor. She kept up lists of debutantes and of eligible young men, and arranged parties and weddings for her clients. It might cost fifteen thousand dollars to have Mrs. Phelps arrange a ten-thousand dollar coming-out party for your daughter, but nobody complained; the extra cost ensured attendance by other ambitious debutantes, and by young men who at least came from the best colleges if not from the best families. None of her clients complained, either, about the fact that the old families of Philadelphia society never sent their children to these affairs. Her clients did not really know who the old families were, because the latter led such quiet social lives. Newcomers to Philadelphia society never realized that, when you held an established position in Philadelphia, you did not have to give parties to prove it.

But all that success was in the future, on the spring day in 1928 when Mrs. Hoyt Phelps thought about Mrs. William DeWitt Lawrence. Mrs. Phelps also thought about a Friday afternoon dancing class which was held at the Bellevue Stratford Hotel and which had been withering for some years. Mrs. Phelps knew that the elderly lady who ran the class was ready to sell her interest in it. Mrs. Phelps proposed to Mrs. William DeWitt Lawrence that they take over the class. Anthony's mother was horrified by the financial risks, but even in those days Mrs. Phelps was a great saleswoman, and so she agreed to try it.

Mrs. Phelps knew exactly which families in the upper middle class, and in the lower ranks of society, had children in their early teens and would be impressed by the Bellevue Stratford Hotel, by invitations engraved at Caldwell's, and by a charge of two hundred dollars. The invitations stated, in a dignified script:

Mrs. William DeWitt Lawrence and Mrs. Hoyt Phelps
announce that a limited number of places
are available for the 1928–29 season
of the
Friday Afternoon Dancing Class
at the
Bellevue Stratford Hotel

There was an R.S.V.P., and Mrs. Phelps' name, address and telephone number. Mrs. Phelps did not trust anyone else to handle the delicate matter of the two-hundred dollar charge (one hundred on application, one hundred midway through the season) or the even more delicate matter of deciding which applicants should be turned down. The latter were more important to Mrs. Phelps' plans than the people who were to be accepted. She realized clearly that an activity gains the appeal of exclusiveness not because of who belongs but because of who is not allowed to belong.

So, in November of 1928, seventy-one girls aged thirteen, fourteen and fifteen, and forty-nine boys of the same ages, began attending the Friday Afternoon Dancing Class. Among the boys was Anthony. It was a proof of Mrs. Phelps' skill that she had even managed to impress Anthony's mother with the desirability and exclusiveness of the class. Mrs. Phelps accepted Anthony for only half of the regular fee.

In November and December the dancing class was very successful. In January, however, its directors sensed that trouble was building up. Anthony's mother became so worried that even Anthony was faintly aware of it, although at the age of fourteen he did not ordinarily notice things that were happening to other people.

As they walked to the Bellevue, on a crisp afternoon in January of 1929, his mother said, "Anthony, do you often dance with Peggy Vandeventer?"

"Huh?" he said. He had been far away, running ninety-nine yards for winning touchdowns against Episcopal Academy and Penn Charter, and the cheers beating in his ears drowned his mother's words. He resented being dragged back to the present, because it was only at moments like these that anybody cheered for him.

"I'm talking about Peggy Vandeventer. She likes you. Do you always make it a point to dance with her?"

"She's an itch," he said, flatly and finally.

"But do you dance with her?"

"Once in a while." Peggy had a thin ugly face and bobbed hair that stuck out like a feather duster. She was always making smart cracks that he was never able to answer, and whenever he danced with her she kept bumping her old stomach against him.

"I wish you would dance with her at least once every Friday. And see if you can coax some of your friends to dance with her too, will you?"

"Aw gee, Mother. What for?"

"I'm afraid if something isn't done she won't come back for the second half of the season."

"Hooray."

"I know how you feel," his mother said, "but I'll explain what I'm worried about. Some of the girls and their mothers are dissatisfied. It all boils down to the fact that we don't have enough boys. No dancing class ever does. We have about three girls for every two boys, and sometimes it seems there are even fewer boys than that. I suppose they're present, because I count them when they arrive, but there never seems to be the full number around at any one time."

"Oh, they're around," Anthony said. "They're all there, Mother." He watched her face and saw that she accepted his statement.

"Well, some of the girls have been talking among themselves and complaining to their mothers. Mrs. Phelps and I think the Vandeventer girl is behind it. She's a natural leader, at any rate in causing trouble. And her parents have so much money that some of the other girls toady to her and their mothers encourage it."

"If they have so much money they ought to buy her a new face," Anthony said. He was pleased with that remark. It ought to make Eddie Eakins laugh when he told Eddie.

"Anthony, if she drops out of the class she might draw fifteen or twenty girls with her."

"Well, you said there were too many girls."

"I didn't put it that way. I said there were not enough boys. Anthony, I hate to discuss things like this with you, but Mrs. Phelps and I are counting heavily on a good attendance the second half of the season. We didn't make much profit the first half because we were buying out the woman who used to have the class. Now that's all paid. If everybody comes back for the second half we'll do very well. We need about seventy members to cover the cost of the Rose Ballroom and the orchestra and refreshments and other things.

Everybody over that is clear profit for us. If we lose twenty girls, there goes two-fifths of our profits. And heaven only knows what might happen if twenty dropped out. Maybe others would think the class was a failure, and drop out too."

"All right," he grumbled. "I'll dance with her."

"And, just for my sake, try to be charming, will you? Most of the time you go around with such a closed blank face that anybody would think you're bored to death."

"What do I have to do, grin at her like an ape?"

"Just be nice to her. And try to get your friends, like Eddie Eakins, to be nice to her."

"Eddie will love that," he said grimly. "I'll ask him but I know what he'll say."

That afternoon, just before the first dance, he went over to Peggy Vandeventer. He bowed from the waist, as they taught you to do, and said, "May I have the honor of this, uh, of this dance, Miss Vandeventer?"

She jumped up like a jack-in-the-box. "Hello, big boy," she said. "It's about time you got around to little me. How's your conduct? Don't tell me. I can see it's too good."

That was the way she always talked, in a whirl of comments and of questions which she answered herself. "How ya been?" he said.

"You only ask because you want to find out," she said archly, tossing her feather duster mop of hair. "What are they going to play, something droopy? They need a hot drummer and a good sax in that band. Oh listen. They're starting "I Can't Give You Anything But Love, Baby." Won't that be a funeral, the way they play it. Do you know how to do the Trenton Hop?"

"No."

"They wouldn't let us do it here anyway. They ..."

She kept on like that while he marched her slowly and painfully around the floor. He could dance all right with some girls but not with Peggy. She had a jerky way of throwing her body around. Sometimes she would be two feet away and the next moment she would give a couple of twitches and her thin bony body would come bumping up against him. He couldn't keep time, the way she danced. Her right hand always felt cold and a little damp, too, and it squeezed his left hand nervously every moment or so.

Over her shoulder he caught a glance from Eddie Eakins, who was dancing with another girl. Anthony took his right hand off Peggy's shoulder blades and turned it palm up toward Eddie. Eddie nodded once, held up one finger and wiggled it. Anthony nodded and held up his thumb. Those were some of the signals of their secret club. Eddie nodded again, and swung his partner away to look for one of the other club members and give him the signals. Eddie was president of the club and a kid you had to look up to, because Eddie always knew the score. "Do I know the score?" Eddie would say sometimes. "Look, kid, I *made* the score." Eddie wasn't talking about football, of course, because he didn't go in for football at school. Probably he could make the team if he ever felt like it, Eddie said, but it was too much trouble.

Eddie was a really smooth kid. He had dark brown hair that he parted in the middle and slicked down with Stacomb, and he was always the first kid at school to know what was being worn in colleges and to start wearing the clothes at school. This year at school Eddie was wearing blue coats and gray flannels and dirty white buckskin shoes, because that was the latest thing. He and Eddie were both in the Fourth Form at Franklin Academy, which was like being in freshman year at a high school. Eddie was fifteen and he was fourteen. It made a big difference in his life when Eddie let him be friends, because he had never really had any friends at school. There was always that handicap of his grandfather being head of the Latin Department, and of not being good at sports or anything much else, and of not having anything like the money most of the kids had.

"Don't you ever say anything but uh-huh and uh-uh?" Peggy said, dancing close against him.

"Yeah, sure," he said, yanking himself back to the present.

"I can't give you anything but love, baby," she crooned, peeking up at him out of her thin wise face. "I bet you don't know what love is. I bet you think it's playing post office and spin-the-plate. I think you're cute. Did anybody ever tell you you're good looking? I like the way that black hair of yours gets a funny sort of dark red color in it sometimes."

He didn't like it when she talked like that and wiped her hips against him. It made him feel hot and uncomfortable. "It's kind of a nuisance," he said. "It stands up all the time."

She went off into silent squirms of laughter, and butted her stomach against him twice.

"I'm talking about my hair," he said furiously.

"I bet you weren't," she said. "Oh, bad Tony, talking dirty to little Peggy. Shame on you."

"I don't want to dance if you're going to talk like that."

"Oh I was just kidding you. Look. That's the end of the dance. Let's sneak out onto the roof and smoke a cigarette. Nobody will see us."

"I can't," he muttered. "I gotta go to the washroom. I'll see ya, Peggy." He turned and ducked away, feeling that her sharp black eyes were watching him all the way across the room.

The Rose Ballroom of the hotel was on the top floor. There were many other rooms for dancing and banquets up there too, with corridors winding every which way and a lot of doors in tricky places. None of the other rooms were ever in use during the Friday Afternoon Dancing Class, and if you knew your way around you could get out of sight easily. Usually he didn't leave the Rose Ballroom by the main doorway, because it was dangerous for too many of the club to sneak out the same way. But this time, with Peggy watching, he had to walk through the main doorway because that was the route toward the washroom. Outside the doorway he made a couple of turns and came out by the elevators and waited there for a minute, so that boys heading for the washroom down the main corridor would be out of the way when he was ready to slip past the washroom.

As soon as he figured everything was clear he returned to the main corridor, hurried by the washroom and turned into an empty corridor lined with potted palms. He was just starting to relax when somebody jumped out at him from behind a potted palm and said, "Got you!" It was that Peggy.

"Hey," he said. "What's the idea jumping at a person like that?"

There was a thin smile on her face. "I knew you were looking for little me," she said. "So I decided not to be mean, and to stop hiding."

"You know I was going to the washroom."

"It's back there, Tony," she said in a singsong voice. "Is poor Tony lost? Should Peggy take him back and show him where it is?"

"I can find it. I was thinking about something else and took the wrong turn. I'll see ya."

He whirled and ran back down the corridor, although Peggy called angrily for him to wait because she wanted to talk to him. He darted past the washroom, peering back to make sure she wasn't in sight. This time there was no use waiting by the elevators and then trying the same route again, because Peggy might still be waiting. He returned almost to the Rose Ballroom, turned left into an empty banquet room and crossed it, cut across a corridor and through another empty room. Behind a row of gilt chairs there were several doors. He opened one of them, crossed a third empty banquet room and stopped before the door of a coat room. It was a wooden door built so that either the top or bottom half, or both, could be opened. A puddle of light oozed under the door and he heard a murmur of voices. He rapped three times, paused, rapped twice, paused, rapped twice. That was his own secret knock. Each of them had his own signal. Inside the door a key turned in a lock. The bottom half of the door swung inward and he stooped and went in.

It was a large coat room. Five members of the club were in it: Eddie Eakins and Bill Holley and Joey McAllister from Franklin Academy, Bill Gillespie from Haverford School and Artie Engleman from St. Luke's. They had brought in chairs from the banquet room, and were using the small table that was always kept in the coat room. Eddie and Bill Holley and Bill Gillespie and Artie were playing blackjack with matchsticks for chips. Joey was lolling on one chair with his feet on another, drinking a Coke and smoking a black Benson & Hedges cigarette with a gold tip.

"What the hell kept you?" Eddie said.

"That Peggy Vandeventer was hanging around one of the corridors laying for me."

"Haw, haw, haw," Artie said. "Laying for you. I bet she would, too."

"She got any suspicions about us?" Eddie asked. He was taking drags on a Camel, which he said was a real working man's cigarette.

"I don't think so," Anthony said. "She's just mad because we don't dance with her enough. My mother says she might not come back next half of the season, and wanted to know if you'd be nicer to her, Eddie."

"Nicest thing I could do for her," Eddie said, getting out a comb and running it through his shiny hair, "is push her out the window."

"With all the dough her family has got," Anthony said, "they ought to buy her a new face."

Eddie looked at him, nodded solemnly. "That's not bad, Tony. Buy her a new face."

A warm glow of happiness crept through Anthony's body. It wasn't often Eddie praised a kid. It was wonderful to have something to belong to like the club. "It just popped into my head," he said modestly.

"You want to take a hand?" Eddie asked. "Twenty-five matchsticks for a quarter. You owe Artie ten cents for the Cokes."

"I'll just sit around a while," Anthony said. He got out a pack of Camels just like Eddie's and lit one. The first drag made him a little dizzy, as usual. "Are Marsh and Fats back in the ballroom dancing?" he asked.

"Yeah, they're holding the fort," Eddie said. "Artie and Bill Gillespie will take over from them in ten more minutes."

Anthony nodded. They had a swell system. Now and then all eight of them got together when there was something to vote on, but mostly only six of them sneaked out at a time. At the start, every Friday, Eddie signalled the members who were to come to the club room after the first dance, and they drifted out of the Rose Ballroom singly and took different routes to the coat room. The two members of the club assigned to stay in the Rose Ballroom and dance made sure that Mrs. Phelps and Anthony's mother saw them. A couple of dances later, two members would come back from the coat room and take their places. And so on through the afternoon. That way, just when somebody might begin wondering what had happened to one of them, there he was back on the floor, dancing like mad and smiling at Mrs. Phelps and at Anthony's mother.

It had been a break, at the start of the season, finding a key left in the coat room door. They swiped the key, so they were always sure of getting in and locking up from inside. Best of all, there was a back door into the coat room and the same key worked on it. If the wrong person ever came to one of the doors, and didn't have the right signal and tried to get in, they could sneak out the other door. And, because each of them had his own secret knock, nobody could spy on one of them and repeat his secret knock and get in. All you had to do was look around and see if the secret knock belonged to somebody who was already in the coat room; if it did, you knew a spy was trying to get in. Nothing like that had happened yet, but every once in a while, without warning, Eddie tested them by having a club member give the wrong signal, and they all sneaked out quietly the other way. It was like holding a fire drill, only exciting.

Now if, Anthony thought, Peggy had managed to follow him and heard his three two-two knock, it wouldn't do her any good to come to the door and repeat it. Because there he was, already inside.

That girl was an itch. He wondered if she had been suspicious. It wasn't good, the way she had hidden along that corridor past the washroom. She must have watched some of them on other days, and trailed them that far. A girl like Peggy was likely to go blabbing to his mother or to Mrs. Phelps if she really suspected anything. He thought about that, and got fidgety.

"Hey, Eddie," he said.

Eddie peeked at his down card. "Yeah?"

"I think I better go back to see what that Peggy is up to. I don't like the way she was hanging around that corridor waiting for me. She might start poking through all the rooms."

"All right, Tony, good idea," Eddie said. "Give Marsh the signal to break away when he has a chance. Two dances from now I'll send Artie in to look you up. Show him four fingers held straight out if things are clear. O.K.?"

"O.K., Eddie."

Anthony unlocked the door, peered out. Nobody was in the room beyond, so he slipped out and heard them lock the coat room door behind him. He hurried back to the Rose Ballroom and saw Peggy near the entrance, jabbering with another girl. He went up and asked Peggy for a dance. She smiled at him, and the tip of her tongue licked a corner of her mouth the way a cat might do after lapping milk.

She started dancing with him but almost immediately said, "Come on out on the roof."

"I don't want to smoke," he said. "I gave it up. What's the matter with dancing?"

"I want to talk with you. Come on out."

She didn't say it in that way she had of trying to act cute, but as if she was telling him what to do and he'd better do it. Maybe he'd better, too. They slipped out onto the roof, although Mrs. Phelps and his mother didn't approve of that, and he waited for what Peggy had to say. It was funny the way she was looking at him, as if she thought she owned him or something.

She said in a taunting voice, "I'm going to let you kiss me."

"What do you mean?" he said in alarm. "I don't go around kissing girls."

"Why were you sneaking down that corridor when I caught you?"

"I told you! I was thinking of something else and went past the washroom and—"

"Oh, shut up. Either you were sneaking down there to do something you shouldn't do, or you saw me walk down there and decided to grab me and kiss me. I wonder which your mother would think you were planning to do, if I told her? Wouldn't it be better to kiss me and not ask her what she thinks?"

He was so mad he could have pushed her in the face, but there was a scared feeling fluttering in his stomach, too. "I don't know much about kissing girls," he muttered.

"It's done like this," she said.

She put her arms around his neck and pulled herself close against him. Her lips were kind of thin and clammy. And her tongue—yes, her tongue, ugh!—came out and poked at his mouth. It was enough to make him throw up. At the same time it was exciting and his heart began thumping harder.

She drew back and said, "Who was trying to tell me he gave up smoking? You just had one. I can smell it."

"All right. What if I did?"

She yawned delicately and patted her mouth. "Who are you going to signal he can sneak out, when you get back on the dance floor? Marshall Emmert, or that fat boy whatever his name is?"

He gulped, stared at her. "What are you talking about?"

"I'm talking about that club you have. You and Marshall and that fat boy and Eddie Eakins and Bill Holley and Bill Gillespie and Joey McAllister and that nasty Artie Engleman."

He was really scared now. "We haven't got any club. What gave you the idea?"

She grabbed his arm and her fingers bit into it until they hurt. "Listen to me, Tony Lawrence," she said in a mean tone. "We know all about it. Don't think eight of you can keep sneaking off without anybody noticing. We've got a club too, fifteen of us, except we didn't start it so we could sneak out by ourselves and smoke and do things we shouldn't. We got up our club to watch the eight of you. I can tell you every signal your bunch uses for sneaking out. The only thing I don't know is where you sneak off to. Oh my, and won't your mother and Mrs. Phelps love to hear about it."

His legs were shaking and his tongue felt like an old blotter, but at least she didn't know the important thing. "That's a lie!" he said. "We don't have a club or anything and you can't prove it."

"Maybe I can't prove it to your mother or Mrs. Phelps. But I can prove it to my mother. The other girls can prove it to their mothers. We're all going to tell our mothers that half the boys in the dancing class sneak off every time to smoke and probably to do nasty things, and that we don't want to go back because there aren't enough boys to dance with. How do you like that, Tony Lawrence?"

"Why should I care what you do?"

"Why?" she said in a lilting tone. "Why? Doesn't little Tony know his mother needs the money she gets from us? Won't little Tony feel bad when his mother goes broke with her dancing class?"

Those were awful things for her to say. Of course his mother had said almost the same things, walking with him to the hotel that afternoon, but somehow it hadn't touched him then. To have an outsider say it made him feel horribly ashamed. It frightened him, too. If outsiders talked about how his mother needed money, he guessed things must be pretty bad. He couldn't even imagine what happened to people when they went broke. Maybe they went to jail or had to sleep in the street or something.

"Look," he said faintly. "I won't sneak out any more, Peggy. I'll dance every dance with you if you like. I'll—"

She waved her eyelashes at him. "You like me, don't you?" she cooed.

"Sure I do."

"You think I'm beautiful and want to kiss me, don't you, Tony? Do you want to kiss me some more right now?"

"Yes," he said, and reached out for her, squeezing his eyes shut. She wasn't there, though. He opened his eyes and saw her smiling mockingly at him, a step out of reach. "What's the matter?" he said pleadingly. "Don't you want me to kiss you?"

"Where does your club meet?"

"I can't tell you that, Peggy. Aw come on and—"

"Don't try to get around me, Tony Lawrence. Do you know what you're going to do? You're going to walk right into the ballroom and go up to your mother and Mrs. Phelps and tell them all about your club."

"You're crazy! Why should I do that? That would make me a ... a ... a traitor or something!"

"What do you want to be, a traitor to your bunch or a traitor to your mother? Either you're going to do what I say or there isn't going to be any Friday Afternoon Dancing Class left. And your mother will go broke. And won't I laugh?"

She was almost laughing right now. She was jiggling up and down with excitement and there was a wide thin grin on her face and her black eyes had sparks in them. "Aw, Peggy ..."

"Make up your mind, Tony Lawrence. Give you a minute."

He shut his eyes and watched waves of light and blackness flicker against the inside of the lids. "I'll tell them," he said in a toneless voice.

She took his arm firmly and led him back into the room and across the dance floor. He was not seeing very well, and kept bumping into couples. His mother and Mrs. Phelps were sitting at a little table near the main doorway. His mother looked up and smiled, but Mrs. Phelps just gave them a cool quick glance and went back to some cards she was checking. Mrs. Phelps was always nice to him but you never quite knew where you were with her, because she was so brisk and busy.

Peggy nudged him, and said, "Tony has something to tell you two."

"Yes, dear?" his mother said.

Mrs. Phelps flicked another glance up at him but went back to her cards. After his first words, though, Mrs. Phelps was listening. He recited what he had to say, like a poem memorized for school, rushing through it in a flat tone. "Eight of us have a club," he said. "We've been sneaking out, six at a time, every Friday. We lock ourselves in a coat room on the other side of the building and smoke and play cards and talk and drink cokes. I guess it's made some of the girls sore because we haven't been around to dance with them. It's hurt the dancing class and I'm sorry."

"Oh, Tony," his mother said softly. "And we worked so hard to make a go of this."

"I was sure of it," Mrs. Phelps said in her cool voice. "But I couldn't put my finger on anything, the way they kept drifting in and out. Well, I think this will solve our problem and keep the girls happy."

"I don't know about that," Peggy said loftily. "I don't know whether my friends and I will want to stay."

"Don't make me laugh," Mrs. Phelps said. "When I get through with them, you'll have eight boys under your thumbs. If I know girls, that will be heaven, and I couldn't drive you out of the class. Where is this coat room, Tony?"

His mother said, "You're not going to insist on catching them there, are you? Couldn't Tony just pass the word that we know and—"

"I want an eye-witness report," Mrs. Phelps said. "My own eyes. I want to handle this personally, if you don't mind, Kate. Where is this coat room, Tony?"

He started to describe where it was, and got mixed up, and stammered something about having to give secret knocks or everybody would sneak out another door, and finally Mrs. Phelps said briskly that he would have to take her there and give the secret knock.

"You can't make him do that," his mother protested. "They'll never speak to him again."

"They'll know anyway, Kate. Come on, young man."

Peggy cried, "I want to go too. I'm the one who found out. I want to see them when you walk in."

"Sorry," Mrs. Phelps said. "You're staying here. I'm sure you're getting what you want out of this."

Anthony looked at his mother, and muttered, "I'm sorry."

"I'm sorry, too," she said, and then added firmly, "No matter what it meant to us, you shouldn't have told on your friends."

He hadn't been looking for any credit, but he hadn't expected to be blamed more for telling than for belonging to the club. He lowered his head, and shuffled off beside Mrs. Phelps. It seemed like an endless walk down the long red carpets of one corridor after another. Mrs. Phelps only made one remark the whole way. Once she looked at him curiously and said, "Did you fall for that Peggy Vandeventer or something? If so, I suggest you find somebody a little more your speed. You'll never keep up with that little number." She didn't seem to expect an answer so he didn't try to give one. He led her across the last empty banquet room and gave the three-two-two knock on the coat room door. The key clicked and the door opened. Mrs. Phelps stooped and went in like a cat after mice.

"Hello, boys," she said. "Having fun? I can see you are. Smoking, gambling and heaven knows what. It's too bad some of the girls aren't having fun too, but they don't have anyone to dance with. Eddie Eakins, I wonder what your mother will say if I tell her? She was so hopeful you would meet some nice girls here. Artie, if your father finds out you smoke, won't there be fun! Bill Gillespie ..."

She went right down the line, talking to each of them. It was startling how much she knew about all their parents. And she seemed to know exactly what would upset the parents of each one the most. Mrs. Phelps flung back the top half of the door, and Anthony saw the bunch sitting there like they were waiting for the dentist.

"Well now," Mrs. Phelps said finally, in a cheery voice. "This doesn't have to go any further than right here. Naturally I'll expect all of you to show some real interest in the girls from now on. So let's go back, shall we? Don't take it too hard, either. If you ever knew how most of those pretty little girls just dream and dream about you smoothies, you'd feel good about it and would want to pay them some attention. All right. Here we go."

The last things she said must have cheered up the bunch, because they came out of the room sort of red-faced but grinning and nudging each other. The grins flicked off as they passed him, though, and Artie tried to kick him in the shins. He guessed he didn't have any friends left now.

He trailed slowly after them to the Rose Ballroom. There was only one tiny bit of comfort in the whole awful business. It looked as if a girl thought he was pretty keen. Of course Peggy wasn't the kind of girl he would have picked, all by himself, but probably not many kids had their lives wrecked by a girl just because she thought the kid was pretty keen and because she wanted him for herself. When he got back to the ballroom he looked around for Peggy. She was in a corner, talking to Eddie Eakins. He couldn't escape seeing Eddie at school so there was no use trying to duck him now. He walked up to them and asked Peggy for a dance.

Peggy looked at him coldly. "Do you think I should dance with him, Eddie?"

"I wouldn't think so," Eddie said.

"And besides," Peggy said, slinking up close to Eddie, "I like the smooth type. I think you're smooth."

Eddie tilted an eyebrow wisely at her. "I can't give you anything but love, baby," he chanted. "Maybe we oughtta show them how to dance, huh?" They swung off together, gazing into each other's eyes and finding in them something for which they had been searching.

3

IN 1924 FRANKLIN ACADEMY had sold its old brick buildings in the center of town, and joined the great migration to the suburbs. The trustees bought an estate in Wynnewood on the Main Line. The mansion on the estate had been erected in the Eighteen-nineties by the owner of a Manayunk steel mill, who had the castle-building urge so common in those days. The result of his efforts had been a heap of battlements, turrets, bastions and buttresses which looked like a stone quarry turned inside out. It was just the thing for resisting either a siege in the Middle Ages or modern schoolboys.

Taking the radical step of moving to the suburbs encouraged bold thinking among the trustees. They retired Doctor Luther Hay Whitney, who was getting into his seventies, and gave him the title of Headmaster Emeritus. For the new headmaster they not only went outside the ministry but even outside of Philadelphia, and brought in a man from New England. His name was Lowell McClintic, and he held Bachelor's and Master's degrees from Harvard. Although he was only thirty-five, he already had a reputation in New England preparatory school circles.

Several of the older trustees worried about the Boston background of the new man, because Boston had a lot of Reds in it these days, like those Sacco and Vanzetti fellows, and you couldn't tell who might be tarred with that brush. Wiser heads pointed out, however, that Boston had also produced President Coolidge, who was a good safe chap. So McClintic was made headmaster. His lack of a doctorate was remedied within a year; the trustees canvassed the colleges from which they had been graduated, and found one that was willing to bestow an honorary degree of Doctor of Literature on the new headmaster, who in fact had written a very nice booklet titled "Admission Practices and Procedures at Andover and Exeter." It made the trustees feel happier and more secure when they could address their new man as Doctor McClintic.

In all this upheaval one thing was not changed. The faculty of Franklin Academy left many old furnishings and a few old ideas behind in the move to the Main Line, but they brought along a short strip of worn green carpet. This they placed reverently in front of the new headmaster's desk. He was a bit startled to find it there when he began his new job. Next to the carved oak furniture and panelling of his office, the carpet looked as out of place as a battered fishing hat worn to a Board of Directors' meeting.

When he asked about it, the gaunt old head of his Latin Department, Doctor Harry Judson, said in his rumbling voice, "I should leave it there, sir, if I were you. That is where the boys stand when it is necessary for you to talk to them. They are used to that green carpet."

The new headmaster was not stupid. He knew that discipline in a preparatory school is the result of many subtle influences, and that an old green carpet might well be such an influence. He did not move it. When the fall term began, a wave of unrest and mischief swept through the student body, because of the change of location and of headmasters. Many boys thought that a new, free era was beginning. One by one, that fall, they met the new headmaster in his office to discuss what they had done. Some came in sullenly. Some marched in ready to put the new head in his place. Others arrived full of injured innocence. Then they saw the old green carpet, worn to its threads by a generation of uneasy feet. Something happened to the sullenness and the swagger and the injured innocence. They stood on the carpet, shifting unhappily from foot to foot, and said yes sir and no sir and that they would do better, sir.

Later, when the trustees congratulated him on how smoothly he handled the problems of discipline, the new headmaster won a reputation for modesty by saying, "It's just a matter of hauling them onto the carpet, gentlemen."

In June 1929, Anthony Lawrence stood on the old green carpet, facing Doctor McClintic across the oak desk. Clinky had not invited him to sit in the chair beside the desk, which was where you sat when everything was all right. Clinky let him stand on the carpet, and everybody knew that meant trouble. Anthony shrugged. It didn't matter if one more person wanted to pick on him. Only why didn't Clinky start?

Not until years later did he realize that Doctor McClintic's actions were as perfectly timed and rehearsed as those of a veteran actor on Broadway. There was the dramatic pause, the bits of stage business (such as the crackling of papers and rasp of pen), the keen awareness of the mood of the audience, and the skill at moving the audience to tears or terror or even relief. All Anthony knew at the time, however, was that he began by shrugging and ended by trembling. First Clinky gave him a glance so quick and sharp that he almost ducked to escape it. Then Clinky scratched away with a pen at papers that crackled unpleasantly in the still room. A telephone purred softly, as if afraid to disturb Clinky, and he picked it up and said brusquely, "Yes ... no ... later." Anthony shifted from foot to foot. The muscles at the backs of his legs began aching, and sweat traced an itchy course down from his armpits. He found himself thinking: aw, come on, Clinky. *Please, Doctor McClintic ...*

The man pushed aside his papers and leaned back in his swivel armchair. "Well, Anthony," he said.

The sound of an ordinary human voice broke the spell. Clinky was ready now, was he? It didn't matter to him what Clinky was going to say. Only, Clinky didn't seem quite ready to say it. Clinky fished out his pipe, There was silence, growing slowly more agonizing, while Clinky dipped the pipe in a tobacco pouch and filled it and carefully tamped the tobacco into the bowl. He lit the pipe and puffed, and peered at Anthony through an omnious blue mist of smoke.

"Well, Anthony," he said again, and now it wasn't an ordinary human voice any more. "I'm sorry to see you under these conditions. I've always thought you had a great deal in you. I'd hoped that the only times I'd see you in here would be to congratulate you for fine work of one kind or another."

Anthony had lined up a number of excuses in his mind, as replies to what Clinky might say to him. None of them seemed to be good answers right at the moment. "Yes, sir," he muttered.

"Can you quote the motto of the Academy, Anthony?"

"Uh, yes sir. Mens sana in corpore sano."

"And it means?"

"A sound mind in a sound body, doesn't it, sir?"

"That's right." The man peered down at a paper, and said, "If you had translated your Caesar that well in your final exam, you would not have scored thirty-seven in it."

"I guess that means I flunked Latin?"

"I'm afraid it does. I have your report here. Can you guess how many subjects you passed?"

He hadn't really thought of his marks. It had been unpleasant to consider what they might be, so he had avoided the thought. Now that he couldn't avoid it any longer, his mind came up with a shocking idea. "Gee," he said, gulping, "maybe I only passed one or two."

Doctor McClintic said gently, "You didn't pass any."

Not any. It was hard to take in that idea right away. It was like waking from sleep and finding yourself falling through black space, and not knowing where you were falling or what you would hit.

"With most boys," Doctor McClintic said, "we would have the problem of how to break the news to their families. But of course, with your grandfather on the faculty, your family already knows."

"They didn't say anything to me about it."

"I asked them not to, until I had a chance to talk to you. A sound mind in a sound body. You haven't done very well on the first part, have you?"

"No, sir."

"Now about the sound body. What teams have you gone out for this year, Anthony?"

Why did Doctor McClintic have to ask him that? Clinky must know the answer. He couldn't have made any teams, anyway. Something had happened to his body in the past year. It got tall and lanky. It went around living a life of its own, bumping into things. It had turned weak on him, too. Last winter, in gym class, he hadn't been able to chin himself once, and in trying the wall climb all he had done was hang there helplessly while the other kids snickered. "Gee," he mumbled, "I couldn't make any varsity teams."

"We have junior teams in all sports, Anthony. You could have tried for the hundred-and-thirty-five-pound football team, for the wrestling squad in your weight class, for the Fourth Form basketball team, for the track or baseball squads. They didn't appeal to you, I suppose."

"Uh, no sir."

"We have a program of donating voluntary work hours to projects on the school grounds. How many hours have you donated this year?"

"I guess none, sir."

Doctor McClintic leaned back, and studied him. This, as Anthony learned years later, was the start of a careful probing process. It was designed to break through the fogs and barriers of adolescence, to find out what his loyalties were, and then to use those loyalties to move him in a desired direction. "You're a scholarship student," Doctor McClintic said. "We expect more of our scholarship students than from other boys. We expect a lot of you. But you've let the school down badly."

What had the dumb old place ever done for him? "Yes sir," he said, without much interest.

"One of the finest members of our faculty is your grandfather. He's taking this very hard, Tony."

His grandfather. Old Nearums, the boys called his grandfather. It was a nickname whose origin was forgotten, except for a rumor that he had come close to being headmaster once many years ago. Some of them even said "Old Nearums" as if they liked him. He didn't feel strongly one way or another about his grandfather. He was just a stooped old man who wandered around home and the school, saying things in Latin as if he liked the sound of his booming voice. Mostly his grandfather didn't pay much attention to him. When he did, his grandfather would blink and stick out his wrinkled turkey neck and study him for a moment as if asking himself who this boy was. "Yes," Anthony said, "I guess Grandfather doesn't like it much."

"You'd probably feel badly," Doctor McClintic said, "if you had to drop back a form while all your friends moved on."

His friends. That was a laugh. What friends? "I don't care much about the kids in my form," he muttered.

"However," Doctor McClintic said briskly, "it isn't a question of letting you drop back a form. I might permit an ordinary boy to do it. But not a scholarship student. What we're discussing, Anthony, is not the matter of dropping back a form but the possibility of leaving school."

That shook him a little. It was a dumb old place but he had been at Franklin nine years and he guessed he was used to it. "Gee," he said, "if I didn't come back here where would I go?"

"There's a high school in town not too far from your home. You must know of it. Central High School. Many private school people might give you a discouraging picture of it, but I don't feel that way. You might find yourself a bit lost in their enormous classes, after our small ones. Unless you tried hard, the teachers would take no personal interest in you, as they do here. The boys you met would be rather different from ours, but I imagine you'd find some rough diamonds in the lot."

Anthony frowned. Who did Doctor McClintic think he was kidding? Anybody with brains could see Clinky thought the place was a hole. And that junk about rough diamonds. Sometimes he passed gangs from Central on the streets downtown and Clinky was anyway half right in what he said. They might not be diamonds but they were rough, all right. No matter what you said against the Academy, at least they didn't let the big kids beat up smaller kids. Not that some of the fresh brats in C and D form didn't need a swift kick in the tail.

"I don't think I'd like Central much," he said.

"Well, perhaps not." Doctor McClintic paused a moment, drew on the pipe and peered out keenly through the swirls of smoke. "I don't imagine," he said gently, "that your mother would like seeing you go there, either. She thinks the world of you, Anthony. She's worked very hard to give you a real chance to get ahead."

Anthony tried to freeze his face into cold lines but it was twitching on him. Doctor McClintic didn't have to bring his mother into this. "I guess she has," he muttered.

"A couple of times in the past I've happened to meet her when there were some good things in your record I could talk about. Her eyes really light up when she hears good reports about you. Nobody in the world means as much to her as you do."

Inside his head, a voice began screaming at Clinky to shut up about his mother. "Oh, I don't know," he muttered.

"Well, I do know. She's very proud of you, Anthony."

She wasn't proud when he told on the club at dancing school last winter. She couldn't be proud of him now. Probably she would never be proud of him again.

The man across the desk went on relentlessly, in a soft voice, "You've let her down, Anthony."

He couldn't take any more of this. He was shaking all over and there was a hot pressure behind his eyes that meant he wanted to start bawling. He wanted to throw himself in the chair beside the desk and start blubbering about all the things that had gone wrong: the dancing class and his mother's scorn and not having any friends and hanging on the climbing wall in the gym with the class snickering and everything else. During the past few months he had managed to keep all those things pushed out of his mind. He had found a way to retreat inside himself and not let anything close enough to bother him. But now the man across the desk had dragged him out. If he broke down and blabbed all this he was going to hate Clinky. Only it was hard to keep it back. It—

The man across the desk got up abruptly, walked to the window and stood there with his back turned. "Well," Clinky said in a brisk voice, "got any suggestions, Tony?"

He took a deep shuddering breath that felt like ice going into his lungs. "Could I go to summer school or something?" he pleaded. "You could give me exams just before school starts like you sometimes do for kids."

"That would mean you'd have to give up the summer camp you had been planning to attend."

"I wouldn't mind that. Honest! I know the Academy doesn't hold summer school, but maybe somebody does in the city." He was talking with desperate haste now. Doctor McClintic didn't seem quite set on flunking him out. "Or maybe I could ask my grandfather to help me. That would save money, wouldn't it? Oh, and I just remembered. My grandmother taught school once. She was good at English and things. I guess she'd help if I asked her."

"You'd have six subjects to make up. That's a lot."

"I could do it, sir. I know I could do it."

Doctor McClintic turned slowly. "I like your spirit," he said. "I'm inclined to give you a chance. But there's something else you'd have to do. I'm not sure you'd want to try it."

"Gee," he said earnestly, "at least tell me what it is, sir. How would you know I wouldn't want to do it unless you tell me?"

"Anthony, this past year you had a scholarship. That means the school paid for you. But the school got nothing from you in return because you didn't do the work or enter into things. So to earn another chance you'd have to repay the school. You can do it by working here part of the day, all summer. We're putting in a new track around the football field, and laying a few walks and removing some old trees. A contractor has taken on the project, but he's really doing it just to give a couple of Penn football players a summer job. They'll need somebody to run errands and give them a hand. The work will last from June twentieth to August twentieth, when the Penn boys leave for pre-season practice. You'd have to work here from nine in the morning until three in the afternoon. Your only pay would be carfare and lunch. You'd have to do outdoor work most of the day and study at night. I'm not sure you'd want to take it on."

It would be tough, all right. But at the same time it would be like finding a long straight path in front of you when you felt like running. "I can do it," he said quickly. "Will you let me try?"

"All right," Doctor McClintic said. "You just made a sale, Tony. Go ahead and try." Then he smiled and added, as if forced to admit it, "By George, you might even make it, too!"

It turned out to be not a bad summer at all. His grandfather and grandmother were nice about helping him, and he got to know them much better. His grandfather knew more Latin than Caesar ever did, and he could get you interested in it if you didn't fight not to be interested. Now and then they all played a game at the dinner table at which you took turns asking the others questions in Latin, and everybody had to give a sensible answer in English. The first person who gave three wrong answers had to do the dishes, except that his grandfather wasn't allowed any wrong answers. They caught Anthony a lot at the beginning of the summer but not so much at the end, and one wonderful night they caught his grandfather, and they all almost died laughing.

Several of the subjects he was making up—Sacred Studies and Math and Science—he could handle himself once he decided to work at them. Math was kind of fun when you knew what you were doing, because you could line up numbers and make them do things just like soldiers on parade.

His grandmother was good at English and History. He had never talked to her much before that summer, because all she usually talked about was did he have his rubbers on and what was he doing for that sniffle, and those things certainly weren't worth talking about. But when she read poetry she had a voice you liked to hear, kind of husky and soft, like somebody fooling with low notes on the school organ. They memorized poems and recited them at each other, and then talked about what they meant. One night in the living room she recited a poem in a way that gave him gooseflesh. It had some lines in it that went: "She walks in beauty, like the night of cloudless climes and starry skies; and all that's best of dark and bright, meet in her aspect and her eyes." His grandfather must have noticed how good it sounded, too, because he made a queer noise in his throat and dropped the book he was reading and came over suddenly and kissed Grandmother, and for a moment they looked at each other as if they were far away.

He had always had trouble with History, because dates in history skidded around in his mind like soap in a bathtub. But his grandmother fixed that. It was easy, once you knew the trick. You just got straight in your mind what was happening in Philadelphia at any given time and then you tied in other dates with that. For example, a thing called the French Revolution began in 1789. Well, who could remember a date like that, floating around all by itself? But you could remember that they wrote the U.S. Constitution in Philadelphia in 1787, and that the French Revolution started only two years later. It was lucky that so much of history had been made right here in Philadelphia, because that gave you a lot of dates to tie other dates to.

It was easy to learn Philadelphia history because it was so important and because you sort of owned it yourself. His mother and grandmother took him around, weekends that summer, to see right where a lot of history had been made. His mother had a new Model A Ford, because the dancing class had worked out pretty well, and so they could drive all over on history trips. They even took one weekend trip to Washington, D.C., which was where they had moved the national government after Philadelphia had started it going properly between 1790 and 1800. A lot of people from all over the country were taking history trips that summer. Some of them certainly didn't know much about Philadelphia.

Like the woman who came up to them outside the Capitol in Washington and said, "Hello, folks. I'm from Ohio. I see by your license you folks are from Pennsylvania."

Anthony said quickly, before his grandmother or mother could reply, "Oh no, we're from Philadelphia."

The woman looked puzzled and said, "They haven't moved it from Pennsylvania, have they?"

His mother and grandmother laughed politely, so the woman wouldn't feel badly about being ignorant, because of course Philadelphia was in Pennsylvania, but you weren't from Pennsylvania, you were from Philadelphia. He guessed maybe out in Ohio there were no important places to be from, so you had to be from Ohio.

So the studying went pretty well that summer, and the work at Franklin Academy on weekdays turned out even better.

The two Penn football players who were doing the work on the quarter-mile track and walks and trees were Joe Krakowicz and Al Horder. They were great big guys with muscles that looked almost too heavy to carry around. They worked without their shirts and did a lot of laughing and kidding. Right from the start they began calling him Tony and kidding with him too, and let him do some of the heavy work besides just running errands. That first afternoon, when three o'clock came and they were through work, Joe brought out a football and threw it to Al. Anthony was starting into the gym to change his clothes to go home, but Joe yelled, "Hey, you Tony, stick around," and threw him a pass. He didn't want to mess up their fun, but they wanted him to stay and pass and kick with them, so of course he did and it was swell. After that they threw the football around and kicked it every afternoon after work.

Early in July they were playing on the football field, inside the quarter-mile track they had been working on, when a Pierce-Arrow drove up beside the track. A big red haired man climbed out and walked over to them.

"Hello, Joe. Hello, Al," he said. "How's everything going?"

"It go fine, Mr. Callahan," Joe said. "How it look to you?"

"We got a couple hundred feet of the track already graded and the crushed stone base on it," Al said. "Say, Mr. Callahan, here's a kid who's doing a good job helping us. He goes to the school. Hey, Tony, come here a minute."

Anthony had recognized the man he used to call Uncle Mike as soon as he stepped from the car. He had been edging away from them, hoping Uncle Mike wouldn't see him. He didn't remember exactly what had happened between them a long time ago, but he knew it had been unpleasant. He had been upset or something about Uncle Mike coming around to see his mother. He hadn't seen Uncle Mike since that time, and the memory of the trouble had faded like the memory of toothaches faded. When Al called him, Anthony came forward scuffling his feet and looking down at the ground.

Al said, "This is Tony Lawrence, Mr. Callahan. The school asked him to help us out."

Uncle Mike's face lighted up. "Well, Tony," he said, shoving out a big hand. "You've grown so much I wouldn't have known you. Al, I used to know this young man when he was a little kid. Nice to see you, Tony."

Anthony looked up and grinned a little and shook hands. Uncle Mike had spoken in a casual way, so maybe he had forgotten the trouble too. They talked for a few moments, and Uncle Mike asked how his mother was, and Anthony said she was fine. He was relieved when Uncle Mike seemed to think that covered everything, and turned back to ask Joe and Al about the work. They took him around and showed him what they were doing on the track. Apparently Uncle Mike was the contractor who had taken on the job.

"This is all very good," Uncle Mike said, "but what's this business of running around on the football field throwing passes and kicking?"

"Well, you told us to quit at three every afternoon and get in a football workout," Al said. "It's three-thirty, Mr. Callahan."

"Sure I did," Uncle Mike said. "But what sort of a workout is this? Are you guys going out for the backfield next fall?"

Al and Joe grinned, and scuffled their feet the way Anthony had done a few minutes earlier.

Uncle Mike turned to Anthony and said, "These two lugs are guards, Tony. Best ones Penn has, too. The coaching staff at Penn will kill me if I let a couple of star guards turn themselves into lousy backs. Now look, Tony, I'm going to appoint you manager of this team. You must know where they keep the tackling dummy here. I want you to string it up every afternoon so these two can get in a real workout. I'll send around a load of sawdust for the tackling pit. I think I can find a charging machine and I'll send that around, too. Will you take charge of all that?"

Anthony said he would, and in a little while Uncle Mike left. Anthony felt proud of being given a responsibility like that, but at the same time he was sorry that the passing and kicking had to end. Now there would be nothing for him to do except stand around and watch.

"It too good to last," Joe Krakowicz said gloomily. "Now just work work work."

"Ah, you like it, you big Polack," Al said. "Besides, don't grumble in front of the manager."

"Ha!" Joe said, poking Anthony in the ribs. "He think he stand around and just manage, that big laugh. What you play on this school team, Tony?"

"Oh gosh," Anthony said. "I'm not on the team."

"Yeah?" Joe said. "Why this?"

"Well, I'll only be fifteen in a couple of weeks, and I only weigh a hundred and forty-five, and—"

"Ha, we get through with you, you throw them all around," Joe said. "How this, Al? He manager, us coaches. What position we teach him to play, huh?"

"All kids like to run with the ball," Al said. "He ought to be a halfback or something."

"Halfback!" Joe snorted. "You got chance turn boy into man and you want to keep him boy? Look, you Tony, up front is where men are. Backfield all boys. Bunch of cheerleaders is all. You come up front with men."

"Now wait, now wait," Al said. "Tony, you might as well know they say guards are just fullbacks with their brains knocked out. If we put you on this charging machine, and give you all the exercises for linemen, your muscles will get set for line work. You'll end up just a dumb guard at the bottom of the pile-up."

"I'd like to be a guard," Anthony said shyly. This was all just in fun, because of course he would never make the Academy team, but it would be nice to pretend to be what Al and Joe were.

The next day Al and Joe brought out football uniforms. Old Mr. Callahan the caretaker (who was of course Uncle Mike's father, although Anthony never thought of him in that way) rummaged through the gym and came up with some old shoulder pads and pants and helmet and cleated shoes and other stuff that fit Anthony. So they began practicing after the regular work. It was pretty good fun. When you learned how to hit the tackling dummy just right, coming in low and hitting it with your shoulder and driving hard with short choppy steps, it didn't hurt you a bit. Sometimes he did it exactly right and knocked the dummy off the spring hook. Joe and Al knocked it off every time. The charging machine had pads, and you put your shoulders against them and dug with your feet, and tried to push the machine back.

Blocking was like tackling, except you couldn't use your hands, and you weren't allowed to block a man from behind because that was clipping and might break his legs. They all practiced blocking the dummy as well as tackling it.

"This stuff is called fundamentals," Al said. "But there's a lot more to football than that. Take tackling, now. The dummy stays right there to be socked. But your ball carrier will either slam into you or try to fool you. He'll fake going one way and take off in the other. He'll show you a leg and pull it away as you dive for it. So you never come roaring full speed at the ball carrier. When you get near him you shorten your steps. You widen your stance so you can go either way. You watch for his fakes and try to fake him too."

They practiced things like that on each other, but with Al and Joe doing it very gently with Anthony so they wouldn't hurt him. They practiced two-on-one charging, and even though they tried to be gentle Anthony had his wind knocked out a few times. They showed him how to use his hands, on defense, to get through the offensive linemen. They showed him how to fake other linemen out of position and catch them off balance, and how to charge low and hard to spill everybody when the interference was driving at you.

"A good lineman," Al said, "charges across the line of scrimmage and then holds his position until he spots the ball. Then he goes for it."

So the summer passed, and most of it didn't seem like work at all. Anthony was sorry when August twentieth came and Al and Joe were finishing up. It had been a swell summer but there was one angle of it that he didn't feel good about. Al and Joe took it for granted that he would go out for the Academy team and make it, and of course he'd never be able to do that. It hadn't been honest to pretend all summer that he agreed with Al and Joe about making the team. He wanted to tell them the truth before they left. The chance came late that final afternoon, after they had showered in the gym and were finishing dressing.

"Well, Tony," Al said, "it's been a good summer. Come on down and see us play some Saturday. We'll send you tickets. Wish we could see you play, but they'd never let us skip practice to come out."

Anthony said, "I ought to tell you something. I've just been kidding about going out for the team and making it. It wouldn't do any good to try."

"What this you give us?" Joe growled.

"Well, gee," Anthony said, "I guess you don't realize I'm ... I'm kind of weak. I can't even chin myself."

"Oh, crap," Joe said disgustedly. He walked up to Anthony and grabbed him under the arms and hoisted him up toward a pipe running below the ceiling. "Take hold pipe," Joe said.

Anthony grabbed it and hung there miserably.

"What you wait for?" Joe said. "Go on chin."

He hated letting them see how weak he was. But he would try, anyway. He tensed his muscles. All of a sudden a startling thing happened. His body floated upward and his head bumped the ceiling. "I did it!" he screamed, hanging there with his head touching the ceiling. "I did it!"

"That only one," Joe said. "Now more."

He lowered himself and tensed and went up again and down and Joe began counting slowly three ... four ... five ... and then things got a bit blurred and the next thing he knew Al was lifting him down and a pink mist was slowly fading from before his eyes.

"You trying to kill the kid, Joe?" Al said.

"I'm all right," Anthony gasped. "I did five, though, didn't I?"

"Nah," Al said. "You did ten and this dumb Polack would of kept on counting till you dropped." He set Anthony on his feet and smacked him on the tail and said, "You'll make it, Tony.'

Years later, Anthony finally got around to wondering how much of the happenings of the summer had been carefully planned, and who had planned them. It might have been his mother, or Doctor McClintic. Or it might have been Uncle Mike, picking up school news from old Mr. Callahan, the caretaker, and moving in quietly to set the stage. Or it might have been everybody working together. It couldn't all have been coincidence. But none of the actors in the little summer drama ever let slip a hint. Certainly Joe Krakowicz and Al Horder played their parts to the end, waving goodby to him as they left the locker room for the last time, and never knowing—or perhaps they did?—that when they were out of sight a fifteen-year-old boy sat down and cried the first happy tears of his life.

4

FOOTBALL PRACTICE BEGAN a week before the Academy opened. Anthony came on the field the first afternoon wearing the old pads and helmet and jersey and football pants and shoes that he had worn so often during the summer. He should have been used to them but they felt strange on him now, like a costume you might wear to a Halloween party. It had been one thing to fool around with Al and Joe all summer, knowing they weren't going to hurt him. It was very different to try out for the team. Boys from the upper forms, who looked just like anybody else when you passed them in the school hallways, now seemed strange and menacing in their black helmets and bulky shoulder pads. He didn't think it would impress them to learn that he could chin himself ten times.

For a while, that first afternoon, they did exercises and sprints up and down the field. Anthony couldn't get his body moving right. It felt as limp and soggy as the old tackling dummy. He tried to tell himself that he was nervous only because of worrying about the results of the make-up exams, which he had finished taking that morning. He couldn't make himself believe it, though. He felt pretty good about the exams. You could usually tell how you would do by whether you got a sick feeling when you saw the questions, or were eager to start writing the answers. He had felt eager when he saw the questions on each test. But right now, with football coming up, he felt sick.

The head coach was starting to sort out guys to play different positions. He came up to Anthony and cocked his head on one side and said, "Your name is Lawrence, isn't it?"

"Yes, sir," Anthony said.

"You've never played football, have you? Or any other sport?"

"Uh, no sir."

"What brings you out for the squad, Lawrence?"

"I guess I just want to play, sir."

"What's your weight?"

"I gained ten pounds this summer," Anthony said. "I weigh around a hundred and fifty-five. I want to go out for guard."

"That's a new one on me," the coach said. "Somebody wants to play guard. Lawrence, that's a tough position. You get a lot of bumps at guard. You ever taken any bumps?"

When you came right down to it, he never had. He kicked at the turf with his cleats and shook his head.

"Well, let's see if you can take them," the coach said. "It's not very fair, doing this to you the first afternoon, but I might as well find out fast. Hey, Creighton, Arnold! Come here a minute."

Two of the varsity men trotted up. They were both from the Sixth Upper, which was the same as senior year in high school. One had played guard and one had played tackle on last year's team. They didn't tower over Anthony the way they once had, a year or so ago, but they still looked awfully big.

"Here's a Fifth Form boy named Lawrence," the coach said. "He has an idea he wants to play guard. He's never done any sports. I want a few two-on-one charges, with him trying to get through you. Now look, Lawrence, here's what you do ..."

The coach showed him how to get into charging position and how to try to get through the two linemen, as if he were a defensive guard. Of course he had been doing this all summer with Al and Joe.

"I'm going to call one-two-three-hike," the coach said, "and on hike you charge. Let's go."

Creighton and Arnold settled their helmets snugly, and their faces seemed to turn cold and hard. Anthony crouched in front of them. Their padded shoulders looked like the fenders of trucks. Al Horder and Joe Krakowicz had looked bigger but they had always grinned at him and he had always known they wouldn't use their full strength. Creighton and Arnold were digging in solidly, jaws set, eyes narrowed.

"One ... two ... three ... Hike!"

Something awful happened. It was like an explosion. A huge force slammed into him and rolled by and left him lying on his back with his helmet jammed down over his eyes.

The coach picked him up. "You all right, Lawrence?"

"Yes, sir," he gasped. "That wasn't very good, was it? I ought to do better than that."

"All right," the coach said. "Try it again."

On the second try they mashed into him and knocked him flat and something cracked into his face and made it feel numb. He got up slowly and wiped a hand over his face. A red smear came away on his hand. He stared at it. Why, that was blood! It was his very own blood, horribly bright and red.

The coach took a look at him. "You have a nose-bleed, Lawrence. It doesn't look bad but maybe you'd better call it for the day, hm?"

"I don't want to call it," Anthony mumbled. He would bleed to death on the field in front of them all, and they would have a special service for him in the Academy Chapel, and *that* would make everybody very sorry.

They tried the two-on-one charging again. Creighton and Arnold didn't smack into him quite so hard that time, but they still pushed him back five yards. He felt better after that charge. The sawdust feeling had gone from his body, and he knew what he had been doing wrong. He had been standing there letting them plow into him. He hadn't been charging at all. He asked for another chance, and the coach said all right but this would be the last.

Crouching for the final charge, Anthony began remembering some of the things Al and Joe had taught him. With two guys trying to take you out of the play, you didn't just charge straight into them. You used different tricks to split them. He waited with his muscles tightening.

"One … two … three … Hike!"

He started a split-second before Creighton and Arnold. He charged at a slight angle, ramming a shoulder into Creighton and using his hands to jar Arnold off stride and then bouncing off Creighton and driving into Arnold from the side, digging hard and keeping his legs churning. It went faster than you could think, just thud-thud-thud and there he was through them and slowing and setting his feet wide and looking for the ball carrier, although of course this time there wasn't any.

"O.K.," the coach said. "That's it."

"Now wait, coach," Creighton pleaded. "We were taking it kind of easy. Give us just one more."

"Yeah, come on, coach," Arnold said. "No Fifth Former can do that to me."

"What do you think, Lawrence?" the coach said.

Anthony peered at the other two. They weren't going to like it much if he walked away now. On the other hand, they might be hard to handle on the next charge. They wouldn't let him get away again with that trick of handling them one at a time. "I'm all ready," he said. Maybe one of those other tricks Al and Joe had taught him would work.

They got down into charging stance. Anthony set himself as if he were going to try the same stunt again. The way they took position, three sets of shoulders would crash together on the same level. But just as the Hike signal came, Anthony went in low and hard, under their shoulders. He came up between them with his legs giving him an explosive push and caught one on each shoulder. They went sprawling, one on each side of him, with the force of their own charge helping to flip them over.

Anthony swung around and saw Creighton getting up slowly and Arnold with his legs doubled up into his stomach. "Gee," he said, running back to Arnold, "are you all right? Gee, I didn't mean to hurt anybody."

"Just … my … wind," Arnold gasped. He staggered to his feet. "Who said," he muttered gloomily, "that no Fifth Former could do that to me."

Creighton slapped his back. "You're all right, Lawrence. Hey, coach, I think you got yourself a guard here."

"Gee," Anthony said, staring wide-eyed at the coach, "can I really stay on the squad?"

The coach grinned. "You don't have to take my regulars apart, to make the squad. You made it when you tried again after that nosebleed. All right, you three. Jog a lap around the track and then go in and shower."

Two days later Doctor McClintic called him into the office and had him sit in the chair by the desk and said that he had passed the make-up exams, and could have his scholarship back.

"By the way," Doctor McClintic said, "I hear you gave Creighton and Arnold a little lesson in charging, the other day." He chuckled and added, "Wish I'd been there to see it. Keep on charging that way, Tony, and you'll do all right."

That fall, for the first time, he found himself accepted by the other kids, although Eddie Eakins and his bunch still looked through him as if he didn't exist. He wasn't worried now about what Eddie thought. There were a couple other Fifth Formers on the football squad and he became friendly with them. He played on the second team for a while and then one of the varsity guards came up with a bad knee and suddenly there he was on the varsity, playing shoulder to shoulder with Creighton and Arnold. Of course he wasn't very good. He had started the season with a big advantage, because he had been getting his muscles in shape for football all summer. As the season moved along, the other guys got in shape and he didn't have that edge on them any more. But with Creighton and Arnold sort of keeping an eye on him in the games he didn't make any awful mistakes and nobody opened up any big holes through them. So he even got his letter that first season.

The next fall he was a Sixth Former and his weight was up in the hundred and sixties. Early in pre-season practice the coach took him aside.

"Tony," he said, "I'm going to have to count on you a lot this year. You're the only regular I have left, from tackle to tackle. Now I want to give you a choice. I can either let you play in the line on both offense and defense, or pull you out on defense to back up the line. What would you rather do?"

"Well," Anthony said, "I don't know that it matters. I'll play either way you want."

The coach scrubbed a big hand over his face, and seemed to be arguing something out inside himself. Finally he said, in a resigned tone, "All right, I'll come clean with you, Tony. I need you in the line, offense and defense. We're awful light and inexperienced through the middle. If you're in there on defense, they won't come pouring through. But I got to warn you, you won't look too sharp in there. That's because you'll be carrying part of the load for the other guard and for the tackle next to you. You'll just be a guy at the bottom of a lot of piles, only the piles won't be more than a yard or two gain on us most times."

"I've been under pile-ups before, coach."

"Yeah. Now let's look at the other side of it. If I give you the linebacking job, everybody will see you on every defensive play. You're a good tackler. And the way they'll gallop through our line you'll get lots of chances to make tackles. I wouldn't doubt you'll intercept some passes and grab off some fumbles. You'll look good. I wouldn't be surprised if it got you elected captain for next season."

Anthony blinked a few times. "I'll look good but the rest of the team won't, huh? Is that what you mean?"

"That's about the size of it."

He had never thought about being captain so it really wasn't hard to give up the idea. "Gee, coach," he said, grinning, "I wouldn't know what to do up in the daylight. I'll go back to the bottom of the pile."

"You'll see lots of them this year," the coach said grimly. "All right, Tony, thanks."

The coach hadn't been kidding about those pile-ups. It was a rugged season, without guys like Creighton and Arnold in the line. Sometimes the games turned into a blur, and all he could remember was throwing himself at waves of interference and feeling dull shocks on his body and going down under squirming heavy masses and dragging himself up slowly and repeating it all over again. They had a five and three season, tying for second in the Interac League, and after it was over the team elected Bill Klepner from Anthony's class as captain for the next year. Bill was a halfback and a nice guy. Only for a moment did Anthony think about the choice the coach had given him at the beginning of practice, and wonder if he had been a dope.

It was a lot different season in his Sixth Upper year. The Academy had almost the whole line back, and they were all bigger and stronger. They didn't have a very good attack, so it was mostly a matter of getting a touchdown on breaks and then digging in. They dropped the opener to Frankford High, took Central and Perkiomen and West Philly and then crunched slowly through the Interac League by one- and two-touchdown margins and came up to the final game with Penn Charter needing only that win for the title.

It was one of those games where nobody could get a drive going and you waited for a break and nobody got any, and it was nothing to nothing in the last quarter. The Penn Charter line was tough, and all through the game they had two guys blocking him out whenever Penn Charter kicked. He wanted to get through on one of those kicks because that might be the break they needed. But the Penn Charter line knew that too. At the beginning of the second half he began following a set pattern on his charge whenever Penn Charter had to punt. He lined up opposite the Penn Charter guard and tackle, and charged the tackle each time. Twice he almost got through, and the Penn Charter back guarding the alley to the kicker edged out a little farther each time to make sure he would be in the right spot to block him.

Then it was the final quarter, and Penn Charter was ready to punt from its own forty. He lined up again in front of the guard and tackle, watching the ball from the corner of his eyes. The center snapped it. This time he went in low between the guard and tackle, the way he had done once with Creighton and Arnold, and came up hard and split them and churned on through. The back was a step too far to the left, and Anthony streaked down the alley and saw the kicker's foot swing up and flung himself into the air and felt the solid chunk of the ball bouncing off his chest.

There it went, back down the field, tumbling crazily. He sprinted after it, mouth open, arms pumping. In three years he had never had his hands on a really loose ball, only a few fumbles in pile-ups. He had never had a chance to score. He was going to now, though. Bouncing wildly ahead of him was his personal football. It was—

Not quite his, yet. The back who had missed the block on him was roaring up from one side. Farther over was Billy Edwards, the Franklin left end, a fast kid coming in like a streak. Anthony would get to the ball maybe a step ahead of the other two. And then what? Pick it up and be tackled by the Penn Charter back? Fumble it? Boot it around? Yeah, everybody would say, they had a chance to win the game but a dumb guard got there first and didn't know what to do with the ball.

He had all those thoughts in a flash and then swerved and threw the hardest block of his life at the Penn Charter back. They went down and rolled over and over. As he came out of the roll he saw that was it. There was Billy scooping up the ball without breaking stride and whizzing to the goal line, and that would be the game and he was where he belonged, flat on the ground.

They kicked the point and came trotting back up the field and suddenly he realized that somebody was yelling his name. Not just one person, either. The Franklin stands were giving him a locomotive, and they hadn't given a locomotive to anybody but the team itself for years and years. He couldn't help glancing over. There was Doctor McClintic, yelling. There was his grandfather yelling. And there, of all people, with his mouth open in the final scream of LAWRENCE-LAWRENCE-LAWRENCE was Eddie Eakins. Anthony grinned. He guessed it had been worth it.

5

MOSTLY YOU KNEW where you stood with nearly all the masters who taught at Franklin Academy. First there were the ones who had been at the school twenty-five or thirty or forty years. The battering of a generation or more of boys had taken a lot out of them. They ran their classes quietly and it was not really good form to try any wild tricks on them. They did not mourn when a fair student failed their courses or rejoice loudly when a poor student improved enough to pass. Now and then a boy who was brilliant in such a man's course came along, and the master would hover over him the way an old prospector might guard a claim where he had finally struck it rich. Aside from that, nothing excited these veteran masters except winning Interac football games and greeting old grads at reunions.

Then there were the masters who had taught more than five years but less than twenty. They had great energy. They prided themselves on knowing all the tricks a boy could pull, and so of course it was a point of honor with many boys to try to invent a new trick. It was an insult to them if you failed to pass their courses. If you worked hard to pass, they felt very good about it.

Finally there were the new masters, who hadn't yet been patted and hammered into the Academy mold. Some of them went at teaching like an angry man trying to chop down a very knotty tree. Some went at it like mothers worrying over the health of their sons. A few looked on teaching with big shining eyes which, under the circumstances, sometimes filled with tears.

Mr. Glenmor was a new master who did not resemble any of the recognized types. He never got upset or flustered. He didn't seem to care whether you passed or flunked his courses in English. He managed to keep his classes off balance, and even the wildest boys found themselves watching for tricks that Mr. Glenmor might pull, instead of planning tricks of their own. You didn't get the feeling that he was trying to teach you English. Mr. Glenmor put on a star performance at the front of the room, and you were an audience rather than a class. A number of the older students, including

Anthony, began to copy the way he drawled, and started to use the knowing Glenmor smile that only touched one side of your face.

Early one May afternoon, Anthony sat in one of the worn leather chairs in the Masters' Room watching Mr. Glenmor read the Salutatory which Anthony had written and was to give at graduation. Mr. Glenmor had been assigned to coach him in the delivery of it. As Mr. Glenmor read the Salutatory, a knowing smile crept up the right side of his face. Sometimes that smile made you feel that you and he were engaged in a gay conspiracy. Sometimes it made you feel that you were being childish.

Today the smile worried Anthony. "Doesn't it sound all right, sir?" he asked.

"It sounds," Mr. Glenmor said, "exactly the way Franklin Academy would want it to sound."

"Then it's all right, sir?"

"Ah," Mr. Glenmor said, with no expression at all in his voice.

That was the sort of disturbing thing he did all the time. Mr. Glenmor had already said the Salutatory sounded exactly the way the school would want it to sound, so you would think it must be all right. If it wasn't all right why … why then the school couldn't be completely all right. Was that what Mr. Glenmor was hinting? Was it possible that the school could be wrong about anything, or even a lot of things? It was a very disturbing thought, and one that he had never had before. Mr. Glenmor was a great one to give you new thoughts.

"I don't think you like it," Anthony muttered.

"I suppose you've memorized it," Mr. Glenmor said. "Let's hear you give it, or perhaps we should say declaim it."

Anthony got up from the chair. Even under the best of circumstances he would have felt uncomfortable, up here in the Masters' Room. There was the faint aroma of tobacco, forbidden elsewhere in the school except in Doctor McClintic's office. There was the feeling that you had invaded a sacred place, where men gathered to forget there were such things as boys. All that would have been bad enough, but it was worse to see Mr. Glenmor studying him as if he were a bug on a pin in Science Lab. He cleared his throat and began.

"Centuries ago, in the age of chivalry," he said, "a young squire about to receive the honor of knighthood would await that event with mingled feelings of joy and awe."

When he had written that first line of the Salutatory, it had throbbed in his head like the sound of drums and trumpets. Now, for some reason, it seemed to squeak.

"It was a momentous occasion," he went on. "It was the culmination of effort, of self-discipline, of self-denying service. With some such feelings we have awaited the coming of graduation day; for to us this ... uh ... for to us ... how does it go from there, sir?"

Mr. Glenmor slouched deeper in his chair and gazed at the ceiling. Without a glance at the paper, he spoke the next few lines. "For to us this occasion is momentous," Mr. Glenmor chanted. "It, too, marks a culmination of effort. And as the mind of the young squire was filled with great projects of achievement, his imagination fired with the desire for knightly deeds; so, too, are the minds of us aglow with high resolve and happy anticipation." He paused, looked at Anthony and gave him that side-of-the-face grin.

It was like Mr. Glenmor to pull a trick like that: to read a paper a minute and then recite the whole thing from memory. His voice had really been something when he recited it, too. It had sounded like the Philadelphia Orchestra playing quietly. And yet ... and yet there had been an odd twist in some of the musical tones of his voice, as if a flute had gone scampering off by itself, sticking out its tongue at the rest of the orchestra.

"Should I go on with it?" Anthony asked.

"Oh, please do."

"Um ... um ... oh yes. I got it now. The last mile of our trail here is finished. Now, we come to the parting of the ways, where the Class of 1932 pauses for a few brief hours before it is swept away and scattered by the winds of destiny. This parting, this breaking of ties, fills us with sadness for all that we leave behind. Yet—joy prevails, joy inspires the occasion, and it is in this spirit that we rejoice in your presence. Ladies and gentlemen, we bid you—welcome."

"Yes," Mr. Glenmor murmured, "I can see you doing it quite well. With full round tones for such words as joy and rejoice. And perhaps—oh, definitely yes—an outflung right arm when you say welcome."

An ugly prickling crawled over Anthony's skin. Mr. Glenmor had been making fun of him all along. "It's awful, isn't it?" he said miserably.

"It depends on the viewpoint, Tony. It's exactly what the school expects of you. It's safe, sound and doesn't mean a thing. Do you know anything about knighthood?"

"Well, uh, it grew up in the age of chivalry. You had to pass a lot of tests and promise to defend the weak against the strong and—"

"Medieval History, Sixth Form course in," Mr. Glenmor said, yawning.

"Well, gee, sir, what was it?"

"Like all other institutions for training the young, it was a system for preventing the young from doing any independent thinking. Any time young men think independently, there is grave danger that they may realize they are stronger than old men. That thought might lead to the blinding truth that all they have to do is throw the old men out and take over, much as a young bull will fight an old bull and beat him and take over his herd. So old men develop institutions that will coax young men to play up, play up, and play the game. In other words, kindly wait until I die, young man, before you take over. And please don't hurry the process by bashing me over the head."

"Gee, I see what you mean," Anthony said eagerly. "In promising to defend the weak against the strong, the young knight was really promising to protect the weak old men who ran the place against themselves, the young knights, that is."

"Anthony, I have hope for you."

A happy glow toasted his body. "Do you really, Mr. Glenmor? I guess I never did much thinking before."

"You have a good brain. It just hasn't been used. Now let's take that phrase about self-denying service. How many of your classmates have done any?"

"Gosh, when you put it that way, it's hard to say."

"And as the mind of the young squire was filled with great projects of achievement ... would you like to run through the list of your class checking that point? I'll pick a couple at random. McKane Edwards. What's his great project of achievement?"

"Girls, I guess. That's all he ever talks about."

"Connell?"

"He wants to be a doctor like his father. He says there's real money in it if you get the right kind of practice. He says ear-nose-and-throat is the thing in Philadelphia."

"Hetherington?"

"Let's see. He isn't going to college. His father has a big plumbing supply business and he's going in it. I see what you mean about great projects of achievement. I guess mine isn't very good, either. I'm hoping for a scholarship to Princeton."

"And then what are you planning to do?"

Anthony hesitated. He knew very well what was expected of him. He could close his eyes right now and see his great-grandmother lying in bed, thin and transparent, and hear her saying, "I hope you know what you have to do, Anthony. You're the boy we've been waiting for, the three of us ..." It was hard to put into words what was expected of him, but he knew, all right. Not even for Mr. Glenmor was he going to talk about that. "I'm not sure," he said.

"Well, I won't pry. You have a lot of drive and intelligence. You might come closer to having a great project of achievement than any of the rest. All I'm interested in doing is making you think a little. Now, just for fun, let's see what kind of a Salutatory you would write, if you gave it some real honest thought. Shall we?"

This time Mr. Glenmor's smile was the kind that made you feel you and he were engaged in a gay conspiracy. "Yes sir!" he said happily, and sat down to work it out with Mr. Glenmor.

They talked and wrote until the final school bell rang, and other masters began drifting into the room. Mr. Glenmor winked at Anthony, and said maybe it would be fun to work out the ideas a little more in their next session.

Each time when they met after that to rehearse the real Salutatory, they spent some time on the one they were doing as a joke. It was wonderful having a secret like that with Mr. Glenmor. It was an education doing the new speech, too. It opened his eyes to a lot of things he had never seen before. Finally Mr. Glenmor suggested that it might be fun to hear Anthony give the secret Salutatory when nobody was around, so Anthony memorized it.

The next meeting, which happened to be the final one before graduation, he stood up before Mr. Glenmor in the Masters' Room and recited the private speech.

"Ladies and gentlemen," he said. "As all of us know, the young male of the human species begins life as a small screaming savage, intent on getting his own way. If this young savage were permitted to grow up unchecked and untrained, life for the rest of the human race would be uncomfortable and in fact downright dangerous. All human societies have, therefore, developed ways of taming this savage before he becomes too big and strong to be handled. The various methods of taming, known in some countries as education, are always designed to fit the young man into the existing order of things without disturbing that order. The objective is to produce a young man who will come into adult society without thinking of knocking over either his elders or their beliefs. If this often produces young men who go through life without thinking at all, that is regrettable but cannot be helped.

"You see before you, on this platform, the Class of 1932, about to graduate from Franklin Academy. For some years, now, the school has been working to make us fit to enter your society. It has, we hope, done this job with its usual success. We have been trained to do the right thing, or at least to have the decency to know it if we do the wrong thing. We will produce our share of lawyers and doctors and engineers and businessmen, and will not embarrass you by turning out to be poets or rebels.

"We have learned a great many things here, all of them right and proper. We have studied the workings of the Electoral College and have not studied the workings of the human spirit. We know the important names of the Revolutionary War, like Patrick Henry of 'Give me liberty or give me death' fame, and have ignored the unimportant people of the Revolution like Tom Paine. We can recite 'The Charge of the Light Brigade' and have been spared learning any lines from someone named Karl Marx.

"We know that Philadelphia is not generally recognized as the center of the universe, but we also know that this is only because of the narrow-mindedness of people who live elsewhere. We are aware of the fact that there are other parts of the United States, notably the seashore and Princeton to the eastward, the Poconos and Maine to the north—with Yale and Harvard up there someplace—Florida to the south, and a vast area called the Midwest which begins not far beyond the limits of our own Main Line.

"We realize, of course, that our education has not been completed. College lies ahead for nearly all of us. It is possible to bump into new and upsetting ideas in college, but we have been so well grounded here that we are not likely to lose our balance.

"You can count on us to respond automatically to certain stimuli: becoming patriotic about things like the Flag, Our Country, and Beating Penn Charter; reacting with due gravity to words like duty, honor and property rights; bristling at things which can be labelled radical, traitorous or bad form.

"We have adopted as our creed the words: 'What will people think?', and by that we mean what will you, our parents and friends, think. We hope that you will always think as highly of us as perhaps you do tonight. Ladies and gentlemen ... welcome." When he finished, there was a hush in the room, and he was afraid to look at Mr. Glenmor for fear it hadn't sounded very good.

"Wonderful," Mr. Glenmor said softly. "Wonderful." His eyes were glowing. If Mr. Glenmor had been a young knight, and if there had been anything to knighthood, you would have said he was seeing visions of a Quest.

"Gee," Anthony said, "you mean it's not bad?"

"It's probably the finest and most honest thing of its kind ever written. Tony, I'm proud of you."

Hearing Mr. Glenmor say that was like getting your varsity letter for the first time, except that varsity letters were all part of the scheme for taming the young male savage. Anyway it made him feel great.

"And the best thing about it," Mr. Glenmor said, "is that you worked out those ideas for yourself. You did some thinking for the first time in your life."

"Golly, thanks, Mr. Glenmor. Did I really do much of it? I know we talked things over and—"

"I merely gave you a few hints. I just unlocked a few doors in your mind."

"I didn't forget any of it or trip even once, did I, sir?"

"You gave it beautifully. Well, graduation is tomorrow night. So I guess we can't play with it any more. But we had fun, didn't we?"

"I had a great time fooling around with it, Mr. Glenmor."

Mr. Glenmor slouched way down on the back of his neck, and put the tips of his fingers together, and peered through them at Anthony. For a moment he looked rather like a wise monkey peering through the bars of a cage. "Well," he said casually, "which one are you going to give tomorrow night?"

Anthony stared at him. "Gee," he said uneasily, "you must be kidding, Mr. Glenmor."

"Am I?"

"We ... we did this as a joke."

"Perhaps we did. Truth is often treated as a joke."

"I know, but gee, Mr. Glenmor, what—"

"What would people think," Mr. Glenmor cut in, grinning up one side of his face. "How does that line go? 'We have adopted as our creed the words: what will people think?' Well, Tony, I'll tell you. It would be over the heads of at least half of your audience. Some of the others would be oddly disturbed, without exactly knowing why. Some would be angry. A few might start to think clearly and honestly, just as you did. You would be doing a tremendous favor to those few, because nobody else might ever give them another chance to think."

"That ... that makes it sound like a pretty serious thing."

"It is a serious thing, Tony. The choice between giving or withholding knowledge is the most important choice a man ever faces."

It was almost like being in church to hear Mr. Glenmor talk to him as solemnly as that. "I guess I backed into something pretty big without really knowing it, sir."

"Perhaps you did, Tony." Mr. Glenmor got up, and put a hand on his shoulder. "I'm not going to try to influence your decision," he said, with a rare both-sides-of-the face smile. "You know both speeches equally well. You can give either one. It's a very simple choice, between honesty and hypocrisy. I'll be in the audience, waiting to hear what your decision has been. Good luck, Tony." He walked out of the room.

After a few moments, Anthony slowly followed. Every once in a while, when things seemed to be going smoothly, life caught up to you and gave you a jagged decision to make. It had been wonderful playing a mental game with Mr. Glenmor, and gradually winning his respect. Once you had won the respect of Mr. Glenmor you wanted to fight to keep it. What would Mr. Glenmor think if he gave the old hypocritical Salutatory about squires and knights and that junk? Mr. Glenmor would never say anything, of course, but he would sit there in the audience with a smile sliding up one side of his face and he, Anthony, would carry a burden of shame all through his life.

As Mr. Glenmor had said, it was a simple choice. He would of course give the new, honest Salutatory ...

The next night was graduation. Anthony paraded into the gym with his classmates, marching solemnly and a little out of step to the music of Elgar's "Land of Hope and Glory," played by the Academy orchestra. They climbed the steps to the platform and fanned out into the rows of chairs and faced the hundreds of proud upturned faces below them. The Elgar music ended and they had the invocation and then began singing a hymn.

Anthony mouthed the words of the hymn but no sound came from his dry throat. After the hymn it would be his turn to give the Salutatory. To his left, down the row of figures in blue serge coats and white flannel trousers, was McKane Edwards. Mac would be awfully puzzled by the Salutatory. "What's Tony jabbering about?" Mac would wonder. Down the row to his right was Eddie Eakins, looking so smooth and confident you wouldn't guess he had just squeaked through for a diploma. What Eddie thought or didn't think had not meant much to Anthony for a long time, but Eddie would probably poke the classmate next to him and whisper, "The guy's nuts."

In the audience he saw his mother's shining face. She was trying, in the embarrassing way that all mothers had, to catch his glance and exchange proud smiles with him. Next to her was his grand-mother, blinking as if she had trouble trying to see very far. The new Salutatory was probably going to bother them a lot, because they had worked awfully hard to help him get through school and here he was making fun of the Academy. Down in the first row of the audience, with others of the faculty, was his grandfather. Masters always knew about their nicknames, and his grandfather must have known all along that the boys called him Old Nearums. If you believed the rumor that his grandfather got the nickname when he just missed becoming headmaster, it must have been given to him in ridicule. But he had carried it patiently all these years, and now it had become in the minds of everybody a sort of badge of honor. The Academy meant everything to Old Nearums. He would be hurt by the new Salutatory.

Down there was his football coach, too. He could picture the coach listening to him, and frowning, and wondering what had happened to him. "There he was," the coach might say later, "one of the best guards we've had lately, standing up there poking fun at the idea of beating Penn Charter. I don't get it."

Down there, finally, was Mr. Glenmor, catching his glance and giving him a wink. That seemed to say, as clear as anything, "It's the two of us against the world, Tony." Of course it was, too. Not many people believed in speaking or hearing the truth. Everybody else might be upset by what he said tonight, but at least Mr. Glenmor would be proud of him.

The "Amen" of the hymn died away, and there was a clatter as people sat on the folding chairs. It was time for the Salutatory, and silence crept across the big room like a tiger stalking him. He walked on wobbly legs to the center of the platform, muttering the opening phrases of the speech under his breath: "Ladies and gentlemen, as all of us know, the young male of the human species begins life as ..."

He stopped in shocked surprise. Why, those weren't his words at all. They were Mr. Glenmor's words. So were all the other words and ideas in the new Salutatory. Mr. Glenmor had pretended that he, Anthony, had done it but that wasn't true. The whole thing was Mr. Glenmor's Salutatory, not Anthony's. He didn't know whether the ideas in the new Salutatory were the truth or not. But if they were, they were Mr. Glenmor's truth—not Anthony's, not his family's, not the school's.

He squared his shoulders and looked out over the audience and said, "Ladies and gentlemen: Centuries ago, in the days of chivalry, a young squire about to receive the honor of knighthood would await that event with mingled feelings of joy and awe."

He paused for a breath. That had the sound of drums and trumpets in it, just as it did when he first wrote it. He went on, confidently. Toward the end he allowed himself a glance at Mr. Glenmor. There was no smile of any kind on Mr. Glenmor's face, and somehow Anthony got the idea that Mr. Glenmor was hoping he would forget the next line and go uh ... uh ... uh ... in front of everybody. But he wasn't going to do that. He found he didn't like Mr. Glenmor now, and to point that out he put full round tones into the words "joy" and "rejoice" as he gave the final lines: "Yet—joy prevails, joy inspires the occasion, and it is in this spirit that we rejoice in your presence. Ladies and gentlemen, we bid you—welcome." As a final touch, he used an outflung right arm when he said welcome. Mr. Glenmor winced.

Anthony sat down with applause rattling pleasantly around his ears.

After the ceremonies were over, Doctor McClintic dodged away from some parents and drew Anthony aside. "Tony," he said, "I have a graduation present for you. The Princeton Club is going to nom-inate you for one of its scholarships."

Anthony tingled. That was like getting your armor and being knighted. "Gee," he said, "that's wonderful, sir. I can't thank you enough."

"You deserve it, Tony. Of course the scholarship can't actually be awarded until the results of your College Boards come in, around mid-summer, and until Princeton accepts you. But I have no worries about any of that. You're as good as in. By the way, I'll let you have the pleasure of telling your family. Oh, and before I forget it, nice work on your Salutatory. A good sound piece of writing and delivery."

There was a small rust spot on his armor. "About the Salutatory," Anthony said hesitantly, "there's something I think I should tell you, except there's somebody else involved."

"Ah yes," Doctor McClintic said, smiling. "Mr. Glenmor. I know the whole story."

"My gosh, sir, you do? About the second one I wrote, and all that? But there were only two of us who ever knew about it, and I didn't say a word to anybody."

"Mr. Glenmor did, though. He told me about it. He has an excel-lent memory, and he recited the whole of the Salutatory which you didn't give."

"I don't understand it," Anthony said. "Wasn't he taking a big chance telling you, sir? I mean, about his job here?"

Doctor McClintic got out his pipe and began slowly packing it. "Perhaps knowing the whole story will add something to your edu-cation," he said. "To start with, Mr. Glenmor is not returning next year. That was decided before any of the Salutatory business began. He doesn't fit into the school. I made a mistake hiring him, as I sometimes do. So he wasn't risking a thing by coaxing you to work on that second Salutatory."

"You mean he was trying to get back at the school? But why would he tell you, sir? You could have called me in and laid down the law to me, or given the Salutatory to somebody else."

"It wasn't as simple as that, Tony. In some ways, Mr. Glenmor has a rather subtle mind. He presented the thing to me as a challenge. Two challenges, in fact. First, did I dare let you make the decision for yourself. Second, what would your decision be. In other words, did I dare rely on the training the school had given you, or didn't I? It was a challenge to test his way of teaching against ours. Mr. Glenmor had two chances to win. He would win if I refused to let you make the decision, and he would win if you gave his Salutatory. He's an interesting person, Tony. Not our kind of person, but still interesting. What did you think of him?"

"I guess he's sort of a rebel, sir."

"Yes, but not of the usual type. You'd never find him leading a mob against a barricade. He'd be peering out from a doorway, thinking what idiots they were on both sides of the barricade. The man might be dangerous if he really believed in anything, but he doesn't. It's like a devil who doesn't want the bother of running a hell."

"I guess it's taught me not to trust people too far unless I know them pretty well, sir. Why ... why if I had given that Salutatory of Mr. Glenmor's, I bet you would have called off my scholarship to Princeton. Wouldn't you, sir?"

Doctor McClintic laughed. "The thought didn't enter my head, Tony. I'll tell you a secret. Mr. Glenmor never had a chance of winning that little contest we had. Now run along and tell your family about the scholarship." He patted Anthony on the shoulder, and moved off to greet more parents.

Anthony watched him for a moment, wondering whether it was true that Mr. Glenmor never had a chance of winning. In his conscious mind Anthony had not made the decision until the last possible moment. But had it actually been made much earlier? Had there, in fact, never been a decision to make? He did not have the answers to those questions.

6

IN MANY WAYS, Anthony's four years at Princeton were like being buried under one long pile-up in football.

At Franklin Academy it had only taken a little extra work to become one of the top students in the class. But at Princeton a little extra work didn't mean much. In each class there were usually twenty or thirty guys with genius ratings, and they went at studies the way football players went after a fumbled ball. Guys like that, Anthony found, were so far ahead of him that he didn't even rate carrying their schoolbooks. It was all he could do to get Second Group marks and hang onto his scholarship.

Football was worse. In an ordinary year he would have been a good 170-pound guard trying to beat out good 200-pound guards for a varsity job. At best he might have made second string. But he entered Princeton at a bad time for good 170-pound guards. For once in its history, Princeton had closed its eyes while the alumni did a little quiet recruiting. Anthony's Class of 1936 was three or four deep in every position with prep school captains and All-State players. His class went through its four years in college with the loss of only one game, and Princeton rated tops in the nation in his sophomore and senior years. He was lucky to make the scrubs. He didn't even get one of those courtesy letters in his senior year, by going in for a couple of plays against Yale, because by then he had a trick knee and was out for good.

Of course there were other ways than studies or football to make your mark at Princeton. If you came from a top family socially, and had gone to one of the gilt-edged prep schools like Groton or St. Marks or St. Pauls (or even the blue-chip ones like Lawrenceville and Hill and Andover and Exeter), and if in addition you were presentable and modest about your advantages, you automatically became a marked man on campus. During Bicker Week in spring of sophomore year, when the upperclass eating clubs picked their new sections, you might well hope for a bid from Ivy or Cottage.

Or you could take the Freshman Herald and memorize the nicknames of the seven hundred men in your class, and flash a winning smile as you used each nickname, and you might be elected to class offices and get a bid to Cap and Gown.

Finally you could throw all your energies into working on The Daily Princetonian or in the Triangle Club, or into going out for manager of a major sport, and if you clicked you were up there with the sports heroes and the smoothies and the politicians.

Anthony didn't have the family background, or the smile and memory of nicknames, or the extra time and energy to win a rating in any of those ways. His scholarship only covered tuition. He had to earn the rest by waiting on tables in Commons and doing other jobs around the campus. Making a few dollars in those depression years was like trying to run down rabbits. He didn't have any energy left over, after earning money and studying and playing scrub football, to try to be a big man on the campus. There were others like him in college: anonymous, hurrying figures about whom people sometimes asked, "Now who the hell is he?"

Along with two-thirds of his class he made one of the upperclass eating clubs in spring of his sophomore year. It wasn't one of the top clubs, and he didn't get an original bid to it, just a secondary. But even that was sheer luck. Each club had the right to take in one man who would get meals and membership free in return for helping to manage the club. These club "scholarships" were generally used as bait for desirable men who might otherwise go into higher-ranked clubs. On Bicker Monday of Anthony's sophomore year, one club found it had lost both its first and second choice scholarship men to other clubs. No third choice had been made. Monday of Bicker Week was very late to look for a new scholarship man. In desperation, a club committee visited the head of the Student Employment Bureau and asked sadly if there was an unbid sophomore who was presentable, intelligent, hard-working, a good mixer and in fact an all-around nice guy, to whom they could offer a scholarship. The head of the Bureau brought out the records and photos of half a dozen men. The committee was not impressed by any of them, certainly not by a sophomore named Anthony Lawrence who had gone to one of those small Philadelphia prep schools and had done nothing on campus.

"Isn't there anything outstanding about any of these guys?" the head of the committee asked.

The head of the Bureau thought for a moment, and chuckled. "You might not believe it," he said, "but this man Lawrence has some kind of a drag with whoever runs the big deb parties in Philadelphia. He told me once he could get a dozen guys invited to most of the coming-out parties, but he doesn't have time to round up the right kind of guys. Does that sound outstanding to you?"

"You kidding?" the head of the committee said.

Fifteen minutes later Anthony made a club.

The committee had to take the debutante angle on faith, but it turned out very well indeed. The Friday Afternoon Dancing Class had not survived the depression, but by the time it faded, Mrs. Hoyt Phelps was already becoming established as a social counselor. She had taken Anthony's mother into that line of work as her assistant, because she liked her and because she could trust Mrs. Lawrence not to walk away with part of the business and start her own counseling service. Mrs. Hoyt Phelps did need stags for dances: presentable ones from good colleges, and lots of them. Depression or no depression, people were still giving big coming-out parties ("Look at all the work it creates for needy people, my dear") and more and more the success of such parties depended on the size of the stag line. Every deb hoped for a party at which there would be at least two men for every girl. If you weren't too free with the champagne, a two-to-one ratio guaranteed a fair number of extra men around the dance floor. Mrs. Hoyt Phelps was glad to have Anthony produce some of them.

So the club was very pleased with Anthony. In fact its rating on Prospect Street went up a notch after he began taking members of his club to dances in Philadelphia.

Anthony knew he had been lucky. Getting a scholarship to a club let him give up working as a waiter in Commons and other odd jobs. And, when he became undergraduate manager in his senior year and had a junior as his assistant, he had some time he could call his own. The free time was important, because it was in December of his senior year that he became interested in Joan Dickinson.

It all started when he cut in on her at a dance somebody was giving at the Merion Cricket Club. She switched on a brilliant smile and gave half of it to the man she was leaving. "Goodby, Princeton," she said. Then she swung into Anthony's arms and gave him the other half of the smile and said, "Hello, Princeton."

He happened to know that the guy she had just left was named Allison and went to Penn, and the loose way she used the name of Princeton offended him. "I'm sorry," he said, "but I'm from Kansas Aggies."

"Oh dear," she said. "I can't ever remember names and colleges, so I just call everybody Princeton and usually that pleases everybody except Yale men. How wonderful to meet someone who goes to Kansas Aggies! What do you take there?"

"Animal husbandry," he said. "I'm majoring in Hoof and Mouth Disease, with a minor in Stoppages of the Udder."

"That's marvelous!" she cried, looking up at him from wide brown eyes. "So many boys just go to college to use up some time. It's wonderful to know somebody who is practical and knows what he wants to do in life. Do you have a football team at Kansas Aggies? I bet it's a good one."

"No, ma'am. We got a mighty nice milking team, though. It's—"

"You're going to have to tell me all about it," she crooned. "Tell me how you happened to go there, and what the boys are like and every thing!"

He started inventing a wildly improbable campus and student body, and got a grim pleasure out of the way she took it all in. It was a crime the way they let these girls give all their attention to their bodies and none to their brains. This girl probably spent more time on her fingernails than she spent on books. She was a pretty kid, with a shining brown page-boy bob and a slender body that swayed with the changing pressure of his arm. But under the page-boy bob she was a refugee from the Jukes family.

He didn't have time to get very far with his imaginary campus, because after a minute someone cut in. She gave Anthony the first half of the brilliant smile, and said, "Thank you, Mr. Lawrence," and turned the other half of the smile on the newcomer. Anthony was almost back to the stag line before he remembered that he hadn't told her his name. He scowled in her direction. At that moment another guy was cutting in on her, so Anthony waited a few moments and then cut back in.

"Oh, goody," she said. "I bet you came back to invite me to the Senior Corn-Husking Bee."

"You've been taking me for a ride," he said.

"Why, Mr. Lawrence, you were the one taking me for a ride. A hayride, I would call it."

"How do you know my name? I didn't tell you."

"Oh dear. It's a long story, and somebody will cut in before I really get started, and you wouldn't want to take me outside on the porch because that would hurt your sense of duty. You feel that when you go to a dance you should show your appreciation to the hostess by staying on the dance floor. Right?"

This girl could tie you in knots. "Yes," he said, "that's right. But how do you know?"

"I go to Miss Moriarty's School for Delinquent Girls, and major in Mind-Reading and Man-Snatching."

"How about coming out on the porch and talking?"

"Just a moment while I read your mind," she said. She stared at him, then nodded "Okay," she said. "Your intentions are strictly conversational. Let's go."

They went out to the big enclosed porch of the Cricket Club. She asked for a cigarette. When she bent forward to get a light from him, the top of her evening gown leaned forward more than she did. She had quite a body: sleek polished shoulders, firm breasts. She peeked up at his face and saw where he was looking and laughed at him.

"Sorry," he said, getting a bit red. "Don't practice the mind-reading for a moment."

"You don't have to apologize for being a man," she said. "After all, I can wear long woollen underwear if I hate that sort of thing."

"Now what's this business about you knowing my name and all that?"

"Why, I remember everybody's name, and what they like and don't like."

"Nuts. You meet five hundred guys a month, and most of them hand you the same fast line that every popular deb gets, and you call them all Princeton because you haven't the faintest idea who the hell they are."

"And then," she sighed, "along comes Mr. Anthony Lawrence who does go to Princeton, and I have defamed Old Nassau."

"Maybe I stepped on your toes at some dance or other, and so you went to a little trouble to learn who that lout was."

"You see? You're the one who meets so many girls he can't keep them straight. You've forgotten our moment of passion, Mr. Lawrence. Correction. My moment of passion. You practically snored in my face."

He wanted to grab her and shake a permanent wave into that page-boy bob. "Look," he growled. "You're Joan Dickinson. You came out last June and I was in the mob scene. I've seen you at maybe twenty dances since then and cut in on you at each of them and danced a few steps with you before someone else took over. I bet we've had a minute and twenty-seven seconds altogether with each other. Now what gives with this moment of passion line?"

She curled one shoulder forward and looked at him across it. How To Be Provocative, Lesson Five. "About the seventh time you cut in," she said, "you began to look slightly familiar to me. By the tenth time, I noticed that you never seemed to drink too much. Around the twelfth time I realized that you didn't hand me the usual heavy line—you know, the one designed to break a girl into small quivering pieces in ten seconds flat. I was slightly insulted. So I dug up who you were. Then one time you cut in on me after I had just developed a blister on my right big toe and wanted to go outside and let it cool off, and I asked you to take me outside, and you gave me that lofty sentiment about staying on the dance floor because it was your duty to the hostess. My goodness, you might have thought I'd offered to rape you."

He couldn't help laughing. "If your offer had been that good, I might have taken it."

"I don't believe it. Not unless the hostess gave you permission first. What is this devotion of yours to dancing?"

For some reason he began telling her about the time at the Friday Afternoon Dancing Class when he played traitor to Eddie Eakins and the club. He didn't really mean to give her the whole long story, and he had never told it to anyone else, but Joan kept poking questions at him and listening eagerly. It was a rather amusing story, now that he could look back on it as something that happened to a kid long ago.

"So that," he said finally, "ended my career of crime."

Joan began choking, and held out a hand and said, "H-handkerchief, please."

He didn't like her to laugh quite so hard at him. He gave her a handkerchief, and said irritably, "What's so side-splitting about it?"

"Nothing," she gasped. "You've got me bawling, you big idiot."

It was amazing. She really was crying. He couldn't help putting an arm around her. She snuggled up against him for a minute, trembling and sniffling, and he patted her and said he was sorry and please stop crying.

She drew back at last and blew her nose and said, "You can't do this to me. I bet I look like something the cat dragged in. Oh, I could kill that girl!"

"What girl?"

"The one at that damn dancing class of yours who started all the trouble."

Sometimes it was hard to follow the way a girl's thoughts jumped around. "She really did me a favor," he said. "Because after that I started getting in trouble at school and—"

"Oh, shut up," she said angrily. "I can't take any more sob stories right now. You're so dumb and nice and innocent it breaks me up. I think I'd like you to kiss me."

He started to look around, to see if anybody was on the porch watching them. He didn't get much of a look. She put her arms around his neck and said, "What do I care if somebody's looking at us?" and came up on tiptoes and kissed him. It was an odd kind of kiss, soft and quivery and faintly salty from her tears, friendly in one way and sexy in another. It scrambled his emotions badly.

After she moved away, he said huskily, "I don't think you know what you're doing to me."

"No, I don't. All I know is what I'm trying to do."

"I've never really had a girl. I wish you wouldn't play around."

She laughed unsteadily. "You don't have to tell me. It's written all over you that you never really had a girl. I guess I'm trying to make it up to you. What are you doing this Christmas vacation?"

"Going stag to dances, the way I always do."

"No you're not. You're going to take me."

"Oh now look," he said. "Christmas vacation is just starting. You've had dates booked for every afternoon and evening for months. I know how a girl like you gets rushed in her season as a deb."

"I just lost my engagement book."

"I hate to tell you this, but I haven't got any money or a car or much of anything."

"Oh God," she said. "He's working his way through Princeton selling magazines. Listen. I'll take subscriptions to all of them. I've got a car. Who needs money going to dances?"

"You're tired and upset and I caught you off balance with a corny little story. Why don't you think this over?"

"If you weren't such a nice sweet thing I'd show you what swearing is, Tony Lawrence! You know what I'll do? I'll go to that precious Mrs. Hoyt Phelps of yours and tell her to drop you from the stag list. I'll—"

"Damned if I don't think you would."

"Yes, but she wouldn't do it, of course. She doesn't let any of us run her business. But Tony, I'm not going to take no for an answer."

All of a sudden he felt very light and carefree and happy. "Miss Dickinson," he said, "may I have the pleasure of escorting you during the Christmas rat race?"

She linked an arm through one of his, and said gaily, "You've just argued me into it. Now you can drop me at the ladies room for a repaint job, and wait for me, and then you and I are walking out on this party. And I do have a car here."

"What about the guy who brought you?"

"I wish you'd stop making a career of being honorable. A lot of us came together from a dinner party, and my hero has been passed out for the last hour. Now let's go before you hear any more calls of duty."

They found an all-night restaurant on the Pike where they sat eating scrambled eggs and buttered toast and drinking coffee, telling each other the story of their lives. There wasn't anything complicated about Joan's, because life can be smooth for a girl who has good health, good looks, and a family with a good deal of money. She had been graduated from Baldwin School the previous June. She didn't want to go to college. She didn't have any urge for a career. She was, she said, an out-of-date creature who merely wanted to get married quickly and have four children without delay, two boys and two girls.

"I've had the names picked out for years," she said, peeking at him from the corners of her eyes. "Arthur, Jonathan, Elaine and Betsy. But now that I've met you, I've decided you can name one of the boys and one of the girls." At the look of horror on his face she collapsed into giggles.

He realized it was all a joke, but just to be on the safe side he said casually that he would be going to Penn Law School next year, which of course meant three years more of studying and then a few more years to get properly started in the practice of law.

"Why law?" she asked.

He explained that to get anywhere in Philadelphia he would have to make money, and he didn't want to take forever making it, either. In banks, or in big corporations, you could spend twenty years getting to be assistant to the vice president in charge of the water coolers. Of course if you turned out to be a genius at management you might shoot up fast, but he didn't think he had that talent. He didn't have the specialized skills needed for engineering or architecture or advertising. He didn't have the family connections and the background of money that would push you along fast in insurance and in the investment business.

He added, "That leaves things like law. Connections are important in law, but it's still a line of work where a guy can go up fast if he knows his stuff, and gets a few breaks. If I have any talent at all, it's for law. I like digging up the facts about a problem, and thinking about the angles that affect it, and then figuring out an answer that fits all the rules and precedents."

"Oh God," Joan said. "Please don't ever treat me like a problem."

"In your case," he said seriously, "I don't think any rules and precedents would help me."

"Good. Just be emotional about me, please. You're planning to practice law in Philadelphia?"

"Yes, and that's another reason why I like law. A big corporation might send me anywhere. I want to stay in Philadelphia. I wouldn't feel at home anywhere else."

"I don't suppose you know Daddy's a lawyer. Quite a good one."

"A lawyer? Dickinson? Oh yes. Dickinson and Dawes, I bet." It wasn't one of the big legal factories downtown, but Judge Dawes was a director of The Pennsylvania Railroad and a trustee of the University of Pennsylvania, and you didn't get things like that peddling apples on street corners. He felt suddenly uncomfortable. Mr. Dickinson might figure that a would-be lawyer who chased Joan might be hoping to catch Dickinson and Dawes. "I think you just became a problem," he muttered.

"I've been reading your mind again, and please don't be stuffy. You haven't even met Daddy yet. Now you can take me home before I get to be any more of a problem."

The Dickinsons lived in one of the newer houses in Penn Valley. It had been built in the late Twenties, when people were busy collecting antiques and ancestors, and wanted houses that looked as if the owners had been landed gentry for at least a century. Nobody could pretend that English castles and French chalets and Italian villas had been around Philadelphia very long, and so architects came up with the Pennsylvania farmhouse. The Dickinson house was a low and rambling structure of fieldstone and clapboards, which almost succeeded in giving the impression that Washington had slept there.

Anthony drove Joan's car up to the entrance, wondering if a suggestion about phoning for a taxi would sound as if he were inviting himself in.

"Tea dance tomorrow," Joan said. "You might come here at two or thereabouts." She started to get out of the car.

"Wait a minute. Where do I put the car? I'll get a taxi but—"

"Take the car with you. The owner's card is in the glove compartment."

"I can't borrow your car. I—"

She leaned over and kissed him. "As long as you've got my car I know you have to come back to return it," she said calmly. "I'm not taking any chances with you." She waved and went into the house.

He sat there for a moment, frowning. He didn't like the idea of driving off with her car. It gave her a little more claim on him than he wanted her to have just yet, and of course people always lifted their eyebrows when a man began sponging on a girl. Still and all, if you had no money and wanted to play around with girls like Joan, you had to do it on their terms. They weren't likely to settle for a joy-ride in a trolley and two straws in a chocolate ice cream soda. He started the car and drove home.

His affair with Joan was one of those improbable things that should have ended in a week, with Joan switching to another man as casually as she might change her nail polish. It didn't work out that way, though. He was with her almost every day during Christmas vacation. Being an escort was very different from being a stag. You got in on the little dinners before big dances, and on opera and theatre parties, and you met people in their homes rather than merely in big ballrooms. You began to be accepted as a person instead of as part of the furnishings of a large dance. Of course his acceptance was on a very special basis. After he had been going with her for about a week, he noticed that he was not being introduced as "Mr. Lawrence" but as "This is Joan's man, Tony." It took him a while to get used to that label.

After he had been going with Joan for ten days, her family began to study him carefully. During times when he was waiting for Joan, they asked questions about his background. He knew they weren't satisfied with it, and he suspected that from time to time they told Joan she shouldn't get too serious about him and to remember that there were other men in the world. He liked her parents, though, and he thought they had a liking for him that was perhaps unwilling but still real. By spring vacation Mrs. Dickinson had unbent enough to start telling him about the antiques she was collecting, and Mr. Dickinson would sometimes complain to him about the New Deal and that man in the White House.

He saw Joan at least once every weekend while college was in session, and had her up for Junior Prom and House Parties. She became a very necessary part of his life. He had tried to prevent that; his future relationship with Joan was a problem he didn't know how to solve, and when you couldn't solve a problem it was a good idea to keep the right to ignore it. But you couldn't keep any rights like that if you wanted to go steadily with Joan. He tried to tell her once that they shouldn't get so serious, because it would be years before he could think of marrying anyone.

"Don't be so horribly practical," she said.

"Sometimes," he said, "I get the feeling that I have to be practical for both of us."

"Hmm," she said.

At the moment they were sitting in Joan's car beside Lake Carnegie in Princeton. It was a night in late spring, with the air as soft as apple blossoms. As Joan said "Hmm" she moved into his arms and kissed him, and crazy things started happening. She had always kept their petting within certain limits: he could kiss her whenever he wanted; he could put a friendly hand on her legs but not an exploring one; if he led up to it carefully and heard her breathing quicken he could slide a hand down inside her dress and touch her breasts and their erect nipples. But that night the limits were brushed aside. She not only encouraged his hands to explore her but also—and unthinkably—her hands began wandering over his body. Before he really knew what was happening, he was trying to take off her clothes and was begging her to get out of the car and lie down with him on the blanket.

Almost as if she had turned a switch, her breathing calmed and she drew back from his arms and said no and began adjusting her clothes. When he kept on begging, she patted his cheek and murmured, "Sometimes I get the feeling I have to be practical for both of us."

He never knew whether she did it to prove that he wasn't so practical after all or to punish him for being stuffy. If she did intend to punish him she was successful. After being aroused like that, and then halted, he felt almost as if he had been kneed in the groin in a football game. He never again tried to lecture her on being practical.

Probably, in his subconscious mind, he had known all along that his affair with Joan was building up to a climax, and that it would arrive long before he was ready to meet it. Since the problem was too hard to solve, he had ignored it. On the day before graduation from Princeton he found he had to solve it anyway.

He was finishing breakfast in the club on Prospect Street when Joan walked in. She looked as if she had just come out of a beauty shop which had put an extra luster in her hair and a special light in her eyes. He had invited her for graduation but that wasn't until tomorrow.

He jumped up and said, "This is a nice surprise. What brings you here?"

"I'd tell you it was somebody named Tony Lawrence," she said, "but I hate to let a man feel too sure of me."

"I couldn't feel too sure of you. I don't quite know how to say it, but there's something elemental about you, like spring coming. A guy can wait for spring but he can't feel he owns it."

"How nice! I feel I've just been elected Miss Nature of 1936. About why I came. Tomorrow your mother and grandparents will be around, and I'll feel like a pair of stockings that don't match. I decided I wanted you all to myself today. I'll take a cup of coffee if you'll give me one."

They sat down and had coffee. She took a couple of sips and studied him over the top of the cup.

"Brace yourself," she said. "I'm going to tell you how to feel sure of me."

"Yes?" he said, beginning to feel uneasy.

"A town named Elkton, Maryland, is less than a hundred miles away. Tony, we can be there by one o'clock. We can get a marriage license without waiting. By two o'clock we can be married by a justice of the peace. By five o'clock we can be back in Trenton, and I made a reservation at the Stacy-Trent for Mr. and Mrs. Anthony Lawrence. My bags are all packed in the car."

While she had talked, his body had started to produce hot and cold running shivers. "My God," he said slowly.

"You're supposed to fall at my feet babbling gratefully."

"Joan, there's nothing I'd rather do, but—"

"I can give you all the buts," she said. "What will my family say? How are you going to get through law school? How are you going to support me? Wouldn't it be safer to wait? Tony, I can answer everyone of those questions, but not a thing really matters except getting married today."

"Your family will have a fit."

"Of course they will. I'm their headstrong little daughter throwing myself away on the first man who came along. So what? They'll get used to it."

"But marrying a guy who has three years of law school ahead of him—"

"What's the difference whether you leave every morning to go to an office or go to classes?"

"But without any money—"

"Tony, I have two hundred a month from what my grandfather left me. On top of that my family would help out. Why shouldn't they? It isn't going to ruin me and it shouldn't bother you. If you want, you can look on the whole thing as a loan you'll pay back when you get on your feet, just as your scholarship to Princeton is a loan you're expected to repay when you're able."

"You make it sound too easy," he muttered. "I know there must be some flaws in it. Dammit, you've got to give me a few minutes to think."

"I don't want to give you minutes to think! I'm nineteen. You're almost twenty-two. A hundred years ago people younger than us were driving covered wagons west and having families and starting homes. What's wrong with us having our chance while we're young?"

"Only one thing. That's no covered wagon you have parked outside. It's a 1936 Cadillac sports convertible."

"All right. Let's get back to 1936. Who's going to be your preceptor in law school?"

He was a bit startled that she knew about preceptors. To enter law school, you had to get a member of the Philadelphia Bar to sponsor you. Your sponsor agreed to give you advice while you were in law school and to give you a job for at least a year or so after you finished. "I don't have a preceptor yet," he said. "I planned to talk it over with the headmaster of my prep school and see if he had any suggestions. I'll get one, but it will take a little time. The trouble is, I don't have any connections."

"Tony, within a week after we're married my father will offer to be your preceptor."

"I wouldn't be too sure of that. If he gets mad, you won't push him around."

"No girl with any sense tries to push men around, not even her father. It just takes a little coaxing. And Tony, don't you see what it means? There's your career. Judge Dawes has a son but Daddy doesn't. He'll end up as proud of you as if you were his son. He—"

Someone tapped Anthony on the shoulder, and the colored doorman said, "Beg pardon, Mistuh Lawrence. Gentleman to see you."

Anthony looked up. A middle-aged man was standing in the hallway outside the dining room, sunlight glinting on his steel-gray hair and sharp profile. A pulse started thumping in Anthony's stomach. "Maybe you'd better practice up on that coaxing," he muttered. "There's your father."

Joan took out her compact and studied her face: the traditional move of a woman preparing for a crisis. "Don't get upset," she said. "I suppose he found out some way what I planned to do, but that needn't stop us if you'll keep your head. Just remember one thing. He's a lawyer and he's going to try to win a case. And if he wins, we lose."

They went into the hallway and Joan kissed her father calmly and Anthony shook hands.

Joan said, "I guess we don't have to ask, do we, Daddy? How did I give it away?"

He smiled and patted her shoulder. "The bureau drawers in your room, honey. They looked as if a hurricane had rummaged through them. We're all familiar with the way you throw things this way and that when you're packing. And you hadn't said anything about being away overnight. Your Mother and I have been sort of on the lookout for something like this."

"Damn," Joan said. "You should have trained me to be neater. Just to get things straight at the start, Daddy, I'm over the age of consent."

"Not in Pennsylvania, my dear. It's twenty-one."

"We're in New Jersey, Daddy. Here it's eighteen for girls."

"Spoken like the daughter of a lawyer," her father said, chuckling. "You're wrong if you think I'm going to argue with you. I merely want to talk to Tony for a few minutes, and get his ideas about the proposed elopement. I'm not here to play the heavy father, either. Merely a friendly discussion."

"Tony," Joan said, "don't believe a word of it. If Daddy were a district attorney instead of a corporation lawyer, that's the way he'd lead up to a demand for the death penalty."

Her father said, "Tony, there are times when a man ought to take the stand for himself. I hope you won't mind talking it over with me. And Joan, I'd like to talk to Tony alone. After all, you had your chance this morning. It's only fair to give me one."

"I'm not interested in being fair," Joan said. "All I'm interested in is getting married. However, I'll go upstairs for half an hour. And Tony—" she looked at him steadily, then blinked away dampness in her eyes "—don't forget you're up against a professional." Her voice broke into husky little notes on the last words, and she swung around and ran upstairs.

Years later, Anthony remembered distinctly what it was like to be up against a professional, and began to use the technique himself. A professional like Mr. Dickinson first made sure he knew everything possible about the strong points and weaknesses of his opponent. Then he worked little tricks to put you at a psychological disadvantage. He edged in on you slowly and quietly, so that he wouldn't alarm you, and coaxed you to make a foolish move. And when you did, he acted with the smooth grace of a judo wrestler to turn your own strength against you.

But that morning Anthony was not conscious of the skilled technique back of everything Mr. Dickinson did. Mr. Dickinson suggested going into the living room of the club, which was empty at that hour. It was a big room of the English manor type, with a beamed ceiling and leaded windows and a large fireplace of sculptured stone at the far end. It was Anthony's club and ordinarily he would have felt more at home and confident in it than a visitor would have felt. But Mr. Dickinson reversed that situation quickly.

"Do sit down, Tony," he said genially, becoming the host and making Anthony the guest.

As he spoke, he sat in a big leather chair placed by itself near a window. Anthony stood for a moment, half remembering an old green carpet before the headmaster's desk at the Academy. No other chair was near enough so that he could sit down. He didn't want to lug one of the other leather chairs halfway across the room, so he got a straight wooden chair. As a result, when they were settled for the talk, Mr. Dickinson was relaxed and at ease in a comfortable armchair while Anthony sat squirming on a hard wooden one.

"I must apologize for upsetting you this way," Mr. Dickinson said. "I really don't usually drop everything and go chasing Joan into the homes and clubs of her friends, like this."

Anthony thought, as he was intended to think, that it took a remarkably fine and thoughtful man to look at this from the angle of how much Mr. Dickinson was upsetting Anthony. From all normal points of view, Mr. Dickinson had more right to be upset. Anthony felt obliged to explain that to Mr. Dickinson, and began floundering in a self made swamp of apologies.

"Oh, let's not mention that," Mr. Dickinson said. "The important thing here is not whether Mrs. Dickinson and I are upset, but what is the best thing for you and Joan. You don't have to tell me, Tony, that you love her very sincerely and that she is very much attracted to you, because that's evident. Nor do you have to convince me that you're a fine young man who will some day make a name for himself. In fact, Tony, if I had a son I couldn't ask for one better than you."

This was very disarming, and at the same time it made Anthony feel uncomfortable. He hoped he could live up to that fine reputation. "Thank you, sir," he said earnestly. "I hope you'll never have to change your mind."

"I'm sure I won't, Tony. Now I suppose you and Joan have done some talking this morning about the problems involved. It would be helpful to me to know how you two looked at those problems."

It was difficult to talk about that to Mr. Dickinson, but he had to try. "I guess the main problem is that I'm going to law school and don't have any money," he said. "Joan thought that could be handled one way or another."

"Oh yes," Mr. Dickinson said brightly. "She has a modest income of her own. A bit over two thousand a year, I believe. Then of course she'd expect us to help out. How did all that strike you?"

"Well, the way Joan put it, it was like my scholarship here. It would be a sort of loan that I could repay when I got on my feet."

"You and I," Mr. Dickinson said, leaning forward confidentially, "are a lot alike, Tony. So I wonder if your reaction to that was somewhat like my own. Did that sound just a shade too smooth and easy to you?"

"Uh, yes sir, I guess it did. I said something to Joan about there being a flaw in that arrangement that I couldn't quite put my finger on at the moment."

"Well, Tony, let's see if there is a flaw. Now I happen to remember the first night you had a date with Joan. I remember it because her car wasn't in the garage the next morning, and I asked her about it. She said she'd lent it to you so you could drive home. She also laughed and said it was one way of making sure you'd come back to see her. Did you have any special reaction to that loan of the car, Tony?"

"I felt kind of funny about it. As if I didn't want to give her that much claim on me right at the start. And of course I felt it was sort of sponging on her."

"I knew we were alike," Mr. Dickinson said, beaming at him. "That's the reaction of a man who isn't really happy unless he's standing on his own two feet. I won't deny there are plenty of young men who are merely out to marry money who would never get that feeling at all. Now then, if you felt that way about the car, how would you feel if, instead of tossing you the car keys, Joan tossed you an apartment for two, and new suits every few months, and a twenty-dollar bill so you could drop in at the Princeton Club and have a good time with the boys? Would your reaction be the same?"

"I don't know," Anthony muttered. "It might be different, being married."

"Or it might not be different. Right, Tony?"

"Yes sir, it might not be different."

"Now let's look at it from Joan's point of view. You're a senior at Princeton. It's a glamorous place. You're a good dancer, Tony. On your dates with Joan you're both excited and all set to have a wonderful time. Now all of a sudden we take away the glamor. Instead of a Princeton senior taking her out on dates you're a law student coming home tired from classes and then buckling down to books half the night. That's asking a debutante to make a big transition. One moment you mean adventure to her. The next, you mean housework to her, and staying out of your way while you plug at books. How will she react to that?"

"Well, but look, Mr. Dickinson, don't most girls have to make that transition when they get married?"

"Indeed they do, Tony. But most of them would have a great advantage over Joan. They may have lost a carefree sweetheart, and the adventure he brought into their lives, but they have gained a breadwinner. And Tony, you wouldn't even be bringing home crumbs."

"I guess it's a gamble, all right," Anthony muttered.

"As I say, Tony, I think we're much alike. I don't care for big gambles. You and Joan might work it out. But it might also end with one of you walking out on the other. There wouldn't be the mutual respect that you have to have in any successful marriage. Do you want to take that gamble with Joan's life and your own?"

"I see what you mean," Anthony said miserably. "It's not the sort of gamble people ought to take. If I could see some other way out of it—"

"Tony, I'm proud of you. You're looking at this thing clearly and honestly. Now, instead of a gamble, I'd like to suggest what I would call a sure thing. Tony, I'd like to be your preceptor for law school. In whatever spare time you have, I'd like you to work as a law clerk at Dickinson and Dawes. As soon as you pass your Bar exams, I'd like you to marry Joan and join the firm. I'll guarantee you a salary that will let you support Joan properly. How does that sound?"

For twenty minutes, Anthony had been led slowly and carefully through a sort of Chamber of Horrors. Now, suddenly, the doors at the far end were flung open and there was sunlight and happiness. "It sounds wonderful," he said solemnly. "I only hope I can live up to that chance you're giving me."

Mr. Dickinson got up quickly: a lawyer who knew that when you won over the jury you rested your case immediately, before you said or did something that might change their minds. "I know you will," he said. "I couldn't feel more sure of that if you were my own son. I'm going to run along now, my boy. Joan's going to be a bit difficult for you to handle, but this is a good time to start learning how to do it. Good luck, Tony. Drop into my office as soon as you get back to town, and we'll get the preceptor business under way and let you meet Judge Dawes." He shook hands briskly and left.

Anthony went bounding up the stairs to the second floor, calling for Joan. She had been standing by one of the tables in the pool room, arranging the pool balls in different designs.

She looked up when he rushed in, and held up a hand so that he couldn't take her in his arms. "I don't like it," she said. "You're too happy."

"But Joan," he cried, "your Father was wonderful. He—"

"I'll bet he was wonderful. I've seen him work on people. He ties you in knots and leaves you feeling that he just straightened you out. What sort of knots are you tied in, Tony?"

"Not any, Joan, honest! He did straighten me out. Everything's going to be fine for us. It—"

"No it isn't," she said. "I was hoping you'd come up here with your face red and your jaw stuck out and mad as anything. That would have meant you'd won. What bill of goods did he sell you?"

He explained what they'd talked about, and the wonderful offer her father had made, and how the other thing would have been an awful gamble with both their lives, and couldn't she see that?

"Of course I saw it," she said. "I was willing to take the gamble. Oh Tony, I shouldn't have tried to talk you into marrying me! I should have coaxed you out for a ride and just argued with my body. Don't you see what's happened? We had a very simple question to settle. I wanted to marry you today. Daddy didn't want me to marry you today. Well, he won. Maybe I should try again to convince you but I don't think I have a chance. Besides I don't feel like trying again. So Daddy won, you think you won, and I know I lost."

"I wish you wouldn't take it that way."

She started walking slowly downstairs. "I won't stay here today, Tony, if you don't mind. I'll come back tomorrow to see you graduate."

He walked with her out to the car, telling her earnestly how much he loved her and how hard he would work to make her proud of him. She cheered up a little, and said that of course she loved him too and maybe the three years would go quickly. But, as she started the car, Anthony noticed that she stared vaguely into the distance and that her lips were silently forming the same series of words over and over.

"What are you saying to yourself?" he asked.

She looked surprised, and then smiled wanly and said, "I didn't realize my lips were moving. Oh, it was just a silly idea. I was saying: Arthur, Jonathan, Elaine and Betsy. You remember? Those were the names I had picked out for my four kids. I had a sudden crazy notion that I'd better repeat them a few times, so I wouldn't forget them in the next three years."

That was a strange thing, and Anthony thought about it after she drove away. For the first time he began to suspect that Mr. Dickinson had coaxed him into making a bad trade. It would have been a gamble to have married Joan immediately. But it was a much worse gamble to bet that a girl who wanted four children, and had already named them, was going to wait three years for anybody.

7

LOOKING BACK LATER, it seemed to him that graduation from college marked the end of a sort of nursery period of his life. Up to that time there had always been people around to make sure that he didn't stub his toes too hard or fall out of his crib. Even at Princeton, where they gave you adult toys to play with, the university tried to keep you from playing with the toys too roughly or cutting yourself badly on the sharp edges.

After he left Princeton there was no more nursery. For one thing, law school was very different from college. The law professors threw stuff at you and walked off without waiting to see if you could catch it. For another thing, there were changes at home.

All during the years, his grandfather had kept on at Franklin Academy, ignoring hints about retiring. He would have been replaced as head of the Latin Department except that it was slowly ceasing to be a department; Latin was not only a dead language but also the study of it was dying. Harry Judson worked hard to keep it alive, seeking out students for his few remaining Latin classes like a football coach recruiting players.

One day, during the autumn of Anthony's first year at law school, his grandfather came home from the Academy with a bad cold. The next day it was worse, and Harry Judson had to stay home, delivering orations against his ailment like Cicero fulminating in the Roman Senate. Gradually the cold turned into pneumonia, and the rolling thunder of his voice faded to a mutter. For two days he lay silently in bed. Then there was one fierce and final burst of energy. He sat up, fighting off restraining hands, and gave one last oration. His words, however, were fogged with delirium. He might have been daring the germ that gripped him to do its worst. Or perhaps he was Horatius, defending the Sublician Bridge against Lars Porsena and the Etruscan army. Or possibly he was merely exhorting the Franklin Academy eleven to score on Penn Charter. The oration ended with a triumphant shout of "Ave atque vale!" and Harry Judson sank back and died. He would have been glad to know that his last words were spoken in Latin.

At the funeral, Anthony's grandmother was quiet and pale and trembling, and Anthony's mother stayed close to her, watchfully.

"You needn't be so worried, dear," his grandmother said in a low voice. "I shall not collapse. It has always seemed to me that dying at a funeral is not good form. It is the sort of thing that is best left to the wives of Hindus and other emotional races. I do not care for dramatics."

Anthony's grandmother kept her promise. She waited for two full months, and then died one night in the parlor of the house on Spruce Street, slumping quietly in the old wing chair where for so many years she had done her embroidery. There was nothing dramatic in her passing, unless you wondered about the book that was open on her lap. It contained poems, and apparently she had just underlined a stanza of Byron's that began: "She walks in beauty, like the night ..." Neither Anthony nor his mother knew whether these lines had any significance. Probably nothing, they thought, that you could call dramatic.

The house seemed very large and empty after that, and Anthony's mother sold it and they took an apartment on Walnut Street just beyond Rittenhouse Square. At about the same time Miss Rogers' Select School, which Anthony's mother had once attended, needed a new headmistress and offered the job to her. She took it, glad to escape from the bright hard efficiency of Mrs. Hoyt Phelps and her social counseling service. But the new job took more of her time than the job with Mrs. Phelps had taken, and it gave her an interest in which Anthony had no part.

So, in a very brief time, his life was greatly changed. At first he had a feeling that he had been uprooted and that all his ties with the past had been snapped. But eventually he realized that was a nursery school type of thought. You did not sell your memories with a house, or bury them along with coffins. Part of his mind still lived in the old row house on Spruce Street, sitting in its heavy walnut furniture, looking at its pictures of Roman and Grecian ruins and of Galahad in his armor, listening to his grandfather's booming voice and hearing his grandmother reminding him to wear his rubbers. Whatever he did in the future would be governed to some extent by the part of his mind that still lived in the past.

There was one other change in his life. During that first year at law school he and Joan moved slowly apart. They saw less and less of each other. For a time each of them felt guilty about it, and would apologize to the other for not having called. But as the months went by Anthony realized—and suspected that Joan did also—that the course of their affair had been firmly charted on a June day in Princeton, just before graduation. They were merely following that course now.

But you can see something coming and still be hurt when it arrives. He had been working as a law clerk for Mr. Dickinson in his spare time, and one day in late spring Mr. Dickinson called him into his office.

"There's something I have to report to you, Tony," he said. Then, staring out of the window, he added, "Joan is going to be married next month."

Anthony felt a twitch of pain go through his body. It was not a new sharp pain but slow and throbbing, as if an old hurt that went back to last June had stirred again. "Well," he said, "I suppose I've seen it coming."

"I hope you won't blame Joan," Mr. Dickinson said. He was still looking out of the window, and Anthony knew that Mr. Dickinson really meant not to blame him. "She wants a home of her own, and a family. It's natural enough."

"Arthur, Jonathan, Elaine and Betsy," Anthony murmured.

"What's that?"

"I thought perhaps you knew. She had those names all picked out for her four children."

"I hope she doesn't go at it in such wholesale fashion. Four children is almost an indecent number. So she had the names picked out, did she?"

"Yes sir." It was silly of him, but he was glad Mr. Dickinson hadn't known about the names. That meant Joan had not been very close to her father, and indicated that he hadn't known her well. Perhaps Mr. Dickinson had been wrong, a year ago, in thinking that a large gamble would have been involved if Joan had married him. "Who is she marrying, Mr. Dickinson?"

"A very nice young fellow. Carter Henry, his name is." Mr. Dickinson turned and looked earnestly at him and continued, "I want you to understand, Tony, that you compare quite well with him, from my point of view. In a couple of years or so, after you passed your Bar exams, I'd have been delighted to see the whole thing work out the way we discussed it. But Carter Henry is in a position to get married now. He's about your age. Out of college a year, and working for his father. The senior Henry owns the Quaker City Battery Works, a business which I believe grosses upwards of fifteen million a year. The boy will be a vice president in a year or so."

"I hope she'll be very happy."

It was the conventional thing to say, but Mr. Dickinson seized the remark as if it was the noblest sentiment anyone had expressed since Nathan Hale regretted that he had only one life to give for his country. Apparently Mr. Dickinson was feeling very guilty. "That's a mighty fine way to take it," he said warmly. "I hoped you would react that way, Tony. It does great credit to you. I'll tell Joan what you said, and I know it will mean a great deal to her. She felt so badly that she said she couldn't face you, and begged me to break the news instead. It was not, I can tell you, a pleasant task."

"You've been very thoughtful and considerate, Mr. Dickinson. I appreciate it."

"Thank you, Tony. Thank you. Now," he said briskly, "I want to assure you that this need not disturb our personal relationship one least bit. I'll be glad to continue as your preceptor, and I'm looking forward to having you join the firm after you pass your Bar exams."

Anthony thanked him, and told him how much he appreciated it, and that ended the discussion. It was clearer than ever to him, however, that he had still been in nursery school on that June day in Princeton. He had been a child, listening wide-eyed to the words of grown-up Mr. Dickinson. From now on he would peer more closely into the motives back of words, and examine them like a bank teller studying a queer-looking bill.

A little examination now hinted that his future with Dickinson and Dawes might not be bright. Mr. Dickinson felt guilty. People do not like to feel guilty. In time, Mr. Dickinson would begin to dislike the person who was making him feel guilty. It would be wise, Anthony thought, to begin planning for the day when that would happen.

He did not try to get in touch with Joan. There was nothing to say except that he had been an idiot, and probably she knew that already. He sent her the best wedding present that he could afford but did not go to the wedding or reception. Gradually the hurt faded and became one of those things, like his trick knee from football, that you had to poke at deliberately to prove that way down deep some damage had not been repaired.

Fortunately for his morale at that time, law school was turning out very well indeed. The classic gripe about law school, passed on from one generation of students to another, was that in your first year they scared you to death, in the second year they worked you to death, and in the third year they bored you to death. But Anthony enjoyed every minute of it. There was a neatness to the study of law that appealed to him. When you ran up against a problem you could go to the library and dig out the decisions and precedents bearing on it, and work out your answer in the light of the answers which other men before you had found proper. Learning how to become a lawyer was much like learning how to become a Philadelphian.

Some of the students in his class—Jews fighting for the coveted title of professional man, Italians from South Philadelphia aiming at politics—were brilliant in ways he could never hope to match. The Jews looked on law as a sort of chess tournament; they wanted to be Grand Masters, inventing new gambits. The Italians went at it emotionally, as if trying a case were like singing an aria from Rigoletto. Rather to his surprise, Anthony, who liked law because it was law, found he could match them in marks even if not in brilliance. He ranked in the upper tenth of his class, when the marks came out after his first year, and was one of the few who were invited to try out for the Law Review.

He did even better in his second year, and by the end of it knew there was some talk of naming him editor of the Law Review for his final year. When he finished his last examination and handed it in, the monitor said that the Dean wanted to see him. He reported to the Dean's secretary, who asked him to wait and went into the inner office. The Dean himself came out.

"Hello there, Lawrence," the Dean said. "How did you hit that one?"

"I hope all right, sir," Anthony said. "But I wasn't quite satisfied with my discussion of circumstantial evidence. There was one decision I wanted to cite, Commonwealth versus Webster in Massachusetts, that I couldn't recall as exactly as I should have."

"Well, well, I'm sure you did excellently. There's a gentleman in my office I want you to meet. A Mr. Wharton, John Marshall Wharton, in fact. Of Morris, Clayton, Biddle and Wharton."

The Dean breathed those four names almost the way you might recite a Psalm in church. That, of course, was quite proper. Morris, Clayton, Biddle and Wharton was one of the great law firms. But it was more than that. When you said Morris, Clayton, Biddle and Wharton you were reciting chapters of Philadelphia history.

The first Morris in Philadelphia, an Anthony Morris, had been the second mayor of the city. His son had also become mayor—all this, of course, back in Colonial days when it was respectable to be mayor. In the third generation had come Captain Sam Morris; as founder of the Gloucester Fox Hunting Club he enjoyed hunting foxes, and as captain of the Philadelphia Troop of Light Horse in the Revolution he enjoyed hunting the British. The Claytons were related, in the maternal line, to several Colonial mayors of the city; a Mr. Logan Clayton had been one of the great Nineteenth Century bankers, and his son Glendenning had been an expert on Constitutional law. The Biddles were as symbolic of Philadelphia as cinnamon buns and scrapple and planked shad and Fish House Punch; a famous anecdote dealt with the pardonable confusion of the Prince of Wales (the one who later became the Duke of Windsor) who was not quite sure whether you visited Philadelphia to meet Biddles and eat scrapple, or to meet scrapple and eat Biddles. The Whartons had been everything you could think of: bankers, mayors, lawyers, and so on. Throughout the history of Philadelphia they had also speculated in its real estate, although their method of speculation was to hold property a hundred years before putting it on the market.

Meeting a member of the firm of Morris, Clayton, Biddle and Wharton was, therefore, rather like having the statue of William Penn atop City Hall bow gravely as you passed.

"I feel highly honored," Anthony said.

The Dean said, "Mr. Wharton wants to discuss a certain matter with you. I came out here so that I could tell you, before you meet him, that the decision you will be called on to make is entirely in your hands. There are pros and cons to it. I would not really want to advise you one way or another. Now let's go in, shall we?"

Mr. John Marshall Wharton was a tall slender man of about sixty, with wavy silver hair that might have looked theatrical if it had been allowed to grow an inch longer than normal. Naturally he kept it cut a quarter-inch shorter than normal. He talked pleasantly and casually to Anthony for a few minutes. Then he said, "At my time of life, many of us in the legal profession get an urge either to go on the bench or to write a book. My weakness is a desire to write a book. It will discuss the evolution of the Sherman Anti-Trust Act through court decisions. I need a bright young man to help me with the research."

"Yes, sir," Anthony said alertly. It was much too early to risk showing a reaction other than alertness. He had been called a bright young man, and he could prove that he was by avoiding puppy-like moves at this point.

Mr. Wharton nodded, perhaps in approval of his caution. "It seemed to me," he went on, "that such a job might well appeal to a law school student who gets excellent marks, who has had Law Review experience, and who is not unwilling to earn a modest fee. The Dean tells me that you qualify on all those grounds."

"That was very good of him," Anthony said, allowing a few degrees more warmth to creep into his tone. "Thank you, sir," he said, looking at the Dean.

"Now I suspect," Mr. Wharton said, with a tiny smile, "that before you came in here the Dean also whispered to you that there are pros and cons to this matter."

The Dean got a bit red, and chuckled. Anthony grinned.

"Perhaps I don't have to go into the pros very deeply," Mr. Wharton said, giving Anthony credit for knowing Philadelphia history. "I'll be glad to pay you fifty dollars a week, starting this summer. I will be at my lodge in Maine during the summer, planning the framework of the book. I would expect you to spend the summer here, digging up everything you can find on Sherman Anti-Trust decisions. Starting in the fall, we would begin work on the book, and no doubt it would require most of your spare time. I hope to finish the book within a year."

"It's hard to see," Anthony said, "how the cons could outweigh the pros, sir."

Mr. Wharton said, "The main objection, of course, is that it would require a great deal of your time. Perhaps it would be no more than you would put into work on the Law Review, but you couldn't do both this and the Review. And that's a fairly big point. In fact, as I understand it, it would mean giving up a fairly good chance to be editor of the Law Review. You know as well as I do what that means in terms of prestige."

Anthony realized that this was a tricky decision. The editor of the Law Review could be sure of getting a bid to a good law firm. On the other hand, that type of prestige didn't last forever. A few years after you got out of law school nobody would care whether or not you had been on the Law Review. But the prestige gained from helping John Marshall Wharton to write a basic textbook, on Sherman Anti-Trust Act decisions, would last a long time. Then there was another angle. Unmentioned, but clearly understood on both sides, was the fact that if he did a good job he might be invited to join the firm of Morris, Clayton, Biddle and Wharton.

Anthony looked at the Dean, hoping for guidance, but the Dean merely smiled and shrugged. Also unmentioned but understood was the fact that, if he did not satisfy Mr. Wharton, he would not get a bid to Morris, Clayton, Biddle and Wharton, and would have given up the prestige of Law Review work in exchange for nothing.

"There is one other point," Anthony said, "that I ought to consider. In my spare time I've been working as a law clerk with Dickinson and Dawes."

"I know about that," Mr. Wharton said. "I'm afraid you would have to give that up, too. I would be willing to call Mr. Dickinson and explain the matter to him. Naturally I wouldn't want to raid his office without his permission. I'm sure he would consent, but perhaps he might not like it. So you see," he added, with a sudden, charming smile, "I'm asking you to give up a lot. But I'm selfish enough to want only the best. And the best man for a job is always busy with other things."

It was a skillful and disarming touch on Mr. Wharton's part to admit that he was being selfish. Because of course he was. He was asking Anthony to gamble a sure thing, the Law Review, against fifty dollars a week and a hope. Mr. Wharton also thought he was asking Anthony to gamble his future with Dickinson and Dawes against the same fifty dollars a week and the hope, but that wasn't the case. During the past year, as Anthony had foreseen, Mr. Dickinson's interest in him had waned. There was less law clerking work to be done. Judge Dawes' son had joined the firm, along with a classmate from Harvard Law. Mr. Dickinson would not exactly break his promise to take Anthony into the firm, but he might bend it into the shape of a question mark.

Mr. Wharton said, "Would you like time to consider this?"

Two years before, Anthony had allowed himself to be frightened away from taking a gamble. That hadn't worked out well. "I don't need any more time, sir," he said. "I'd feel greatly honored to have a chance to work with you."

"Good," Mr. Wharton said. "I'm sure that both of us have all the pros and cons firmly in mind, and I hope neither of us ever regrets the decision."

They smiled and shook hands, not realizing that the future would bring a pro and con which had not been discussed at all, and which would turn out to be far more important than all the others combined.

During the summer Anthony lived so closely with the Sherman Anti-Trust Act that everything else in his life began to seem faintly unreal. Mr. Wharton returned from Maine early in September and fired a machine-gun series of questions at him, designed to probe his knowledge of famous anti-trust cases, such as the Standard Oil case of 1911. Anthony began answering.

Mr. Wharton listened for ten minutes, then laughed and held up a protesting hand. "All right," he said. "I merely wanted to see if you had been working. You've almost convinced me that you wrote some of those decisions. That's fine. Now we can get down to work."

At first they worked together, a few evenings a week, at the Racquet Club or at Mr. Wharton's office. Then Mr. Wharton began coming in Sundays. Finally Mr. Wharton asked Anthony to come out to his place weekends so that they could get more work done. And that opened an entirely new life to Anthony.

The Wharton mansion was old Philadelphia, even though it was far out the Main Line in the Radnor Hunt country. Six generations back, in the 1790s, a Wharton had built the house as a refuge from the yellow fever epidemics that kept burning through the city in those years. The architecture was Georgian, and over the years its pale bricks had taken on the mellowness of sunshine. The house seemed to rest lightly on the land, as if it were floating on its unruffled green lawns. Inside, it was a place filled with soft gleams: the amber glow of mahogany and satin-wood and cherry furniture, the bluish flames of old silver, the deep shine of Wedgwood and lustre ware. In some ways, Anthony thought, living there seemed almost as irreverent as picnicking in the Parkway Museum. But of course Mr. Wharton was used to it.

On his first visit to the house Mr. Wharton led him into a study and said, "Pull up a chair and we'll start."

Anthony pulled up a chair with wooden arms and leather seat, and started to sit down and then leaped up almost in panic. There was no mistaking the smooth feel of the chair arms, the lyre back with its shell motif at the top, and the cabriole legs with their claw-and-ball feet.

"What's the matter?" Mr. Wharton asked, a bit impatiently.

"I'd better get another chair, sir. This is Chippendale, isn't it?"

"If it isn't, my great-great-great grandfather was stung. Probably made by William Savery or Jonathan Gostelowe or another of those fellows of the Philadelphia Chippendale school. Nothing wrong with it, is there? Legs aren't wobbly?"

Anthony couldn't help grinning. "No sir. I just happened to think that this must be worth at least several thousand dollars."

"Very likely. Fiske Kimball was out here once and almost cut my throat, trying to get a pair of these for his damned museum."

"I'd feel more comfortable in another chair."

"Nonsense. Chairs are made to sit in. Now let's get going."

Mr. Wharton had no children. He had not married until he was forty-five; the panic of 1907 had disturbed the Wharton fortune and John Marshall Wharton, with a first-things-first air, had put all his energies into restoring them, postponing marriage. Mrs. Wharton was considerably younger. Anthony thought she was perhaps several years younger than his mother, although in his eyes that still made Mrs. Wharton quite middle aged. She might have been in her early forties.

He was aware of her first as a slim graceful shadow moving about the house, unobtrusive as a candle flame. Later he sometimes found himself watching her profile at the dinner table, at which she sat to his right, usually looking at her husband at the other end of the long mahogany table. Her profile was clean and cold, like a design cut in ice by an expert figure skater. She had black hair, cut short and brushed back in dark wings from her temples. There were glints of silver in her hair. Either chance or the genius of a hairdresser had arranged for the silver strands to be a trifle longer than the black ones, so that the effect was as if the black hair had been lightly frosted at the ends.

Now and then, while her husband was talking at dinner about the Sherman Anti Trust Act, she would find an opening to drop in a hopeful comment or question about art or music or modern novels. This, Anthony saw, was like trying to upset a steam roller by scattering flowers in its path. But Mrs. Wharton's profile never changed its expression as the Sherman Anti-Trust Act rolled forward and mashed her efforts at conversation.

More than a month went by, from the time he began spending weekends there, before he ever really talked to Mrs. Wharton. Then one Sunday morning, before the Whartons had come downstairs, he decided to explore the huge library in the west wing. Its shelves were filled with books in magnificent bindings of morocco and other fine materials, and at first he looked suspiciously for the uncut pages that you often found in large private libraries. But of course that wasn't the case here. The Whartons bought things for use, not for show. John Marshall Wharton was not, however, much of a reader, so obviously the library dated back to Whartons of past generations.

He was examining an early edition of *Robinson Crusoe* when Mrs. Wharton came in. "I beg your pardon, Mr. Lawrence," she said. "I didn't realize you were in here."

"Just admiring things," he said. "How are you this morning, Mrs. Wharton? This is quite a library, isn't it?" He closed the copy of *Robinson Crusoe* and replaced it.

"Yes, it is nice. Not very modern, though. John's father and grandfather were great readers, but John never went in for it."

As she spoke, her hand moved, apparently without conscious thought, to the copy of *Robinson Crusoe* and turned it over on the shelf so that its spine faced up instead of outward. Her action reminded Anthony that the book had been turned over that way when he took it from the shelf. In fact, now that he noticed it, at least a hundred of the many books in the library were turned upward.

"Do you mind if I'm curious?" he asked. "Why did you turn that book over? And why are so many turned over on the shelves?"

"Well," she said, "I understand that some years ago, perhaps around 1910, John's father made a thorough survey of this library. He needed more room on the shelves, and he was going to dispose of books which no longer interested him or for which he had duplicates. So he turned over the ones he was considering giving up. But he debated about it for a few years, and then died. Naturally no one has disturbed the arrangement, although it is very hard to train new servants to leave the books as they are."

Her tone implied that this was a very solemn matter, and Anthony knew he should treat it in the same way. But actually it struck him as very funny. He fought to keep his face under control but it got away from him and began grinning. Mrs. Wharton looked at him in shocked surprise. Then suddenly she giggled. It was such a delightful little sound, breaking through the cool calm mask she had always worn, that Anthony let himself go and began laughing. Mrs. Wharton started laughing too, and then in a few seconds they were both slightly hysterical.

"Oh dear, oh dear," Mrs. Wharton wailed finally, dabbing at her eyes. "I haven't laughed like that in years. Oh Tony, it is the funniest thing, isn't it?"

"It's wonderful," he choked. "I'm sure it could only happen in Philadelphia."

"All those b-books lying solemnly that way since 1910 ..." And she was off again into hysterics.

They were just recovering when Mr. Wharton walked in, looking slightly offended. "House sounds full of maniacs this morning," he grumbled. "What's so funny?"

Anthony didn't dare tell him for fear of losing control again, but Mrs. Wharton managed to explain in between fits of laughing and weeping.

Mr. Wharton said, "If my father thought it was a good idea I can't see what's so funny about it. I—" He stopped. The muscles of his face, working against his will power, wrestled his mouth into the hint of a smile. "Come to think of it," he said, "it is ridiculous. It—" Then he looked startled, and up from his chest came a big booming laugh, and then they all began howling madly. In the middle of it Mr. Wharton gasped, "Let's put the damned things back the way they belong," and all three of them ran around wildly and happily standing the books up properly on end.

After it was all over they were a little abashed at having been so unrestrained, and were not quite ready to meet each other's glances. There was no talk at breakfast. A Sunday newspaper was at each place. Mr. Wharton read the editorials in *The New York Times*. Mrs. Wharton looked at the department store ads in *The Philadelphia Inquirer* and Anthony pretended to study the sports section of *The Philadelphia Record*. He took in very little of the news. What had happened in the library was a startling thing, and one which would make a change in their relationships. He did not know what the change would be, and he wanted to move cautiously until the actions of Mr. and Mrs. Wharton gave him a clue.

The clue appeared early that afternoon. He and Mr. Wharton were in the study, where they usually had a luncheon tray and then worked through the afternoon. But when a knock sounded on the door it was not the maid with the tray, but Mrs. Wharton. "I've decided to take a firm stand," she said pleasantly.

"Yes, dear?" her husband said vaguely, making another note about an anti-trust decision he had been discussing with Anthony.

"You didn't hear me but I'm not going to be put off," she said. "John, you're working this boy too hard. I'm sure he's had no exercise or relaxation for months. Have you, Tony?"

"Well," Anthony said, "I've been pretty busy and—"

"You see, John? You can set your own pace, and keep yourself in fair condition. But Tony not only has to keep up with you but also with the pace they set at law school. Why don't you two take the afternoon off, and get some fresh air and exercise? You know you're way ahead of schedule on the book."

"Perhaps you're right," Mr. Wharton said. "Tony, you are getting a little thin and pale. Can't have that. Don't know how I could handle this book if you got sick. Well, what do you suggest, Carol?"

"What about horseback riding? Do you ride, Tony?"

"I like riding," Anthony said, "but I don't suppose I'm any good. We had Field Artillery R.O.T.C. at college and had to learn to ride, but the horses were awful brutes."

"Take him out this afternoon, John."

"I'm a bit afraid of that sacro-iliac of mine, dear."

"I forgot," she said, sighing. "Tony, we have two magnificent jumpers in the stable. John and I used to ride with the Radnor Hunt, but he took a spill a year ago and came up with a bad back. The horses haven't been ridden much since. I walk them every day, riding one and leading the other, but it's not much fun for them or for me. We ought to sell them, but it's like the books turned over in the library. We do something for a reason, and then the reason vanishes, but we keep on doing it because by that time it's a tradition. Now we have a tradition of keeping horses even though we don't ride them."

"No reason why you can't take Tony out," Mr. Wharton said. "Do you good to get in a decent gallop."

"I suppose I could," she said, looking uncertainly at Anthony.

Before the episode in the library he would have backed away from that, because Mrs. Wharton had seemed as awesome as a glacier. Now he smiled at her and said, "I'd like it."

So that afternoon they dug up riding breeches and boots of Mr. Wharton's which didn't fit him too badly, and went down to the stable. The two jumpers, a chestnut named Topaz and a black named Captain, whinnied and began toe-dancing in their stalls. They saddled and rode off on a bridle path through woods. It was a crisp afternoon in early December. The horses kept trying to break out of the walk, jetting impatient puffs of steam from their nostrils. Anthony, up on Captain, realized that this was a very different type of horse from the brutes in Field Artillery. It was like sitting on a rocket that wanted to go off. Up ahead, Mrs. Wharton swayed gracefully on the chestnut, turning now and then to smile at him. There was a color in her face he had never seen before.

After fifteen minutes she stepped up the pace to a slow trot and then a trot, and they moved smoothly along the bridle path and finally came out on the edge of the rolling fields of the Radnor Hunt. Up ahead were brown meadows and low stone walls and rail fences.

"Are you game?" Mrs. Wharton called.

He had done a little jumping, in the riding hall at Princeton, but always over barriers that went down if your brute hit them. The walls and fences up ahead wouldn't topple in that convenient way.

He hoped the black package of dynamite under him knew more about jumping than he did. "Let's go," he shouted.

The chestnut took off like a scared cat, and the black quivered and danced. Anthony leaned forward slightly. That was all the black was waiting for. The ground blurred and the wind scraped at his face as they raced across the first field. Fifty yards ahead, Mrs. Wharton's chestnut stretched smoothly and soared over a stone wall. Anthony took a deep breath. Back in the riding hall at college you kept your weight forward and didn't pull on the reins and then, if you were lucky, the brute of an artillery horse would go over the jump like a couple of freight cars buckling in the middle. The wall swooped at him and the muscles of the black horse rippled and they floated over the wall. It was like rocking in a porch swing except that it made you drunk.

They went galloping on and on over the hunt country. The black caught up to the chestnut and matched stride for stride, and at two fences they glided over together as if each horse were a mirrored reflection of the other. At last Mrs. Wharton lifted a hand. She and Anthony brought the horses down to a walk and moved along side by side.

"Oh, weren't they glorious!" she cried. "Like small boys let out of school. It's been so long since they've had a run. And so long since I've had one, too." She reached out a hand and touched his arm, lightly. "Tony, I'm so grateful to you."

He laughed. "I'm the one who ought to be grateful. Why should you be?"

"Because today you either added ten years to my life or took ten off my age, I can't figure which."

He looked at her curiously. There were pink banners in her cheeks. She had taken off her cap, and her short black hair with its silver frosting tumbled around her face. She was breathing quickly as a result of the exercise, and her breasts strained against the jacket. The belt of her riding breeches accented her slim waist. For the first time he saw that she had a good figure. He was surprised to have a thought like that about a middle aged woman, but there it was, anyway. On an impulse, he said, "You look about eighteen."

The pink banners in her cheeks turned crimson. "I wasn't fishing," she said. "And I didn't just mean this ride, either. It all started with that wonderful crazy laugh in the library this morning. Tony, have you ever felt like a piece of crystal that's vibrating nearer and nearer to the cracking point? I've been getting closer to that point for months. I felt like one of those silly books, turned on its side since 1910, becoming a dead tradition."

There were subtleties in that which he didn't understand. Furthermore, he didn't want to understand them. He tried to figure what to say, and for a few minutes they moved along with no sound but the creak of leather and clop of hooves and the deep slow hiss of the horses breathing.

"I'm sorry," she said. "I'm afraid I shocked you. Did I sound disloyal?"

"No," he said, "it wasn't that. If I was shocked, it was mainly because suddenly you became a real person. You know, with problems like everybody else. All I ever saw before was just the shine on the outside of that crystal you mentioned."

"You weren't a real person either until today, Tony."

"Me?"

"You were a stuffed shirt. You were the classic bright young man, printed on cardboard. Oh, I shouldn't have said that!"

He chuckled. "I deserve it. I've been so busy with my own affairs that I haven't given a thought to anyone else. I bet this book-writing business has been awfully dull for you."

"I'm very much in favor of John writing the book, really I am. You see, he spent most of his life patching up the family fortune. He was forty-five when we were married, and we haven't been able to produce any children. John has never had time to do the sort of things that might have brought him a really good appointment to the bench, and now he's sixty-two and wants to leave some kind of a monument behind. That's where the book comes in."

"It's going to be a good one. They'll remember him a long time for it. But it's left you pretty much out of things, hasn't it?"

"It merely came at the wrong time for me. Just when John was giving up all the things we used to do together, riding, trips and all that. And I used to be active on all kinds of committees but in the last year they began boring me to death. I don't want you to think I'm disloyal. John means more to me than anybody ever could. I admit I married him for security. I was twenty-five, and nobody in my family had earned a penny for seventy or eighty years, and we all liked nice things and soon there wasn't going to be any money for them, so ... but John's a wonderful person. I couldn't be fonder of him, and it's not just the security any more."

"I'd have felt badly if you didn't care for him. He's a mighty fine guy."

"Tony, I hope you won't make the mistake he did."

"What mistake is that?"

"He was trying to save the Wharton position. You're trying to create one. Don't get so involved that you wait until forty-five to get married."

"I'll try to remember that."

"I've never heard you mention a girl, and I don't know when you'd have time to go out with any. Has there been a girl, Tony?"

He smiled faintly. "I had one, and got talked out of her."

"Who was she, and how did it happen?"

It was rather pleasant to talk this way with an older, understanding woman, and so for the first time he found himself telling someone about his affair with Joan Dickinson. He didn't really mean to give her the whole long story, but she kept poking questions at him and listening eagerly. The memory of it didn't hurt badly, now that he could look back on it as something that happened to a college boy more than two years ago.

"So that," he said finally, "wound up my little romance."

He looked at her and smiled, and saw that she was crying quietly. He remembered that a scene like this had happened once before, on the night when he told Joan about his boyhood tragedy at the Friday Afternoon Dancing Class. Joan had cried, and that had marked the beginning of their affair; perhaps if he hadn't told Joan the story she would never have become really interested in him. Apparently women reacted quite strongly to sad little stories, and it might be a good idea to pick your audience carefully, if you didn't want the girl to get emotionally involved with you. Fortunately you didn't have to worry about such problems with an older woman.

Mrs. Wharton said, "Now I've had a good cry to go with that wonderful laugh this morning. It's been a big day. I think we might trot the horses a little and then walk them the last half-mile."

After that day, it became an accepted thing that he and Mrs. Wharton would ride every Saturday and Sunday afternoon. There was still plenty of time to work on the book, which was coming along nicely. He enjoyed the rides not only for the exercise but also because it was a new experience, and very pleasant, to have a sexless friendship with a woman.

The winter passed smoothly, and spring came, and one Saturday night Mr. Wharton pushed aside their manuscript earlier than usual. He walked to the window and opened it and sniffed the air. "Dogwood and violets," he said. "I don't suppose they have a scent, but I can smell them anyway. At my age I shouldn't have spring fever but I don't feel like working any more tonight. I'm going to bully you into taking a walk with me. And while I'm changing clothes, why don't you look up Carol and see if she'll come?"

Anthony went out into the hall. There was music floating up from the first floor, and as he went downstairs he identified it as The Philadelphia Orchestra's recording of "The Blue Danube." It was coming from the record player in the living room. He walked to the doorway of the room, and paused in surprise. Mrs. Wharton was dancing by herself in the big room, drifting around like a leaf caught in idle swirls of air. She wore a gown that seemed to be woven of moonlight. Her head was thrown back and her eyes were partly closed and dreamy. Anthony was about to move away, because watching her seemed like spying on a girl taking a bath, but one of her pirouettes brought them face to face and she saw him. The dreamy expression on her face didn't change. She came forward as if she had been expecting a partner and, without quite knowing how it happened, he found himself dancing with her.

For a few moments he felt embarrassed to be dancing with an older woman, and Mrs. John Marshall Wharton, at that. But then, slowly and shockingly, he realized that this was not an older woman at all. Not if you judged by her body. She was not wearing any of the clever things of cloth and elastic and boning that usually armored women, in their war with mirrors and scales and dress sizes. Where his hand rested on her back he felt nothing but two thin layers of material which let him trace every ripple underneath. There was a slim sheath of muscle on each side of her spine and a delicate groove between which bent like a wand as they danced. It was a fascinating thing to feel, and his hand wanted to move around and touch her shoulder blades and ribs and the curve at the small of her back.

His face was getting quite hot, and he tried to forget about Mrs. Wharton's back. That was a mistake. It left his mind free to consider the touch of her breasts and the soft pressure of her stomach and the way her thighs and knees brushed his legs. He tried desperately to call back his picture of her as an older woman but it was like trying to prove that springtime was old. His body began to feel as if it were dancing against flames. It was becoming hard to breathe. He looked at her face and saw that her eyes were no longer dreamy and partly closed. They were wide and dark and questioning, and seemed ready to accept whatever answer he wanted to give.

The music stopped.

He stepped back, and forced himself to laugh and to say casually, "I'd almost forgotten how to dance. And I did forget to give you a message from Mr. Wharton. He's going for a walk and wants to know if you'd like to come."

She stared at him almost blankly for a moment, and then abruptly her glance flickered over his shoulder and she said, "I'd love a walk. Will you wait for me to change, John?"

Anthony managed to turn slowly so that he did not appear to be startled. Mr. Wharton was standing in the doorway. "Of course I'll wait," Mr. Wharton said. He moved aside to let his wife pass, and looked after her with a slight frown. He turned back to Anthony, and seemed to study him, and then flashed his rare and charming smile. "That was very nice to watch," he said. "I'm sorry I don't dance any more."

During the next few weeks Anthony took care not to let anything like that happen again. But it was much easier to keep his body away from Mrs. Wharton than to keep his mind away from her. He became sharply conscious of all her actions: the click of high heels as she entered a room, the tiny sharps and flats in her speaking voice, the changing curves of her body as she moved. When you became so aware of another person you tried to read significance into little things. When they rode side by side, did her knee brush against his by chance or intention? If he helped her down from the saddle, did her hands remain in his a few seconds longer than necessary? Was that a friendly smile, or were her lips parted invitingly?

The situation was his own fault. He had built his relationship with her on the stupid idea that she was an older woman, that older women were sexless, and that therefore he could have a comfortable friendship with her. Then, when his body suddenly disagreed that she was sexless, his mind was unable to throw up defenses quickly. Of course, even at that, he was safe if there was no invitation in the brushing of knees and pressure of fingers and the giving of smiles. Now that he had been warned about the way his body reacted, he could control himself. But he didn't want to test his ability to control both himself and Mrs. Wharton.

There was one definite change in the way she was acting. Originally she had been cool and poised in whatever she did. Now, from weekend to weekend, she showed more signs of tension. She dropped things. She stared off into space. Her laugh was pitched too high. She rode the big chestnut horse more recklessly each time they went out.

One Saturday in May, when they had been riding for about half an hour, she deliberately swerved the chestnut away from a break in a stone wall and rode him at a nasty place that was partly masked by bushes. The chestnut made the jump, but Anthony heard the rattle of a stone kicked off the wall. He sent the black horse over the break and galloped up to her.

"You'd better take it easy," he called. "Topaz nicked that wall."

"Good old Tony," she cried. "Always playing it safe. I'll race you to that big tree on the next rise."

He didn't like the wild note in her voice, and he cut in toward her to make a grab for her reins. "I'm tired," he yelled. "Slow down, will you?"

"You're not tired. You're just afraid. If you want to stop me you'll have to catch me first."

His grab at the reins came too late. She nudged the chestnut with her heels and shot away from him. He swore, and sent the black after her. It was useless because she was both a better and a more daring rider than he. She pulled steadily away from him, taking another wall and pounding downhill to a stream and jumping that and heading across a flat meadow toward a rail fence. She was pushing the chestnut too hard. She wasn't giving the horse a chance to time its jumps; she was spurring it at a crazy dead run and hoping the timing would come out right. Or maybe she wasn't even bothering to hope. He yelled at her, but the wind stuffed his words back down his throat. He saw exactly what was going to happen at the rail fence. The timing wasn't going to come out right. The chestnut saw it too. At the last moment the horse broke its run with a horrible stiff-legged slide and sent its rider in a pinwheel spin out of the saddle.

It seemed to take hours to gallop across the field toward the unmoving crumple of clothes and casual sprawl of arms and legs that marked where she had fallen. He got there at last, and leaped off the black and nipped the reins over a post and vaulted the fence. She was lying face down. Her jumping cap, its stiff crown dented, had fallen off, and her hair fanned out around her head like the petals of a black flower. Something he had read flashed crazily into his mind: amateurs should not try to move someone who has been in an accident because they may make an injury worse. Sure, he would leave her lying here and ride two miles and get back two hours later with a doctor. Pretty soon he'd be worrying about the way he was walking on somebody's grass.

He studied the position of her arms and legs, and decided that there couldn't be any complete break or dislocation. He didn't know about her neck. It wasn't twisted, but that didn't mean it wasn't broken. She had hit her head and he couldn't tell how much of the shock the cap had blotted up. He kept his mind busy on practical little thoughts like those, so that it wouldn't go screaming off the way it wanted to do, thinking of the way she had giggled at him that time in the library, of the pink banners in her cheeks the first day they rode together, of her body drifting in a lonely dance around the living room. He arranged her arms and legs carefully and then rolled her over, letting her head come to rest in the crook of his arm.

She was breathing, and her color looked all right. There was a scrape on her forehead but only a tiny swelling under it, and he couldn't feel any lumps on her head that might mean a fracture or a bad concussion. She was wearing a shirt and necktie, and the collar was too tight. He undid the necktie and unbuttoned the top of the shirt. She sighed and took a deep breath and opened her eyes and looked at him.

"Oh, Tony," she said weakly. "I was so bad, wasn't I?"

He couldn't help what happened. She looked soft and young and helpless, and he bent and kissed her. For a moment she rested limply in his arms. Then her body arched toward him and her arms slid around his neck. She was lying in the curve of his left arm; his right hand was free and began wandering over her body. He wanted to call it back but it seemed to be living a life of its own, unconnected with his brain. It traced the curve of her hip and the soft hollow under her ribs and then it moved up and examined the rise and fall of her breast. She trembled. One of her arms left his neck and her hand ripped at the shirt and freed her breast and pulled his head down to it. The nipple quivered and rose like a bud pushing out to meet springtime. He managed to recover a little sanity, perhaps from the simple action of bending his head down and getting some blood back into it. He untangled himself from her arms and sat up and began buttoning her shirt with shaking fingers.

She looked at him, almost pouting, and said, "You don't have to treat me like a little girl who doesn't know what she's doing."

He wanted to explain that he was treating her like Mrs. John Marshall Wharton. But that would sound stuffy, and besides, she might decide to prove that she had never heard of the woman. "Listen," he said, "you may have a broken collarbone and three busted ribs for all I know."

"There's nothing wrong with me but a bad temper, Tony. And you've been the cause of it. Are you really as cold as you've been acting, this last month or so?"

"I'll give you a rundown on my sleepless nights, if you want."

"You really did kiss me all on your own, didn't you?"

"I was afraid I was running out of reasons for sleepless nights. I wanted a new one."

"Sometimes I feel like breaking that stiff neck of yours. Do you think it could bend down once more?"

He had to say something to jolt her out of this. It couldn't be noble and stuffy, and it couldn't be something practical about getting her to a doctor. She was not in a mood to be noble or practical. A good coarse remark might do the trick; she wasn't the kind of person who liked men's room humor. "There's no percentage in this," he said coldly. "Not even a couple of acrobats could go wrong in boots and riding breeches."

"Tony!" she said angrily. Her face flamed and she twisted away from him and sat up. "If you'll get the horses, I can ride back."

They rode home without speaking. Whenever he looked at her she was staring straight ahead, her profile as cold and remote as a face stamped on a silver coin. He had a suspicion, however, that the long dark lashes veiling her eyes sometimes hid a glance that studied him carefully. He wished he knew what to do. Law books didn't tell you how to handle a situation of this type; they merely pointed out the various legal results of letting a thing like this get out of control. If he wanted to consult a book he'd better write his own, and write it fast.

When they got back to the house Mrs. Wharton went to her room, refusing to call a doctor and saying that she merely needed some rest. He and Mr. Wharton ate dinner alone, and worked for a couple of hours on the final pages of the manuscript. His imagination kept telling him that Mr. Wharton was studying him in the same secret way that Mrs. Wharton had done. They ended work early, because Mr. Wharton said he was tired. Anthony took the manuscript to his room and tried to polish it a little, but the Sherman Anti-Trust Act and the problems of bloodless corporations couldn't hold his attention.

His mind examined the case of Lawrence vs. Wharton from all its angles. There seemed to be only three courses of action open to him. He could pretend to be called home by an emergency, and then in one way or another avoid visiting the Whartons again. However, Mr. Wharton was not a fool and might guess the reason for such a sudden break. So he would hurt Mr. Wharton, and of course kill his own chances of being invited to join Morris, Clayton, Biddle and Wharton. He would also—and this was a point to consider—hurt Mrs. Wharton. The second course of action was to follow the prompting of his body and have an affair with her; it would be a wild disorderly business that would leave three lives blowing around like waste paper in the street. The third course of action involved saying loftily to Mrs. Wharton, "How then can I do this great wickedness?" A man named Joseph had used that line once with a certain Mrs. Potiphar, and it hadn't worked out at all well for Joe.

There ought to be a fourth course of action but at the moment he couldn't find it.

It would have been handy if he could have found it, because someone was rapping lightly at his door, and it was possible that Lawrence vs. Wharton might be coming up for trial. He opened the door and saw her standing there. For a moment he was quite willing to lose the case. She was wearing a wisp of negligee over a glimmering black nightgown. Her dark hair with its silver frosting was brushed back in clean pure lines from her face. Her lips were very red and gave him a small trembling smile.

She said in a faint voice, "I thought you might be worrying about me, Tony. Were you?"

"I've been worrying about you for a couple of months," he muttered.

She slipped into his room and closed the door quietly. Women were amazing creatures, he thought; she had probably never done a furtive act in her life, but here she was gliding into his room with what you might call professional skill.

"Tony," she said, "this is awful of me, isn't it? I couldn't help myself. Do you have to stand there looking at me like a judge?"

"I'm trying to think. I—"

"I don't want you to think!" she said with a flash of anger. She moved close and fitted her body against him softly, and rubbed her face against his chest and murmured, "That was an awful thing you said, back in the field after I took that fall. About boots and riding breeches. But I couldn't get it out of my mind. I ... I wish I hadn't had them on."

There was no use lecturing her on the moral and legal points involved. Women never cared much about such things; in general, they only approved of laws and rules of behavior which supported them in what they wanted to do. Right now Mrs. Wharton wanted to go to bed with him. If he hoped to stop her without getting into the Joseph-and-Potiphar's-wife mess, he'd better find something she wanted to do that conflicted with the notion about bed and which was much more important to her. Like all women, Mrs. Wharton was practical and put a high value on security. She admitted having married for security. She was also a Philadelphian, and the last time the top people in Philadelphia had gambled with their security was, he believed, in 1776. And perhaps even then what many of them had fought for was more security. He wondered what would happen if he asked Mrs. Wharton to trade in her security for a series of romps in bed. It might be worth while to find out. No matter what happened, it couldn't make things much worse.

"What do you want?" he said hoarsely. "Just a quick little affair? I'm not going to settle for that."

She looked up at him and pouted slightly. "Why do we have to think about that now, Tony?"

"I've got to. This can't be a hit-and-run thing with me. Will you go away with me? Tonight? For good?"

He was holding her tightly now, and she put her hands on his chest and pushed herself back slightly. "Tony! You're so abrupt and hasty. There are so many things to consider."

"All we have to consider is a divorce."

"But Tony darling, we can't just jump into something like that. At least we have to be civilized and think about John's position and our own. You won't be through law school until next month and then you have your Bar exams and—"

"We'll get along somehow. The hell with law. I can do something else. I know I can't offer you anything but we can rent a little apartment and make out. I know it's asking you to give up a lot, your position and husband and home and all that. I know people will sneer at us and not understand. But—"

She put a hand against his lips. "You don't know what you're saying, my dear. Forget about this for a moment. Can't we just have each other tonight and then think of what's best to do?"

It was very difficult to keep his body under any control, standing pressed against her like that. He let himself slip down onto his knees before her, breaking the contact of their bodies, and stared up at her pale face and said earnestly, "I love you too much for that. I've got to have you completely if I'm going to have you at all. It's bad enough the way it's been the last few months. But I can take that. I can't take the business of having you and then walking off." He stopped, buried his face in the skirt of her negligee, and waited.

The seconds ticked past in a slow, stumbling file. Then at last her hand reached down and moved softly through his hair and touched his hot face. "You're such a sweet boy," she murmured. He looked up at her. There was a smile on her face: a lovely quiet smile with a hint of satisfaction in it.

"But I'm a boy, though. That's what you're thinking."

She patted his cheek. "Of course you are. And I've been silly and selfish. I've got to think of what's best for you, Tony. And this isn't right at all. You have your whole life and career ahead of you, and I'm not going to wreck it. Now stand up, like a good boy, and look at me for a moment."

He got up, feeling his legs tremble as if their muscles had turned into old rubber bands. "You're so lovely," he muttered.

Her laugh had crystal tones in it. "Just knowing that you think so is enough," she said. "I want you to keep your hands at your sides and not touch me, because I don't want you to get upset." She tilted her head and kissed him briefly and gently. "I'm sorry I've been so bad and thoughtless. I hope you'll go on being very fond of me, but keep all the rest for that wonderful girl you'll marry some day. Good night, Tony." She touched his cheek once more, and went out of the room.

He listened to the small final click of the door latch, and went to the bed and threw himself on it face down. Joseph should have tried that with Potiphar's wife. Except, of course, that Joe might not have liked it, if his body had raged at him this way after it was all over ...

Two weeks later he and Mr. Wharton finished the manuscript of the book, and Mr. Wharton said happily, "Well, we did it, didn't we? Nice work, Tony."

"Thank you, sir."

"How do you feel about the book, Tony?"

He smiled a trifle grimly. He felt nothing about the book except relief that it was finished and that he could clear out. In the queer way that human nature worked, now that he had tricked Mrs. Wharton into giving him up, he wanted her more than ever. And there wasn't the slightest chance of getting her. Nowadays she purred around her home and husband and position in society like a mother cat who has just collected her strayed kittens. And inside this purring creature, warm and comforting as the contents of a saucer of cream, was the knowledge that she was lovely and desirable and that she had sacrificed herself for Anthony's good. Nobody was going to rob her of any of those delightful things. He was glad it had worked out so well for her, but he didn't want to hang around yowling on her back fence.

"I think you've done a fine job on the book," he told Mr. Wharton. "There isn't a corporation law firm in the country, or a law school, that doesn't need a book like this."

"That's very flattering, Tony. And of course you've contributed a great deal to it. Now that we're through, I'd like to express my thanks in a practical way. Perhaps the thought of joining Morris, Clayton, Biddle and Wharton has crossed your mind?"

He was yowling on the back fence but they weren't going to throw things at him. He, too, could have a saucer of cream. "Well, naturally, I've thought about it," he said carefully. "But of course I realize you can take your pick of a lot of men."

"I've made my pick," Mr. Wharton said. "You're it, Tony, if you'll accept. Of course Mr. Dickinson has been your preceptor, and in theory he would have the first right to you. But I think he would join us in agreeing that his interest in you is not as deep as it once was. He won't object. But I do want you to understand the conditions under which you'd join us. Perhaps you can figure out a few of them yourself."

"Yes sir, I think I can. You have a big firm. It's a sink or swim proposition."

"Exactly. You'll have to make your own way. I'll do my best for you but it won't be much. I'm going to retire in a year or two, and Mrs. Wharton and I plan to get in some travelling. That's much too soon for me to try to swing any of my clients over to you. It might take ten years to do that. So in a year or two you'll be on your own in a big cold law factory. Are you willing to risk it?"

"The way I look at it," Anthony said, "is that in a big firm it's a tough climb to the top but a mighty nice view if you can get there. I don't want to get to the top in a small firm and find I still can't see over the heads of the crowd. I'll take my chances in a big firm."

"I'll watch your career with interest. Personally I think you'll end up with a mighty nice view."

"Thank you, sir. That's good to hear."

"My reason for saying that," Mr. Wharton said, studying the ceiling, "is that you have an unusual skill in dealing with people, and of course the practice of law is nine-tenths people and one-tenth law. I am not unaware of the fact that there have been certain under-currents in our relationship. Neither you nor I, I'm sure, wish to discuss them. I merely want to say that you have handled yourself very well."

Anthony nodded gravely. Mr. Wharton, too, had an unusual skill in dealing with people. A saucer of cream, and a pat on the head. Perhaps he was being sentimental, but the pat on the head meant a great deal.

8

HE GRADUATED FROM law school in June, took his Bar exams in July, and learned four months later in the columns of the Legal Intelligencer that he had passed. That was in the summer and fall of 1939. Meanwhile untidy things started to happen in Europe. It became evident that people like Second Lieutenant Anthony J. Lawrence, F.A., Res., would not be able to concentrate on law careers very much longer. He had to mark time at Morris, Clayton, Biddle and Wharton, without a chance to make any real progress. Mr. Wharton suggested that he might join the legal staff of one of the alphabet agencies that were spreading like crab grass over Washington. But both of them realized this would only be temporary; he would be called to active duty in the Army sooner or later. Anthony decided that, as long as he had to go, he might as well get in early. Besides it didn't seem fair to let the Army train him for a possible war and then try to back out as soon as one came along. Late in 1940 the telegram came:

> You will proceed on December tenth to Fort Bragg North Carolina reporting to Commanding Officer Field Artillery Replacement Training Center for duty.

He went off feeling slightly heroic, because he was going to get a battery and lead it galloping bravely into action. But it turned out that the Field Artillery was no longer galloping, and anyway there wasn't a battery waiting for him. When Pearl Harbor came, he was on the West Coast nursing a hatch of barrage balloons near San Francisco. Barrage balloons were the sort of things you might produce by crossing a whale with a bucking bronco. It was hard and dull and lonely work. Other officers his age were going overseas. The ones who were both smart and lucky would come back with promotions and two or three rows of fruit salad on their jackets, and for a year or two after the war everybody would try to give them the breaks in business. Lawyers a few years older than he were moving into the War Production Board and other agencies in Washington. They would negotiate contracts with big corporations, and win the respect of business leaders, and when the war ended they would be sitting pretty.

When the war ended he would just be sitting. All his plans for a career were slowly collapsing around him, like so many barrage balloons losing their gas.

As soon as you got the barrage balloons flying nicely at the ends of their cables there wasn't much to do, so he started reading Army Regulations. The Army had a regulation for everything, just as, in a way, Philadelphia did. But of course in Philadelphia the regulations didn't have to be written down because the social organization was old and stable, the personnel didn't change rapidly, and you could absorb things by example and precept. The Army had to write down its regulations because its personnel came from many different places and changed rapidly. The result was the same both in Philadelphia and the Army: an orderly society which seldom moved in the wrong direction and sometimes did not move at all.

Up in the Western Defense Command, a few people heard about the second lieutenant in barrage balloons who read Army Regulations for pleasure. Probably they made jokes about it at first. Then someone found out that he was also a lawyer. By March of 1942 he found himself being detached now and then from barrage balloon duty to act as defense counsel in various courts martial held by the Defense Command. Regular Army officers didn't like that assignment; if they became really interested in a case, they might put up too vigorous a defense and step on the toes of superior officers. When reserve officers were brought in to defend people, they were often incompetent because they didn't know Army Regulations, or else they were brash and clever lawyers who tried to win by any means at all, just as if they were trying a case in a civil court.

From the Army point of view, Second Lieutenant Anthony J. Lawrence was a perfect defense counsel. He knew his ARs. He was aware of the fact that courts martial were not at all like civil courts. He had a knack of making every officer on a court martial feel like a Commanding General, and at the same time he won an amazing number of acquittals. This gave him a reputation not only for knowing Army Regulations but also, and much more important, for knowing how to get around them. By August of 1942 he was promoted to First Lieutenant and transferred to Defense Command headquarters.

Then, in October, a new Corps Commander came boiling out of Washington on his way to the Southwest Pacific Area, snatching up a staff as he moved. He paused in The Presidio in San Francisco, raiding right and left. There was a bright young lawyer in the Defense Command who knew how to get around the ARs, was there? Hell, a man who knew that might be worth a battery some day. Grab the guy. Salt him away in G-1 until we need him. Let's go, goddamit. There's a war on. Who says I can't ask for an officer by name? You want me to take it up with Marshall?

Orders whipped through the purple ink of the mimeographs like bullets through a machine gun, and First Lieutenant Anthony J. Lawrence, F.A., was on his way to Port Moresby.

The new Corps Commander was Maj. Gen. Buckley D. "Buck" Brimmer, and Anthony worked quietly on the staff of his 19th Corps while the Buna and Gona battles were fought on the north coast of New Guinea. Nobody had told him why he had been grabbed for overseas duty, so he was startled one day in January of 1943 to be called in for a conference with General Brimmer. The CG was sitting in his Quonset hut before a wooden field table, scowling at a sheaf of papers as if they were soldiers who didn't know how to salute. He was a solid man who had once played a lot of fullback at The Point, and he had a red face that stubbornly refused to take on the yellow color that everyone else picked up from the atabrine. Nobody else was in the hut except his aide, Major Thomas Strang, a lean West Pointer who had been in the Class of 1936.

"Lawrence, sir," Anthony said. "The General sent for me."

General Brimmer glanced at him, turned to his aide. "You're sure this is the one, are you?"

"Yes sir," Major Strang said. "It was back in The Presidio and you—"

"You don't have to tell me," the General said. "I never forget these things. Somebody said there was a first lieutenant in the Defense Command who knew how to get around regulations, and

I said grab him and salt him away in G-1 until we needed him. All I want to know is, is this the man?"

"Yes sir, he's the one."

"All right. I just don't want to waste time. Pull up a chair and sit down, Lawrence. You know Major Strang, my aide? Now as I said I grabbed you because somebody said you knew how to get around the ARs. I got a problem for you. What do you know about Major General Oliphant?"

This was pretty high-level stuff, and Anthony decided he'd better be up on his toes. For a Corps Commander to ask a first lieutenant about a division commander was like handing you a grenade with the pin out. Actually he knew a lot about Major General Oliphant, just as he knew a lot about General Brimmer and Major Strang. He liked finding out all he could about people and their motives. But he thought he would move carefully, and try to hand the grenade back to the CG.

"Well, sir," he said, "General Oliphant is commander of the so-called Thunderhead Division, which got its name back in the First World War. National Guard, of course. I believe it was mobilized late in 1940, along with General Oliphant. The General is a big feed and grain man in his home state, and the National Guard has been his lifelong hobby. It was probably a dream come true for him when he found himself commanding his state's National Guard division when it was mobilized. Of course now there are a lot of out-of-state draftees in the division, but it's still about fifty percent home state in its personnel. That's about all, sir."

General Brimmer looked at his aide, jerked a thumb at Anthony, and growled, "This guy knows a lot and says goddam little."

"General," Strang said, looking in dislike at Anthony, "I don't trust these cautious guys."

"It's all right," the General said. "He's walking on eggs and I don't blame him. Now look, Lawrence, nothing I say is to go beyond this room. Question. If you were in my shoes, how would you get rid of General Oliphant?"

Anthony allowed himself to grin. In one way that was taking a liberty, but it showed he wasn't too cautious. "General," he said, in an almost familiar tone, "are you waiting for me to look at you wide-eyed and ask why don't you just relieve him from command?"

"I was waiting for it, all right," the General said. "And if you'd given me that crap seriously, tomorrow you'd have been laundry officer on Snafu Island. Now go ahead. And don't worry about breaking a few of those eggs you're walking on."

"Sir, I'd like to feel my way a little bit. You've probably thought of all these things but I'll have to run them through the meat grinder.

Would GHQ take him on? I mean, would General MacArthur ask him to do some terribly important job, like cementing our relations with the Aussies back in Brisbane?"

"Yeah, Mac would do that for me."

"But you've tried it, though, haven't you, General? And you found that General Oliphant balked?"

"Yes, goddam it. What's your next try?"

"Sir, this New Guinea climate is very unhealthy. Men pick up diseases they hardly know they have, and get dragged down without quite realizing it. If General Oliphant were up here for a conference, and if your staff doctor happened to notice a queer color in his eyes, it would be natural for the doc to insist on an immediate physical exam. Then if he found some very serious things wrong, you'd be forced, much against your will, to send General Oliphant Stateside to recover."

"It won't work," the General said. "He's onto that trick. If he hadn't been, they'd have snatched the Thunderhead out from under him back in maneuvers in Louisiana. The son of a bitch has a Mayo Clinic hotshot in his division who checks him all the time and keeps giving him a clean bill. If I tried your idea it just ends up as a squabble between doctors. What else you got?"

"General, you're not only making me walk on eggs but also you're making me do it in the dark. I'd have a better chance of coming up with something if you'd give me the picture first."

Major Strang said abruptly, "You National Guard, Lawrence?"

"No sir. Reserves."

"I could have told you that, Tom," the General said. "Now lay off the lieutenant. He's doing all right. O.K., Lawrence, here's your picture." He thrust the pile of papers across the desk. "Don't read the whole mess, just enough to get the idea."

Anthony scanned them rapidly. "Wow!" he said.

"Yeah, wow," the General said bitterly. "I've drafted orders relieving him from duty for failure to carry out orders, failure to press home an attack, God knows what all. If he demands a court martial I got the papers ready. All right, that gives you the picture."

"If the General will pardon me for asking," Anthony said, "can you prove those charges?"

"Damn right I can. Oliphant treats that division of his like an only child. He's soft with them. They're boys from his own state and he doesn't want them killed. Goddam it, people get killed in a war. The softer they are, the more of them get killed. Oliphant had that Lona River job to do. He didn't push home the attack because his boys were getting killed coming up against those dug-in Jap positions. So he got a mess of casualties and still didn't force the

Lona River, and the Aussies had to do it for us and they'll never let us forget it. Oh, I can prove it, all right."

"Unfortunately, sir," Anthony said, "you won't be court-martialing General Oliphant. You'll be putting the National Guard on trial."

"You're telling me."

"In addition, sir, you'll be putting his state on trial. As I understand it, there are three war correspondents out here from big newspapers in his state. General Oliphant treats them like kings. They think he's wonderful."

"Goddam it, Lawrence, I know all that. I didn't call you in so we could all cry on each other's shoulders."

"Sir, I'm just trying to chop away the underbrush so we'll have a clear field of fire. General Oliphant is also one of the few division commanders who believes in public relations. His PRO setup is the best in any division out here. They send back bales of hometown stories to papers in his state. Every time a private gets upped to Pfc., a story goes back to the kid's hometown paper saying, 'Major General Arthur C. Oliphant announced today that Private Elmer H. Caskie, of 223 South Sycamore Street, Midland City, has been promoted to Private First Class. Pfc. Caskie is a member of the state's famous Thunderhead Division, now fighting in the Southwest Pacific Area under General Oliphant's command.' Sir, I strongly recommend against a court martial. General Oliphant's home state will scream murder, and the Pentagon will ask what size noose you'd like around your neck."

"Lawrence, you have now arrived at the point I'd reached just before I called you in. O.K. I don't dare get rid of him in any regulation way. If you're the hotshot they said you were, back in The Presidio, tell me how to get around the regulations."

Anthony fumbled through his memory. A little less than three years ago he had been backed into much the same type of corner. He could almost hear once again Mrs. Wharton's soft rap on his bedroom door, and feel the creeping chill of panic as he considered and vetoed all the usual courses of action. "General," he said, "when you've got to get rid of somebody and the usual ways won't work, you can try to trick the person into getting rid of himself."

"Yeah? How?"

"Well, sir, General Oliphant wants very much to go on commanding the Thunderhead Division. We've got to find something he wants to do even more. Have you any ideas?"

"Sure," the General growled. "He wants to be Governor of his state. He'll swap his division for that."

"Do you know when the next election is?"

"Next fall. The primary is this spring."

206

"Sir, why doesn't he go home and run for Governor?"

General Brimmer got up and began stamping around the hut like a bulldozer with a loose track. "Oh, goddam it, goddam it, goddam it," he said furiously. "That's been my only hope and nothing came of it. Here he is, a natural politician, a shoo-in to win, a guy who's invented an entirely new method of baby-kissing, and not a single bastard in his state has asked him to run for Governor. I guess they're glad he's tied down over here so he can't come home and take the governorship away from them. I've had friends of mine in Washington checking into it, and there hasn't been a whisper about getting him to run. All right. Now what do you say?"

Anthony braced himself. He had done all right so far. He had proved he could think the problem through as well as General Brimmer had done. Now he could shrug and back out. But he liked this big red-faced man who was clanking up and down the room. The guy was trying to do a job, and Oliphant was messing it up. So he ought to try to help. A plan that might work had slipped into his mind, along with thoughts of what would happen if he tried it and it went wrong.

"General," he said, "we ought to remedy that oversight on the part of the politicians. We ought to start a Draft-Oliphant-for-Governor campaign."

General Brimmer stopped as if he had just run over a land mine. "Godamighty!" he gasped. "You don't know what you're saying!"

"Yes, sir. I know all the regulations barring Army officers from engaging in politics."

"Um. How would you go about this, Lawrence?"

"Sir, do you think you should know? If anything goes wrong, you'll have to cut my throat. The less involved you are, the better."

"You serious about this?"

"Yes sir."

"How long will it take?"

"General, it will either work fast or not at all."

"Do you want any help from me?"

"I'll need some orders detaching me for temporary duty, sir, and travel orders."

General Brimmer turned to his aide. "Give him whatever he wants, Tom. And don't get involved, because you're too close to me. All right, Lawrence. You're on your own."

Anthony left the hut with Major Strang, and had orders cut which detached him for temporary duty and gave him top travel priority by air throughout the theater. Strang handed him the orders and said, "Sorry I snapped at you a few times, Lawrence. I read you wrong."

"That's all right, Major."

"The Old Man's a great guy," Strang said. "If he wasn't, I'd have yelled long ago to get back to troop duty. If he has to cut your throat, he'll be sorry as hell about it."

"As I hang out the day's wash on Snafu Island," Anthony said, "that will be nice to remember."

He jeeped to the Buna air strip and grabbed the first plane for Port Moresby on the south coast of New Guinea. The men he wanted to see might not be there, but it was the forward echelon of GHQ and a logical place to start looking, and he didn't dare get people curious by sending radio queries. When he reached Moresby he hunted up the Public Relations Office of GHQ and made a few quiet inquiries. He learned that one of the war correspondents from General Oliphant's state was in Brisbane and two were in Moresby. That night, timing himself carefully, he hung around the PRO mess hall until he could slip into a vacant chair beside Bill Cleamer, war correspondent of the *Menapolis Herald* in General Oliphant's home state. He introduced himself and started a casual conversation with Cleamer.

"You're new around here, aren't you?" Cleamer said. "Are you one of the censors or something?"

"I'm just visiting," Anthony said. "I'm from G-1 at the Nineteenth Corps."

"G-1, huh? That's intelligence, isn't it?"

"No. G-1 is Personnel. G-2 is Intelligence."

"Oh. I don't know the Army set-up very well. Not that it matters about strategy and tactics and all that. My paper didn't send me here to compete with the Associated Press. My paper wants human interest stuff. And what I say is, if a guy can cover people on a courthouse beat, he can cover people in the Army."

"That's the right way to look at things. We have your state's division in the Nineteenth Corps, haven't we? The Thunderhead?"

"Yeah. Great bunch. I got some swell human interest stuff about the way the boys in the Thunderhead busted through the Japs on the Lona River. Anything cooking now up north?"

"It's kind of quiet," Anthony said. "Mostly mopping up. Of course I never hear much about operations in G-1. We just deal with people, like you do, from privates right up to generals like Oliphant. Well, to be exact, G-1 doesn't really do much when it comes to generals. A message came in from Washington last night on General Oliphant and all we did was file away an information copy. The action copy went to General Brimmer. Listen, do you think it would be right to let a guy out of the Army so he can run for governor of a state, especially when he's commanding a division?"

Cleamer choked suddenly on his food. Then he glanced around the mess hall, perhaps looking to see how close a correspondent named Johns, of the *Midland City News*, was sitting. "Well, it all depends," Cleamer said in a very casual voice. "You're talking about General Oliphant?"

"Yeah. You probably know all about it. It's that quiet little movement back in your state to draft him to run for Governor. They're keeping it under wraps because I suppose it's a touchy thing to talk about grabbing a division commander from a combat zone to run for Governor. You must know him well. Would he make a good Governor?"

"Jeez," Cleamer said, "come to think of it, he'd make a hell of a good Governor. That is, I don't mean I've just thought of it, because like you say a war correspondent has to know those things, but I mean I've just thought of it in connection with him maybe getting out of the Army. Do you think he's going to get out?"

"I wouldn't know. This message I saw, it was one of those top level things from the Pentagon. I guess some big shots from your state have been putting the heat on the Administration about breaking him loose to run for Governor, and the Administration took it up with the Joint Chiefs and they messaged GHQ asking what the hell they should do about it. What I think is, unless a guy is badly needed back home, he ought to stick to his job out here."

"Yeah, but a guy can serve his country in more ways than one. The home front is important too. I wonder what General Oliphant thinks about it?"

"He may not even know," Anthony said. "This wasn't a message to him. For all I know, what with him doing such a good job commanding the Thunderhead Division, they might try to quiet things down back home so they can keep him. Wouldn't you handle it that way if you were the top brass out here?"

"It's hard to say. You don't know what they're going to do, huh?"

"No. This is too high level for me. Say, I just happened to think, maybe I shouldn't have told you all this. Not that there's any story in it, of course, but I shouldn't be talking about the messages we see in G-1. Still and all, I suppose you war correspondents get the inside dope on a lot of things, so anything I've said is safe with you."

"Oh, sure," Cleamer said. "Most of us know more of what's happening out here than a lot of high-ranking officers do. Well, I got to run along and do some work. Nice to have met you, Lawrence."

After Cleamer left, Anthony waited a few minutes and then walked to the press room. Yes, there was Cleamer jabbing busily at his portable.

Now the problem was to make sure that Cleamer's story got through censorship. Previously Anthony had not had any direct dealings with the Public Relations Office, but it was an interesting side of the Army and he had learned as much about it as he could. In the Southwest Pacific Area, press censorship was one of the duties of the PRO. And, unlike most other theaters, the Southwest Pacific censored for accuracy and general policy as well as for military security. The story Cleamer was writing might worry the censor who got it. But there wouldn't be any directives covering such a story, so the censor might take it up with the Chief News Censor or the Exec of the Public Relations Office or the PRO himself. Anthony thought he'd better tag one of the bases in that chain of command.

He asked some questions and learned that the PRO, Colonel Thompson, was in Moresby at press headquarters. Thompson was said to be a sharp guy: Regular Army, of course, but not a West Pointer. It was good not to have to deal with a West Pointer in a matter like this, because a lot of them thought public relations was something to be avoided, like scrub typhus. According to report, Thompson had been in the Philippines and rated high with MacArthur. So Thompson was a good bet both to figure out the right decision and to have guts enough to make it.

He went into Colonel Thompson's office and introduced himself. Thompson asked what he could do for him. That was a good sign; plenty of Regular Army colonels would never think of asking what they could do for a first lieutenant.

Anthony said, "Colonel, if one of your censors gets a story that has some political angles in it but no military security of any kind, what would he do with it?"

"He's supposed to use his judgment. He might pass it. He might bring it to me. Why do you ask?"

"I think one of your censors is going to get a story like that pretty soon. I'm hoping it will be cleared."

Colonel Thompson was a sort of bird-like guy, but much more hawk than canary. He got a look in his sharp black eyes that said he was ready to pounce. "That's an interesting thing to tell me, Lawrence," he said briskly. "Are you here just representing yourself, or somebody else?"

"In a way, just myself, Colonel."

"That would make you pretty stupid, Lawrence. You don't look stupid. So I don't believe it. You say you're from G-1 of the Nineteenth Corps. How come you're back here in Moresby? What sort of orders are you carrying?"

Anthony dug out a copy of his orders. "They're a bit vague, Colonel," he said.

Thompson glanced at them. "Vague, hell. They let you go any damn place you please for as long as you want, within theater limits. That's quite a set of orders. Now what's the deal?"

"Colonel, the less you know about it, the better. Would it be out of line to ask you to let things ride that way, until and unless the story comes in to you?"

Thompson glared at him for a moment, then chuckled. "Lieutenant," he said, "you sound like a red alert to me. I ought to be sending out the alarm right now for that story. But I'll take a chance. If it gets past my boys, O.K. If they bring it in here, we'll see. You can wait if you like."

Anthony thanked him, and settled down to wait. This was the key part of the operation. It had been easy to trick Cleamer into writing the story; all he'd had to do was pretend to let the story slip out. But nobody was going to feed birdseed to this hawk of a PRO. He waited. Fifteen minutes went by. Twenty. Then a tall black-haired first lieutenant came in. He had the crossed sabers of the cavalry on the collar of his suntans and the big First Cav patch on his shoulder, and he looked like the kind of guy who would have enjoyed riding with Custer.

"Got a story here I'd like you to see, Colonel," he said, holding out two typewritten pages.

Thompson read the story quickly. Finally he pushed the pages across the desk to Anthony. "This it?" he asked.

Anthony began reading. At first he had a little trouble, because the dispatch was written in the choppy cablese that correspondents used in order to save radio and cable tolls. It began: "Brass here hints politicos homeward casing Oliphant governorship. Reported topmost Washington asks can fightingest division spare Lona hero ..." Probably that would be translated into: "It was learned on high authority here today that top political leaders of the state are exploring the possibility of drafting Major General Arthur C. Oliphant, Commanding General of the Thunderhead Division, to run for Governor in the coming spring primaries. The movement, it was understood, has reached the point of high-level queries from Washington as to whether General Oliphant, the hero of the Lona River battle, could be spared from the state's hard-fighting division ..."

It went on like that for both pages, hinting, speculating, guessing. Without actually saying so it gave the impression that FDR, Marshall and MacArthur were devoting their closest attention to it and trying to decide what would be best for the country. The dispatch ended with a lot of stuff about how the division under General Oliphant's heroic leadership had smashed the impregnable Jap lines along the Lona River, opening up the whole northeast coast of New Guinea for further Allied advances.

"Yes sir," Anthony said, keeping his face blank. "This is it."

Colonel Thompson drummed his fingers on the desk in machine-gun bursts. "I could query General MacArthur on this," he said. "It certainly implies that he's involved, doesn't it?"

"Yes sir," Anthony said. "But of course it doesn't say so directly. I wouldn't urge you to check it with him."

"Lieutenant," Thompson said, "this is one of our censors, Lieutenant John L. York, Jr. Jack, this is Lieutenant Lawrence. He's from G-1 of the Nineteenth Corps. By an odd coincidence he was here waiting to see if this story would come in."

"Hello, Lawrence," York said. Then he grinned at Thompson and said, "For once I was smart, huh, Colonel? This thing looked hot to me. Bill Cleamer's out there bleeding all over my desk, trying to get it through."

Thompson nodded. "It'd be a big story for his paper. Look, Lawrence, would I have to hunt very far to find the high authority, the reliable source, the theater spokesman who cannot be identified, who gave this yarn to Cleamer?"

"No sir," Anthony said. "You wouldn't have to hunt very far."

"Jack," the Colonel said, turning back to his censor, "this Lieutenant Lawrence has the damnedest set of orders. Corps Head-quarters is letting him go anywhere in the theater and stay as long as he wants, with his mission confidential but not specified."

The young Cavalry lieutenant said gravely, "I guess they want to make sure that the hero of the Lona River gets everything that's coming to him. I'll have to tell those Aussie correspondents to quit writing stories about how they saved our skins on the Lona River."

"If General Oliphant went home," the Colonel said gravely, "it would be a great loss to the theater. Please don't misquote me. I'm talking about the Southwest Pacific Theater, not the professional stage. However, our loss would be the country's gain, wouldn't it, Jack?"

"Yes, Colonel. I felt that way all along."

The Colonel frowned. "Well then for God's sake don't bring stories in to me that any damn censor ought to have brains enough to pass. As far as I'm concerned, you're going to do what you think is right, and you never asked for my opinion."

"Oh hell," York said disgustedly. "I mean, oh hell, sir. Why is it always the lieutenants who have to stick their necks out?" He took the story and marched grumpily out of the room.

"Goddam poor discipline we have around here," Colonel Thompson said. "Have to do something about it some day. Well, Lawrence, anything else I can do for you?"

"Can I hang around a few days, Colonel, and see what happens? Might be some interesting developments."

"Sure. Ask Jack York to take care of you. I won't be able to help. As a matter of fact, I left for Brisbane a couple hours ago, so I didn't even meet you. Good luck, Lawrence. I hope we're about to contribute a Governor to the country's welfare."

Anthony settled down in PRO headquarters to see what was going to happen. As it turned out, things moved fast. Anthony was able to keep track of them because the Army controlled all press communications, and Lieutenant York grabbed copies of incoming messages and outgoing stories for him. With a little deduction you could get a good picture of the course of events.

The first morning after the story went to the *Menapolis Herald*, Cleamer took off for headquarters of the Thunderhead Division. Early that afternoon a message came in from Midland City, in General Oliphant's home state, for Johns of the *Midland City News*. It was from the editor of the *Midland City News* and it said bitterly: MENAPOLIS HERALD BANNERING CLEAMER STORY ON SECRET DRAFT OLIPHANT GOVERNORSHIP STOP WHY YOU KEEPING IT SECRET TOO QUESTION MARK FILE STORY SOONEST. Johns caught the next plane for the Buna strip and Thunderhead Division headquarters. Next came queries from the AP and UP to their correspondents, and traffic to the Buna strip took another jump. Then, over Signal Corps radio circuits, stories began to come back from Thunderhead Division headquarters. First General Oliphant told Cleamer of the *Menapolis Herald* that it was all news to him and that his place was at the fighting front but that naturally he was honored to be considered for the state's highest office.

Then came Johns' dispatch to the *Midland City News*, beginning: "Oliphant denied ambitions governorward today exclusive interview this correspondent but readiest bow popular decision ..." Next came the AP and UP stories in which General Oliphant rather unwillingly admitted that certain quiet approaches had been made to him which he had of course rejected, because it would take a real grassroots movement to convince him that his duty lay elsewhere than with the Thunderhead.

Meanwhile, far south in Brisbane, the third correspondent from General Oliphant's state—Sundstrom, of the *New Oslo Times*— had been caught far off base. Knowing that he couldn't reach Oliphant in time to compete with Cleamer and Johns and the wire services, he was furiously filing stories from GHQ. All he could get from GHQ were flat denials of any pressure from Washington to release Oliphant. But Sundstrom, who had covered the State

Legislature at home, knew how to make stories out of flat denials, and managed to give the impression that GHQ knew much more than it would admit and that the pressure was growing every hour.

Anthony could not, of course, trace exactly what was happening in General Oliphant's home state, but on the basis of messages from editors to their correspondents he could guess at it. Political leaders in the state had obviously been badly jolted by the first dispatches. A secret move had developed to draft the state's war hero, and they had been left out of it. Worse than that, Oliphant would be hard to beat. There was, however, one saving feature. The draft movement had been launched so secretly that nobody knew exactly who was in it. So who could prove you were a liar if you stepped out in public and claimed you were one of the top political leaders who had started the secret draft? Why, you could take over the movement from whoever had launched it! All over the state, that white-hot truth burned into the minds of party leaders: the incumbent Governor, one of the state's U.S. Senators, the Speaker of the Assembly, assorted city and county bosses. A dozen of them came out for Oliphant with almost military snap and precision, like a drill team counting off by the numbers. Then, noting in surprise how much company they had, they broke ranks and began a wild scramble to get word to Oliphant that each was the original and most important leader of his cause.

Anthony spent a week in Moresby watching all this develop. It was an interesting lesson in practical politics and he enjoyed it. He realized, of course, that he deserved very little credit. Chance had stacked up a lot of firewood and kindling, and all he had done was walk around the pile and touch a match to the right spot. He said goodby to the Cavalry lieutenant and went back to Nineteenth Corps headquarters and reported to Major Strang.

"Major," he said, "I think the show is on the road."

Strang came out from behind his desk as if shot from a bazooka, and grabbed his hand and shook it. "Lawrence," he said, "it's done better than that. It's reached Broadway and it's a smash hit. Take a look at this message that came in a couple of hours ago."

Well, there it was. A week ago he had pretended that such a message existed. Now it did: "FROM MARSHALL FOR MAC-ARTHUR FOR BRIMMER. TREMENDOUS PRESSURE DEVEL-OPING TO DRAFT MAJOR GENERAL ARTHUR C. OLIPHANT TO RUN FOR GOVERNOR OF HIS HOME STATE. YOUR REC-OMMENDATIONS DESIRED AS TO WHETHER HE CAN BE RELEASED FROM ACTIVE DUTY WITHOUT DAMAGE TO WAR EFFORT."

Major Strang said gleefully, "Three guesses what the recommendation will be."

"I hope you'll be a bit reluctant, and make General Oliphant beg for it," Anthony said.

"Indeed we will. General Brimmer is practicing a heartbreak right now."

Two weeks later, Anthony was permitted to watch a small ceremony at Corps headquarters, during which General Brimmer awarded the Distinguished Service Medal to Major General Oliphant and wished him all kinds of luck back in the States. After the ceremony was over and General Oliphant had left, Major Strang caught Anthony's arm. "Don't run away," he said. "We have another little ceremony."

He led Anthony into General Brimmer's office. In a few moments General Brimmer came in and said to his aide, "All right, Tom. Read it."

Major Strang took out a paper and read: "Citation for Bronze Star Medal. First Lieutenant Anthony J. Lawrence, Army of the United States. For meritorious achievement in connection with military operations against the enemy in the Southwest Pacific Area from 28 October 1942 to 19 January 1943. As an officer attached to G-1 of the Nineteenth Corps he was assigned a personnel problem of the most important nature. By his exceptional ability, broad knowledge of human nature, and sound judgment, First Lieutenant Lawrence contributed immeasurably to the success of combat operations in the Nineteenth Corps Area."

General Brimmer stepped forward and pinned the Bronze Star Medal on Anthony's shirt, and shook his hand. "Congratulations, Captain," he said.

Anthony gulped. "Did you say Captain, sir?"

"Yep. Strang has the order promoting you. Well, that winds it up. I'm only sorry about one thing. Do you know what I'm talking about, Tom?"

Major Strang grinned. "Yes sir. The wrong guy got the DSM."

9

DURING HIS LIFE Anthony had never really had a close friend of his own age. For a time, back in the Friday Afternoon Dancing Class, he had thought of Eddie Eakins as a friend. There had been Creighton and Arnold on the Franklin Academy football team. At Penn Law he had spent some time with a classmate from South Philadelphia named Louis Donetti. They had been completely unsuited to each other in background and temperament, and they were always on the opposite sides of arguments, and it was graduation time before they realized that they had actually been friends instead of enemies. But none of these friendships had been close.

Now, in the Southwest Pacific, he and Major Strang became close friends. It was one of those friendships that can only happen in an all-male society, under pressure of an activity, like war, which dominates every thought. One moment they were strangers. The next, after going through the Oliphant business together, they were brothers. They began hunting each other up at mess time. They arranged to share quarters. They played fierce two-handed games of gin rummy. They pooled shirts and beer and the occasional bottles of liquor that came through on the fat-cat planes from Australia. They went off on leave together and found that Australian girls were just as friendly and easy to please as everybody claimed; they headed back from Brisbane feeling heartbroken, and forgot all about it as soon as one of them brought out the gin rummy cards on the plane trip north.

From Anthony's point of view it was an easy friendship to maintain, because he always knew exactly how Tom Strang would react to any situation. West Point turned out three basic types of officers: the thinkers, the doers, and the sitters—the latter being officers whose main ambition was to stay out of trouble. You could get various combinations of the three types, and you could get one type in various degrees of intensity; in the case of the sitters, lack of intensity. Tom Strang was a doer, high intensity. He was as direct and uncomplicated as a bullet coming out of a gun. You could win his respect either by doing things as well as or better than he could, or by proving you were a thinker. After the Oliphant affair, Tom looked on Anthony the way an Indian brave might have looked on the tribe's medicine man.

At first Anthony wondered why General Brimmer kept a guy like Tom at headquarters instead of on troop duty. He learned the answer after General Brimmer promoted Tom to lieutenant colonel and made him G-3 of the Nineteenth Corps, and brought in Anthony as his own aide.

"Tom keeps nagging me all the time for troop duty," General Brimmer told Anthony. "Maybe this will keep him quiet for a while. If I can ever get him to realize that there's more to war than leading a charge, he'll have a chance of going far. Not that he'll ever be a guy who plays all the angles, but he could develop into another Georgie Patton. The Army could use more guys like Georgie. He really rolled them up in Sicily, didn't he? Don't say anything to Tom about this, understand? But whenever you get a chance, keep selling him on how he needs more experience in staff work."

So 1943 went by, with the Nineteenth Corps making leapfrog assaults along the north coast of New Guinea, and with Anthony and Tom becoming more necessary to each other every day.

In January of 1944 came a directive from the Joint Chiefs of Staff which, to every officer in the Southwest Pacific Area, meant that Washington favored the Navy and was more interested in bottling up MacArthur than in beating the Japs. The Joint Chiefs drew a line on the map north of New Guinea. Above that line, only the Central Pacific forces under Admiral Nimitz could operate. Below it, the Southwest Pacific forces under MacArthur could go on playing leapfrog, completely and forever shut off from Japan and Formosa and the Philippines. The staff of General Brimmer's Nineteenth Corps couldn't have felt gloomier about the directive if the Army had just been sold to the Marines.

A few days after the JCS directive arrived, there was a staff meeting in General Brimmer's headquarters to discuss the next leapfrog operation. Tom Strang, as G-3, sketched the operation on an overlay of a map which showed the north coast of New Guinea. It was a leapfrog landing which would take them another hundred miles along the coast to Salananda. It would pinch off ten or fifteen thousand Jap troops. Strang mapped the convoy route, and drew in the blue symbols of the Nineteenth Corps assault units and the red symbols of the Japs. He showed by dotted lines the Jap air raids that could be expected from the Royalty Islands, a group of smallish islands about two hundred miles north of Salananda. Everybody on the staff knew the Royalties well and unfavorably; Vals and Zekes and Bettys from those islands had been working them over recently.

General Brimmer said irritably, "Can't we neutralize that goddam airfield? There's only one in the Royalties, isn't there?"

"Yes sir, there's only one," Tom said. "The Fifth Air Force flies a mission against it once a week, but we can't really neutralize it, not with the limited strikes we can make. Air Intelligence says the Japs don't base their planes on that field. They stage them in for a raid, and fly them out afterward. So nearly all the time there's nothing to hit but the runway and fuel dumps. They can repair the runway in a couple of hours, and the fuel dumps are dispersed through coconut groves around the airfield."

G-2 said, "Nothing will knock out that airfield short of taking it, General. The Navy's going to hit the Royalties this summer, as you know."

"Yeah," Brimmer growled. "The whole Pacific fleet, two divisions of Marines and one Army division. Meanwhile we take it on the chin from Jap planes for five more months. Well, I guess that's all we can do. Your Salananda operation looks all right, Tom. Think the Thunderhead Division can handle it?"

"Yes sir. They're a real scrappy outfit these days."

General Brimmer stared glumly at the map for a minute, while everybody waited for his decision. "Oh hell," he muttered. "What does it all add up to? Boxed in the way we are by that goddam directive, we're like a halfback who's running wide but can't turn the end. All we do is run straight along the coast of New Guinea and beyond that we hit the out-of-bounds markers where the Southeast Asia Command starts. We can't make a yard across the line of scrimmage, because Nimitz owns everything up north. Jeez, I wish we could hit those goddam Royalties."

"They're in the Central Pacific Theater, General," Tom said.

"I know, goddam it."

Anthony had been attending the meeting as General Brimmer's aide. He hadn't been saying anything, but now an idea was stirring in his mind. In the Army people often got boxed into jobs or places that they didn't like. He himself had been boxed into a dull job in barrage balloons. He got out of it by chance: first by studying Army Regulations, then by serving as defense counsel on courts martial, and finally by winning a reputation as a guy who knew how to get around regulations. It had been a one-step-at-a-time process. Sometimes you could get out of tough situations in the Army that way, whereas if you tried to jump out, somebody would crack down on you. Right now the whole Southwest Pacific command was in a box like the barrage balloons. He wondered if they could sneak out of it step by step.

He cleared his throat and said, "General, may I make a few comments?"

General Brimmer frowned at him, probably thinking that aides should be seen and not heard at staff meetings. "Yes?" he said impatiently. "What is it?"

"General," Anthony said, "in regard to the Royalties, there's nothing in the directive to prevent you from reconnoitering them."

"Oh, what the hell, Tony," General Brimmer said. "We reconnoiter them all the time."

"That's by air, General. I'm talking about a reconnaissance by troops. You could do that, couldn't you?"

"I could send in a platoon or so. But where does that get us?"

"General, if you're permitted to reconnoiter at all, there's nothing in Army Regulations or the Field Manuals to prevent a reconnaissance in force. Let's say, a force strong enough to raid that airfield and knock off the fuel dumps. The field is five miles inland from the main beaches, but only a mile inland from a tiny beach on the other coast. If you hit that little beach with a battalion, without warning the Japs by a series of air strikes and a big naval bombardment, the battalion might break through to the airfield. We all know how the unexpected will knock the Japs off balance."

The General was staring at him now, eyes as hot as jets from a flame-thrower. "Yeah?" he snapped. "Go on. Go on."

"Well, sir, if the battalion actually does take the airfield by surprise, would you pull it out? That airfield is the only thing of military value in the Royalties."

The G-2 officer broke in angrily, "Now look, Captain, our reports show that there are at least twenty thousand Japs in the Royalties. You want to throw one battalion against them?"

Anthony said, "If ten thousand of those Japs are on smaller islands in the Royalties, how are they going to reach the main island if we're in there with PT boats and destroyers?"

"You've still got ten thousand Japs against one battalion."

"The Japs will be scattered at first," Anthony said. "They'll be off balance. We all know they have lousy communications, and probably their signal center is at the airfield. If we knock that out, it'll take twenty-four hours before they can mount a coordinated major attack."

"And then," the G-2 officer said, "goodby battalion."

"What the hell," Anthony said, "is General Brimmer going to take that lying down? Not even the Navy would expect him to do that. At the moment when he stages a reconnaissance in force of the Royalties, he's ready for the Salananda landing. The whole Thunderhead Division is combat loaded. All he has to do is divert them north to the Royalties."

There was silence in the room. Men glanced at each other, looked away quickly. At the field desk, General Brimmer put a big hand up to his face and kneaded it into Halloween grimaces. Nobody had to spell it out any further. What it amounted to was a complete and utter flouting of the directive of the Joint Chiefs of Staff. It was one of those situations that might come up once or twice in the career of an officer. If you got away with it, your career was made. If you flopped, they might give you a chance to retire rather than face a court martial.

"Five months from now," General Brimmer said softly, "the whole Pacific Fleet, two assault divisions of Marines and one Central Pacific Army division are going to hit the Royalties. And we're talking of hitting them without air preparation, without a fleet bombardment, and with one goddam battalion."

Nobody said anything.

"If it worked," the General muttered, "we'd never hear anything more of that Navy fence north of us. The way back to the Philippines would be open."

Nobody spoke.

"One goddam battalion," Brimmer muttered.

Tom Strang wheeled back to his map overlay. He made a quick arc with blue crayon starting at their present base and ending at Salananda on the New Guinea coast. The letters "D-Day" leaped out in blue on the overlay at Salananda. Then the crayon raced north from their base up to the Royalties: a harsh blue line cutting across the Navy fence. The symbol "D minus 3" jumped out at the little beach in the Royalties. The crayon snapped suddenly: a pinpoint of sound in the quiet room.

General Brimmer said quietly, "I'll buy it."

For three weeks the Nineteenth Corps staff worked on top secret plans, with headquarters sealed off as carefully against the Navy and the Aussies as against the Japs. Nobody was permitted to leave except General Brimmer, who made a flying visit to Moresby where he may have seen MacArthur. The Thunderhead Division began combat loading for the Salananda landing. Meanwhile Task Force X was brought together. It was a little gem of a force: two crack rifle companies and two heavy weapons platoons from other Nineteenth Corps divisions, a Ranger platoon that could work in the dark with knives, and a team of frog men for underwater demolition. They began practicing assault landings on a quiet area of the New Guinea coast, under the impression that they were to spearhead the Salananda landing.

Tom Strang and his staff in Operations worked out plans down to the last round of ammunition. D-Day was the Salananda landing. D-Day minus three was the Royalties landing. At sunset on D minus four, there was to be an air strike at the Royalties' airfield; nothing big, nothing startling, just the regular weekly strike, but timed to give the Japs a lot of work after dark. H-Hour at the Royalties was dawn. At H minus three, the frog men would swim in to clear any obstacles protecting the tiny beach a mile from the airfield. At H minus two, the Ranger platoon would land from rubber boats. At H minus one, three old destroyers— four-stackers from World War I—would lay down a bombardment fifty yards inland. At H-Hour, dawn, the assault battalion would hit the beach from their LCIs. Task Force X would ram through to the airfield a mile away without stopping to consolidate or mop up. Then it would dig in around the perimeter of the airfield and see how long it would take before there was hell to pay.

Meanwhile, at dawn on D minus three, the Thunderhead Division would sail for the Salananda landing. The convoy would curve a hundred miles north to stay well out of sight of Jap coast watchers. At sunset, D minus three, the convoy would be eighty miles south of the Royalties. If Task Force X had taken the airfield, if it was still in existence by sunset, if Task Force X said it could hold on during the night, the convoy would wheel north and hurl the Thunderhead Division at the tiny beach at dawn on D minus two.

It was a beautiful plan, delicate and precise as the jeweled movement of a fine watch. Of course, fine watches often got broken in a war.

Three days before everything was to start, Tom Strang came leaping out of General Brimmer's office and rushed to Anthony's desk and began pounding him on the back. "I did it!" he gasped. "I did it! I put it up to the Old Man and he gave in and said yes!"

"Outside of beating me to death," Anthony said, "what is it that you did?"

"I got Task Force X!" Tom cried. "It's mine! I'm commanding it! I put it to the General that I haven't had troop duty for a year and a half, and that nobody knows the timing of this operation the way I do, and that I ought to have the command. Finally he gave in and said yes."

"That's swell. This is really what you've wanted, isn't it?"

"It's perfect. And look, Tony, I want you to go with me. You've never seen a real scrap and you'll get a big kick out of it. You deserve a chance to be in on it, too. This started as your baby."

Anthony grinned. It would be an experience to hit the beach with a guy like Tom. It was the sort of wild thing he had never done in his life, and it would be fun to do something crazy just once. Especially since he could do it with Tom. "Would I be any damn use at all?" he asked.

"You would have to think of that, wouldn't you? Sure you'd be useful. You know this operation almost as well as I do. We'll have a lot of briefing to do on the way there, and you can help. And when we get ashore it'll be handy to have a guy beside me who knows the score and can help me keep my eye on the ball. How about it?"

"Think I can get an okay from the General?"

"Sure you can. Go in right now, Tony. Don't take no for an answer, either. He'll start by giving you all kinds of hell."

"You're on," Anthony said.

They shook hands happily, and he went in to see Brimmer. The General was slouched behind his desk, peering over the In and Out baskets like a rifleman in a foxhole. He scowled at Anthony and said, "Request denied."

"My gosh, sir," Anthony protested. "I didn't say a word yet."

"You're going to, though. You're going to ask if you can go with Tom. He's just been putting you up to it. I knew exactly what he was going to do when he ran out of here. Hell no, you can't go with him."

"But General, you haven't even let me ask! You must have listened to Tom when he came in and asked for Task Force X. It's only fair to listen to me."

"I listened to Tom because he's a Regular Army officer. He needs a combat job on his record. I don't think he's ready for this one, but I can't hold him off forever. You're just a goddam civilian in uniform. I don't have to give a damn whether combat is on your record or not. You wouldn't be a single bit of use with Task Force X."

"But General, Tom says I can help him with the briefing. I can be a sort of special Exec to him after we hit the beach. I—"

"Screw that."

"General, he's my best friend."

General Brimmer hitched his arms and shoulders over the desk like a tank waddling into position. "Now look, Tony," he said, "you can make this hard for me. I know he's your friend. I know I owe you something, for the Oliphant business and for this Task Force X deal, if it works out. You can make me feel like a louse if you keep on arguing. Maybe in the end, to stop from feeling like a louse, I'll say yes. But I tell you, you won't be a bit of use on that operation. And you've been goddam useful here. I'm just an old bald-headed bastard and I'll retire after the war is over and nobody will ever hear of me again, and I don't expect you to look on me as a friend or anything. But I'm gonna ask you something man to man as if I didn't have these two stars on. Leave it lay, will you? Do me a favor and leave it lay."

Anthony stared at the big red serious face across the desk. Brimmer was a son of a bitch to deal with. He was one of those guys, like Joan Dickinson's father or John Marshall Wharton, who could sense your weak points and drive right in at them. Nobody would ever want Buck Brimmer as a friend; he'd sell you out in a second if it would help him get on with his job. But you had to respect him for it. He didn't pretend to be a good guy.

"All right, sir," Anthony said slowly. "I withdraw the request."

"Good boy," Brimmer said, almost casually. He never wasted time enjoying a victory. "By the way," he added, with a small grin, "you might like to know that our little reconnaisance is all cleared with the Central Pacific, naturally just in vague general terms. A little scouting party to check on how good the air reconnaissance has been. They'll stay completely clear until our scouting party gets out. Nice, huh? If it works, they won't have grounds for a single squawk."

Anthony agreed that was nice, and walked out of the office and back to his own desk, where Tom was waiting. He looked at Tom and shook his head and then looked down at the floor.

Tom said angrily, "You couldn't have put up a real fight. You weren't in there long enough. He just wrapped up his no with a little crap about needing you, and you took it. Didn't you?"

"I guess I did," Anthony muttered.

Tom said in a hurt tone, "Probably you didn't want to go with me very badly."

Anthony looked up and tried to smile but his face seemed frozen. "Sorry," he said.

Tom stared at him for a moment as if seeing someone he didn't quite recognize. Then he smiled and slapped Anthony on the shoulder. "Don't worry about it," he said. "I know how the Old Man can work on people. Well, see you later."

Anthony watched him walk out of the Quonset hut. In spite of the smile and slap on the shoulder, he had a feeling that the only close friendship of his life had just ended.

In the early morning hours of D minus three, Anthony sat in the Quonset that housed Operations, watching one of Tom's G-3 officers work on the overlay of the map of the Royalties operation. The guy had drawn symbols indicating that Task Force X was closing in on the beach, and sending in the frog men and the Ranger platoon. It didn't mean anything, of course. It was merely guesswork, because Task Force X had been under radio silence since leaving New Guinea. The last message you could hang anything onto had been the report of the modest Air Force strike at the Royalties' airfield at sunset. Since then, nothing.

He slipped through the blacked-out doorway and watched the eastward sky begin to pale and the teeth of the Owen Stanley Mountains begin to gnaw into it. If everything had gone according to plan, and often things didn't, the assault battalion's LCIs would be streaming toward shore. Tom would be standing with the coxswain of one of the leading LCIs, peering over the ramp at the dark beach. Or would the beach be dark? Would tracers be flaming out from a score of machine gun nests? Would the hills be winking with artillery fire? Would the LCIs be moving through a white forest of shell splashes and now and then vanishing in a gust of dirty pink smoke? The little beach shouldn't be defended like that. The Japs shouldn't be set for a landing. But you never knew.

A messenger from Signal Center ran into Operations, and Anthony followed him. Radio silence had broken. One word had come crackling south. It was a code word from the old four-stacker destroyers, and it meant: OPERATION PROCEEDING

ACCORDING TO PLAN. AM BEGINNING BOMBARDMENT AT H MINUS ONE. Anthony began sweating. It was good news, of course, but it was stale. At this exact second, dawn was rolling over the Royalties and the assault waves were hitting the beach and the bombardment would be lifting and starting to probe through the coconut groves toward the airfield.

An hour went by. Another code word. It meant: TASK FORCE X LANDED ACCORDING TO PLAN. AM LIFTING BOMBARDMENT.

But right at that moment Tom and about eight hundred guys, or what was left of them, would be bursting out onto the airfield. Their lungs would be burning for air and they would be black with sweat and there would be Japs running around like ants. That is, they would be bursting onto the airfield if they ever got that far. These plans looked neat and clean when G-3 put them on paper and maps, but they seemed a lot different when you thought of them in terms of guys who ran fifty feet and flopped back of a kindly tree and then forced themselves to get up and run toward clumps of brush that might mask the snouts of Nambu machine guns.

For a long time there was nothing from the assault battalion. The air waves started to fill with other messages. From the destroyers, pounding targets of opportunity. From the PT boats lashing in and out of the channels between the Royalty Islands, looking for Jap barges. From the Fifth Air Force, alerted now to something big, and throwing in an air cover of fighters and strikes with B-25s. Nothing from the assault battalion.

Anthony went back to headquarters. General Brimmer was checking messages and mapping the slow northward curve of the Thunderhead Division convoy, en route to the Salananda operation. There were a lot of touchy parts in the Royalties job, but the trickiest would be the decision whether or not to divert the Thunderhead to the Royalties. There were only a few hours around sunset when it could be done. After that, the big convoy would be curving west, away from the Royalties, and you couldn't stop it out in the Pacific while you made up your mind.

The Japs were reacting now. Fifth Air Force fighters were tangling with Zeros coming down from the Carolines. The landing beach had taken a pasting from a formation of Bettys. One of the over-age destroyers was damaged by a near miss. The PTs had sunk four Jap barges heading from smaller islands of the Royalties to the main island.

Noon dragged by. 1300. 1400. At 1430 a messenger came in from Signal Center. The destroyers had picked up a single code word from the assault battalion. It wasn't much of a code word if you knew the operation, because you could decode it for yourself. It meant that the battalion had taken the airfield and dug in around the perimeter. It was a single small word with the sound of trumpets in it: JACKPOT!

General Brimmer swallowed once. He looked at Anthony and wiped sweat from his face and said, "Son of a bitch. They made it."

Then, from time to time, there were brief messages from the battalion. Mopped up infiltrating squad. Repulsed attack in platoon strength. Taking sporadic fire from mortars. Bombed. Repulsed two platoons attacking in waves. Mopped up infiltrators. Bombed. Bombed. Repulsed attack in company strength.

The western sky was reddening now. Two hundred miles north, on the airfield in the Royalties, the battalion was waiting for night and the screams of banzai charges. A hundred and ten miles north, the Thunderhead's convoy was lacing white trails across blue satin water. General Brimmer had two hours in which to make a decision.

Enlisted men moved around the headquarters shutting the blackout curtains. Sunset and night came fast in the tropics.

A messenger came in from Signal Center. The destroyers had picked up a message in the clear from the battalion and without waiting to encode it had flung it south to Nineteenth Corps. It said simply: JESUS CHRIST THERE ARE A LOT OF JAPS HERE BUT WE CAN HOLD OUT UNTIL NOON TOMORROW.

"All right, Tony," General Brimmer said. "Take down these three messages and run them to Signal Center for encoding and transmission. To Commanding officer Task Force X. Thunderhead Division will land at dawn. End message. To Commanding Officer Salananda Convoy. Open sealed orders and execute Plan B. Confirm repeat confirm. End message. To Commanding General Thunderhead Division aboard Salananda Convoy. Open sealed orders and execute Plan B. Confirm repeat confirm. End message. That's it, Tony."

He typed them out fast and ran to Signal Center and listened to them go rattling out over the short-wave channels. The confirmations were back in thirty minutes. A hundred and twenty miles north, the ships of the Salananda convoy were curving north instead of west, and the Thunderhead was on its way to the Royalties.

He stayed up all that night waiting for the big message. It came through at 1000 on D minus two, from the CG of the Thunderhead: LANDED ACCORDING TO PLAN AND HAVE RELIEVED TASK FORCE X WHICH TOOK CASUALTIES OF EIGHTY PER CENT BUT HELD AIRFIELD LAST NIGHT AGAINST BANZAI ATTACKS BY ESTIMATED FOUR THOUSAND ENEMY.

Well, that was it. They had the airfield, and the Japs would never get it back now. They had the key to the Royalties. They had smashed through the Navy fence. An assault battalion and three over-age destroyers had done what the Pacific Fleet and three divisions were to have done five months later. Back in Washington the Joint Chiefs of Staff would make some harsh comments, but only among themselves, because who could argue with victory?

There was just one thing wrong with all this. Anthony looked at General Brimmer and said, "Eighty percent casualties."

The General appeared to be a lot older today. "Tony," he said softly, "it's a cheap price. We'd have lost that many men in bombing raids from the Royalties, in hitting the beaches at Salananda."

"I wonder how Tom made out."

General Brimmer tilted his head back and stared at the ceiling. "Before this started," he said, "I left word at Signal Center and Operations that you weren't to see a certain type of message if it came in. Well, it came in. Tom caught a package."

It was the sort of thing that didn't register very clearly at first, "Do you know how it happened, General?"

"Yep. Tom went in with the Ranger platoon, before dawn. He had no right to do it, but he did it anyway. While the Rangers were getting in some knife work, Tom and a sergeant made a patrol inland. They shouldn't have been there. They got caught in the destroyer bombardment. The first assault wave found them a hundred yards inland, all chewed up by a shell burst. I'm sorry, boy."

Anthony said dully, "He always did want to be way out in front of everybody. Maybe if I'd been there I could have—"

"The hell you could!" the General said sharply. "He was that kind of guy and I tried to teach him differently and couldn't. You'd have been right there with him. Now I want you always to remember this. That day you asked to go with him, I asked you not to go, as a favor to me. You made a decision. It was the right one. Don't ever let that fact get away from you. Understand?"

"Yes sir," Anthony said.

Of course it was the right decision, but he would never feel good about having made it.

10

HE CAME HOME from Japan in October of 1945 wearing the gold oak leaves of a major, the Legion of Merit, Bronze Star, Asiatic-Pacific

Theater campaign ribbon with three battle stars, American Theater ribbon, World War II Victory ribbon, and the Philippines Liberation ribbon. That impressed everybody at Morris, Clayton, Biddle and Wharton, and they gave him an honor, too. It consisted of putting his name on the right-hand side of the firm's letterhead along with the names of eleven other lawyers. This also entitled him to a small office of his own. Before the war he had been assigned to the bull-pen where the younger lawyers worked in the open, and of course then he had not rated the letterhead.

All that was very nice. But the right margin of the letterhead was farther from the left than you might think, if you were looking at it only in terms of inches. On the left side were two groups of names. First came the five senior members of the firm. Then there was a discreet white space, and the five associate members of the firm. You could leap from the right-hand side of the letterhead to the lower group on the left if they liked you and if you could bring in about fifty thousand dollars worth of fees and retainers a year. You could jump the half-inch of white space between the lower and upper groups on the left side if your name was respected in U.S. Supreme Court circles or in the best homes in Philadelphia. The latter was considered harder to achieve than the former.

It was quite possible to work for the firm all your life without ever getting a chance to move to the left-hand side of the letterhead, which the bullpen lawyers, with a lack of reverence, called the Happy Hunting Grounds. Anthony didn't intend to spend the rest of his life on the wrong side of the letterhead. He had already lost too much time, and now he had to move fast to make up for it. The war had come at the worst possible moment for him. It had forced him to mark time during his first eighteen months out of law school. It had taken him away from his career for five years. Now he was thirty-one, and just starting. He still had to make a reputation, and make money, and find a wife who could help him to get ahead. He had no reputation as a lawyer, and no money. While he had been away in the Army, the eligible girls he had once known had married. There was a new crop of debs and post-debs, and he didn't know any of them. Once he had been a college kid who was presentable and danced well, and therefore had little trouble getting around with the right kind of girls. But by the time you were thirty-one the post-debs expected something practical from you, like money or position or at least solid prospects. The right-hand side of the letterhead of Morris, Clayton, Biddle and Wharton wasn't likely to make any of them swoon.

His mother tried to help him get started again socially. As head-mistress of Miss Rogers' Select School, she knew a number of girls of good families. She dug up half a dozen for him, but the two inter-esting ones were not interested in him and the other four, frankly, did look as if they had been dug up.

The John Marshall Whartons took an interest in him which was flattering but not very helpful. Mr. Wharton was enjoying a quiet retirement, and was only able to throw a few small bits of legal work his way. Mrs. Wharton was as lovely as ever, although the sil-ver frosting had crept deeply through her hair. She was contented and happy, and it seemed like a century ago rather than seven years since they had taken that last wild ride together. She worked hard on the problem of marrying him off to the right girl, and kept making up lists and then sadly crossing off the names.

"Any of them would be wonderful for you, Tony," she would say. "But we've got to get you a big client or something first. Oh dear, I wish John would do something about that."

It was highly unlikely, Anthony thought, that her husband could get him a big client no matter how hard he might try. A big client was one who either gave you a steady flow of profitable work, or else paid you a large retainer for the right to call you if and when he needed help. There weren't many clients like that around. When you added up the big companies in business and industry, and the banks and insurance companies and the large estates, and a few miscellaneous enterprises, there probably weren't more than a thousand big clients in the Philadelphia area. It was no easier to get a law firm to give up such a client than to get a member of an old Philadelphia family to give up his ancestors.

Besides, you couldn't go out and try to lure a client away from another lawyer. Long ago, wise old lawyers had made sure that hungry young lawyers couldn't raid their client lists. They had adopted a code of conduct which banned "unprofessional conduct." One of the worst types of such conduct was intermeddling with another lawyer's client. The penalty for that could be disbarment, ending your legal career. Or it could be suspension for an extended period. If big corporations had adopted a system like that to con-trol competition, it would have been called conspiracy in restraint of trade, and lawyers would have been the first to swing the axe of anti-trust suits. But lawyers were not going to swing axes on their own private method for controlling competition. The young lawyer was encouraged to respect the rules which in turn would help him in his twilight years.

Anthony needed a big client. He didn't have family connections that would produce one, and nobody was going to give him one, and he couldn't go out and fight for one. All he could do was set out his wares in the marketplace and wait hopefully beside them.

He needed some highly attractive wares, and he spent a lot of time trying to decide what they should be. Some years ago, the big money in law came from helping corporations in their wars against each other. The lawyer's job was to help his clients make money. Now, however, a new field of legal work was developing. Taxes of many kinds—income, corporation, inheritance, gift, capital gains, personal property, excise, and so on—had grown tremendously under the New Deal and during World War II. It was possible to have a very large income or big gross profits and still end up with little after taxes. The most promising legal work now was not helping clients to make money but showing them how to keep it. Lawyers were starting to specialize in one type or another of tax laws. But Anthony didn't think that was the answer. A specialist might save a client money in one field of taxation but lose it for the client in another. What was needed were lawyers who knew all forms of taxation, and could use one tax to take the sting out of another.

He was going to be a lawyer like that.

All during 1946 he buried himself in tax laws and decisions: federal, state, county and city. And then, in December of 1946, Mrs. J. Arthur Allen walked into his office, and gave him the chance for which he had been waiting.

Christmas came on a Wednesday that year, and on the Tuesday morning before Christmas Anthony was in his office doing a small job for one of the senior members of the firm. Office parties were starting, downtown, and many people had already left their desks for the day. Anthony had been invited to a couple of office parties, but when a job came his way from a senior member of the firm he liked to do it quickly. He was one of the few members of the staff working at his desk that morning, and the receptionist knew it, and so it was natural for her to think of him when somebody who sounded like a nuisance walked in and wanted to see a lawyer.

The receptionist came to his office and said, "I'm awfully sorry to bother you, Mr. Lawrence, but it's hard to find anybody today. There's an elderly woman outside who seems a bit eccentric and wants to see a lawyer."

Anthony said, "What does she have on her mind?"

"Oh dear. I knew you'd ask me that, and honestly I can't coax her to tell me much. It's something about a will she wants to make for a dog, if you can believe that. I told her it was hard to get anybody the day before Christmas, but she said for all she knew she might drop dead on Christmas and then what about her dog? I know it will wreck the rest of the morning for you if I bring her in. Shall I just say nobody is around?"

Anthony looked at the work he still had to do, and sighed. The visitor sounded like a screwball, but even if she wasn't, it was probably a nasty little job that would take hours and for which you'd hate to charge more than a few dollars. However, he disliked the idea of slamming the door on the woman the day before Christmas. She might worry about the will all day Christmas. People would put off thinking about a will for years and years, and then decide something had to be done and be miserable unless it was done the next minute.

He said in a resigned tone, "Call me Santa Claus, and bring her in."

"You're just too nice," the girl said. "Someday Santa Claus ought to visit you for a change."

She went back to the reception desk and returned with a brisk little old lady. Philadelphia was filled with little old ladies like her. They wore dresses that had been in bargain sales thirty years ago, and hats that looked like badly battered coal scuttles. They clutched shabby handbags as if they were carrying a million dollars. You saw them whisking in front of clanging trolleys and putting their heads down to dive through streams of autos. Somehow they never got killed in traffic or dropped dead from over exertion. They gave you a faint impression that perhaps they had ridden into the center of town on broomsticks. This was one of those little old ladies.

"How do you do?" Anthony said. "My name is Lawrence. Please sit down and tell me how I can help."

"Well," the little old lady said, "so you're a lawyer. I was beginning to think nobody was practicing law any more in Philadelphia. I'm glad to see somebody is. I want a codicil added to my will. I want it done right now. Will you do it?"

"Yes indeed. Now your name is ..."

"I'm Mrs. J. Arthur Allen."

He printed the name slowly on a pad of paper. Was there something vaguely familiar about it? Or was it merely the fact that she said the name as if it ought to command respect? Ten to one she was a widow; most of Philadelphia's little old ladies were. But, after they had been widows a few years, most women started using their given names. Mrs. Allen was still using her husband's name, and with considerable pride. J. Arthur Allen. J. Arthur Allen. There must be hundreds of J. Arthurs in the city and a great many Allens. Nothing significant about the names in themselves.

"All right, Mrs. Allen," he said. "Suppose you tell me just what you want done."

"Well," she said, "when I got up this morning my collie—her name is Beauty and she's a lovely dog—came bounding in to say hello.

And I suddenly wondered what Beauty would do if I weren't here to get up in the morning. Who would take care of her? Well, of course the servants would for a while, but after that what? So—"

"Just one moment," he said, "while I make a few notes."

Servants. The servants. How many people nowadays had a plural number of servants? He scribbled on a sheet of paper: "Look up the name J. Arthur Allen in the Social Register and in Poor's Register of Directors and Executives, and bring me the answer in writing quickly." He made a few more notes, to cover up the fact that all he had wanted to do was write the message. "Now would you go on?" he said.

"So I thought about my will, and realized that I hadn't said a thing about Beauty in it. So, really, anything at all might happen to Beauty if I died the next minute. This may sound like a little thing to you, Mr. Lawrence, but you can get very attached to a dog like Beauty and she means a lot to me."

"I think you're quite right," he said warmly. He slipped the note into his Out box, and pressed a button for a girl from the stenographers' pool.

"Now of course I realize," Mrs. Allen said, "that Beauty wouldn't be shot or anything if I died, but she might be sold or given to someone who wouldn't appreciate her. I wanted to make sure she would go to the right person, and my grand-daughter Grace would love her and take good care of her. So I want a codicil to my will giving Beauty to Grace. That sounds odd, doesn't it? Giving Beauty to Grace. Make sure you don't mix up those two names, young man."

Anthony chuckled, and said he'd keep them straight. The girl from the pool came in, and he pointed at the Out box. She took the note and left with it.

"Well, so anyway," Mrs. Allen said, "I took the train in town and walked here from the station, and my goodness it's a cold walk in this weather, and do you know what, I suddenly realized I had been so upset I hadn't had any breakfast. So I went to the Automat, where they don't stick you with awful prices the way some places do, and had breakfast and came back."

"Here?" Anthony said. "You mean our office? Does a member of our firm handle your work, Mrs. Allen?"

"Oh no, no. I went to my own lawyer's office. But everybody I knew was out, and they have some stupid girl at the reception desk who didn't know me and seemed to get all confused, and I simply wasn't getting anywhere. So I went down to the lobby and looked over the names listed on the directory board to see if I could recognize any. And I saw your firm's name. Anybody who knows

Philadelphia knows you can't go very far wrong with names like Morris, Clayton, Biddle and Wharton, and I decided you could handle my codicil for me satisfactorily."

"Do you mind if I ask who is your lawyer?"

"Mr. Dickinson and Judge Dawes. Perhaps you know them."

"Indeed I do. I even worked there for a time, while I was a law school student. Would you like me to call Dickinson and Dawes, and explain that you're here? I'm sure I can clear up any misunderstanding the girl at their desk may have had. You see, one lawyer isn't supposed to snatch a client from another lawyer."

"You're not snatching me, young man. I came in here of my own free will, and if it worries Mr. Dickinson and Judge Dawes a little, I won't mind at all. The next time the girl at their desk will know who I am."

"All right, Mrs. Allen. But you understand I'm just doing this to be helpful to Dickinson and Dawes."

"If you're smart," she said sharply, "you'll stop worrying about them, and help me."

"I certainly want to, Mrs. Allen. Now if—"

The girl from the stenographic pool came in and laid a typed note on his desk. He glanced at it. A suspicion had been forming in his mind, but the note still was a shocker. He couldn't have been more startled if Mrs. Allen had suddenly turned into Miss America of 1946, in a bathing suit. The note said: "Mrs. J. Arthur Allen is listed in the Social Register. Her home is 'White Pillars,' in Haverford. Poor's Register of Directors and Executives lists her as a director and principal owner of Allen Oil Company, of Camden." The note didn't have to tell him that Allen Oil Company, although not as big as Atlantic Refining or Sun Oil, was a mighty nice hunk of property. Principal owner! He was glad he had cleared himself already by offering to notify Dickinson and Dawes that she was here. After reading the note it would have been quite a battle to force himself to offer to do that.

"Now if," he said, "you can give me the date of your will, I'll get right at the codicil."

She fumbled in her handbag and brought out a mass of carbon copies bound in blue legal paper, and riffled through them. "It's June 6, 1941," she said.

"And the full name of your grand-daughter Grace, who is to get the collie?"

"Her name is Grace Shippen."

That was another jolt. You couldn't live in Philadelphia very long without hearing or reading something about Grace Shippen. They called her the Golden Girl. She was or would be an heiress to three fortunes. Way back, one of her ancestors had been related to the Peggy Shippen who married Benedict Arnold. She was an ash blonde of about twenty-five. She was God's gift to the Speed Graphic cameras of newspaper photographers, because no matter what angle or lighting they used she always came out looking cool and clean and beautiful. You never saw her name linked more than a few times in a row with the same man.

All this had left him a bit dizzy. If he didn't watch out he might make the mistake Mrs. Allen had warned him against, and give and bequeath Grace to Beauty instead of the other way around.

"I'll call in a girl and dictate the codicil," he said. "You can check me on the details." He pressed the button again to call a girl from the pool. The telephone rang just then, and he picked it up and said, "Lawrence speaking."

"Hello, Tony," a voice said softly. "This is Logan Clayton. Hold the receiver closely to your ear so my voice won't carry beyond you."

Logan Clayton was one of the five senior members of the firm. "Right, sir."

"Tony, I hear you have quite a visitor. The whole office is buzzing."

"That's right, Mr. Clayton."

"You have fifty to a hundred million dollars sitting across from you. This is dynamite if it's not handled properly. We must keep our skirts completely clean. There mustn't be a breath of suspicion that we are disturbing the client-lawyer relationship between Mrs. Allen and Dickinson and Dawes. I realize you can't say much, so I'll phrase my questions for a yes or no answer. Did you notify Dickinson and Dawes that she is here?"

"No sir."

"Did you suggest doing so?"

"Yes sir."

"I'm glad of that. But she didn't want you to do it?"

"That's right."

"Well, to make absolutely sure that we stay in the clear, Tony, I'm going to try to locate Mr. Dickinson or Judge Dawes on the phone. If I can locate one of them, he'll break his neck to get here. Take your time with whatever little thing Mrs. Allen wants, and hold her in conversation. That will give me more chance to find her lawyers. And remember, Tony, the good name of Morris, Clayton, Biddle and Wharton means a lot more to us than any new client. Not that we'd have a prayer of getting Mrs. Allen. Right?"

"Right, sir."

"Goodby, then."

As he hung up the phone Anthony felt a tingle of anger. It hadn't been necessary for Logan Clayton to lecture him about professional ethics. It was all very well for Clayton, with fees of a hundred thousand or so a year, to be high-minded. Logan Clayton had never been a hungry young lawyer. He had been a fat young lawyer with all the power of an important family back of him.

The girl from the pool had arrived by that time, and Anthony swivelled around and began dictating to her. "This is a codicil to a will," he said. "Let's have an original and four carbons. Ready? Be it remembered that I comma Mrs. J. Arthur Allen comma of quote White Pillars unquote comma Haverford comma Pennsylvania comma being of sound and disposing mind comma—"

"Young man," Mrs. Allen broke in, "how did you know my address?"

He had been caught off base, so he might as well admit it. "I sent out a note and had you looked up," he said.

Mrs. Allen bobbed her head vigorously. "You're a smart young man," she said. "Good for you. Now you may go ahead."

"Being of sound and disposing mind comma memory and understanding comma—"

"I understand a lot more than people have ever given me credit for," Mrs. Allen said.

"I'll bet you do," Anthony said. "Now let's see. We stopped at understanding comma. Take this, please. Make comma publish and declare this to be a capital C Codicil to my last capital W Will and capital T Testament dated June 6 comma 1941 period."

"I like codicils," Mrs. Allen said. "It always worries Mr. Dickinson and Judge Dawes when I make another codicil. But I don't care. I have a perfect right to do it if I want. Besides, it keeps my nieces and nephews and my grand-daughter on their toes."

"And besides," Anthony said, grinning at her, "It's fun, isn't it?"

Mrs. Allen looked startled for a moment, and then giggled. "You know," she said, "it really is. You're the first person I've ever met who saw that. Everybody else treats a codicil as such a solemn thing. They always act as if it's rather shocking of me to make another codicil."

He smiled at her. He wasn't going to be stupid enough to tell her just to drop in any old time and they would have fun with codicils. That might end his career as a lawyer in one big bang. But they couldn't disbar him for an encouraging smile. "Now let's see where we are," he said. "New paragraph, please. By my said capital W Will I made certain specific and pecuniary bequests comma but I did not make provision with respect to a certain collie named Beauty period. I give and bequeath the said collie to my grand-daughter comma Grace Shippen comma in the hope and belief that said Grace Shippen will give said collie the home and affection to which the said collie is accustomed period. How's that, Mrs. Allen?"

"That's just beautiful."

"All right, then," he said to his stenographer. "Please add the usual paragraph about in all other respects ratifying etcetera said Last Will and Testament and codicils of date previous to this, and add the usual signed, sealed, published and declared paragraph, and bring it in. You and I will witness Mrs. Allen's signature."

The stenographer left, and Anthony turned back to Mrs. Allen. He had come to a very big decision. He was going to try to steal Mrs. J. Arthur Allen and the Allen Oil Company from the firm of Dickinson and Dawes. If he made any important mistake, he might find himself facing disbarment proceedings. If he made the slightest mistake, he might be asked to resign from Morris, Clayton, Biddle and Wharton. This was one of those jobs like General Brimmer deciding to go after the Royalty Islands and to hell with the Joint Chiefs of Staff. You couldn't attack in full force. You had to make it appear that you were just walking innocently along, and the Royalty Islands or Mrs. J. Arthur Allen happened to fall into your pocket. If he won, without any taint of unprofessional conduct, his career would be made.

What he needed first was to find a soft spot at which to aim his attack: a spot like that little beach in the Royalties. He had no G-2 working for him to bring in facts. He had nothing to go on but the information he had picked up in studying Mrs. Allen and listening to her for the past thirty minutes. He had already made a few remarks, like the one about the fun of making codicils, which had pleased her. But personal charm wouldn't be enough to win this battle. Mr. Dickinson knew how to use charm, too, and would pour it on as soon as he found out what a dangerous thing had happened to his most important client.

No, he needed to offer Mrs. Allen a lot more than charm. He had to give her a solid practical reason for changing lawyers. He thought back over remarks she had made. She had servants, so she wasn't a miser. But she had walked in cold weather from Suburban Station to the office building, a distance of five blocks, instead of taking a taxi. She had eaten breakfast at the Horn and Hardart Automat because most places charged too much. Obviously she liked to save money. If he could show her ways in which Dickinson and Dawes had failed to save her money but in which he could, he would have a very strong case. But it would have to be done delicately, if he didn't want to be disbarred or at least thrown out of Morris, Clayton, Biddle and Wharton.

He started drawing her out in conversation, keeping alert for any fact that might give him the opening he needed. He began by asking if Beauty was a smart collie. That sent Mrs. Allen off on a long happy monologue about Beauty's tricks and intelligence. He learned that Beauty was registered with the American Kennel Club and had five champions in her immediate ancestry, although Beauty herself had never been shown. From there, Mrs. Allen went on to other dogs she had owned, and to the difference among breeds. Anthony began feeling sick. He was getting nowhere. If this went on, he might just as well limp away with his tail between his legs.

Mrs. Allen moved from breeds of dogs to the fact that dogs were man's best friend, in spite of the fact that many people did not treat dogs properly. "It certainly is a good thing," Mrs. Allen said, "that we have the S.P.C.A. to protect dogs and other animals. I'm a great believer in the S.P.C.A. I contribute a thousand dollars a year to them. I—"

That was the sort of fact he had been praying for. He leaped at it like a stray hound at a bone. "Do you contribute that in cash?" he asked.

"Why, of course. How else would I contribute it?"

"I don't mean to pry, Mrs. Allen, but I assume you own quite a few shares of stock of one kind or another? I don't mean of Allen Oil Company, but of General Electric, General Motors, companies of that type."

"Yes, I do, but I don't see the connection."

"Well," he said, "even though we did have a break in the stock market this year, it's likely that there are some very large capital gains in some of the shares you own. You can't sell those shares without paying a capital gains tax. So you're locked in. But you could give a thousand dollars worth of those shares to the S.P.C.A. without paying a penny on capital gains. The S.P.C.A. could sell the shares at full price. And you could deduct the full present market price as a charitable contribution. And you still have your thousand dollars in cash. In other words, you wipe out a capital gains tax liability at no cost to yourself. Have you ever thought of that?"

She cocked her head on one side, like a bright-eyed bird studying a handout of crumbs. "My goodness," she said, "that certainly is interesting. I like that idea very much. Now why didn't Mr. Dickinson or Judge Dawes ever explain that to me?"

It was time to cover his tracks, fast. He said smoothly, "I'm sure they would have done so, if the subject had come up."

"Yes, but it didn't come up. They don't seem to like sitting down and chatting with me, the way you've been doing. If they had, maybe the subject would have come up. They're such busy people, and probably I'm a nuisance and they're a little afraid of me, so they try to get rid of me quickly. They—"

236

The girl came in with the typed copies of the codicil, and Mrs. Allen cut short her comments and put on her bifocals and read it word by word. "Very good," she said.

She signed it, and Anthony and the stenographer added their names as witnesses. Anthony was about to suggest sending a copy to Dickinson and Dawes when he realized that wouldn't be necessary. From the corridor came a familiar voice, assuring the receptionist that he knew exactly where to go. The voice was not as mellow and controlled as Anthony remembered it. It was pitched a few notes higher than usual and it was breathless. You heard voices like that on movie sound tracks, when the captain of U.S. Cavalry was ordering his men into Indian country to save a wagon train of settlers. Out in the corridor, Joan Dickinson's father was riding to the rescue of a hundred million dollars.

Mr. Dickinson came galloping into the office, and gasped, "My dear Mrs. Allen! I was so terribly upset when I heard what had happened at our office this morning. It couldn't have happened except on the day before Christmas and with a new girl at the reception desk. We will never forgive ourselves."

Mrs. Allen peered up at him. There was a smile of mischief on her face, and for a moment you got the impression that she was eight years old and had caught a teacher in a mistake. "Why, there's nothing to forgive yourselves for," she cooed. "I've been taken care of ever so well by this nice young man."

Mr. Dickinson looked at Anthony from eyes that might have chipped from a glacier. "Well, Tony!" he said. "It's so nice to see you again. Tony and I are old friends, Mrs. Allen. Originally, in fact, I was his preceptor in law school. So it's no surprise to me that he's done a good job. Perhaps I might even take a little credit for it. Tony's a fine lawyer."

Mrs. Allen said, "If he's so good, why didn't you take him into your firm?"

Anthony tried to hide a smile. The settlers were shooting at the rescuing column of U.S. Cavalry. Perhaps the Indians ought to rescue the Cavalry. "It was just one of those things," Anthony said. "In my last year at law school I helped Mr. John Marshall Wharton with a book he was writing, and we became good friends and so it was natural for me to join Morris, Clayton, Biddle and Wharton. But Mr. Dickinson had been most helpful to me and would have continued to help me, I'm sure, if it had been necessary."

You could see that Mr. Dickinson didn't like the Indians to act so nobly. However, he smiled bravely, and said, "Yes, I've always regretted losing Tony. Now, this was a codicil you wanted, Mrs. Allen?"

"It's all finished," Mrs. Allen said. "Done very well, too."

Anthony said, "Naturally I was going to send a copy to you, Mr. Dickinson."

"Yes, yes, of course. Well, Mrs. Allen, perhaps we could go down to my office, and file the original in our safe with your other papers, and make sure that everything else is in order."

Mrs. Allen sighed. She had obviously enjoyed this and was sorry to close out the incident. "Mr. Lawrence was very helpful in another way," she said. "I mentioned that I always give a thousand dollars each year to the S.P.C.A., and he suggested using a few shares of stock in which I have large capital gains, instead of using cash. In order to wipe out the capital gains tax liability."

"It just happened to come up as we talked," Anthony said. "I pointed out that you would have suggested the same thing, if the subject had ever come up between you."

"Yes, naturally," Mr. Dickinson said. The expression on his face said that the U.S. Cavalry would love to scalp a few Indians. "Thank you very much, Tony. May I say that you have not only done a fine job but also conducted yourself very well, professionally?"

"Thank you, sir."

Mrs. Allen got up slowly. "Young man," she said, "I hope you'll send a good fat bill to Mr. Dickinson for, as he points out, taking care of me so well. I'm sure my retainer will cover it, Mr. Dickinson?"

Mr. Dickinson wanted to scalp the settlers, too. "Indeed it will, Mrs. Allen."

"And, young man, if you get any other ideas for saving me money," Mrs. Allen said, "I hope you'll let me know."

Mr. Dickinson held his breath. This was it, Anthony knew. He had to say exactly the right thing. He had to avoid unprofessional conduct and at the same time leave the door open a crack. He had to use shadowy words that would haunt Mr. Dickinson, and make him think that the silhouette of a bush in the dark was really that of a crouching Indian. If Mr. Dickinson worried enough, he might make the error of trying to convince Mrs. Allen that she should pay no attention to his own worries.

Anthony picked his words like a jeweler selecting diamonds for a necklace. He said, "Mrs. Allen, you're a client of our good friends at Dickinson and Dawes. I'm sure they give your affairs their closest attention. It would be unprofessional conduct on my part to suggest that I could do something for you that they can't." Let Mr. Dickinson and Mrs. Allen think that over. It protected him completely. And yet, if you analyzed the statement, you might find in it a hint that perhaps he could save money in other ways for Mrs. Allen.

"Very high-minded of you, I'm sure," Mrs. Allen said, a bit petulantly.

"Thank you, Tony," Mr. Dickinson said in a very thoughtful tone. He was already beginning to examine the shadows in those words. He took Mrs. Allen's arm and led her from the room.

Anthony paid a Christmas call the next afternoon on the John Marshall Whartons. After they had talked for a while he told them, casually, about Mrs. J. Arthur Allen's visit. Mr. Wharton laughed heartily.

"That's wonderful, Tony," he said. "I'll have to run down to the Union League for lunch tomorrow and tell that story. I think I will call it the Case of the Collie's Codicil. People will laugh themselves sick, thinking how scared Dickinson must have been. He's not very popular, you know."

Mrs. Wharton said indignantly, "I don't think it's a laughing matter at all! You mean poor Tony had to let Mrs. Allen go without trying to land her as a client? When he needs a big client so badly?"

"My dear, you don't understand these things," her husband said. "Of course Tony couldn't do that. They'd bring charges against him in the Bar Association. I assume that Tony closed the thing out quite firmly. Right, Tony?"

"Yes, quite firmly."

"Oh Tony, you idiot!" Mrs. Wharton said.

Mr. Wharton looked at him with a faint smile. "You don't fool me," he said. "The fact is, you baited a hook and dropped it in the water somewhere, didn't you?"

"Did you, Tony? Did you?" Mrs. Wharton cried. "Please tell us about it."

"He's going to," Mr. Wharton said. "In fact, much as Tony may like to see us, I believe he came out today for advice. Now confess about that hook, young man."

"It's a very small one," Anthony said.

"But with a big gob of bait on it, I'll bet. What's the bait?"

Anthony explained about the S.P.C.A. and his recommendation, and then reported how Mrs. Allen had said, just before leaving, that he must call her up if he had any more ideas for saving her money.

"Very interesting," Mr. Wharton said. "Dickinson was there at the time, wasn't he? What was your reply to Mrs. Allen's suggestion? The exact words, if you can remember."

Anthony dug the words out of his memory. "I said, 'Mrs. Allen, you're a client of our good friends at Dickinson and Dawes. I'm sure they give your affairs their closest attention. It would be unprofessional conduct on my part to suggest that I can do something for you that they can't.'"

"Magnificent," Mr. Wharton said.

"If there's a hook in that," Mrs. Wharton complained, "it's too small for me to see."

Her husband said, "Carol, there's not only a hook in it, but also what they called in the war a booby trap. If Dickinson starts taking that statement apart, it may blow up in his face."

"It's too deep for me," Mrs. Wharton said. "And I suspect for Mrs. Allen too."

"The beauty of it," Mr. Wharton said, "and I'm not talking about Beauty the collie, is that Dickinson may make the mistake of trying to explain Tony's statement to Mrs. Allen. And if he does, she'll end up by seeing the hook in it."

Anthony said, "You think I'm in the clear, then?"

"Oh, definitely, my boy."

"Do you feel that I should drop the whole thing and make no further efforts at all? What I mean is, if the hook catches anything, should I cut the line?"

"Are you asking my opinion of your ethics, Tony?"

"Partly that."

Mr. Wharton chuckled. "Your ethics are delightfully bad. But nobody can make a charge of unprofessional conduct stick, so far, unless you choose to plead guilty."

"I'm also worried about my standing at the firm, if anything more develops. Logan Clayton was quite upset yesterday."

"He's a damned old woman," Mr. Wharton said. "There's too much banking blood in that Clayton family. All he thinks of is avoiding risks and building reputation. He ought to be running the Philadelphia Saving Fund Society. I'll go talk to Logan tomorrow. I think I can promise that, if you handle yourself as well in the future as you did yesterday, he'll go along."

"Grace," Mrs. Wharton murmured thoughtfully. "Hmm. Grace."

"Saying grace, dear?" her husband asked.

"I think I will go see Grace Shippen."

"My dear, please stay out of this."

Mrs. Wharton protested, "Grace is on my hospital committee and I have every right to see her. And if I happen to tell her about the Case of the Collie's Codicil, which is being talked about all over town, I dare your Bar Association to do anything to me."

"Perhaps you have a point. Of course it's most unethical to discuss a person's will."

"Women have no ethics," Mrs. Wharton said. "That's the sort of excess baggage only men like to carry. Grace has a wonderful head for money, even better than her grandmother. I think I can make sure that Mrs. Allen will understand that careful statement Tony made."

Mr. Wharton shrugged. "Take to the hills, men," he said. "The women have broken loose."

"I've never met Grace Shippen," Anthony said. "What is she like?"

"She's delightful," Mrs. Wharton said. "She's lovely and rich and smart. She's a hard worker for charity and a good sportswoman. She has a nice sense of humor and she's fun to be with. There's only one thing wrong with her. I don't think she has a heart."

"How ridiculous can you be!" Mr. Wharton said. "Of course she has a heart. It's just that nothing has ever touched her deeply."

"Well, if she has one," Mrs. Wharton said, "she keeps it locked in the safe deposit box with other valuables. It's not easy to touch something that's protected by tons of chrome steel. I hope Tony doesn't like her."

"If she resembles her grandmother," Anthony said, "it will be love at first sight. Mrs. Allen is wonderful."

Mr. Wharton said, "You'd better start trying to figure ways to save Mrs. Allen money. Although how you can do it without an exact knowledge of her affairs, I don't know."

"I don't know either," Anthony said, "but I've got to do it. That's the key to everything."

11

FOR THE NEXT ten days he spent most of his time picking up scraps of information about Mrs. Allen and the Allen Oil Company. It wasn't easy. The company's stock was not listed on the Big Board or the Curb. It was closely held by a very small number of people. Finally, however, in checking through the will of J. Arthur Allen in the records at City Hall, he discovered that fifty shares of company stock had been left to Mr. Allen's secretary. He learned that she was retired, tracked her down at an apartment in Haddonfield, New Jersey, told her that he was thinking of investing in the company and asked her opinion of the stock as an investment. Like most faithful old employees of a company, she loved to talk about it. She gave him a great deal of information, and allowed him to borrow copies of the company's annual reports for the past ten years.

Meanwhile he was digging into every recorded public fact about Mrs. Allen's financial affairs: transfers of real estate, newspaper stories about her contributions to this or that cause, the inventory of her late husband's estate, and so on. He would have given anything for copies of her income tax returns, but there wasn't a chance of getting those. He did succeed, through a devious route, in getting some information about her county personal property tax returns.

None of this turned up any obvious ways to save her money. Not that he had expected to find any such ways. Dickinson and Dawes may have handled her affairs in routine fashion, without really digging to see how much could be done, but it was too good a firm to make any glaring errors.

So he was not well prepared when, a few days after New Year's, he found that the bait had been taken and that the hook was deeply imbedded. The phone in his office rang and Logan Clayton asked him to come down the hall to his office. When he arrived he saw Mr. Dickinson, waiting for him with one of his most charming smiles. Years ago, those smiles had won his trust and cost him Joan Dickinson.

"Nice to see you again, Tony," Mr. Dickinson said, shaking his hand cordially. "How are you?"

"Fine, thanks. You wanted to see me, Mr. Clayton?"

Logan Clayton always acted as if his desk were a high court bench. He nodded solemnly and said, "Yes, Tony. Sit down, will you? Mr. Dickinson has come to us with a rather grave problem."

"It really isn't serious," Mr. Dickinson said. "In fact it has its amusing angles. It's in connection with my client, Mrs. J. Arthur Allen. A charming person. Rather an active imagination, though."

"I wouldn't have suspected that," Anthony said. "She seemed quite practical to me."

"Well, let's say impressionable, then. You recall that small suggestion you made, in regard to a contribution of stock rather than cash to the S.P.C.A.?"

Logan Clayton said, "Before you go on, do you have any objection to the fact that Tony made that suggestion? As I understand it, the idea merely popped out in casual talk."

"Oh, no objection at all. However, the amusing thing, and what made me use the words imagination and impressionable, is that Mrs. Allen has built up that tiny suggestion into a feeling that Tony could save her money in other ways."

"Surely you can talk her out of that," Anthony said smoothly.

"Tony, elderly ladies nearly always look on taxes as a personal insult. They respond eagerly to the idea of avoiding the insult. It's not easy to talk them out of it. I might have done so, even at that, but for a few unfortunate remarks you made at the close of her visit."

Logan Clayton said, "Please choose your words carefully, Mr. Dickinson. I don't care to have any reflections on the good name of this firm. What were these alleged unfortunate remarks?"

"Mrs. Allen, in leaving, asked Tony to let her know if he got any more ideas for saving her money. Tony said, and I believe I quote exactly, 'Mrs. Allen, you're a client of our good friends at Dickinson and Dawes. It would be unprofessional conduct on my part to suggest that I could do something for you that they can't.' On the surface, that sounds very nice and proper. But if you read between the lines, you'll find that statement doesn't go very far. In fact, it leaves things wide open, although I'm sure Tony didn't intend it that way."

Logan Clayton said, "Yes, that was a weak statement, Tony. I might almost agree it could be called unfortunate."

Anthony smiled. "In reading between the lines, I'm afraid Mr. Dickinson missed one that was actually present. In the middle of that statement I also said, quote, I'm sure they give your affairs their closest attention, unquote."

"Come to think of it, you did say that," Mr. Dickinson said.

"Well, my dear sir, what more do you want?" Logan Clayton complained. "Tony gave you what is almost an endorsement. Now I'm almost inclined to say he went too far in your behalf."

"We lawyers do haggle about words, don't we?" Mr. Dickinson said blandly. "Nonetheless and notwithstanding, Mrs. Allen did come away with a feeling that Tony implied he could save her money if she were not a client of Dickinson and Dawes. May I term this regrettable?"

"You're drawing an extremely fine point," Mr. Clayton grumbled.

"Not too fine, I trust, when the reputation of Morris, Clayton, Biddle and Wharton is concerned. You see, I can't prevent Mrs. Allen from going around saying that you have a bright young man who wants her business and hinted he could save money for her on taxes."

"On that basis," Logan Clayton said, "it is a bit awkward. But I don't know what we can do about it."

"It's a very simple thing," Mr. Dickinson said lightly. "All Tony has to do is write me a little note. In it, he regrets any misunderstanding that may have arisen, and asks me to assure Mrs. Allen that he does not know of any further ways to save her money. A friendly little note, merely stating the facts."

"I see no harm in that," Logan Clayton said, handing down a high court decision. "How do you feel about it, Tony?"

The U.S. Cavalry, Anthony thought grimly, was doing well today. The Cavalry was using ambush tactics, and it looked as though the Indians had had it. But it was an outrage to let Mr. Dickinson get away with this. Logan Clayton ought to tell the man to handle his own clients and not come around asking them to do it for him. But

Mr. Dickinson had used the shrewd trick of pretending that the reputation of the firm was involved, and Logan Clayton's motto was: In Morris, Clayton, Biddle and Wharton We Trust.

If he agreed to write such a letter, Mr. Dickinson would use it to kill Mrs. Allen's interest in him. If he refused to write it, he would have to give a reason. Logan Clayton probably wouldn't let him use the natural reason, and tell Mr. Dickinson to run along and handle his own clients without their help. There was only one other reason he could give. That one involved playing Russian roulette with a revolver pressed to his head. But instead of merely one of the six chambers being loaded, five of the six would be ready to fire when he pressed the trigger. It was the nastiest kind of an ambush. Just as had happened years ago, he had been a little too wide-eyed and innocent in dealing with Joan Dickinson's father.

"Aren't you taking quite a while to decide, Tony?" Mr. Dickinson said pleasantly.

Logan Clayton said, "I can't see that it's worth all this thought. Come, come, Tony."

"I don't care to write such a letter," Anthony said.

"Very interesting," Mr. Dickinson murmured. There was a razor-thin smile on his face.

"I'm afraid you'll have to explain your attitude," Logan Clayton said.

There was no harm in trying to get away with the explanation that wasn't loaded. "Sir," Anthony said, "you yourself agree that my statement to Mrs. Allen went even further than necessary, and in fact was just about an endorsement for Dickinson and Dawes. If any misunderstanding has come up, I suggest that it is Mr. Dickinson's fault. Why should we bail him out of trouble he's having with his client?"

"I admit," Logan Clayton said ponderously, "that it's asking us to go quite far. But when the reputation of the firm is involved, even though it is not through any fault of our own, nothing is too much to ask. Tony, on behalf of the firm, I ask you to write that letter."

He had tried, anyway. Now for the Russian roulette. There was a chance that Mr. Dickinson might be scared off when he lifted the revolver. "Sir," he said formally, "the firm wouldn't ask me to write a letter which tells a lie. It would be untrue to say that I don't know of any further ways to save Mrs. Allen money."

"My God!" Logan Clayton said.

Now, would Mr. Dickinson back away from that? He stared at the man, and saw that once again he had not judged him correctly.

Mr. Dickinson's face was flaming. He got up and pointed a trembling finger at Anthony. "You'll prove that! And if you can't, I'll bring charges against you before the Committee of Censors. You're accusing me of incompetence."

This was quite interesting. Mr. Dickinson had a weakness, after all. It was his self-esteem. If you attacked that, he lost control. But of course he was a very dangerous man even when he lost control, and you'd better be ready to defend yourself. Anthony wished he knew exactly how to do it. Right at the moment he didn't have the weapon he needed, even though he was sure it existed somewhere in the complicated tax affairs of Mrs. J. Arthur Allen.

"I don't say that you're incompetent," Anthony said. "I happen to be specializing in tax laws and regulations. I know more about them than you do, just as you know more about other fields of law than I."

"I won't accept that," Mr. Dickinson said furiously. "A cub lawyer telling me he knows more than I do. You're going to prove your statement or eat it."

Logan Clayton said pleadingly, "Tony, what is this way to save money for Mrs. Allen?"

"She's not my client," Anthony said. "I don't work for Mr. Dickinson. I'm not going to tell him, and let him present it to her as his own idea. If he wants to bring charges, I'll answer him at the hearing."

"Surely we can keep this … this unpleasantness out of the Bar Association," Logan Clayton gasped. "There must be some other way to settle it. Some—"

Mr. Dickinson broke in. "I challenge you to repeat your statement in the presence of Mrs. J. Arthur Allen, and to prove it. With Mr. Clayton and myself as witnesses."

Mr. Dickinson was pretty far gone to make an offer like that. Of course, Mr. Dickinson didn't think Anthony could come up with anything. But even so, it was a direct invitation to solicit Mr. Dickinson's client under remarkable but quite ethical conditions. "Any time," Anthony said.

"You're bluffing, Tony. And I'm going to tear you to pieces before we're through. If I can arrange it, will tomorrow morning be suitable?"

"Fine with me."

"In my office, if you don't mind."

"I do mind," Anthony said. "I won't take any action that might look as if I'm going out of my way to solicit your client. I'll see you in my office or nowhere." He wasn't going to have any tricks of lighting or placement of chairs worked on him. He was going to fight on his own grounds, where he would feel the greatest amount of confidence.

"Where we meet is immaterial to me," Mr. Dickinson snapped. "Mr. Clayton, thank you for your courtesy. I will telephone you about the arrangements." He marched out of the office.

"Tony," Logan Clayton said weakly, "this is a hell of a mess. That is, unless you really can back up your claim. Can you?"

"Don't worry, sir," Anthony said. "We'll be all right."

He went slowly back to his office. The way the U.S. Cavalry was operating these days, he knew how the Indian must have felt in that painting called The Vanishing American. Only, damn it, he wasn't going to be a Vanishing American. Between now and the next morning he was going to find what he needed among the jumbled facts he had gathered about Mrs. Allen. He shut his office door, cleared the desk and got out the fat folder on Mrs. Allen's affairs.

In mid-afternoon Logan Clayton interrupted him and said that the meeting was set for ten the next morning. Anthony nodded; Mr. Dickinson wasn't going to give him any extra time. Logan Clayton looked at the masses of paper on the desk, started to say something, swallowed with difficulty, and left. Mr. Clayton was probably afraid to ask if the paper work meant that things weren't quite in shape.

At four-thirty Mrs. John Marshall Wharton telephoned, her voice husky with excitement. "Tony," she said, "Grace Shippen just phoned me. She says there's to be a showdown between you and Mr. Dickinson tomorrow at ten, with Mrs. Allen present. Are you ready for it?"

"Oh, sure," he said. That wasn't a lie. A man could be ready for his own funeral, couldn't he?

"I thought you'd like to know that Grace is coming, too."

"I'm flattered."

"She's heard so much about you she's getting curious. Don't count on any support from her, though. I'm sure Mrs. Allen will be for you. But Grace doesn't take sides. She only cheers after there's a winner. Don't fall for her, Tony."

Lady, the corpse seldom falls for anyone. "I'll have other things on my mind," he said.

"I'll be praying for you. Good luck, Tony."

He hung up and went back to work. Later, he hurried out for a hasty dinner and returned to the office. As the hours went by he began to feel desperate. He was studying the Allen folder fact by fact but was getting nowhere. Yet there must be ways to save money for her. Within the past ten years the tax laws had stretched their spiderwebs in every conceivable place where the unwary dollar might try to go. Few lawyers had been able to keep up with all the tax laws, especially not general corporation and estate lawyers like Dickinson and Dawes. Anybody who had holdings as big and complicated as those of Mrs. Allen must be losing money somewhere in the spiderwebs.

The trouble was, he only had scraps of information about her affairs. The chances were a thousand to one that he lacked many key facts.

After he came to that dead end, he stopped examining each fact by itself. He began playing a sort of jigsaw puzzle game with all the facts, fitting them against each other, balancing them, and figuring the effect of one type of tax on other types which Mrs. Allen was paying.

And suddenly, there it was.

One small move of his hand in weighing one tax against another, and he had it. It was like watching a breeze roll the clouds away from a distant mountain peak. There the answer was in all its simplicity and grandeur.

He was too tired to feel elated. He swept the papers into a drawer. He walked slowly out of the place, more like a man who was ending his career than one who has just seen a limitless future opening ahead of him.

At nine the next morning he was back in his office, setting the stage for the meeting. Since the person to impress was Mrs. Allen, who didn't waste money on frills, he removed a vase of flowers, a chromium water jug and glasses, and everything else that wasn't strictly business. He dusted his law books. On a small table near the door he laid the Treasury Department's bulky booklet on rules and regulations of the Excess Profits Tax on corporations.

Then, because he remembered vividly how Mr. Dickinson had worked the chair game on him, years ago at Princeton, he spent some time in selecting and placing chairs. One with a deep soft seat for Logan Clayton, so that it wouldn't be easy for him to sit up and interfere. Two chairs with wooden arms and firm leather-covered seats for Mrs. Allen and Grace Shippen, so that they would be comfortable but sitting up alertly. A hard wooden chair for Mr. Dickinson to squirm on, placed so that the light from the window would annoy him.

A little before ten, Logan Clayton came in and began wandering around the room like a man in a strange office building hunting for the men's room. Anthony coaxed him into the deep-seated chair and spoke soothingly to him. Then the receptionist announced their visitors, and he went out to greet them. Mrs. Allen was wearing another bargain basement dress from 1920 but the same mashed coal scuttle of a hat. She took his hand and patted it and said she hoped he had something good to tell her. Behind her was the girl he wasn't supposed to fall for. What was all the shouting about? Grace Shippen hadn't invented the idea of being a tall cool blonde. Behind her was Mr. Dickinson, giving him a look that should have been in a scabbard. He led them into the office and made sure they got the right chairs.

Mr. Dickinson started right off with a cavalry charge. "Well now, Tony," he said, "are you ready to admit this has gone far enough? Sometimes the enthusiasm of youth carries a man away. I think we'd all be willing to overlook that, and not let the thing go further."

Logan Clayton tried to heave himself forward in the deep-seated leather chair, but it was quite an effort and Anthony cut in before the man could say anything. "Do I understand that you're giving up?" he asked pleasantly.

"I was merely giving you a chance to withdraw gracefully. You don't seem to realize the spot you're in."

"Mr. Dickinson, you suggested this meeting. You came to me with a challenge. You have brought Mrs. Allen here. I can hardly withdraw from my own office."

In the depths of the deep-seated chair, Logan Clayton nodded.

"You're just juggling words, Tony," Mr. Dickinson said. "Either tell us whatever wild idea you may have dreamed up, if you've actually gone that far, or else admit you've been bluffing. And I can assure you I won't let you get away with any vague unsupported promises."

"Mr. Dickinson, will you tell Mrs. Allen exactly what your challenge was?"

"She already knows about your ridiculous boast. But I'm willing to repeat what I said. I challenged you to make good on your boast that you knew some further ways to save her money. I challenged you to prove it in her presence."

"If I may correct one thing," Anthony said mildly, "it was not a boast. You asked me to write you a letter stating that I did not know of any further ways to save money for her. I refused. I had to refuse, because any such statement would have been untrue."

"Prove it."

"Oh yes," Mrs. Allen said eagerly. "Do let's hear about it."

Anthony smiled at her. Then, perhaps by a trick of lighting, he found his attention caught by Grace Shippen. She seemed to attract a great deal of the light in the room, almost as if she were an actress picked out by a baby spot. She was dressed rather plainly: dark blue tailored suit with white collar and cuffs, blue hat with a small white bow, white-gloved hands folded on her lap. She had lovely legs, and she sat with her knees together and one foot neatly crossed in front of the other. There was a look of mild interest on her face. He remembered his grandfather telling him how the Vestal Virgins of Rome would sit quietly in the Coliseum, watching gladiators thrust and parry on the sands below. Grace Shippen would have felt at home with them.

He took a deep breath and cleared his head of distracting thoughts.

It was necessary to lead up impressively to the idea he was going to present. Lawyers had nothing to sell but their thoughts. If your thoughts seemed to come too easily, people tended to feel that they weren't worth much. So he began with a general talk on taxation, explaining how it was a constant battle between the unwilling taxpayer and the needs of governing bodies for more and more money. There were lawyers on each side of the battle: trying to invent new forms of taxation and trying to find refuges for money, helping taxpayers to slip through loopholes and helping governing bodies to close the loopholes. The result was a maze of laws and regulations and court decisions in which most people were lost.

Mr. Dickinson squirmed on his hard chair. "You're not saving anybody money with this lecture," he said. "You're just costing us time."

"I'm trying to show Mrs. Allen how complicated the tax problem is," Anthony said gravely. "I wouldn't want her to think that the money-saving idea I have for her was simple to uncover, and that you should have found it, too."

"Don't condescend to me, Tony. You haven't produced a thing yet."

"What we have in Mrs. Allen's case," Anthony said, "is a large and complicated fortune harassed by large and complicated taxes. We can't wrestle blindly with those taxes and hope to win, because they are too many and too strong. We have to adopt the tactics of judo wrestling, and turn the strength of our opponents against themselves."

Mr. Dickinson said, "Really, Mrs. Allen, I hate to subject you to this."

"Now please don't worry about me," Mrs. Allen said, her eyes bright and happy. "I don't understand half of what he says, but he says it so nicely."

Grace Shippen let a smile glide across her lips. She had the calm clean features you might find in an old cameo. Some people liked that sort of perfection but it seemed rather bloodless to him. You couldn't conceive of her ever having a smudge on her face. He suspected that she understood every word he said, and knew why he was saying them, and was not in the least impressed. A flourish of weapons in the arena meant nothing to her. She was only interested in the kill. He didn't know why he was bothering to think about her.

"I would like everybody to understand," he said, "that I am only using publicly known facts about Mrs. Allen's affairs. That's all I have. We start with the generally-accepted belief that Mrs. Allen owns about fifty million dollars worth of the stock of Allen

Oil Company. It may be more, it may be less, but let's work with that figure."

On the hard wooden chair, Mr. Dickinson frowned and tried to get more comfortable. He was starting to look a bit worried. Mr. Dickinson had perhaps thought the money-saving idea would either deal with vague buried treasure or with the specific saving of a few hundred dollars. He didn't like the sound of fifty million unburied dollars.

"Mrs. Allen lives on the Main Line, in Haverford," Anthony said. "County personal property taxes are four mills on the dollar. She pays that county tax on her fifty million dollars worth of Allen Oil Company stock. That's a tax of two hundred thousand dollars a year. No small sum, if I may say so."

"Come on, Tony," Mr. Dickinson snapped. "Don't throw these figures around as if they mean something."

"They mean something to me," Anthony said. "I don't think she should be paying that two hundred thousand a year."

"Oh my!" Mrs. Allen gasped.

"You must be crazy," Mr. Dickinson said. "She has to pay. It's the law."

"It really is, you know," Mrs. Allen said. "The county assessor is very nice and pleasant, but he wouldn't let me get away with anything."

"Assuming that you own, let's say, some General Electric stock," Anthony said, "you're not paying county personal property taxes on it."

"You don't know the first thing about her affairs," Mr. Dickinson said. "GE owns property in Pennsylvania and does business here and pays Pennsylvania taxes as a foreign corporation. So its stock is not subject to the personal property tax. Allen Oil Company, as you do not seem to realize, is a New Jersey company. It does no business here and pays no taxes here. So any resident of Pennsylvania who owns its stock has to pay county personal property taxes on it."

"Quite so," Anthony said. "Now let's see if we can't change all that. Did you ever hear of a company called J. Arthur Allen, Incorporated?"

Mr. Dickinson began to sweat. He still didn't see the bonfire waiting for him but he could feel the heat. "Yes, of course," he said nervously. "J. Arthur Allen Incorporated does do business in Pennsylvania. It owns and operates tank trucks here. It owns and leases service stations there. It buys oil and gas from Allen Oil Company. But it's not a part of Allen Oil."

"Allen Oil owns nearly all its stock."

"What difference does that make? It's another company!"

"But it's not just any other company," Anthony said mildly. "Allen Oil controls and directs all its activities. It would be a simple matter for Allen Oil to take over part of its operations in Pennsylvania and do business here. Allen Oil would pay a proportion of the tax J. Arthur Allen Incorporated has been paying, with those taxes coming out of the same pants but different pockets. And that would save Mrs. Allen two hundred thousand dollars a year, because she would no longer have to pay county personal property taxes on her Allen Oil Company stock."

Mr. Dickinson looked badly shaken, as indeed he should be. For years he had been handling Mrs. Allen's affairs in a routine manner, doing the obvious things for her but not looking for extra work and trouble. Now he had a lot of explaining to do, and there really wasn't a good explanation.

Mr. Dickinson jumped up. "Mrs. Allen," he cried, "this is a wild and reckless idea! I'm sure you trust the management of Allen Oil Company. You wouldn't use your voting power to force the officers to do a crazy juggling act. This isn't a matter for lawyers. It's up to the officers of your company. If it had been a good step to take, the officers of Allen Oil would certainly have taken it long ago."

"They never thought of it," Anthony said. "It's not their headache if Mrs. Allen loses all that money every year."

"I don't really understand this," Mrs. Allen said breathlessly. "It would be wonderful to save all that money. I understood the S.P.C.A. thing. But this is so complicated." She turned to her grand-daughter. "Do you understand it, Grace?"

This time a full smile moved over the girl's lips. Watching it, Anthony knew that she had followed and understood every word. The fight in the arena was over. The Vestal Virgin could see that one gladiator was down, unarmed and squirming, while the other looked up for the signal.

"Yes, Grandmother," she said. "I understand perfectly. The whole thing is quite simple, and I'm surprised that Mr. Dickinson never thought of it. Mr. Lawrence is using Pennsylvania taxes on corporations to knock out the county personal property tax. He has just saved you two hundred thousand dollars a year."

"How wonderful!" Mrs. Allen gasped.

"My dear Mrs. Allen," Mr. Dickinson stammered. "Even if this idea does turn out to be practical, I hope you won't feel that Dickinson and Dawes have been remiss. We have devoted our best efforts to your interests. This idea involves so many things beyond what a lawyer might be expected to do, such as major changes in company policy, that we could hardly be blamed for not suggesting it. A mere hunch by an outsider, a lucky guess that could never be repeated again, should not be held against us."

"I—I don't really know," Mrs. Allen said. "You understand it, Grace. What do you think?"

The girl's face was very calm. That was probably the way the Vestal Virgins had looked, peering into the arena and giving the thumbs-down signal. In her low soft voice, with its cello notes, she asked for the kill. "What I think," she said, "is that you need a new lawyer."

There might have been a chance for Mr. Dickinson to rescue something if he had tried hard. But Mr. Dickinson still had his weakness. If you attacked his self-esteem, he lost control. He stood very straight and glared at the girl and said, "First a cub lawyer tries to tell me my business and then a girl presumes to run my client's affairs for her." He turned to Mrs. Allen. "If you agree in any way with your grand-daughter's remark, Dickinson and Dawes will withdraw from the handling of your affairs."

"Well!" Mrs. Allen said irritably. "Grace has a good head on her shoulders. I can't help thinking she has a point."

"We will turn over your affairs to anyone you name," Mr. Dickinson said, and marched out of the room.

"Well!" Mrs. Allen said. "Think of him acting like that."

Let us, Anthony said to himself, stop thinking about Mr. Dickinson and start thinking about that deserving young lawyer, Anthony Lawrence. "I'm sorry you had to witness a scene like that," he said. "However, I hope you found this trip into town worthwhile."

"Worthwhile? My! I should say so! Two hundred thousand dollars! I couldn't get a refund for past years, could I?"

Anthony chuckled. "A delightful idea. I only wish you could. Now, even though I have no further right to offer you legal advice, I should point out that none of this has been accomplished yet. You ought to get someone working on it at once."

"Yes, of course. I need a new lawyer, don't I?"

In the depths of the deep-seated chair, Logan Clayton wrestled with a problem in ethics. Was or wasn't it proper now to drop a hint about Morris, Clayton, Biddle and Wharton? He got a strangle hold on the problem in ethics, and said, "My dear Mrs. Allen, naturally we—"

"Mr. Lawrence is your man," Grace Shippen said quietly.

"I believe he is," Mrs. Allen said, beaming at him. "You're a bit young, but you certainly seem to know what you're doing."

"And if I may say so," Logan Clayton said, "Mr. Lawrence will have back of him the full resources and experience of Morris, Clayton, Biddle and Wharton, in the handling of your affairs."

"I'll be very proud and happy to take on the job," Anthony said. "Now if you want us to move immediately, Mrs. Allen, I suggest that we call in a secretary, and you can get a letter right out to Dickinson and Dawes asking them to turn over all your legal affairs to me."

For the first time Grace Shippen's face came alive. She laughed, and delightful little crinkles fanned out from her eyes, and he realized suddenly why Mrs. Wharton had said the girl was fun to be with. "You don't waste any time, do you?" she said.

"Time is money," he said, grinning at her. "In this case, time is two hundred thousand dollars." He was starting to wonder why Mrs. Wharton had warned him against the girl.

They got the letter out, with Anthony making sure that the wording identified him rather than just the firm in general, and then he and Mr. Clayton escorted Mrs. Allen and the girl to the elevators. Grace Shippen lagged a bit and Anthony found himself walking beside her.

"You were very helpful," he said. "I appreciate it."

"I like a winner, Mr. Lawrence. And you're every bit as good as Carol Wharton said. She has a very high opinion of you."

"She's a wonderful person."

"Now I'm going to shock you," she said, looking at him with wide blue eyes. "Are you still in love with her?"

It took him a moment to recover. Then he laughed and said, "That's one of those have-you-stopped-beating-your-wife questions, which can't be answered yes or no. Do you often throw things like that at people?"

"Only when I'm interested in them."

"I'm not in love with anybody, if that's interesting."

"No strings attached to you? Then, in my shy way, I'm going to ask you to take me to dinner Saturday night."

"That's the nicest legal fee I ever collected. You live with Mrs. Allen, don't you? Shall I pick you up there?"

"Yes. Six-thirty, please."

They caught up to the other two at that moment. There was an elevator waiting, and she stepped into the car and was gone, and he had a feeling that she had taken half the light in the corridor with her. Things were starting to break quickly for him. A big client. An invitation to take Grace Shippen to dinner. And now you, Mr. Clayton, if you please?

Mr. Clayton wasted no time. He said, "A brilliant job, Tony. I do hope, though, that you realize it was only your connection with the firm which first gave you the opening, and then made it possible for you to take full advantage of it."

"I know all that, sir. I want to assure you that I'm completely loyal to the firm."

That was what Mr. Clayton wanted to hear. "We'll have to get you a more suitable office, Tony. I'm sure the other senior members will agree that you should be an associate member of the firm. Your present office is not proper for an associate."

There he went, skipping over to the Happy Hunting Grounds on the left-hand side of the letterhead. "Thank you very much, sir."

"There may be some gossip about Mrs. Allen moving to us from Dickinson and Dawes. But we can take care of it. What was that phrase you used once, in referring to the way all this started?"

"The Case of the Collie's Codicil."

"Delightful. I must use that in discussing this matter. Any criticism of us will be swept away in a gale of laughter."

A big client. An invitation to dinner with Grace Shippen. An associate member of Morris, Clayton, Biddle and Wharton. Anything more just now?

A week later, something more did come. It was a letter in a handwriting which he had once known very well. It said: "Dear Tony. This is a voice from the past. I have just heard about the Case of the Collie's Codicil. I think you've evened things up now with Daddy, and hooray for you. Sincerely, Joan Dickinson Henry."

12

DURING MUCH OF HIS LIFE Anthony had been hanging around the outskirts of Philadelphia society like an eager substitute trying to make a team. Now and then they let him come in for a few plays, and patted him and told him he was doing fine. But he was always sent back to the bench very soon. He was a handy person to have around but not good enough to play regularly.

After Mrs. J. Arthur Allen became his client, everything changed. He could see the change in many ways. It was evident in the actions of the senior members of the firm, asking him to play golf on the East Course at Merion or to have lunch at the Philadelphia Club or to come out to the house for dinner and meet a very nice girl from an excellent family. It was clearly shown by the invitations he received to join people in their boxes at the Academy of Music. It was proved by the new business that began to come to him: wills, an executorship of an estate, retainers from an insurance company and a bank. There was talk at the Princeton Club of putting him up for the university's Board of Trustees in a few more years. One of the smaller banks sent out a feeler to see if he would join its Board of Directors; Logan Clayton suggested turning it down, because there would be better openings later on.

He knew, of course, that there was a lot more back of all this than merely success in business. Philadelphia society had a pattern of its own. It was not like New York society, whose walls had often been breached in the old days by the mere weight of money, and whose low modern fences could be jumped if you were mentioned in enough gossip columns. Nor was it like, say, Detroit, which had an assembly-line society that automatically took in all the top people in the automobile industry. You needed more than money or power to win acceptance in Philadelphia. And if you enjoyed the neon glare of gossip columns you had better stay out of Philadelphia, which preferred candlelight.

People often made the mistake of comparing the social organization in Philadelphia with that of Boston. Once there had been many similarities. But in Boston they had forgotten to take their cod liver oil. They had forgotten that any society gets anemic if it refuses to admit new members. Boston society had closed ranks against the invading Irish and Portuguese and Italians, so it had no new blood. It had lost the knack of making money. The only thing that kept it solvent was the spendthrift trust, developed to protect the old shipping and manufacturing and banking fortunes; Boston society lived on the interest from money its grandfathers had made. To fit into the Boston pattern you had to come from an old family, and accept the kind of taboos that people would call superstition if they saw a primitive tribe following them.

Philadelphia society had long ago worked out a procedure for taking in new members. Money and power were important, but Philadelphia wanted to see if you could produce children and grandchildren who could handle money and power. Marrying well was part of it, but Philadelphia wanted to find out if the blood lines would run true from generation to generation. Proving that you had poise and balance and culture was part of it, but would your children have the same qualities, or would they be freaks and eccentrics? Philadelphia society didn't care for freaks and eccentrics. It had produced very few of them in its two hundred and fifty years of existence. Those few had been removed quietly and quickly, the way a gentleman farmer who was proud of his stock might dispose of a two-headed calf.

Anthony knew that his acceptance was the result of a long series of tests, in which the Allen affair had merely been part of a final examination. He was being accepted because of the approval of John Marshall Wharton and the headmaster of Franklin Academy. Because of his standing with classmates at the Academy and at Princeton. Because of his mother and Miss Rogers' Select School and the long-ago marriage to William DeWitt Lawrence. Because of his grandmother and the years Harry Judson had spent teaching Latin. Because a pretty young Irish girl had come to Philadelphia long ago with a driving urge to better herself. People could trace his family back for nearly a hundred years and see that it had been moving up slowly, meeting setbacks but recovering, having secret troubles but never open scandals. There seemed to be good blood lines that ran true.

All he had to do was march firmly down the path that lay ahead. There were no more barred gates. After he chose one of the very nice girls from excellent families whom he met so easily now, the O'Donnell-Judson-Lawrence blood line would be firmly established in the Philadelphia stud book.

There was only one difficulty. He didn't want one of the very nice girls from excellent families. He wanted Grace Shippen, and he couldn't get her.

It wasn't that she didn't like him or preferred another man. From the start it was clear that she liked him better than anyone she had ever met. They saw each other several times a week, whereas she had never dated other men more than a few times each. They danced and played tennis and swam and rode and went to shows and argued about books and art and music. She was a wonderful companion: laughing, lively, interested in everything. Now and then she would kiss him in a pleasant and sanitary way. After they had been going with each other for several months he asked her to marry him. She patted his cheek and said he was the nicest person in the world but that she wasn't ready to think about marriage and please, would he keep on asking. He kept on. It became a sort of grim joke with him.

"Is it time for me to ask again?" he would say glumly.

"Poor Tony," she would sigh. "Or maybe I mean poor me. I can't seem to decide."

One night in the living room of the Allen mansion he became furious after she had given him one of her sterile kisses. He grabbed her and kissed her mouth and eyes and throat. For a moment she struggled a bit, then lay quietly in his arms. She was wearing a strapless gown that fastened up the back. He found the zipper and pulled it down and peeled her out of the dress, and tried with hands and lips to waken a response in her. At times she watched him with wide curious eyes and at other times she closed her eyes and might have been peering into herself. But her breathing never quickened and her body never responded.

At last she sat up and pushed him away and said, "I'm sorry, Tony. Nothing happened, did it?"

She gave him a sterile kiss and picked up her clothes and left him, a slim white goddess withdrawing to her temple. He never tried that experiment again.

If he had been sensible he would have traded her in for one of the very nice girls of excellent families. Unfortunately this was one of the things about which men were often not sensible. Two minds and two bodies brushed against each other and, by some chemistry, the reaction of desire began bubbling and fuming through one of the minds and bodies. He didn't know why he had to have her. Why did people feel they had to climb Mount Everest? Because it was there. Why did he have to have Grace Shippen? Because she was lovely and intelligent and a good companion and the heiress to three fortunes and a symbol of the very best in Philadelphia? Because she was there?

He knew very well now why Mrs. Wharton had hoped he wouldn't fall for the girl. He didn't agree, though, that she either had no heart or else kept it locked in one of the family safe deposit boxes. He thought he knew the answer to the puzzle of her personality, but it wasn't a very useful thing to know. Grace Shippen could be explained, he believed, by the simple statement that the things she wanted were the things she already had.

Not long after running into this blank wall he took up a hobby which was to produce remarkable and unforeseen results. It involved spending an hour, several times a week, in the magistrates' courts in the central city. One of them was held at Twelfth and Pine Streets police station, not far from his office. He passed it one morning when he was taking a walk to clear his head, and wandered in. It was odd; he had been studying or practicing law for years, and yet this was the first time he had realized that it was something more than just a fascinating game. Because here were people—sweating, lying, sobbing, angry people—at grips with the law. They were prostitutes and dope addicts and drunks. They were people accused of cheating or robbing or assaulting each other. They were people in all the different kinds of trouble people can get into. Some of them deserved it and some didn't. He watched and listened, and went back to his bloodless duels with tax laws, feeling curiously alive and stimulated.

After he had been attending the hearings for a short time he began studying criminal practice. They gave you very little of that at law school, and of course firms like his own shunned it. But he was slightly bored with his own work, much as he had once been bored in the Army when he was assigned to barrage balloons. He began studying criminal practice just as he had once read Army regulations. It was interesting, and it helped to pass the time. He started to understand what was happening, and saw that some people were getting the better of the law and others were getting a great deal the worst of it.

He was thinking about that one day, before the hearings began, when a woman standing near him began crying and telling him her troubles. He hadn't encouraged her, but she had to tell her troubles to somebody, and he was there. The landlord had raised the rent on the two rooms where she lived with her swarm of kids. She couldn't pay that much. An eviction notice had been served on her and they wanted to take her furniture and she had threatened to throw a pot of boiling water on the landlord and so here she was and what happened to her kids if she went to jail? All this in a flood of tears and with gestures like a windmill in a gale.

Without thinking, he said, "I'm a lawyer. I'll take your case if you want."

She backed off, an alley cat spitting at a hand that might be reaching out to grab her. "I don't have no money," she said sullenly.

"This is on me." he said.

It took five minutes to convince her that he was on the level. In fact it took longer to win her confidence than to win the case. It had been obvious from her first few remarks that, although she didn't know it, the landlord was playing tag with the Rent Control regulations. He looked at her eviction notice and saw that it wasn't in legal form. So when her hearing came up it only took a few sharp questions to cut the plaintiff into small bits. There was a good magistrate on the bench that day. He discharged the woman and told her to come back to him if the landlord didn't reduce the rent and make repairs. The hardest part of the whole thing, for Anthony, was getting away from the woman afterward. Now her alley-cat instincts told her to climb onto his lap and purr.

She left at last, and he was about to go back to his office when somebody grabbed his arm and called his name. He turned. For a moment he didn't recognize the person who had stopped him: a plump man in a wrinkled gray suit, who wasn't going to have to comb his hair many more years. Then he noticed the wise black eyes with their heavy, sculptured lids. Those hadn't changed.

"I'll be damned," he said. "It's Louis Donetti. I haven't seen you since law school. What are you doing here?"

"Got a case coming up I want some high bail on," Louis said. "Maybe you didn't know. I'm an assistant D.A. Hey, you went pretty good in there."

"Thanks. It was just one of those open and shut things."

"What's the angle, Tony?"

"Do I have to have an angle?"

"What the hell. I know you're in the chips. Morris, Clayton, Biddle and Wharton isn't chasing ambulances these days. You slumming?"

"I wouldn't call it that."

The wise black eyes studied him. "Funny thing," Louis said. "A corporation hot shot, working the magistrates' beat. If you don't mind some more slumming, let me take you to lunch some day. I'm curious about your angle. I better get my guy held now. I'll give you a bell."

"Sure, fine," Anthony said.

A few days later Louis called, but Anthony explained that he couldn't make it that week and would call back when things looked clearer. Of course he never did. He remembered how Louis and he used to battle each other in law school, and he didn't want Louis grilling him on his motives in taking the woman's case. He wasn't really sure what they had been. Any time you didn't know your own mind, Louis Donetti would make you feel you didn't have one.

He kept on visiting the magistrates' courts and found that an odd thing had happened. He had become a minor celebrity. He never knew whether the woman had spread the word about him, or whether Louis had talked or what. In any case, the result was that people were beginning to ask him for help. A professional bondsman might sidle up to him and muttter, "Guy over there could use you. No dough in it, natch." A magistrate might call him to the bench and say, "How's for defending a case that's coming up? I'm not too sure of the law." The phone might ring in his apartment or office and a low voice might say, "This is the house sergeant at Twelfth and Pine. I got kinda sorry for a kid who was picked up last night." There was nothing sensational about any of the cases, just little people in big trouble, and nobody to make sure they got a fair shake.

One day a reporter asked him a few questions about what he was doing, and he laughed and said it wasn't anything and he didn't want to talk about it. So it was a shock the next morning to open his paper and see a spread on Page 2 under a headline that announced:

Top-Ranked Lawyer Plays Robin Hood
At Hearings in Magistrates' Courts

The lead of the story stated: "Anthony J. Lawrence, a lawyer for big corporations and people with millions, was revealed today as a modern Robin Hood who haunts the magistrates' courts ready to defend people who do not have a dime."

"Oh God," Anthony said.

He went to his office, wondering how soon the phone calls would start. He didn't have to wonder very long. The first buzz was an inside call.

"Hello, Tony? This is Logan Clayton. How are you this morning?"

"Fine, sir. And you?"

"Pretty good, thanks. Just reading the paper."

"Oh yes."

"I suppose you saw that story about you."

"I'm afraid I did."

"Quite a surprise to me, Tony. I had no idea you went in for anything like that."

"Until I read the story I had no idea I went in for anything like that, either. The basic facts are true but the conclusions—well, I don't recognize myself."

"You do come out looking a bit too colorful. I've been trying to decide whether or not this is the sort of thing we ought to be doing. What do you think?"

"Well, sir, from my point of view it's like a surgeon doing some free work for the ward patients." That sort of professional attitude ought to appeal to Mr. Clayton.

"Not a bad way of looking at it, Tony. Well, I suppose one story can't hurt anything. They can't write you up twice for the same thing. And, as a matter of fact, it shows that in our firm we're not untouched by the facts of life, doesn't it? I assume you wouldn't stay with anything messy that's headed for the courts."

"You're quite right, Mr. Clayton."

"Good. See you later, Tony."

Next came the long rings of an outside call. A cool contralto voice said, "So you've been leading a secret life."

"Hello, Grace. You read the damned thing?"

"Yes, darling. What is this sackcloth-and-ashes stunt of yours?"

"It's nothing, actually. The story blows it up out of all proportion. It's merely like your Junior Leaguers doing their charity projects." That ought to present it in a way Grace would understand.

"Oh. Well, if that's all. You stay away from my Junior League girls, Tony Lawrence. Some of them are very cute. I'd rather not have that kind of competition."

"If I thought competition would do me any good, I'd stage a Miss America contest in my office."

Across the line came a soft laugh, like fingers strummed idly over cello strings. "You're a dear. You're not forgetting tonight?"

"You can always count on me. Maybe that's the trouble."

"When I first read the story I began wondering if I could. But I understand now. Goodby, Tony."

Two down, and how many to go? At least the two about whom he had been most worried were under control. The phone bell told him of another outside call.

It was a flat voice and it said, "Hello, Robin Hood."

"Who's this?"

"This is Little John, Robin."

He had it, now. That was the rasping tone, like a file working on a piece of tin, that Louis Donetti used in law school when he was disgusted. "Still scrapping with me, are you, Louis?"

"I didn't call up to scrap," the flat voice said. "I just wanted to compliment you on your publicity man." Louis was dragging out every word in an irritating way.

"I had nothing to do with the damn story."

"Sure. You just got caught with your halo on, that's all. You never had that lunch with me to tell me what your angle is, Tony. It's none of my business, but we always did get under each other's skins back at law school and now you got me curious."

"You just said it was none of your business."

"Yeah, but you bother me, pal. I read that story and begin asking myself what is this guy fixing to do, run for the U.S. Senate or something? Or is the running he's doing just away from himself? If he's fixing to run for something I want to know because I happen to be in that nasty thing called politics. If he's just running away from himself I want to give him running room."

"You make a very simple thing sound complicated."

"The hell I do. It's complicated, and you kid yourself it's simple. If this is a right guy, I tell myself, maybe I can help him to be righter. I can tell him he better trade in that bow and arrow for let's say a 38-caliber Police Special."

"I don't know what you're talking about and I wouldn't be interested if I did."

"There are a couple other angles I'm working on, Tony. I ask myself, is this guy a do-gooder? I hate their guts, see? A do-gooder comes around and acts noble and everybody is supposed to reform quick so they won't put him to any extra trouble. Then I ask myself, is this guy a phony? I like taking phonies apart. They go all to pieces when the going gets rough."

"You're sort of insulting, aren't you?"

"Yeah, Tony, I mean to be. The way you look now, see, you're the lord of the manor bringing a basket of goodies to the peasants, so they can put off starving until tomorrow."

"I have a full day ahead, Louis. Go play with your imagination somewhere else."

"Okay, Tony, okay. Keep fooling around, and maybe some day I'll get a chance to make you prove if you're a phony or not. So long, pal. Don't take any wooden bowstrings."

The flurry of excitement over the newspaper story soon became a thing of the past, and his life went on unchanged until a September day in 1948. The paper that morning had the usual news. The Russians were being unpleasant. Truman had made another speech and was kidding himself that he could beat Dewey. The usual auto accident and crime news. Something interesting, though: John C. M. Stearnes, local investment banker, killed by a shot from his own revolver. Police suspected murder and were hunting a mystery visitor named Howard Jones, who had been with Stearnes just before the shot was fired, according to Stearnes' butler. Stearnes had a big home out in Ithan but the shooting took place in his downtown residence on Delancey Street, where he often stayed overnight. Anthony had only met Stearnes a few times, but what made it interesting was that Stearnes was an uncle by marriage of Grace Shippen. Not on the Allen side of the family, her mother having been the only child of the Allens, but on her father's side.

After breakfast he dropped in at the Twelfth and Pine Streets police station. The cops thought he might be interested in a man they had picked up the previous night. The man's name was Chesley A. Gwynne, and he was charged with being drunk and disorderly, breaking and attempted entering. There were a couple of odd angles about the case that puzzled the cops. Anthony went into Gwynne's cell. Not many people looked good after the cops took away your necktie and belt, and after you slept in your clothes and missed a shave, but this one looked worse than average. He slumped on the cot like a dirty sack filled with rubbish.

"My name's Lawrence," Anthony said. "I'm a lawyer. The boys thought maybe you could use a little help."

The man might have been good-looking once but now he had the thickened nose of the steady drinker and eyes that looked like egg yolks doused with catsup. "You better run along," he said wearily. "I'm broke. I had a little money but I must have lost it last night."

"Your name's Gwynne, isn't it? Gwynne, now and then I take a case just for exercise. Do you mind answering a few questions?"

"They better be few. I'm tired."

"The cops said you claimed you lived in that house where you were caught breaking in. For some reason they believed you, even though the man who lives there never saw you before. Now that's all I know. If you're too tired to tell me about it, they'll give you maybe a year and a day to rest up."

"The cops got it screwed up. Or maybe I told them wrong, I don't know. I was carrying quite a load at the time. What I tried to tell them was that I used to live in that house, years ago. When I took on that load last night I forgot and tried to go back there and figured I had lost my keys and tried to climb in a window."

"What's the address of this place where you lived?"

"Markley Street, near Camac. Just a little block-long street."

"I never heard of a Markley Street," Anthony said. "The place you were trying to get in was 1009 Bendix Street."

"Well, I never heard of Bendix Street. That isn't the right number, either. It was 1015 Markley Street. Listen, why would I make it up?"

"When did you leave the place?"

"Almost twenty years ago, I guess."

"Where do you live now?"

"I've been living in L.A. for years. Great country out there. Warm. The people are warm, too. Not like the cold weather and iced-up people you have here."

It was a crazy story but the guy told it straight and it sounded good. "Why did you come back here?"

"Just got a notion. I thought I might look up some people I used to know."

"What are their names?"

"What difference do the names make? I probably wouldn't be able to find them in the phone book after all these years, and I'd have to go around asking questions to try to locate them."

He didn't sound so good answering that question. "When did you get in town?"

"I came in on the train from Pittsburgh late yesterday afternoon. I dropped into one of those bars near the station and lifted a few and got talking to a couple guys and tied one on and the next thing I knew the cops were grabbing me down on Markley Street."

"Where's your suitcase?"

"Did I have a suitcase? Yeah, I had one. Maybe I walked out of the bar and left it."

"What's the address of the bar?"

"I can't remember."

Queer, the things he could remember exactly and the things he claimed he couldn't. "Well, I can't promise you anything. Best I can do this morning is get you held for a further hearing, and look into that Markley Street business. How do you feel about that?"

"What have I got to lose?" the man said, shrugging.

Anthony left the cell and entered his name with the house sergeant as Gwynne's attorney, and agreed with him and the turnkey
that it was a weird case. When the hearing came up, he asked for
a continuance. The magistrate held Gwynne in a thousand dollars
bail for a further hearing the next morning.

Anthony went back to his office and telephoned the Department
of Public Works. The answer to the Markley-Bendix Street problem
was simple. There had been a Markley Street, covering one block
between Tenth and Eleventh. Bendix Street had ended at Ninth
and picked up again at Twelfth. In 1932, Bendix Street was cut
through and took over Markley Street and the houses had been re-
numbered. There had been a 1015 Markley Street, just as Gwynne
claimed. Anthony sent his secretary on a couple of errands, and by
late afternoon had the evidence he needed.

The next morning he went to the station house a little ahead of
time and gave Gwynne the good news. It didn't seem to make the
guy feel any better. Gwynne was in a jittery mood. He claimed that
during the night the cops had whispered about him and flashed
lights in his face. Nothing but hallucinations, of course; it was
normal for an alcoholic to have them while sweating out the with-
drawal of liquor.

Anthony went into the hearing room and waited for his case
to be called. The magistrate came in and started disposing of the
regular quota of overnight drunks. There was a stir at the back
of the room, and Louis Donetti entered with a group of people.

Louis saw him and came over. "Hello, Tony," he said. "How's that
mean old sheriff of Nottingham these days?"

"I'm a little tired of the joke," Anthony said.

"Guess I got you sore that time I called up, huh?"

"Let's forget it, shall we?"

"You just looking on today, or have you got a case coming up?"

"I have a case."

"Good. I like watching you work. Well, I'll see you. Got to check
on a guy they're holding for me."

Ten minutes went by, and the magistrate's clerk called, "Chesley
A. Gwynne." The turnkey brought Gwynne out and Anthony
joined him.

The cop who had arrested Gwynne and the man who lived at
1009 Bendix Street testified. The clerk swore Gwynne in, and
Gwynne pleaded guilty to being drunk and not guilty to the charges
of disorderly conduct, breaking and attempted entering.

Anthony took over, and said, "Mr. Gwynne, what events led up
to your presence on Bendix Street?"

"You mean about my getting a load on?"

"That's right. Tell the court, will you?"

"Well, Your Honor, I got in town from Pittsburgh that afternoon and dropped into one of those bars near the station and I guess I had a few too many. Anyway I wasn't quite sure what I did after that."

"Do you live in Philadelphia?" Anthony asked.

"I live in Los Angeles. I used to live here about twenty years ago."

"What was your address when you lived in Philadelphia?"

"It was 1015 Markley Street."

It was odd how nervous the guy was. He was getting worse every minute. "After you had those drinks at the bar, did any thought in regard to your former home come into your head?"

"Yes. I wanted to go there. But I forgot it was a long time since I lived there, and just thought I was going home. I got there and looked for my keys and thought I had forgotten them and tried to climb in a side window. This gentleman heard me and called the police."

"You told him it was your home, and gave the address?"

"Yes, but the man who lives there, this gentleman, said he never heard of me and nobody knew of any 1015 Markley Street. They said it was 1009 Bendix Street."

"But in fact it really was your former home?"

"That's right."

"Your Honor," Anthony said, turning to the magistrate, "I submit as evidence these two documents. Exhibit A is an affidavit from the Chief Clerk, Bureau of Engineering, Surveys and Zoning, to the effect that until 1932 there was a ten hundred block Markley Street, which was eliminated in that year when Bendix Street was cut through. The houses on what had been Markley Street were re-numbered at that time, and 1015 Markley Street became 1009 Bendix Street. Exhibit B is a notarized photostat of a page from a Philadelphia Telephone Directory of 1930, showing that a Mrs. J. A. Gwynne had a telephone listed under her name at 1015 Markley Street. Now, Mr. Gwynne, will you tell the court your relationship to Mrs. J. A. Gwynne?"

"Your Honor, she was my aunt."

"And you lived there with her?" Anthony asked.

"Yes, I did."

"Your Honor," Anthony said. "Mr. Gwynne pleads guilty to the charge of drunkenness, but he has already been held in jail a day and a half, which might be considered sufficient punishment if you so desire. The disorderly conduct was merely his shocked reaction to what he considered an interference with his right to enter his own home. As for breaking and attempted entering, there has to be an intent to break and enter. This can hardly exist when a man honestly believes he is merely trying to go into his own home. I feel hopeful that the gentleman who now lives in the house where Mr. Gwynne once lived will not want to press charges under the circumstances."

The magistrate called the occupant of the house to the bench and asked him if he wanted to prosecute. The man said he didn't think it was necessary. The magistrate looked at the district police captain, who shrugged. "Discharged," the magistrate said.

Anthony led Gwynne away from the stand. "Get your stuff from the house sergeant," he said. "Then we'll try to figure how to get you back to Los Angeles or wherever you're going."

Gwynne was still shaking. "That was swell, Mr. Lawrence," he said. "Yeah, I sure want to get out of this town."

Next to Anthony, Louis said in his flat voice, "Tony, it's a pleasure to watch you work. Nice, neat preparation. Did you say you sure wanted to get out of town, Gwynne?"

"Who's this guy?" Gwynne said.

"Friend of mine," Anthony said. "He's an assistant district attorney."

"Oh," Gwynne said. You could hardly hear his voice.

"He isn't going to leave town just yet," Louis said. He peered at Anthony, with just a slit of eyes showing under his heavy drooping lids. "I got a warrant here charging Chesley A. Gwynne, alias Howard Jones, with the murder of John C. M. Stearnes night before last."

"Oh my God," Gwynne said.

The hearing room had become very quiet. There was a little circle of police and detectives and reporters around the three of them. Louis Donetti wasn't looking at Gwynne. He was watching Anthony, and smiling.

"Okay, Robin Hood," Louis said gently. "Shall we step aside and give you a clear path back to the Main Line? Things are about to get rough."

Anthony moved his lips so Louis could read that he was being called a son of a bitch. "How long have you been holding up that warrant?" he asked.

"Only since last night, Tony. The last place you look for a murder suspect is in jail. And we were looking for a Howard Jones."

"You must have found out right away that I was his attorney. You could have called me last night or this morning."

"Well, Tony, it saves us a wee bit of trouble to have the guy swear to being Chesley A. Gwynne. On account of Chesley A. Gwynne is a first cousin of the dead man. We could prove who this guy is, but like I say this saves trouble."

Anthony moved close to him so that nobody else could hear, and said quietly, "You're a goddam liar. You wanted to put me in a spot."

"This is only a bad spot for a phony, pal. Remember me saying if you kept fooling around, some day I'd make you prove if you're a phony or not?"

Anthony looked around. The reporters weren't close enough to pick up this quiet conversation but they would have plenty for a story. He thought about a fact that Louis had mentioned very casually: Chesley A. Gwynne was a first cousin of the murdered man, John C. M. Stearnes. That would make Gwynne a cousin of Grace Shippen's, and probably a relative of several of the leading families of Philadelphia. This wasn't going to be just any old murder case. It was going to embarrass some of the best people in town.

He swallowed, and it was like sending sandpaper down his throat. "What are you doing, trying to set up an easy win for yourself?" he said. "You want a guy to take the case who's never had any criminal court experience?"

"I remember those mock trials we had back in law school," Louis said. "You weren't easy then. I admit a guy can go soft."

"I'll have to think it over."

Louis turned abruptly away from him. "All right, fellows," he said. "Slate Gwynne and take him to the Hall."

A thin, terrified voice cut the air. "Mr. Lawrence!" Gwynne cried. "Don't walk out on me! You've got to help! I know this town. Nobody else will help me. They'll burn me, Mr. Lawrence, and honest to God I didn't do it!"

Anthony walked over to where Gwynne was writhing in the grip of two detectives. "Now listen," he said. "Listen hard. Make no statement. Answer no questions. Don't sign a thing. They'll try to make you but they haven't any right to. Got it?"

"Sure, sure, I got it," Gwynne gasped. "You're going to help me? You'll be my lawyer?"

"I want you to understand something. I'm a corporation and tax lawyer. I've never taken a criminal case to court."

"I'll never get anybody better, Mr. Lawrence! Will you do it?"

"Yes. I'll do it."

"Take him away," Louis said.

The detectives swung Gwynne around and pushed through the crowd to the house sergeant's office.

Louis smiled. "My hero," he said.

"When are you going to produce him for a hearing?" Anthony said.

"You'll look good in the stories the reporters are gonna write," Louis said. "But this is only the start, Tony. It'll be a cheap thrill that'll wear off fast."

"I ask you to produce him for a hearing tomorrow morning."

"Don't get impatient, Tony. This will heat up fast enough for you."

"Tomorrow morning, or I get right to work on a writ of habeas corpus."

"Here I want to talk socially and you're all business. I could keep him on ice for three or four days, moving him from one police station to another."

"You won't like the statements I'll make to the papers."

Louis said in a fond tone, "I always wondered what it would be like to play for keeps against you. You're looking good in your first at bat. This thing goes nine innings, though. I'll produce Gwynne for a hearing tomorrow morning."

"Thanks."

"Maybe by tomorrow you won't feel so brash. This isn't just a little old pig in a poke you bought. This is a rattlesnake in a gunny sack. So long, hero."

13

ANTHONY BRUSHED PAST the reporters, refusing to give a statement of any kind, and returned to the office and went in at once to see Logan Clayton. He told him exactly what had happened. You had to give Mr. Clayton credit; he might be an old woman in worrying about things that might go wrong, but he toughened up when the worst really did happen. He didn't say "I warned you" or "I told you so." He listened to the story with a sort of detached concentration, like a fighter getting the word in his corner.

Finally Mr. Clayton said, "Well, Tony, you were the victim of a very clever job of entrapment."

"Unfortunately," Anthony said, "not the kind of entrapment the courts frown on."

"I assume that the papers will build you up as a colorful and romantic figure. That makes it awkward to withdraw from the case. But you could still pull out, on grounds of lack of experience in criminal practice. The average newspaper reader would accept that as a natural and honorable thing to do."

"I'm not concerned about the average newspaper reader," Anthony said. "I'm worried about what I'll think of myself, if I quit."

"Yes, I realize your pride is deeply involved."

"I'm also worried about what you would think. You might not say anything, but I have a feeling that your opinion of me would drop a few notches."

"I haven't thought it through carefully. My final reaction might depend on just one point: would the interests of the defendant be hurt or helped if you backed out? At the moment I'm inclined to think they would be hurt."

"You think I can defend Gwynne as well as anyone could? In spite of my lack of experience?"

Mr. Clayton said, "Perhaps it's silly for me to hazard an opinion on that. But I've watched you work. Some lawyers only understand the law, and there are great differences between civil and criminal law. Some lawyers understand people, and people are the same whether it's a civil or criminal case. You work in terms of people. My guess is that, if your heart's in it, nobody can defend Gwynne better than you can."

"You haven't said anything about how this might affect the firm."

"It may be damned embarrassing. But as long as you do the right thing, whatever that turns out to be, the firm will back you."

"I appreciate that a great deal, sir."

Mr. Clayton sighed. "I wish I felt that certain other people would give you the same kind of support. But I'm afraid you're in for something. The pressures that will be turned on you will be enormous. Brace yourself for them."

Anthony went back to his office and asked his secretary to start bringing in every edition of the newspapers. He knew almost nothing about Gwynne, and the newspapers gave him a lot of information he needed. Gwynne was forty-two years old. He was a first cousin of the dead man, John C. M. Stearnes. He was a third cousin of Grace Shippen. He was related to many important people. And he was, obviously, one of the freaks that Philadelphia society produced now and then. He had attended several fine prep schools and had been thrown out. He had been expelled from college. His police record began when he was sixteen with arrests for speeding. Before he was twenty he had been arrested several times for drunkenness, disorderly conduct, and brawls of one kind or another. By that time the papers had almost a standing line of type they used in such stories: "Chet Gwynne, the bad boy of Philadelphia Society, was arrested again last night for ..."

Under a 1930 date came a much more serious story. Some valuable antiques had been stolen from the home of Mrs. J. A. Gwynne, 1015 Markley Street. Chesley A. Gwynne was arrested in New York City, trying to sell the antiques to a dealer. His aunt, Mrs. Gwynne, refused to prosecute, and the case was dropped.

At that point a curtain came down over the life of Chesley A. Gwynne, as if Philadelphia society had quietly disposed of its two-headed calf. The curtain had not lifted until September of 1948, when John C. M. Stearnes had been shot with his own revolver while Gwynne was visiting him in the town house on Delancey Street. The newspapers did not yet have any new facts about the alleged murder. They had learned, however, that Gwynne had been back in Philadelphia for at least a month, living in a rooming house on lower Spruce Street under the name of Howard Jones. And last June in Los Angeles he had been arrested, charged with assault and battery on a woman with whom he had been living. That case was still pending in Los Angeles.

The newspaper stories were very kind to Anthony J. Lawrence. Robin Hood had gone out with his bow and arrow to defend the weak, and had found the weak apparently using 32-caliber revolvers. Robin Hood was still in there pitching, determined to make sure that justice was done, although somewhat out of his class in a world that used gunpowder.

In the late afternoon they started turning on the pressure. The phone rang and Grace Shippen was calling.

"Oh, Tony, you poor dear," she said. "What have they done to you?"

"Nothing yet," he said, wondering if Grace would see what he meant. She didn't.

"You've been doing such fine work and it's a shame to have this happen. Of course you're going to withdraw."

"Am I?"

"I don't mean right this second, Tony. But as soon as things cool off a little."

"I'll give it a lot of thought."

"He's a cousin of mine, isn't it awful? You'll probably find out sooner or later that the families involved have been giving him an allowance for years, on condition that he adopted another name and stayed away from the city. Tony, it will be quite easy for the families to get him a good lawyer."

"I'm not a good one?"

"Oh, Tony, don't be stiff-necked. You're a wonderful lawyer. That's why I want to protect you from any unpleasantness. You will be sensible about this, won't you?"

"We may disagree about what's sensible."

"I know you're tired and upset now, darling, and I'm not going to nag at you. Goodby, Tony."

"We had a date for tonight, didn't we?"

"I think you need some rest, Tony dear. Let's call it off for tonight."

"All right, Grace. I'll see you."

He hung up the phone, feeling a bit sick. He hadn't realized that the pressure would be so heavy or take that form. Without saying so directly, Grace had managed to put across the idea that he'd better drop the case if he wanted to go on seeing her.

A half-hour later there was another call. This was from Mrs. J. Arthur Allen. "Hello, Anthony," she said. "You know I'm not one to beat around the bush. I hope you'll find it possible to drop this hot potato you're holding."

"Mrs. Allen, I wish I could, and still feel right about it."

"This Gwynne person is no relative of mine. I don't care about him one way or another. I'm not concerned about most of his relatives, either. Only about Grace."

"Grace and I had a little talk and didn't get very far."

"Anthony, you're one of the nicest young men I know. In general, I'd back you to the limit. But Grace is very close to me. Think it over, will you?"

There were no more calls the rest of the afternoon. But at dinner that night, at the Racquet Club, the chairman of the board of a major bank stopped by to say hello. It was a bank which, he had hoped, might some day invite him to become a director. The chairman chatted with him for a couple of minutes about this and that, mentioned in passing that old Bill Brinkerhoff was likely to retire from the Board next year and do some serious fishing, the lucky stiff, and ended with a casual comment that it was too bad the way those newspaper fellows jazzed up stories, like that one today about Anthony. The chairman smiled pleasantly and moved on. Depending on how you felt, you could make anything or nothing out of that.

When you added up the call from Grace and from Mrs. Allen and the talk with the banker, it looked as if he risked losing his girl and his big client and his prospects for a directorship of a major bank, if he insisted on defending Chet Gwynne. They claimed Philadelphia was slow, did they? This was split-second stuff. It had taken him years to build his career up to this point. They could take his career apart in five minutes, and they were making sure that he realized it.

He went back to the apartment near Rittenhouse Square and found his mother waiting for him, with the newspapers stacked up beside her. He gave her all the other news about the case.

"What do you think?" he said finally. "Am I an idiot?"

She smiled at him, and shook her head. She had a lovely smile, he thought. You didn't ordinarily notice things like that about your parents. The smile and the nice brown eyes and the soft voice and all the rest of it had always been there and so he had never thought much about it. Her hair had been brown once, he remembered. She must have been quite a beautiful girl.

"Should I go on with the case?" he said.

"I can't give you advice, Anthony," she said. "All I can do is tell you something, and hope it won't sound like preaching. A long long time ago, when I was getting ready to spend the summer with Mrs. DeWitt Lawrence, your great-grandmother said something to me that I never forgot. Keep your pride hot and bright, she said, and they'll respect you more for it."

"And did you?"

"I think so. Perhaps many people might say I was foolish. Perhaps you might, too. If I hadn't stood up to Mrs. DeWitt Lawrence, you might have inherited the Lawrence millions. But you might have paid a very high price for them."

"You've never talked much about my father. I suppose he was on the weak side."

"You mustn't think that, Anthony. He was strong and fine. You and he would have, well, liked each other."

"I'm glad to know that."

"And Anthony, you were talking about dirty linen and skeletons in closets, in connection with this Gwynne matter. There's not a family anywhere that doesn't have skeletons in closets. If you looked hard enough you'd find some in ours. Don't automatically condemn anybody just because of the skeletons. It might be a murder victim, or it might only be a dead hope."

"Thanks," he said, getting up and kissing her. "I'll try to stay away from the dead hopes."

The next morning Louis Donetti kept his promise and produced Gwynne for a hearing. Anthony asked for a further hearing so that he could investigate the facts in the case. The magistrate held Gwynne without bail for a further hearing in two weeks. Anthony asked for an interview with his client. The captain of the police district talked it over with Louis Donetti, and said he could see Gwynne that afternoon.

It was a frustrating experience to interview Gwynne. The man was covering up. Either he wouldn't talk about things or he lied. And he wouldn't volunteer anything. If you had a fact, you could use it like an oyster knife to pry an answer out of him, but the answers were flabby things like these:

On his early troubles in Philadelphia: "Maybe I was a little wild as a kid. The newspapers had to make a big thing out of it. I don't want to go into all that."

On why he left the city permanently: "The family figured I'd be better off somewhere else, making a new start. I've been out on the West Coast since 1930."

On the allowance his relatives had given him: "They told you that, did they? For a while it was a hundred bucks a month. During the last eight years it's been two hundred. Yes, they wanted me to use another name. That's why the name Howard Jones. All the checks came to me under that name."

On why he came back to Philadelphia: "Just a visit, that's all. A guy can want to look in on his hometown, can't he?"

On why he visited John C. M. Stearnes that night: "He sent the checks to me. My check for September had been forwarded from L.A. But I couldn't get it cashed without identification, and how the hell can I identify myself here as Howard Jones? I wanted old Johnny to cash it for me, or at least fix it up with a bank."

On the events leading up to the shooting: "I don't have the faintest idea what happened. I'd been hoisting a few drinks. The last thing I remember is talking to old Johnny in his study. The next thing I remember is being picked up on Markley Street. Why would I shoot old Johnny and cut off my checks?"

That was all Anthony could get out of him. None of this provided a defense that would stand up in court. Plenty of lawyers might feel they had a right to walk out on such an uncooperative client. But you still couldn't duck the main issue: was there a reasonable doubt that Gwynne was guilty of murder? So far, in Anthony's mind, there was such a doubt. You couldn't walk out on a guy, carrying that doubt with you.

One morning, a week after the preliminary hearing, Logan Clayton came into his office and asked if he would be available for a meeting that afternoon. Dr. Shippen Stearnes had telephoned. He wanted to come in with his grand-niece, Grace Shippen, and discuss a matter with Anthony and with Logan Clayton.

Mr. Clayton said, "I suppose you know he's the grand old man of the Shippen and Stearnes clans. We'll have to see them, but you'd better be ready for some unusual pressure. Doctor Stearnes is a delightful old gentleman and it won't be easy to say no to him. As for Grace Shippen, well, you know your problems there."

"It's not fair for them to start turning the heat on you and the firm as well as on me," Anthony said."

"Start turning it on?" Mr. Clayton said. "My boy, you don't know what we've had to go through, these last ten days."

"It might be better if I resigned from the firm."

Logan Clayton stuck out his jaw. "We wouldn't accept it," he said.

The meeting began very gently and pleasantly, as any meeting did when Dr. Stearnes was conducting it. He was a wonderful old man of eighty-one. He was worth millions and had devoted his life to studying the effect of heredity and environment on various creatures. His work had won him the top award of the American Association for the Advancement of Science. At eighty-one he was erect and active, and his mind worked as precisely as a well-tested scientific formula.

"My dear friends," he said, smiling at them, "we have all been distressed at this terrible thing which has happened, and the consequences it has brought. May I discuss them with you this afternoon?"

"We'll be glad to discuss them," Logan Clayton said. "But I would like something understood right at the start, sir. If we are to be subjected to more pressure, this meeting will be useless. Mr. Lawrence has been pushed by circumstances into a very unhappy position. He has been doing what an honorable man should do. This firm will not let him down."

Dr. Stearnes said gently, "Let me point out that the pressure brought to bear on you was not the result of any joint plan. People acted on their own, in the belief that they had the best interests of you and others at heart. I assume, my dear young sir, that you were very upset by the pressure."

"I saw everything I've worked for going down the drain."

"Then perhaps this will make you feel better," Dr. Stearnes said, beaming like a Santa Claus in an orphanage. "We have had a formal council of the families involved. I am here to tell you that we approve completely of the fact that you are acting as Chet Gwynne's lawyer." He looked around at all of them, as if expecting to see a row of happy shining faces.

Anthony couldn't see his own face, but he could see that Grace was looking at him almost fearfully. Logan Clayton hunched his head down against his chest, peering at Dr. Stearnes like a bear roused from sleep.

"Astonishing," Mr. Clayton said in a toneless voice.

"I can see this will require some explanation," Dr. Stearnes said, preparing to unwrap the present so they could see how nice it really was. "We start with the fact that the families do not seek an eye for an eye and a tooth for a tooth. We would be ill advised to do so. Much as we might like to deny it, Chet Gwynne is of our own blood. The best thing we can do is to stand aside and let justice take its course."

"He might go to the chair," Mr. Clayton said bluntly.

"True. And, as one who has always upheld the influence of heredity over environment, I would have to admit that the families would bear a certain stigma."

Anthony said, phrasing the question carefully, "And if, by some chance, he was acquitted ... ?"

"We would accept that in the same spirit, my dear young sir. I think I can promise you, however, that we would not in that event turn our backs on Chet as completely as we have done in the past eighteen years. We would accept more responsibility for him. As an alcoholic and a man of generally weak moral fiber, he should not be tossed willy-nilly back into the world. A small place in the country would be best for him, perhaps."

"A sanitarium, you mean?"

"Not exactly, Mr. Lawrence. A place of his own, where he could potter around and even have a few drinks. Well looked after, of course."

Anthony shuddered slightly. It sounded like Eastern Penitentiary, but with nice silverware. "I'm very glad you've come to this decision," he said. "Every man has a right to be defended in court. If I didn't do it, somebody would."

"Quite so. And we are not unaware of the fact that another lawyer might approach this in a very different spirit than yours. Since no great financial rewards could be expected, another lawyer handling the case might seek his payment in headlines, with scant regard for justice."

This was very interesting, Anthony thought. He wondered if Dr. Stearnes was referring to justice for Chet Gwynne or justice for the families he represented. He remembered the nightmare thought that had prowled through his head some time ago. Did the families have some dirty linen they didn't want washed in public? Had they been afraid that he would be able to rummage through the right bureau drawers and find it? It might be worth while to explore that subject very delicately.

"Yes," Anthony said, "I can see what might happen if some lawyers took the case. It's always possible to twist facts, and to make good intentions seem bad."

Dr. Stearnes looked at him with approval. "Exactly. We feel confident that you will deal honestly with the facts of the case. Ah, by the way, what sort of a man is this Assistant District Attorney who will handle the prosecution?"

"Louis Donetti? Louis will play rough."

"He has been investigating the background of the case very thoroughly. In fact, more thoroughly than seems necessary."

So that was it, Anthony thought. Louis and his boys had been poking around and asking pointed questions. The families were worried. He said, "Has Donetti been investigating the immediate background, or the remote background of the case?"

"Both. And, after all, Chet's youthful misdeeds have nothing to do with the present. Some of us have been deeply disturbed by this prying. Donetti apparently sees this case as a chance to make political capital."

"Have you any idea what he has learned?"

"From us?" Dr. Stearnes said, in amazement. "My dear young sir, none of us is involved in the case or wishes to be. He has learned nothing from us. There is nothing to learn. But, judging from the questions, I suspect that he would like to put the Philadelphia way of life on trial, along with Chet Gwynne."

"He can't do it by himself," Anthony said. "The defense would have to open the subject for him."

Dr. Stearnes studied him for a few moments, and during that time the Santa Claus mask hung askew and allowed the scientist to peer out. His eyes were as cold and impersonal as if he were about to dissect a laboratory specimen. "That is why," Dr. Stearnes said finally, "we would like Chet defended by a lawyer who will seek justice rather than headlines."

This might be a good time to rummage through those bureau drawers. He said, "Young Chet Gwynne was obviously a real problem. What were the reasons why he left various prep schools?"

"Lack of study. Pranks. Nothing serious. His aunt—a niece of mine, by the way was a delightful person but unable to cope with him. She is dead now, of course. De mortuis nihil nisi bonum, if I remember my Latin. I shan't criticize her, but she did adore and spoil the boy."

"And when he was expelled from college?"

"He got a girl in trouble. A pretty enough girl, but quite cheap. And of course there was a greedy mother in the picture. The girl was caught in his room at college, and he was expelled. Chet wanted to marry her, but it would have been a tragic and unsuitable thing. We bought off the girl and her mother."

"Did Chet take a job after that?"

"Let me see. Yes, poor old Johnny—John C. M. Stearnes, you know—gave Chet a job in that investment banking firm of his. It didn't work out well. Chet was starting to drink too much. He gambled a lot, too. When some money was missing, a few thousand dollars or so, things pointed to Chet. So we sent him out beyond Strafford to manage a dairy farm which I believe your father owned, Grace. We hoped that would straighten him out. But he wouldn't stay there. No bright lights, you know. He returned to his aunt on Markley Street, although he was warned that we would do nothing for him as long as he took that attitude. Well, you know how he repaid his aunt, because the papers dug up from their files that business of the stolen antiques. She was broken-hearted. At that point it was necessary to take a firm stand with the young man. Poor old Johnny arranged a monthly allowance for him, and told him to get out and stay out. The allowance would stop if he returned to Philadelphia."

"About his parents," Anthony said. "I assume they died when he was very young. Was any money left for him?"

"Not directly. Let's see, now. One of his grandparents, yes, that would have been Edward, was still living and had much of the family fortune. Chet's father died rather young, before he could earn much money or inherit anything, and left his modest estate to Chet's mother. When Chet's mother died, she left part of her estate for Chet's education and general up-bringing, and that was gone by the time Chet came of age. The rest of his mother's estate went to Chet's aunt, his mother's sister-in-law. The intention was that this should go to Chet some day, but when he turned out so badly it became obvious that the money would only be wasted, and his aunt cut him out of her will."

"Thank you very much," Anthony said. "That answers everything."

"I am so glad," Dr. Stearnes said. "And I'm delighted that we have managed to straighten out the temporary unpleasantness. You might thank my grand-niece for her efforts along those lines. She stood up for you like a trooper. Well, my dear friends, that concludes my business."

"Tony," Grace said, "may I see you alone for just a moment before we go?"

Anthony walked with Grace down the hall to his office. As soon as they entered it, she closed the door firmly and moved close to him.

"Tony," she said in a small voice, "I was wrong to treat you that way."

"Don't worry about it."

"But I do," she murmured. Her arms crept around his neck and her long slim body pressed against him. Her kiss was not quite as cool and antiseptic as usual. "Do you forgive me, Tony?"

"There's nothing to forgive. You acted in a very natural way."

She shivered a little. "A murder is such an ugly thing. I hate ugly things. Tony, I felt so proud when everybody decided they could have confidence in you."

"Confidence about what?"

"Why, just as Uncle Ship said, to make sure that justice is done."

"I'll try to make sure of it," he said, trying to keep any note of grimness out of his voice.

"I know you will, Tony dear." She kissed him again, and gave him a bright smile and left.

Two minutes later Logan Clayton walked in. His usually pink face was flaming. "I held myself in," he said. "It was a job, but I managed to do it. That is the damnedest proposition one alleged gentleman ever made to another in my hearing. Do you know what I'm talking about, Tony?"

"I'm afraid I do, sir."

"I've got to give the old gentleman the benefit of the doubt, but by God, it comes hard. He's so steeped in the science of heredity that he thinks he's dealing with chromosomes instead of people. I'm not crazy, am I, Tony? He made the proposal so gently and subtly that it's hard to pin anything down. What was your impression?"

"The same as yours," Anthony said. "Get him off without a scandal, if you can. Otherwise, let him go to the chair quietly, please."

"Is there a way to get him off without a scandal?"

"I haven't seen it."

"How about with a scandal?"

"Doctor Stearnes said a great many interesting things. From his point of view, the families acted honorably and with the best intentions. My client may not have seen it in that light."

"It's a possible line of defense, isn't it?"

"Yes, sir."

"Would you use it, Tony?"

"I can't answer that question now."

Logan Clayton shook a fist under his nose. "Let me make this clear," he said. "If your client is convicted, and if you fail to make full use of any legitimate line of defense, we'll accept that resignation you offered this morning." He turned and stamped out of the room.

Anthony nodded. Yes indeed, there was a real man in the firm of Morris, Clayton, Biddle and Wharton. He didn't know whether there were two of them or not.

14

HE SAT IN THE CELL with Chet Gwynne at Moyamensing Prison and studied the man. The days in jail without liquor had made changes in Gwynne's appearance, but not entirely for the better. Now that his eyes were no longer bloodshot you saw how weak and watery they were. Now that his face had lost its puffiness, it looked like gray cardboard that had been left out in the rain. His hands had stopped shaking, but his body moved with the abrupt jerks of a marionette.

"How are we doing, Mr. Lawrence?" Gwynne asked. "You're gonna get me off, aren't you?"

"If I can, Chet."

"Look, Mr. Lawrence, if a guy blacks out and can't remember anything, how can they prove he meant to kill somebody and went ahead and did it?"

"By circumstantial evidence. Blacking out is no defense, unless it's insanity. Let's talk about that blackout, Chet."

"I'm not going to talk about it! That's what happened, see, and I'll tell anybody. I was drinking and don't remember."

Gwynne was standing up, his body jerking and twisting. Anthony shrugged. Deliberately or not, the man had erased part of that evening from his mind. "Let's go back a bit earlier in the evening," he said. "You were talking to Mr. Stearnes about that trouble of yours in Los Angeles. About the woman who charged you with beating her up. You were telling Mr. Stearnes it was going to cost something to buy her off, and—"

"Don't pull that stuff on me," Gwynne snapped. "I never told you anything like that. What I told you was I wanted him to cash that check for me or fix it up with a bank. Lay off trying to trick me."

"You've got me confused with the prosecuting attorney," Anthony said. "If I don't find out about certain things, they may explode in my face at the trial, and I won't know how to handle them." He got up slowly. "But of course if you won't give me the help I need, you'd better get another lawyer."

Gwynne grabbed his arm. "Now wait, now wait, Mr. Lawrence. Don't get sore. It's just that I'm not used to having anybody on my side. I keep thinking you're against me, too."

"My job is to put up the best defense for you I can. If you tell me something that would hurt your case, it's not my duty to bring it out in the trial. But I've got to be ready if the prosecution brings it out."

"Yeah, I see what you mean. That stuff about that woman I lived with was in the papers, wasn't it? So I guess they'd bring that out in the trial. Well, your guess was right. That was what I was talking about to old Johnny. Five thousand bucks would square her. Out of the lousy two hundred bucks a month they sent me, I couldn't ever save that much."

"You had been in Philadelphia a month before that night. Why did you wait so long before asking him for the money?"

Gwynne's glance flickered around the cell, as if looking for a good answer. "A month, was it? That's right, I had been here a month. Well, it took me a couple weeks to work myself up to getting in touch with him, because he always said no more allowance if I ever came back. Then he put me off for a week or so before he'd see me. Maybe he was checking the Los Angeles angles."

Gwynne had found an answer but it wasn't a very good one. Anthony decided to come back to that question later, from another direction. "Some of your relatives have been giving me a little background about you," he said casually.

Gwynne stiffened. "Who?"

"Doctor Shippen Stearnes, for one."

"That son of a bitch."

"Chet, I've heard their side now, and I'd like to hear yours."

"What did they say?"

"You got a girl in trouble at college and were expelled. The family bought you out of the jam with the girl. John C. M. Stearnes gave you a job. You were drinking and gambling and walked off with several thousand dollars. They gave you a job running a dairy farm and you refused to do it. You carted away some valuable antiques from your aunt's house and tried to peddle them in New York and were caught. It broke her heart. Because of that, she cut you out of her will."

While he had been talking, Chet Gwynne started trembling. Now his eyes were bright and hot. His hands curled into claws and his breath hissed like steam under pressure.

"The bastards," he said. "Oh the God-damned praying bastards. I got a girl in trouble, did I? She wasn't their kind so it couldn't be love or anything but just getting a girl in trouble, and the fact I wanted to marry her didn't mean a thing except I was a wild kid who always wanted to do the wrong thing. Sure, I'll tell you about her. I'll tell you the works."

He paced the cell, four strides up, four strides down, opening and clenching his fists. Anthony sat quietly. The dam was breaking, and if he didn't move or interrupt he would see how much dirty water had been backed up.

"She was a good kid," Gwynne said hoarsely. "All right, she let me get her into trouble. That happens, though, and I don't care which side of the tracks the girl comes from. I got her in trouble and I wanted to marry her, but her mother's a scrub woman and the girl works in a factory and so the family thinks it would be a worse scandal to marry her than it was to get her in trouble. I'm telling you, we'd have made a go of it if we had had the chance. But I let the family make a dirty thing of it and rub her nose in a little money. The bad mistake I made wasn't getting her in trouble. It was letting the family haul me out of it.

"Old Johnny gave me a job in his office. It was one of those jobs where you get paid off in peanuts and a lot of crap about buckling down and showing what you're made of, my boy. Yeah, I started drinking some. Maybe I took a few days off now and then to watch them run at Bowie and Havre de Gras, so there's your gambling. But I didn't take that dough to gamble with. I kept thinking about that girl they bought off for me. It got so bad I took some money and hunted her up and tried to get her back. But she's married by then and spits in my face, and won't even let me look at the kid she had.

"I went on a real bender and blew the money, and old Johnny kicked me out of the office and the family sent me back in the sticks to run a lousy farm. You're damn right I didn't stay there. I was going nuts. I came back to my aunt's, and I didn't have any dough at all and they told my aunt not to give me any. So I walked off with a load of antiques and got caught trying to sell them. You know who owned that stuff? My mother and father. Sure, everything was in my aunt's name but it was supposed to come to me. Then they really turned the screws on me. They gave me a choice of going to jail or getting out of town on a lousy hundred bucks a month. That's a choice, is it? I got out.

"I went to the West Coast and I had one hope left. I was supposed to get some money when my grandfather died and when my aunt died. The family took care of that. I know how they must have worked on my grandfather and aunt to make them cut me out of their wills. If I'd had any sense I'd have got myself a slick lawyer and taken against those wills on grounds of undue influence. Because the money was supposed to come to me. Everybody knew it. But they don't let loose any dough in families like mine to somebody who don't fit their goddam pattern. You know the racket. Play ball, keep your nose clean, marry a girl they approve of, and you get all kinds of nice little things. You inherit dough. You get snap jobs that pay good—trusteeships, executorships, directorships of this or that bank or company the family has its hooks in. A guy from the right family can make a good living even if he's got no brains, no talent, no desire to work, no nothing, just as long as he fits the goddam pattern. But bust loose, like me, and they cut your throat with the best manners of anybody in the world.

"Well, that's it. They took my girl. They took away my money. Then to cap it all you know what they did? Do you? Do you?" He was standing in front of Anthony, his face twisted, his voice cracking like glass. "They took away my name!" he cried. "They stole it from me. They peeled it off me like a coat I didn't have a right to wear. They kicked me out and said there wasn't any Chet Gwynne any more and that my name was Howard Jones. Who's Howard Jones? Who's that bastard? He's a zero. He's a nothing. And that's who I've got to be from then on." He dropped onto the cot in the cell and pushed his face into the mattress. His shoulders twitched and you could hardly catch his muffled words. "Of all the dirty things they did to me that was the worst. They took my name away. They stole my name."

It was quiet in the cell but for the soft thick noises coming from the face pressed into the mattress. It was very odd, Anthony thought. There was Gwynne hating his family and everything it stood for, but clinging to a name that meant nothing if it did not mean the family and its standards and its orderly way of life.

He had both sides of the story, now, and what did he have? A leaf falls from a tree, and one man looks at it and thinks of how leaves make a lawn untidy. Another man looks at it and thinks of the shade that leaves give in summer. You start with a fact. A leaf falls. A man gets a girl in trouble. But then each person looks on the leaf or on the fact in terms of his own reaction to it, and which reaction is the truth? Is one right and the other wrong? Is the truth to be found somewhere else? Or is truth something you vote on, like an election, and declare that whatever receives the greatest number of votes is hereby elected the truth in accordance with the will of the people?

Those were not questions he could answer. He had both sides of the story now, and what he had were a few leaves falling from a tree.

He said gently, "Chet, feeling the way you do, it couldn't have taken you several weeks to work up courage to go to Stearnes. When you came back to Philadelphia, you were ready to fight. What did you do in that month before Stearnes was shot?"

Gwynne lifted his head. His face had the cold blank look of a photograph in the Rogues' Gallery. "You're a smart cookie," he said. "I'm glad you're not the prosecutor. I knew old Johnny. Next to him, stainless steel is soft. He'd have told me to get the hell out or no more checks, if I'd gone to him cold. But I knew something else about old Johnny. He always liked women. There never was a time he wasn't keeping one, and everybody knew it but his wife and kids. He never got his women in trouble and got caught at it. He played it nice and quiet like the family rule book says. So I spent three weeks watching him. At the end of that time I knew the name of the latest one and how often he visited her apartment and how often she sneaked into his town house and everything. So finally I called old Johnny up and said I wanted to see him. He told me to beat it, and hung up on me. I dropped him a note with a few hints in it. He didn't hang up the next time I called. So I went to see him, and told him what I needed and said if I didn't get it I'd let his wife and kids know about the dame he was keeping. You want to call it blackmail? Go ahead. It's a long way from murder, though. Is a blackmailer likely to shoot? Hell, no."

"You must have had quite a row with him."

"I don't know what I had," Gwynne said sullenly. "I took a pint with me when I went to see him. I was drinking. I don't know what happened. I'm not ever going to remember for anybody. Because I'm not a murderer, see?"

"All right, Chet."

"You said you'd never use anything that might hurt me. This stuff I've told you. Would that hurt me?"

Anthony said slowly, "It would depend on how it was presented at the trial."

"Spell it out for me, Mr. Lawrence. Would all this stuff add up to a defense? If you presented it right?"

"I think it would."

"Wouldn't they squirm, though!" Gwynne muttered. "Wouldn't they hate to see all the skeletons dragged out of closets and made to dance in public. Funny thing. I don't like the idea. But I'll tell you something else. I don't like the idea of going to any electric chair. If it turns out that's the only defense we have go ahead and use it."

"We'll see what turns up," Anthony said. He got up and called for the guard and left.

It might be a very good defense, he thought. Juries decided murder cases, and juries were made up of people, and you could do a lot of things when you were dealing with people. He had seen that line of defense emerge hazily, and Logan Clayton had seen it, when Dr. Shippen Stearnes was telling them the families' side of the story. It was a very clear line of defense, now that Gwynne had told his side. You put Gwynne on the stand and let him tell about a persecuted kid who wanted to marry a girl and was forced to leave her. You showed the kid being slowly crushed until there wasn't much left but husk, and then you showed people taking the husk of his name from him and throwing the rest of him away. And you showed that these people were not upright and honest, as they pretended to be, but that they too had stains in their lives which they had managed to conceal. Finally you showed the man who had been crushed returning to his home and putting up a fight in the only way he could fight, by threatening to tell about the stains.

Gentlemen of the jury, who drew out the gun? Did a man who once made a mistake and was crushed for it become maddened into grabbing it and firing? Or did the man who claimed to be righteous reach for his gun and threaten his visitor? Who meant to shoot who? Did somebody see a black and empty future ahead of him and try to commit suicide? Was there a struggle? Who knows? Who can call it murder?

It was a defense, all right. It could be a winning defense. Of course it would leave a few losers in its path. Among them would be Dr. Shippen Stearnes and Grace Shippen and their relatives. Also Morris, Clayton, Biddle and Wharton. Also Anthony J. Lawrence. Was it right for all of them to lose, just to save one man? Perhaps it was, if the truth was on Chet Gwynne's side. And that brought you back to the falling leaf, and the question as to whether the truth was that leaves cluttered up a lawn or gave a comforting shade.

15

AT THE FURTHER HEARING two days later Louis Donetti didn't show his hand any more than he had to. He put on the stand the policeman who had been called to the house, the medical examiner who had conducted the autopsy, and the Stearnes butler. John C. M. Stearnes had been killed by a bullet from his own 32-caliber revolver which had entered his chest from the front and passed through his heart. The bullet had been fired from close range, but it was highly unlikely that the fatal wound could have been self-inflicted. A visitor calling himself Howard Jones was in the room at the time and loudly quarreling with Mr. Stearnes, and said Howard Jones fled afterward, probably through a French window opening onto the garden beyond the room. Donetti asked the butler if he saw Howard Jones in the courtroom, and the butler pointed to Chesley A. Gwynne.

Anthony let the policeman and medical examiner go without cross-examination.

The butler's testimony was the heart of the prosecution's case. Anthony cross-examined him slowly, being careful not to give the butler any cause for alarm or hostility. He wanted thousands and thousands of words of testimony from the butler which he could study at leisure. Perhaps something might turn up. And if it did, and if he could create a trap for use at the trial, he wanted the butler to be relaxed and off guard.

The butler's name was George Archibald. He was thin, of medium height, and combed his hair in precise lines over a bald spot on his head. When he took the stand he looked around the crowded room and frowned slightly, as if wondering how so many people could possibly have bought their clothes at the wrong shops. He had worked for John C. M. Stearnes, he testified, for fourteen years, three months and two days before the evening of the shooting. He had obviously been devoted to his employer, and would not willingly say anything that might reflect on him.

Archibald's testimony was very damaging. He had neither known nor heard of Chesley A. Gwynne, alias Howard Jones, before the evening of the shooting. Stearnes told him that a visitor named Howard Jones would be coming, and that he was an unpleasant person, and that Archibald should stay within call in case there was any trouble. Archibald admitted the visitor soon after eight P.M. and led him, as instructed, to the ground-floor study at the rear of the house. Stearnes was upstairs taking his usual after-dinner nap. Archibald did not like the way the visitor peered around the study; the man was badly dressed and had been drinking and might steal something. Archibald tried to memorize the position of valuable things in the room, before leaving to call Stearnes, so that he would know if anything was missing when he returned.

He notified his employer, who said he would be down in five minutes and told Archibald to offer the visitor a drink. Archibald returned to the study and asked the visitor what he would like to drink. The visitor pulled a half-empty pint bottle from the left-hand pocket of his jacket, and said the stuff Stearnes drank was probably like tea and that all he wanted was a glass, no ice, for his own whisky. Archibald brought a glass to him on a tray. Meanwhile Archibald checked to see if anything had been taken or disturbed. He noticed that the center drawer of Mr. Stearnes' desk was slightly open, although it had been closed when he first brought the visitor into the room. In that drawer Mr. Stearnes kept his revolver. Archibald saw that something heavy was weighing down the inside pocket of the visitor's jacket. When the man leaned over to pour a drink into the glass, the jacket bulged outward and Archibald saw a gleam of metal.

Archibald went back upstairs and warned his employer and asked if he should call the police. Stearnes looked thoughtful, and said that wouldn't be necessary at the moment.

Stearnes went downstairs and spent the next two hours talking to the visitor. Now and then Stearnes rang a buzzer for Archibald. Each time it was to have Archibald carry away two empty glasses on the tray; Stearnes liked to have everything neat and clean around him, and did not like to use a glass twice without having it washed. In fact Stearnes did not even like to have emptied glasses around the room.

Not long after ten o'clock the buzzer rang again. This time Stearnes met Archibald at the door of the study, and handed him a tray with one glass on it. Stearnes said he would not need Archibald any more that evening, and closed the door of the study. Archibald did not like the idea of leaving, but it was unthinkable to stay nearby when he had clearly been dismissed for the evening. He went up to his room at the second floor rear. Half an hour later he heard loud and angry voices from his employer and the visitor. There was the sound of a scuffle, and a shot. He ran downstairs, opened the door of the study and found Stearnes lying on the floor with the revolver two feet away. A French window opening onto the garden in the rear of the house was open. Stearnes seemed to be dead. Archibald telephoned for the police.

That was his story, and it was bad.

In cross-examination Anthony led him back over every bit of it, disregarding the impatience of the magistrate and the attempts of Louis Donetti to hurry him. Archibald made an excellent witness for the prosecution. He gave responsive answers and never tried to evade the question. He had a remarkable memory. Anthony tested it several times, by asking a question requiring a detailed answer and then moving to another subject for a few minutes and finally rephrasing his original question. Each time Archibald could repeat all the details in his first reply. He also repeated them in somewhat different words, which proved he had not memorized his testimony. Archibald was very observant. He gave an exact description of the clothes the visitor had been wearing. He described the contents of the study in enormous detail; Anthony had no way of checking his accuracy on that subject, at the moment, but it seemed likely that he had named and placed correctly every piece of furniture and bric-a-brac in the room. Archibald was evidently proud of his ability to remember details, and liked to demonstrate it. He answered many questions much more fully than necessary.

For example, when asked how many drinks John C. M. Stearnes had during the evening, he replied, "Mr. Stearnes had three drinks while his visitor was present. I assume that he took about an ounce and a quarter each time, because that was his usual amount. He had a Scotch-and-soda, using Glen Murry Scotch, for his first and second drinks. For his third, he had a rather heavier-bodied Scotch, Royal Tartan, with his soda."

Anthony said, "Why do you say you assume that he took about an ounce and a quarter? You must have known exactly, since you apparently served him each time."

"No sir, I did not serve him. Mr. Stearnes kept a liquor cabinet in the study, containing a bottle of Glen Murry Scotch and one of Royal Tartan Scotch, and one bottle of Napoleon brandy. He usually had an ounce and a quarter of brandy in a brandy sniffer immediately after dinner, before taking his nap."

"Mr. Archibald, if you did not pour his drinks and were not in the room, how do you know exactly what Mr. Stearnes had to drink each time?"

"I was able to check on that, sir, from the glass he had used. The aroma of the two Scotches is quite distinctive, and in fact, so is that of the Napoleon brandy. Most good liquor has a characteristic bouquet of its own. In fact, of course, so does bad liquor, although

I hesitate to call it a bouquet. Mr. Stearnes' visitor was drinking a very raw and cheap rye. I do not know its name, but it was easy to tell which glass Mr. Stearnes had used and which glass his visitor had used."

"You sniffed at each glass whenever you took ones that needed to be washed from the room? Isn't that rather unusual?"

"There was a practical reason for it, sir. In that way I could keep track of which bottle Mr. Stearnes was using, and bring a new bottle if it became necessary. By the end of the evening my calculations indicated that there were four ounces of Glen Murry remaining and fifteen ounces of Royal Tartan. By keeping track of the liquor in that way I was able to replenish the supply, without asking Mr. Stearnes if he needed a new supply or fumbling around in the liquor cabinet to see what was left."

"I assume that you are somewhat of a connoisseur of fine liquor, Mr. Archibald."

"Well, yes sir. And, if I may say so, of other fine things as well. To provide proper service to a gentleman like Mr. Stearnes it is necessary to have a rather wide knowledge in the fields of food, liquor, clothing, and so on."

"Do you yourself drink, Mr. Archibald?"

"To a limited extent. I permit myself two drinks a day, of an ounce and a half each, always in the evening after the serving of dinner. Usually one at eight o'clock and the other at ten. Personally I prefer a light-bodied bourbon, unmixed and without ice, with a chaser of water. I feel that ice destroys the bouquet."

"Naturally you had two drinks on the evening in question."

"Yes sir. The first one a bit later than usual, because the visitor arrived at the time I would usually have had it, and the second at about the usual time. I do not care to gulp a drink. I prefer to relax and savor it slowly."

Anthony probed into the details of Archibald's final trip to the study in answer to the buzzer. The door was closed when Archibald arrived. He rapped on it. Stearnes opened the door part-way and handed him the tray holding one used glass. Archibald did not actually see the visitor on that occasion because the door hid him from view. The glass on the tray was one the visitor had been drinking from, because Archibald sniffed it and identified the smell of the raw and cheap rye which the visitor had brought.

Anthony accepted every answer politely and made no attempt to back Archibald into any corners. He took two hours for his cross-examination. Then he said he was not calling any witnesses for the defense. The magistrate held Chesley A. Gwynne, alias Howard Jones, without bail for the Grand Jury.

Two weeks later the October Grand Jury brought an indictment, and Gwynne was arraigned in court and entered a plea of not guilty to the charge of murder. Louis Donetti put the case on the calendar for trial in December.

To Anthony, there was a dream-like quality to the days that followed. On one hand, his life went on normally: tax work, corporation law, Grace Shippen. On the other hand there was the Gwynne case, seeping through his life like a dark stain and coloring everything it touched. The pressure that had formerly been brought against him no longer existed, but there was a new and subtle type of pressure. People did not ask him outright how he was going to defend the case but they kept prying at him gently to see how he felt about it. Wasn't it a shocking thing to happen to fine people like the Stearnes and Shippen families? Did he think the trial would be a long one? How was Chet Gwynne bearing up? Wasn't it a shame that the man hadn't stayed out on the West Coast? Didn't Anthony think that the families had really given Chet Gwynne every possible chance?

They were testing him all the time. What they really wanted to ask was: You're not going to drag fine names in the dirt, are you? We can trust you, can't we?

Meanwhile an odd thing was happening to Chet Gwynne's attitude toward the case. You could tell a defendant a million times not to talk to anybody about his case, but as time went by in jail, waiting for trial, the average defendant would start talking. There were guards, either sympathetic or pretending to be sympathetic. There was the warden and his assistant, coming around to drop soothing comments. There were other prisoners asking questions. After the strangeness of jail wore off, a prisoner usually adjusted himself to a community which had many things in common with other types of communities. For example, the prison community could approve or disapprove of an inmate. The normal prisoner wanted the community to approve of him, just as most people always wanted the approval of their communities. So the prisoner talked, and responded to sympathy and interest. He told parts of his story which showed him in a good light. He sought advice and encouragement.

Gwynne had adjusted himself to the prison community and was talking. He was getting sympathy. Every time Anthony visited him there were more signs of a change in his thinking. First Gwynne had posed as a bewildered victim of circumstance. Then he turned into a martyr. The final step was to become a man with a mission. He was not only going to have a chance to justify himself in public, but also a chance to expose those who had persecuted him. Not that he wanted to, of course, but it was his duty. As one who knew the dark truth about many leading people it was his duty to bring it to light.

Prisons being what they were, Anthony knew that much of this was relayed to Louis Donetti. In fact, he suspected that Louis might have directed the prison campaign of sympathy and advice and encouragement. Now and then Gwynne made a remark that might have come straight from Donetti, such as saying that maybe this case would burn down a few manors around a few absentee landlords. Of course the assistant district attorney was not visiting Gwynne, because that would not be quite ethical without Anthony present. But it would be easy for Louis to conduct his campaign through the warden and guards, and prisoners who wanted to stay on the right side of the District Attorney's office. Louis wanted to put Philadelphia society on trial along with Chet Gwynne.

And the big question was: how did you defend Gwynne without doing just that?

16

THIS WAS THE second day of the trial of Commonwealth of Pennsylvania vs. Chesley A. Gwynne, alias Howard Jones. The Quarter Sessions courtroom was filled with people, whispering and coughing and stirring around as they waited for the judge to come in. Chet Gwynne, seated at the defense table, counted the house and said with satisfaction that it was a sell-out. Gwynne seemed to look on the proceedings as a sort of pageant, like the Mummers Parade, with himself as the center of attraction. He spoke of taking the witness stand as if he expected to receive a prize there.

Anthony glanced around the room, and had the odd sensation that his life was starting to repeat itself. Was this really a courtroom where, in a short time, he might have to make a decision that would affect the course of his life? Or was it the gym at Franklin Academy where Anthony J. Lawrence of the Sixth Upper was trying to decide which of two Salutatory addresses he would give? The faces in the crowd were different, of course. Years ago he had seen Eddie Eakins and his grandfather and grandmother and the football coach. Now he saw Logan Clayton and the John Marshall Whartons and Grace Shippen and Dr. Shippen Stearnes. Instead of the radical master, Mr. Glenmor, there was Louis Donetti at the prosecutor's table. Both Glenmor and Donetti had felt the same hot urge to rip apart the classic pattern of Philadelphia life. But Mr. Glenmor had wanted to destroy because he liked picking things to pieces, while Donetti thought he had to tear down before he could build something better.

There was one link in the audience between that long-ago night and the present. His mother was still trying, after all these years, to catch his glance and exchange proud smiles with him. Years ago he had been embarrassed by that. Today he smiled back at her. He wasn't at all sure, however, that today she would have any reason to be proud of him.

This was the day when he would have to see if the quickness of the hand could deceive the observant eyes of George Archibald, butler to the late John C. M. Stearnes. Donetti had finished his direct examination of Archibald yesterday, and today Anthony could cross-examine.

The prosecution had built a strong case. Some of it was the case which Donetti had presented at the hearing several months ago: testimony by the medical examiner, by the police, by the butler. Yesterday, also, Louis Donetti had brought out his secret weapons, and they had been deadly. Stearnes had been a man who used filing cases the way most people used waste baskets. He had kept the letters Gwynne had written to him throughout the years, and copies of his brief and brusque replies. There were ten letters from Gwynne. Nine of them wheedled, begged and whined, and Chet Gwynne squirmed as they were read into the record. The tenth letter, written by Gwynne a few days before the shooting, was threatening. It said:

> "If you're smart you won't hang up on me next time I call. You don't know it, but I've been back here more than three weeks, watching you all the time. Does that give you the chills? It better. I want to talk to you. I'm in a jam out on the coast with a woman, and I need five thousand bucks to square her. That lousy two hundred a month I've been getting from the family don't mean a thing. This time it's got to be five thousand or you're going to be very sorry."

The letter was handwritten and signed Chet Gwynne.

So now Louis Donetti had his case, and it was as strong as a hangman's knot. Or perhaps, since Pennsylvania used the electric chair, you ought to say as strong as high voltage current.

The jury came in, solemn and intent, and then the judge, and George Archibald was recalled to the stand and turned over to Anthony for cross-examination. Anthony began asking questions.

He gave the man every chance to prove to the judge and jury and the crowded courtroom how remarkable were his powers of observation and memory. Archibald loved it; in fact, he seemed more at ease now than he had been with Donetti. Anthony, of course, was a gentleman who dressed well and respected butlers. Donetti was a South Philadelphia Italian in clothes dusted with cigar ashes.

Anthony devoted a lot of time to questions and answers about the three drinks John C. M. Stearnes had taken during the evening, and the butler's skill in identifying the type of liquor by sniffing the glasses. He went over the details of Archibald's final trip to the study, when Stearnes met him at the door with a tray containing one glass and told him he wouldn't be needed again that evening. Not once in all the questioning did Anthony try to trap the witness in any way. Up on the bench, the judge was looking puzzled; this was no way to defend a man accused of murder. At the defense table, Gwynne looked bored and superior. At the prosecutor's table, Donetti sat on the edge of his chair, tense with suspicion.

"Now, Mr. Archibald," Anthony said mildly, "when you went to the study on your final trip in answer to the buzzer, you found the door closed?"

"That is correct," Archibald said. "I rapped twice on the door, in accordance with my usual custom. Mr. Stearnes opened it and handed me the tray containing one glass. I estimate that he opened the door about two feet in order to pass me the tray."

"And you did not actually see the defendant at that time?"

"No sir. The chair in which he was sitting was not in the line of sight available to me through the partly open door."

"Is it possible that the defendant could have left, and that the glass on the tray was from a nightcap which Mr. Stearnes had just finished drinking?"

"Oh no, sir. In accordance with my usual procedure I sniffed at the empty glass. The aroma was definitely that of the raw and cheap rye which the visitor had been drinking all evening. I would have had no trouble identifying the bouquet of the Glen Murry Scotch or the somewhat headier Royal Tartan Scotch which Mr. Stearnes had been drinking."

"Could you also have identified the Napoleon brandy which, you said, he kept in the liquor cabinet in the study?"

"That would be easiest of all to identify. No sir, the smell of the liquor which had been in the glass was definitely that of the rye which the visitor had brought."

Anthony turned back to his table and signalled to a man who had been sitting there quietly. The man rose and pulled a small table up close to the witness stand. He opened a brief case and placed on the table three small medicine bottles labelled A, B and C, and three plain glasses also labelled A, B and C.

"Mr. Archibald," Anthony said in a friendly tone, "your ability to identify various types of liquor by the aroma is interesting. I wonder if you would mind demonstrating it to the jury."

Louis Donetti leaped from his chair as if he had suddenly found it equipped with electrodes. "Objection!" he snapped. "A test of this type is not material or relevant."

"Your Honor," Anthony said in a hurt tone, "the witness has testified that he believes the defendant was still in the study, at the time in question, because the glass which Mr. Stearnes handed him was reeking with the fumes of the raw and cheap rye which the defendant had been drinking. I submit that it is material and relevant to allow the witness to demonstrate to the jury his ability to identify various types of liquor."

Donetti said, "Your Honor, there can be no real comparison between the witness's ability to identify types of liquor in his normal place of employment, and his ability to identify types of liquor in the stress of courtroom procedure and under the badgering and bullying of counsel for the defense."

Perhaps Donetti realized, the moment he said the words, that he should not have used the phrase "badgering and bullying." But then it was too late. The tension of the courtroom exploded in laughter. Archibald permitted himself a wisp of a smile. Even the judge, pounding for order in the court, was fighting off a grin.

When order was restored, the judge said, "May I say to the prosecutor that never in my career on the bench have I seen defense counsel treat a key prosecution witness with such remarkable consideration and courtesy. Perhaps we might ask the witness if he feels badgered and bullied."

Archibald said, "Your Honor, the gentleman who is counsel for the defense has been most kind and thoughtful. I have no doubt at all of my ability to give the demonstration which has been requested."

"Objection over-ruled," the judge said.

"Your Honor," Donetti said, "I object to the introduction as evidence of various unidentified bottles containing mysterious liquids."

"Your Honor," Anthony said, "I have not introduced the contents of the bottles in evidence, nor may it be necessary to do so. But in good time I will be glad to, if it seems essential, together with the testimony of my assistant, a chemist who bought a bottle of Glen Murry Scotch, a bottle of Royal Tartan Scotch, and a bottle of cheap rye at a State liquor store, who has subjected the contents to chemical analysis, and who has had the various liquids in his possession and control ever since."

"Objection over-ruled," the judge said.

Anthony turned to his assistant and asked him to pour a small amount from bottle A into glass A, from bottle B into glass B, and from bottle C into glass C. While this was being done, Anthony went back to his table.

Gwynne beckoned to him and whispered, "Isn't it about time you lit into this goddam butler? You've been acting like you hope to hire him."

"Suppose you let me try the case," Anthony said.

"Waiting for me to get on the stand and win it for you, huh?"

"Relax," Anthony said. "I might even try to win it on my own."

Anthony waited until the pouring was completed and his assistant returned to the defense table. Everybody was looking at him now. There was a water carafe and glass on the main table. Anthony poured himself a glassful and took a sip and walked back to the witness stand. In a forgetful way he carried the water glass with him, and then noticed it in his hand and put it on the small table containing the three liquor glasses. He picked up the glass labelled A.

"Mr. Archibald," he said, "please test the bouquet of the liquor in this glass by your sense of smell. I'm not going to rush you on this, so do not try to tell the jury what the glass contains until we are both sure you're ready." He handed the glass to Archibald.

Archibald smiled happily. This would be one of the great moments of his life. He put his nose to the glass, and inhaled with delicate little sniffs. "I believe I am ready," he said.

"Let's make sure, now," Anthony said. "Try it a few more times so that you give it a real test."

Archibald bent over the glass again, and sniffed a number of times. Then he nodded.

"Very well," Anthony said. "Please tell the jury what, in your opinion, this liquor is."

"There's not a doubt in the world," Archibald said. "I do not know the brand, but it is definitely a rye which has had a very short aging period. Quite cheap, I would say."

"Thank you, Mr. Archibald," Anthony said, giving him an encouraging smile. "Now here is the second glass, labelled B. Please take plenty of time."

Archibald sniffed. He looked slightly puzzled. He lowered his head again and spent a long time sniffing the aroma. Gradually the puzzled look faded and he began to smile. "I am quite ready," he said. "My delay was not due to any confusion but merely because you asked me to take plenty of time."

"And how do you identify this liquor?"

Archibald said triumphantly, "This is Royal Tartan Scotch. It's unmistakable. Heavy, rich bouquet, with a definite aroma of peat smoke."

Anthony took the glass and said, "Thank you, Mr. Archibald." He put the glass back on the small table, without looking down, and fumbled for the third glass. "Now the third," he said, handing it to Archibald.

Archibald put his nose down and began to sniff. Then his head jerked up and he looked reproachfully at Anthony. "I am afraid," he said, "that you gave me your glass of water this time."

"Did I really?" Anthony said nervously. He looked around, quite flustered. "Are you sure? Did you smell it?"

"Now Mr. Lawrence," Archibald said reprovingly, "I know water when I see it. I tried to smell it and of course there was no smell at all, except perhaps a touch of the chlorine which the city puts into its water."

Anthony said quite irritably, "I'm sure I gave you the right glass. Now please smell it and don't make any mistakes."

Archibald shrugged. He bent his head and sniffed and looked up and said, "I am very sorry, sir, but this is water. I trust you were not trying to trick me into identifying it as liquor."

"How could it be water?" Anthony snapped. "I reached down and picked up glass C and handed it to you."

"If you will note," Archibald said kindly, "this is not labelled C. It is your water glass. If you will pardon me, since my throat is somewhat dry—" He lifted the glass to his mouth.

Anthony held his breath. He had not counted on this.

Suddenly Archibald choked. A strangled cry bubbled from his throat. "It's gin!" he gasped. "It's gin! You tricked me!"

Anthony grabbed the glass from Archibald's hand and, while the courtroom rang with noise, whipped out a sticker and pasted it on the glass. On the sticker was a big red D. Above the noise you could hear Louis Donetti shouting a furious objection. The judge's gavel rapped sharply and the noise died away.

"Your Honor," Donetti cried, "I move that this entire vaudeville act be stricken from the record! It is quite obvious what counsel for the defense did. He—"

Anthony cut in sharply, "Your Honor, you had already overruled the prosecutor's objection to this test. The fact that it became more dramatic than I expected has nothing to do with its relevance."

"You tricked him!" Donetti shouted. "You filled his nose with fumes so he couldn't smell anything. You didn't give him that glass of gin by chance. You deliberately handed it to him."

"Your Honor," Anthony said mildly, "if the Assistant District Attorney wishes to testify, let him take the stand and I'll be glad to cross-examine."

A machine-gun rattle of applause swept the audience. The judge banged his gavel heavily. "If there is another demonstration," he said, "I will have the court cleared of spectators. I order the prosecutor's last remark stricken from the record and I instruct the jury to disregard it. Mr. Donetti, if you have been making an objection, it has not been in a form this court recognizes. Unless you wish to make an objection in proper form, the cross-examination may proceed."

"If Your Honor pleases," Anthony said, "I wouldn't care to be accused later of drugging or intoxicating the witness. Does the prosecution wish to ask for a recess?"

The judge turned to Archibald and asked, "Did you swallow any large quantity of the, ah, liquid?"

"I don't believe so," Archibald said faintly. "I began choking when the first drops went down my throat."

The judge said, "I will entertain a motion for a recess if the prosecution wishes to make it."

Louis Donetti nicked a glance at the jury. He was obviously trying to figure what effect a recess would have on them. In Louis' position, Anthony thought, he would be worrying over whether the recess might seem like a rout of the prosecution, and whether it would give the jury too much time to think about the incident.

Donetti said, "The prosecution does not ask for a recess. I would like to enter on the record, however, my contention that the ability or inability of the witness to identify gin by smell has nothing to do with his ability to identify the types of liquor which were actually drunk during the evening in question. I contend that the incident involving the gin is immaterial and irrelevant."

"Your Honor," Anthony said, "I intend to show that it is far more material and relevant than the worst fears of the prosecutor might lead him to suspect."

"Objection over-ruled," the judge said. "Cross-examination may continue."

Louis Donetti began shuffling back toward his table. He passed close to Anthony, and whispered, "You son of a bitch. I knew you were laying for him."

"Hold your hat," Anthony muttered. "You haven't seen anything yet."

The judge rapped his gavel. "Counsel for the prosecution and the defense," he said, "will make any further remarks openly and in accordance with the rules of court procedure."

Louis nodded sullenly and trudged to his table.

Anthony moved toward the witness stand and studied Archibald. The man was no longer relaxed and happy. He shoved himself back in the chair as if trying to get as far away from Anthony as possible.

"Mr. Archibald," Anthony said briskly, "do you believe that the fumes from the first two glasses may have saturated your sense of smell, and therefore led you to identify gin as water?"

"I don't know," Archibald stammered. "It ... it was, well, perhaps that was the case. I had some difficulty in identifying the second glass, and perhaps that was because of the fumes from the first."

"You didn't tell us that at the time, Mr. Archibald. If you wish, I can have your statement read back to you by the court stenographer. But perhaps you will agree that, in substance, you said your delay in trying to name the contents of the second glass was not due to confusion but merely because I had asked you to take plenty of time. Is that correct?"

"Well, I suppose it is."

"You testified earlier that you generally take two drinks each evening, one usually around eight o'clock and one at about ten. You said you had your first drink a little later than usual on the night in question. You said you had your second drink at the usual time, that is, ten o'clock. Do you agree?"

Archibald had stopped giving long full answers. Now he wanted to escape from each question quickly. "Yes, sir."

"You testified that you like to take your time with drinks, and savor them. Is it correct that you inhale their fumes as part of the enjoyable process?"

"Well, yes, I do."

"You had your second drink, according to my timetable, just before the buzzer called you on your final trip to the study. Thus, if fumes destroy your sense of smell, they had destroyed it that evening when you sniffed at the single glass which your employer handed you on a tray. Is this true?"

"Objection," Donetti said. "There has been no testimony indicating how long or short a time the sense of smell might be affected by the fumes of liquor taken previously."

"Sustained," the judge said. "Strike the question. The jury will disregard it."

Anthony was not disturbed. You could tell a jury to disregard something until you were blue in the face, but they would still remember. "Mr. Archibald," he said, "in view of the test you just took, do you now claim that the empty glass on the tray actually had held a raw and cheap rye? Please remember that this is important as indicating whether or not the defendant was in the room on the occasion of your final trip."

"I—I certainly thought it was that cheap rye," Archibald said hesitantly. "But of course I, well—" He paused, seeking a safe way out, and thought he saw one. "But actually the defendant was in the room!" he said triumphantly. "Don't forget I heard his voice later!"

Was that a slight groan from the table where Donetti sat? It might well be. Anthony pounced at the witness. "Are you trying to tell the jury," he said, "that at ten minutes after ten that evening, you knew the defendant was in the study because a half hour later you heard what you thought was his voice? Do you have second sight, Mr. Archibald? Do you have a crystal ball? How can you make a decision at ten-ten based on something that happens at ten-forty?"

"I see what you mean," Archibald said unhappily. "Of course I didn't have that evidence at the time. Perhaps later the two events ran together a bit in my mind."

"You admit that sometimes you can't keep details straight?"

"I didn't really mean to say that."

"They just run together a bit in your mind?"

"It ... it doesn't sound very well that way."

"It certainly doesn't," Anthony said grimly. "Now, Mr. Archibald, let's discuss that voice you heard. You claim it was the defendant's?"

"Yes sir, I do."

"You were up in your room at the time?"

"Yes. But it is right above the study."

"How much wood and plaster was between you and the voices?"

"There's the floor of my room and the ceiling below."

"A solid, well-built house?"

"Oh yes. Quite solid."

"Yet you claim to identify the defendant's voice?"

"Yes."

"He was shouting?"

"Yes. Rather loudly."

"How many words had you heard the defendant speak, before this episode of the shouting?"

"I can't remember, exactly."

"You certainly had no long conversation with him, did you?"

"No sir."

"Perhaps you heard him speak fifty words?"

"It might have been around fifty."

"How many of those fifty words were shouted at you?"

"Why, none at all."

"Yet, on the basis of fifty words spoken in a normal tone, you claim to identify angry shouts coming through the ceiling and floor of a well-built house?"

"It sounded like his voice."

"Want to make a test?" Anthony snapped.

"No sir," Archibald said, shuddering.

"Then you're not confident of your ability to identify his voice?"

"Objection," Donetti growled. "The witness is in no condition to take such a test. This time perhaps it's obvious that he is being badgered and bullied."

"Sustained," the judge said.

Anthony was satisfied. The jury would remember that point, too. "Mr. Archibald," he said, "let us return to the test you took when, by your own statement, you were not at all doubtful of your ability. You saw me at my table pouring liquid from a water carafe into a glass. Did you assume anything from that?"

"Of course I did," Archibald said eagerly, seeing a chance to justify himself. "Naturally I assumed it was water. You even raised the glass to your lips."

"But your assumption was wrong, wasn't it?"

"Well, yes."

"You even went so far as to assume that you smelled the chlorine with which the water had been treated, didn't you?"

"I guess I did."

"How many wrong assumptions did you make the night Mr. Stearnes died?"

"I—I don't know what you mean."

"After the defendant arrived, you took him into the study. You claim you checked the position of every movable object in the room so you would know if he stole anything. When you returned a little later, you claim that the center drawer of Mr. Stearnes' desk, where he kept his revolver, was slightly open, although you say it was closed previously. You assumed from that small fact that the defendant had stolen the revolver, didn't you?"

"Oh, but don't forget there was a heavy bulge inside his jacket."

"How do you know it was a heavy bulge, rather than a bulge from a large but light object?"

"I saw a gleam of metal when he leaned forward to pour his drink."

"And from those tiny facts, no more significant than the sight of me pouring liquid from a water carafe, you made an assumption. In one case you assumed a stolen revolver hidden inside a coat. In the other you assumed a glass of water. Which assumption was more reasonable?"

"Well, you see I thought—"

Anthony jabbed a finger at him and cried, "What's that in your inside coat pocket!"

Archibald jumped. His left hand grabbed at the pocket. "It's ... it's ... I ... oh, it's my wallet, sir, really it's my wallet!"

"You had to grab for it to find out, did you? What's that metallic gleam inside your coat? I saw it when you leaned forward. Come now! Tell us!"

"A metallic gleam? Really sir, I ... I ..." He fumbled inside his coat and finally gave a sigh of relief. His trembling hand brought out a fountain pen and matching pencil. "This was it, sir. They do have a metallic gleam, don't they? You startled me with those questions."

"The defendant might have had a wallet and a pen and pencil set in his pocket, mightn't he?"

"I suppose he might have," Archibald said weakly. He was blinking and looked ready to cry.

Anthony studied him. He pushed the man hard. He had backed him into corners and slapped him around. Archibald hadn't shown any fight. Perhaps if you offered him a face-saving way to escape, he might take it.

"Now Mr. Archibald," he said in a gentler tone, "isn't it possible that whatever mistake was made was not your fault? Isn't it possible that, while you may be correct about the defendant opening the desk drawer, there was no revolver in it? Wouldn't that seem to tie up with the fact that Mr. Stearnes did not seem very worried when you told him about the disturbed drawer?"

"Oh, yes sir," Archibald said gratefully. "That could very well be the case."

"And doesn't it seem unlikely that Mr. Stearnes would sit drinking and talking quite normally with the visitor, if he really knew the visitor had stolen his revolver?"

"Yes sir, that seems very reasonable. Or," Archibald said, with the air of a man discovering a great truth, "Mr. Stearnes could have coaxed him to give it up. Or a burglar could have crept in and caused the fight I heard. There are really a great many possibilities, aren't there, sir?"

Anthony smiled. He had given the rabbit a clear path to its burrow, and the rabbit had run. "Indeed there are," he said. "Thank you, Mr. Archibald. Let us close on the thought that there are a great many possibilities. No more questions." He walked back to his table.

Gwynne leaned over and said, "You really took the guy. Nice work, Mr. Lawrence."

Anthony nodded. He watched Donetti, looking old and tired, shuffle toward the stand to begin his re-direct examination. He listened to Donetti trying to patch up his case. Louis didn't get anywhere. The rabbit was safe in his burrow and was not coming out.

Finally Louis gave up, and told the judge that the prosecution rested. Anthony said he wished to demur to the evidence presented by the Commonwealth for failure to establish its case as a matter of law. They argued the motion, with the jury excused from the room, and the judge denied the demurrer. Anthony asked that his exception to the ruling be noted, and that the court instruct the jurors that the ruling was merely as to a matter of law and that the denial of the motion was no concern of theirs.

The jury returned and received its instructions, and then the judge said, "It is now twenty minutes of twelve. Does the defense wish to proceed with its case now, or have a recess until after lunch?"

Anthony glanced at Donetti, and saw that Louis was being nagged by an unhappy thought. Louis had the right idea, too. "Your Honor," Anthony said in a confident tone, "with cross-examination of the last witness, the case for the defense has been established. The defense rests."

Whispers scurried around the courtroom. The judge banged his gavel and said, "Court will re-convene at two o'clock for closing arguments."

Chet Gwynne was staring at Anthony with eyes like the bottoms of jigger glasses. "What's the idea?" he said hoarsely. "What's this business of the defense resting? When do I go on the stand?"

"You don't go on."

"What do you mean, I don't go on? That's what I've been waiting for!"

"You can stop waiting."

"Now just hold on. I have something to say about this."

"You'd better say it to another lawyer, then. I only want to win this case once. I'm not going to try to win it twice. Get this through your head, will you? This case is won! I don't care what the jury says now. With what's on the record I could bust a guilty verdict into a million pieces on appeal. So you're not going on the stand while I'm handling the case. And if you got another lawyer and took the stand, you'd be asking for trouble. Sure, you could bring out your sob story. But then Donetti would cut you into bits. You saw what I did to the butler. That would be a tea dance compared to what Donetti would do to you."

"But this was my chance," Gwynne said tearfully. "For once people were going to see what a dirty deal I've had, all along. They were going to look at me and say he wasn't such a bad guy if they'd ever given him a break. They were going to feel sorry for me."

"I'm not interested in people pitying you," Anthony said bluntly. "I'd rather have them envy you because you beat the rap. I'll see you after lunch." He got up and walked away. That was quick and brutal, but it was the way he felt.

When he returned after lunch, a change had taken place in Gwynne. The man with a mission had become drunk on self-pity.

He was almost in a stupor, and you could do anything you wanted with him as long as you were gentle about it. He didn't want to change lawyers. He trusted Anthony. Anthony would get him off, wouldn't he? That was all he wanted. It was sickening to see that happen to a man, but of course to start with there hadn't been much of a man.

Louis Donetti gave his closing argument to the jury. Louis was going down fighting, but he didn't have much punch left. He did as well as he could with the threatening letter and the medical and police testimony and what he could salvage from the butler's testimony. Then he returned to his table like a groggy fighter wading back to his corner.

Anthony made his argument short and easy to remember.

"Ladies and gentlemen of the jury," he said. "There is just one question for you to decide. Is the defendant guilty of murder beyond any reasonable doubt? The job of the prosecution is to prove that absolutely. It is not enough for the prosecution to hint that he might have done it or that he could have done it. The prosecution has to prove that murder was committed, that the defendant committed it, and that no one else could have. You must decide whether or not the prosecution has managed to do that. All I ask you to do is to examine the facts and let them speak for themselves.

"Fact one. The prosecution has made a great point of what it calls a threatening letter. The prosecution would like you to believe that this was a threat of murder. But that is merely an assumption. Is it not just as reasonable to assume that the writer of the letter was threatening suicide? Or that he was threatening to bring discredit on his family as a result of his trouble on the West Coast with a woman? So all we have here are several conflicting assumptions, with no proof back of any of them.

"Fact two. The alleged theft of the revolver. In cross-examination you heard the butler, George Archibald, back away from the assumption that a drawer left partly open and a bulge in a coat meant that the revolver had been stolen.

"Fact three. The single glass on the tray, which at first was assumed to mean that the defendant was still in the study. You saw a test which proved that the witness can make mistakes in identifying the contents of a glass. In the closing argument you have just heard, the prosecution tried to dismiss this test as a vaudeville stunt. It was far more than that. It was clear, direct proof that the witness could draw false conclusions from a set of facts. From a water carafe, he assumed water. From a drawer which he thought had been moved, and from a bulge in a coat, he assumed a stolen revolver. From a glass on a tray, he assumed that the defendant was in the study.

"Fact four. From shouts heard through the floor and ceiling of a solidly-built house, the witness assumed the presence of the defendant, although he admits he had only heard the defendant speak about fifty words and that none of these had been shouted. Once again an assumption, which you as reasonable people have every right to examine.

"Ladies and gentlemen, now I have run out of facts for you to consider. What is left is a major assumption by the prosecution, to the effect that murder was committed and that the defendant committed it. I ask you to consider several other assumptions. Did the defendant attempt to commit suicide, and was John C. M. Stearnes accidentally shot in an attempt to prevent this? Or did Mr. Stearnes, alarmed at something, grab his gun either to protect himself or to force the defendant to leave, and did the defendant in his turn try to protect himself and engage in a struggle during which Mr. Stearnes was shot? Or, as the key witness for the prosecution himself has suggested, did a burglar sneak into the house and cause a fight in which John C. M. Stearnes was killed?

"These are all things which you will want to consider. I can close in no better way than by quoting the exact words of George Archibald, butler to John C. M. Stearnes. Quote. There are really a great many possibilities, aren't there? Unquote. Ladies and gentlemen of the jury, I ask you to find the defendant not guilty."

After that the judge gave his charge to the jury. It was clear and concise, and it didn't do the prosecution any good. The jury was out for thirty-seven minutes and came back with a verdict of not guilty.

A sound made up of dozens of sighs and whispers crept through the room. No applause, this time. The applause in the morning had been a cheer for the underdog, for an inexperienced lawyer who had suddenly started to slug it out with a wily prosecutor. Later it had developed that a wolf was romping around in underdog's clothing. You might admire the skill of a wolf in running down his quarry but you weren't likely to cheer when he succeeded. And, of course, there was nothing heartwarming in the sight of a creature like Gwynne beating a murder rap. So the audience merely sighed and whispered.

There were, however, a number of people who admired skill, and they came up in a steady parade.

Here was Logan Clayton, shaking hands and saying fervently, "Magnificent, Tony, magnificent. I wouldn't have thought it possible, except that once I saw you take Mr. Dickinson apart." One vote for skill.

Here were the John Marshall Whartons, smiling proudly at him and saying that it had been one of the most thrilling experiences in their lives. Two more votes for skill. Here was his mother, looking a little pale and weak, and very relieved that he had come out of it so well. You couldn't exactly call that a vote for skill because it was just a mother's vote for her son, but even she didn't seem to realize what had happened.

Here was Dr. Shippen Stearnes, a delightful old gentleman carrying his eighty-one years as if each were a medal of honor, beaming at him and saying, "My boy, our trust in you was more than justified. We are forever in your debt. You may not know that Mrs. John C. M. Stearnes and two of her sons were in the audience. They did not think it proper to come forward now, for obvious reasons. But I bring you their heartfelt thanks. At some time in the future they wish very much to meet you." Another few votes for skill.

"Thank you, sir," Anthony said. "I appreciate that very much. Now what about ..." He jerked his head toward Chet Gwynne, slouched in his chair like a sack whose contents were slowly draining away.

"Ah, yes," Dr. Stearnes said, with a bright smile. He moved around the table and touched Gwynne's shoulder. "Hello, Chet," he said gently. "How are you feeling?"

The weak eyes looked up and came slowly into focus. "It ... it's Uncle Ship, isn't it?" Gwynne said. His voice might have sounded like that years ago, as a boy who had done something wrong and had been caught at it. "I'm sorry I caused you so much trouble, Uncle Ship. I didn't mean to."

"Everything's going to be all right now, Chet." Dr. Stearnes murmured. "We're not going to turn away from you this time, my boy. We want to look after you. Won't that be nice?"

Gwynne was very tired. "That will be nice," he said.

"Would you like to come along with me now, Chet?"

Gwynne got up slowly and put an arm around Dr. Stearnes' shoulders to steady himself, an old man of forty-two leaning on a younger man of eighty-one. "Will you really take care of me?" he said in a pleading tone.

"Yes, Chet, we'll do that."

Dr. Stearnes looked at Anthony and smiled, and led Chet Gwynne slowly from the courtroom. Anthony shivered. Had that been dear old Santa Claus smiling at him, or the cool impersonal scientist? In any case, there was Chet Gwynne, moving off the stage of life to a quiet little place in the country. He remembered that it had sounded like Eastern Penitentiary, but with nice silverware.

And here, finally, was the golden girl herself, lighting up the drab courtroom like a million candlepower or like twenty million dollars or like the girl he happened to love, whichever you preferred.

"Tony," she said, "I just can't get my breath to talk properly. Darling, it was tremendous. Are you awfully tired? Do you think you could come out to see me tonight? Because by then perhaps I'll have caught my breath again." Another vote for skill.

"I'll be there," he said.

She flashed him the smile that the photographers loved, and went away.

It was odd. All those votes for skill, and nobody had looked behind the skill to ask the basic question which ought to come up whenever a case has been tried. Perhaps nobody was interested in that question unless ... unless ... he watched Louis Donetti amble toward him through the nearly deserted room. Fat balding Louis in his unpressed suit with cigar ashes on the coat. Was Louis going to vote for skill? He didn't think so. It would be unpleasant but sort of refreshing to listen to the vote Louis was going to cast.

Louis said, in that voice like a file scraping metal, "I thought you'd like the worst saved till last. You know I'm not going to congratulate you."

"I wouldn't want you to."

"That stunt you pulled. It'll be one for the books."

"It's already in the books."

"Oh. I thought it seemed a bit familiar. You always were a great guy for research and precedents and finding out how things had been done before. What was the case, Tony?"

"One of those that Bill Fallon handled, years ago in New York City. You've read about Fallon."

"Yeah. Criminal lawyer. Slick as they come. How did he use that trick?"

"He was defending a guy accused of arson. A fireman testified he had smelled kerosene at the fire and had seen a couple of places where it had been splashed around. On the stand, Fallon asked him to identify kerosene by taking some long sniffs of it. The fireman's nose and lungs got full of kerosene fumes. Fallon handed him a glass of water. Kerosene was all the fireman could smell so he called the water kerosene. Not guilty."

"You did a nice job of adapting it. Well, Tony, your Main Line friends ought to pay off good."

"You think so?"

"What the hell, Tony. They're emperors in the last days of Rome. They're too soft to do their own fighting. Outside the palace gate the dirty smelly plebs have been putting on a riot, so the Praetorian Guard marched out and gave the bastards a lesson. You're captain of the Praetorian Guard, Tony. They got to keep you loyal. You might even get to sit on the throne some day. If you remember your history, a lot of captains of the guard made it."

"You make it sound too romantic."

"The Praetorian Guard probably didn't think it was romantic, either. All in a day's work, boys. How do you feel about it, Tony?"

Anthony wrestled his face into a smile. "I feel lousy about it, thanks," he said brightly.

"Don't feel too bad," Louis said. "It's half my fault. I lost sight of the main issue. I wanted to bust the stained glass windows and drag some of your friends out in the open, so everybody could see they weren't cathedral types after all. But to drag your pals into the open I needed your help. I knew I didn't have a prayer of getting it if you saw any other way out. So I set up the goddam case too tight. I tried to nail every door but one shut so you couldn't get a finger grip and would have to use the only door left open. Well, some of the doors didn't fit good. I forced them shut. I let that damn butler try to prove too much. That gave you a chance to mousetrap him. I lost sight of the main issue."

"Just out of curiosity," Anthony said, "what's your idea of the main issue?"

"The issue was to try to get some justice done."

"Do you think he was guilty, Louis?"

"I don't know. I guess you don't either. That's reasonable doubt, so he goes free. Maybe a little justice sneaked in the back door on us. But we never invited it in. All we were trying to do was outsmart each other, and you won."

"You know I took a big chance, Louis. I tried that test on myself, and it worked. But there was no guarantee it would work on the butler. If he had called it gin before he sipped it, school would have been out. Magicians don't look good when their tricks flop."

Louis stared at him curiously. "And if it had flopped, you had only one chance for an acquittal. Tell me. Would the captain of the guard have started burning down the palace? Would you have put Gwynne on the stand, and to hell with the Main Line?"

Anthony sighed. "I wish I knew the answer," he said softly. "I wish I knew."

17

WHEN HE DROVE up to White Pillars in Haverford that evening, all the lanterns along the crushed stone driveway were glowing and the high tetrastyle portico was bathed in light and every window was glittering. White Pillars only turned on all its lights for great events: a wedding, a birth, an important anniversary, the end of a war. So this was quite a special evening. Louis Donetti would probably have said it was the end of a war and that the Praetorian Guard was being welcomed back to the palace.

One of the maids opened the door for him before he could ring the bell, and took his coat and hat as if they had been shining armor. Mrs. Allen came into the hallway to greet him.

"Well," she said happily, "I hear you're a holy terror in a courtroom, Anthony. I wish I'd been there to see it. Did you notice the lights as you drove up?"

"Of course. It's beautiful. I know about the tradition. Tonight must be a big occasion."

"You're the occasion. You're a good boy, Anthony. It's a comfort to have you around. Well, I'm going upstairs and won't be bothering you young folks. You'll find Grace in the living room."

Anthony could sometimes tell what mood Grace was in by the clothes she was wearing. Tonight, if her clothes told the story, she was in a little-girl mood. She wore flat-heeled sandals and a plain white dress with a flaring skirt and a tiny string of pearls. Her bright hair had been pulled back into a pony tail. She looked as if she were going to her first dancing class and was afraid nobody would dance with her.

She said in a low voice, "Hello."

He grinned and said, "Where's that older sister of yours? She's the one I came out to see."

"Don't tease me, Tony. I know I look like a child. I feel like one, too."

"Is that bad?"

"Tony, until the trial was over and I left, I hadn't realized how scared I was."

"What were you scared about?"

"Tony, I don't like being scared. I don't ever remember being scared before. You've got circles under your eyes, Tony. Was it awfully tiring today?"

"A little. The trouble was, my emotions were involved. A lawyer shouldn't let that happen."

"I was scared," she said again. She looked up at him, and blinked, and a single file of tears began coming in solemn procession from her eyes. "I was scared!" she wailed, and threw herself against him, shaking with sobs.

He had never seen her cry before. It was hard to believe that all the poise and glamor could be washed away like so much lipstick, leaving a child bawling as if she had just fallen downstairs. He led

306

her to a couch and sat beside her. She crawled onto his lap and burrowed against him, and gradually the sobs faded into long quivering gasps. Her wet face lifted from his shoulder and her lips followed a trembling course across his cheek until they found his mouth. It was almost like kissing a baby.

He brushed her shining hair and said softly, "What was the trouble?"

She looked at him with eyes that had just opened after a bad dream. "It could have been so awful," she gasped. "We all knew what Chet was likely to say if he went on the stand. He would have lied and lied, but people would have believed him and none of us could have helped being dragged in the mud. And we would have hated you, Tony. We would have blamed you for it, as if it were all your fault that Chet had been weak and bad. We would have tried to hurt you. And if you had kept Chet off the stand and let him be convicted we would have been relieved but then we would have despised you. And I didn't want to hate you! I didn't want to despise you! I wanted to love you! Oh, it could have been so black and nasty, and Tony, I don't like black nasty things. I like everything to be bright and nice. Am I making sense to you?"

"Yes. You're making sense."

"But it ended up all right, didn't it, Tony?"

"Most people would think so."

She sniffled a bit, and said, "I do want to love you, Tony."

"You have too many words in that sentence. It would sound better if you just said I love you. How do you feel about that?"

She sat up perkily on his lap and smiled as if she were looking at a Speed Graphic camera. "Tony," she said, "we haven't played our question-and-answer game in months!"

"You mean it's time for me to ask you again to marry me? Wait till I put on my glum look and brace myself for the pat on the cheek."

"Come on, Tony. You have to ask."

"Do you love me, Grace?"

"That isn't the right question," she said, pouting.

"Sorry. I'm out of practice. Will you marry me, Grace?"

"Yes!" she cried. "Oh yes, I will, Tony!" She threw her arms around him and clung as if she meant never to let go.

This was it, his brain told him coolly. This was Fish House Punch and scrapple and planked shad. It was the Liberty Bell and meeting at the Eagle in Wanamaker's and the annual Assembly Ball. This was Philadelphia rattling into his hands in one great big jackpot. Counting himself, four generations of his family had worked to put him way up here at the absolute top. It turned out to be a rather cool and lonely place. He shouldn't feel that way, he realized. It had taken a wild combination of luck and chance to put him here, because he had fallen in love with a girl who might never, in the ordinary course of things, have married anyone. Long ago he suspected that the answer to Grace Shippen lay in the simple statement that the things she wanted were the things she already had. As far as men were concerned, she wanted the companionship of a man she considered suitable, and that was all. No love, no marriage, no children, nothing to disturb the bright and ordered pattern of her life.

But something had disturbed the pattern. Chet Gwynne had come to town, and black and ugly shapes had troubled her dreams. Beyond the palace gates the dirty smelly plebs had rioted. For a time her clean and germless world had seemed to be in danger. But the man from whom she merely wanted companionship had sterilized everything and put her world back in order. So she would marry him. He was ready to accept her on any terms at all, but it was hard to be ecstatic about it. She wasn't really going to marry a man. She was merely taking out an insurance policy.

18

IT TURNED OUT to be a very nice life, though. He had to give Grace credit. She may have acquired him as an insurance policy but you had to admit that she paid the premiums promptly and cheerfully. She was as delightful a companion as always. She was willing to concede that marriage entitled a man to make love to his wife from time to time. It was not the sort of activity she would have preferred, but then husbands often liked their wives to join them in love-making or boating or hunting or mountain climbing and such things, and it was a good idea to go along with them. Of course love-making could have a rather important result in the form of babies, but that was expected. In the first four years of their marriage she produced two healthy sons, and did it with a minimum of fuss.

They made their home at White Pillars, and that worked out quite well, too. As Grace pointed out, her grandmother was going to leave the place to her and so it would be foolish to buy or build another home. In many cases it might have been a bad idea to move in with his wife's family, but Mrs. J. Arthur Allen was a grandmother, not a mother, and White Pillars was big enough so that you almost had to make an effort to meet each other in it rather than an effort to avoid each other.

Whatever potential problem existed, as a result of living in the same house with Mrs. Allen, it did not last long. In the second year after his marriage to Grace, Mrs. Allen began failing. Not that she ever admitted it. It was the doctors who were failing, the climate was failing, but she herself was as spry as ever. Right to the end of a long illness she fought hard against her ailments, clinging to the worn fabric of her life as if it were one of those ancient bargain-counter dresses which she insisted on wearing. Her mind remained clear, and she had one great pleasure: changing her bequests. She hoisted her codicils and flew them like battle flags in a war against fate, and when she finally died it was necessary to unclasp her frail fingers from the carbon copies of her last Will and Testament.

There was one codicil which she had never changed. That was the famous one in which she gave her old collie, Beauty, to Grace. And there was one new codicil which Anthony had not been allowed to draw up or to see. It left him the sum of five hundred thousand dollars. For the rest, the estate was divided among Grace and a number of nieces and nephews, with Anthony and a bank as the executors. Grace also received White Pillars. Most of the stock of Allen Oil Company went to a charitable foundation which Anthony had helped Mrs. Allen set up. This of course avoided huge inheritance and estate taxes, and made it unnecessary for the estate to throw huge blocks of stock on the market. Naturally Anthony had arranged things so that the voting stock went to the heirs, which kept control of Allen Oil Company in the hands of the family.

At the office, getting ahead became almost as effortless a matter as riding into town on the Paoli Local. Both his career and the commuting trains ran on a dependable schedule, and what you noticed was not the steady record of success but the occasional minor delays. Of course, soon after he and Grace were married, his name moved up across that half-inch chasm on the left-hand side of the letterhead of Morris, Clayton, Biddle and Wharton. Some day, if it seemed desirable, it would be Morris, Clayton, Biddle and Lawrence. He became a director of one of the best banks in the city, and went on the board of a leading insurance company. When you reached that point, new clients began drifting in without any real effort on your part.

Among his new clients was an astonishing one. The man walked in unannounced one day: a huge white-haired man who brushed past the secretary like a bulldozer pushing aside a sapling. "My God," Anthony said, "Uncle Mike! How long has it been?"

Shaking hands with Mike Callahan was like putting your arm into a cement mixer. "It was 1929," Uncle Mike said. "Twenty-three years ago."

"That's right. I had a summer job at the Academy. A couple of steel mill boys you had given to the Penn squad were teaching me football. Let's see. Al Horder and Joe ... Joe ..."

"Joe Krakowicz. Good boys. Joe's a plant superintendent at U.S. Steel. Al was in the Seabees. Got killed in the war. I've seen you since then, though. As a matter of fact I came out a couple times to see you play for the Academy. You weren't bad. Twenty pounds more weight and you'd have been hard to handle."

"Did you arrange that summer job for me? Did you fix things to have Joe and Al there, to take me in hand? I often wondered."

"Me? Why would I do all that? I had no special interest in you."

"Why did you come out later to see me play, then?"

"I got a bit curious after Joe and Al told me you looked good. What is this, cross-examination?"

"Sorry," Anthony said. "Funny I've never seen you around town these last few years. I hear about you. I see those big Callahan Construction Company signs all over the place."

"Well, you and I don't walk exactly the same beat. They wouldn't like me tracking mud into the Academy of Music and the Racquet Club and those other places you hang out. I tracked some mud in just now. See it? I never was trained right."

"Track it over the top of my desk, if you want to. You carry around a good brand of mud."

"That lot is from where the Pennsy is tearing down its Chinese Wall. I'm gonna put up an office building there. I want a separate corporation for it. Thought I might get you to draw up the papers."

"That's the nicest compliment I've ever had as a lawyer."

Mike Callahan let out a grunt. "Yeah? I'll expect you to charge a nice low fee, then. Now here's the deal ..."

After that he saw Mike Callahan quite often, and gradually much of the legal work of the Callahan Construction Company found its way to Morris, Clayton, Biddle and Wharton.

So that was the way things went, at home and at the office. It was a smooth successful life, although nothing about it seemed to be very important. Fortunately there were things to do around the city that kept him interested. Of course he had dropped his hobby of playing around in the magistrates' courts, because he had seen where that could lead. But there were new hobbies to take up. The city was getting to be a fairly lively place. Many old buildings and old ideas were coming down, and new things going up in their places. The Board of Judges and the Bar Association decided to make a study of the magistrates' courts, and asked him to head the committee. A group of top businessmen formed the Greater Philadelphia Movement, and began to get things like the new City Charter done; Anthony helped write the Charter and push it through. There were jobs to be done in connection with City-County Consolidation and Penn Center and the new Food Distribution Center. You could work on projects like those and keep your hands clean; whatever fights you got into were on a pleasantly high level. So it was a nice life, and probably even useful.

He saw Louis Donetti often during those years. Louis was getting ahead; he was in City Council now, and swung a lot of weight in several of the South Philadelphia wards. If you wanted aid from Council on a civic project, Louis was a good man to know, because he played politics the way an expert plays three-cushion billiards. Anthony found him very helpful. He knew, of course, that Louis as a practical politician would expect the favors returned some day, and therefore he was not surprised when the day came.

Anthony's appointment list for that day merely carried the note: "Donetti, 11 A.M.," so he knew something was up when Louis arrived not alone but with Mike Callahan. They sat around for a few minutes telling him how well he looked, which meant that they wanted him feeling strong enough to take a shock.

"Kids fine?" Louis asked.

"Oh yes, swell. Seems unbelievable, but young Tony starts to school next fall."

"Married seven years and only two kids," Mike said. "You'd better get busy."

"Look who's talking," Louis said. "Why didn't you ever get married, Mike?"

"Never got around to it. I'd like to see your kids some day, Tony."

"Come on out to dinner. How about this Friday?"

"Wait till you hear what we came for. Maybe you'll take back the invitation."

"I resent that," Louis said. "This little matter we came about, Tony, is about me. You're not gonna get upset because your old pal Louis wants some help."

"You've got me softened up," Anthony said. "Bring it out in the light and let's see if it tries to crawl into the nearest crack."

Louis smiled at him like a cherub in an old Italian fresco. "Like you may have heard," he said, "I'm kinda in politics."

"Only up to his bald spot, though," Mike said.

"And when a guy's in politics, he likes to get ahead. You know, like a guy in any line of work."

"Okay," Anthony said. "What are you planning to run for?"

"It's not me doing the planning," Louis said, looking abashed. "It's only that some of my friends think I ought to run."

"Lock the vaults, fellows," Anthony said. "Here comes Donetti looking innocent."

"What I'm interested in may startle you a little bit."

"Louis, the only startling thing you could run for would be for cover."

"I'm thinking," Louis said, as if it were being dragged out of him, "of running for Mayor."

"Wow," Anthony muttered.

Mike said anxiously, "What do you think of it, Tony?"

"I'd like to hear what Louis thinks of it, leaving out the stuff about being forced into it at gunpoint. What's back of your idea, Louis?"

"You're a practical guy," Louis said, "so I'll give it to you without any gift wrapping. I'm a politician. I want to get ahead. Maybe in the old days I'd have played the game all the big boys did. Build up a machine. Grab patronage. Buy votes. Play along with me and you get jobs and handouts of coal and food. Shake down everybody for campaign funds. Rake in graft and make the machine bigger. But you know what? That don't go nowadays. Offer them a handout of coal or food? They laugh at you. They got unemployment compensation or relief. Offer them jobs? Most jobs are under Civil Service. Graft? Sure, you can still graft. But nowadays you can't build an unbeatable machine, so you can't be sure of staying in office and covering up about the graft. So the way to play it now is straight, see? Pass out just enough favors and jobs to keep the ward leaders sullen but quiet, and make your real play for the independent vote. That means good government. That's the Donetti platform, like it or stuff it."

Anthony grinned. "Are you sure there isn't a nasty hunk of idealism hiding in that cynicism of yours?"

"If there is," Louis said, in his file-on-metal voice, "as soon as I can get to a doc I'll take a shot of penicillin for it."

Mike said, "What do you think of him, Tony?"

"I think he'd make a good Mayor."

"But what about his chances of getting elected?"

"We never had a Mayor with an Italian name."

"Give it to us straight," Louis said. "You don't think I could win."

"All right. I don't think you'd have a prayer. You're a Republican. The Republican machine in this town is strictly from the junk yard. The Democrats are in office. They have about as strong a machine as you can put together these days. They came in on a reform ticket. They made reforms."

"That was the last four years," Louis said. "Now the boys are a bit tired of their halo. Reform is getting to be a dirty word around the Hall. I'd like to see us Republicans get going again. Even if we didn't win, we could keep the boys in the Hall slightly honest. I got nothing against Democrats. I just like a two-party system, is all. Right now we got a one-party system here, and that's never good."

312

"I couldn't agree with you more," Anthony said. "But that still doesn't elect you Mayor. Don't get sore, Louis, but outside of South Philly they never heard of you."

"I worked it out the same way," Louis said. "So I figured first I would run for District Attorney, and then four years later make a pass at being Mayor."

"District Attorney, huh? That's a better idea. But the way things are, I still don't think you can make it."

"What we want to know," Mike said, "is will you back us up if Louis runs for D.A.? You could pull in the business crowd. You could raise money. Would you do it? Do you think Louis is worth some solid backing?"

"I'll work for him. What about you?"

"What the hell," Mike said. "A machine isn't a machine unless it has a big Irish contractor. The Democrats have Kelly and McCloskey. The Republicans and Donetti need a Callahan."

"I'm with you," Anthony said. "But I still don't think it will work."

"Yes it will," Louis said. "There's one little point we didn't mention yet. We got just the right gimmick to make everything work."

"I don't believe you. What is it?"

"You'll love it," Louis crooned. "First *you* run for District Attorney. First *you* run for Mayor. Nice, huh?"

Anthony jumped up. His body felt as if it had just come from an oven. He said angrily, "That's a hell of a way to try to trap a guy."

A big red face poked close to his own, and Mike growled, "Don't tell me we tried to trap you."

Louis chuckled and said, "You two guys look enough alike to be related, standing there with your jaws poked at each other. Relax, will you?"

"I just don't want him getting any wrong ideas," Mike said, turning away and sitting down.

"I'm sorry," Anthony said. "You threw it at me too fast."

"If any trapping has been done," Louis said softly, "you did it to yourself, pal. You've been building yourself into this trap for ten years. You've been running for Mayor ever since you started playing that Robin Hood game in the magistrates' courts, and it's not our fault if you told yourself you were only out for a Sunday walk. You've been like a dame at a beach sticking her toes in the water and squealing so everybody will look at her. Well, dive in, goddam it, dive in!"

"You guys are crazy."

Mike said, "We've been nursing you along and testing you and working you into city projects for six or seven years. You can't let us down on this."

"What gives you the idea I could win an election?"

"Oh God," Louis said. "On top of everything we have to teach him politics. You got sex appeal, pal. Don't think that people forgot that Robin Hood racket you had. The little guys never forget a big guy who goes out of his way to help them. We plug that Robin Hood angle in the right places, and Robin Hood gets a hundred and fifty thousand votes. We plug that work you did on the study of the magistrates' courts and on Penn Center and the Food Distribution Center, and we get you a hundred and fifty thousand independent votes. Mike, here, twists the arms of some of the ward leaders and you got a hundred thousand organization votes. I pull fifty thousand votes for you in South Philly. You rate with the business and society crowd, and that gives you five thousand votes and all the dough we need. That's four hundred and fifty-five thousand votes, pal. Only seven hundred and seven thousand votes were cast in the last election for District Attorney. You got it made. Four years later you're a shoo-in for Mayor."

Anthony paced up and down the office a few times. The faces of his visitors—one big and red, one plump and sallow—watched him like Jack-o'Lanterns grimacing from windows. He said finally, "Outside of your crazy idea that I've been running without knowing it, and your notion that I could win, is there a single reason why I should run?"

Mike said, "You agreed with the reasons why Louis ought to run, didn't you?"

"Yes, but—"

"They go double for you."

"It was all a gag about Louis running, was it?"

"It's no gag," Louis said. "But I'm not the guy to break the hold the Democrats have on this city. You're the guy. I'll back you for D.A. and run for Council again. When you run for Mayor, I can make it as D.A. When everybody admits you've done a good job as Mayor but hates your guts for doing it, and after you've had a second term if you can take the punishment, little Louis will run for Mayor."

"You certainly make it sound attractive."

"Who wants to make it sound attractive? You'll have to get right down in the middle of the people, pal. A lot of them eat garlic and don't wash enough. All they think of is what's in it for them, and maybe you did them a favor last week but what the hell have you done for them this week? We're not inviting you to a country club. We're asking you to run a big tough city, and we're serious about it."

Anthony said, "I don't even live in the city. I live in Haverford."

"When he grabs for a straw like that," Mike said, "he's getting wobbly."

"We know where you live," Louis said. "It wouldn't matter if you did live in Haverford, because you could move back here in time. But Haverford isn't your legal residence. All these years you kept an apartment with your mother in town. You vote here in town. Do I have to quote the law to a senior member of Morris, Clayton, Biddle and Wharton? A man's domicile is where he has his permanent place of abode. Absence of months or years will not change it, if there is the intention of returning to it. You never got away from us, pal. All the time in the back of your head was the idea you belonged in the city. Of course you'd really have to move back here."

"Grace would never move into town in a million years. You don't know what you're asking me to give up."

Louis said, "If you didn't have to give up anything, you wouldn't be worth putting up for office."

"A lot of people," Mike said quietly, "have given up things to help put you where you are. Your mother's one of them."

He stared at the big old man, and a forgotten thing stirred in his mind. Once long ago, when he was a little kid, he had done something that involved his mother and Mike. It had hurt badly, and his mind had tucked the memory away in a dark corner so that it wouldn't bother him. He didn't want to drag it out now. He had a hunch, though, that if he did drag it out it would prove Mike Callahan was right.

"I'll have to think it over," he muttered. "I'll have to talk to Grace. How much time will you give me?"

"Until tomorrow morning," Louis said promptly.

"You turn on the heat pretty hard, don't you?"

"Listen," Louis said, "you've had your mind made up on this for years. Only you don't know which way it's made up, and neither do we. Whatever it is, you aren't gonna change it. You change about as easy as that statue of Billy Penn on top of the Hall. All you have to do is find out which way your mind is made up, and tell us. You could do it in two hours, but you have a right to see your wife first. Tomorrow morning. Or call Mike any time tonight if you want."

They got up and walked out slowly, without shaking hands or giving him another glance.

19

HE SAT AT the dinner table across from Grace, trying to find the right moment to bring up the subject. The two boys, little Tony and Ship, had hurried through the meal and rushed away to fire off a last skyrocket burst of energy before bedtime. There was no reason for him to wait any longer. It was hard to start, though. He had been married for seven years to this cool glossy creature who sat across from him, but he was no closer to her than on the first day they met. There would never be a right moment to bring up this subject.

"I had a couple of visitors today," he said. "Mike Callahan, of the Callahan Construction Company, and Louis Donetti. You remember Louis."

She gave a tiny shudder. "I certainly do. A very unpleasant man."

"He's all right when you get to know him."

"You do have to work with the strangest people downtown, don't you, dear? Especially in that civic work you do. Sometimes I think you do more than your share of it."

"I wonder what a person's share is."

"I suppose it's a little more than we really have time for. That's the way it works out with my charity projects."

"I hate to look at the things I do as charity."

"Darling, you can look at them in any way you want. Call it volunteer work if it makes you feel better."

"I wonder if we do enough of it."

"Poor Tony. Something's nagging at your conscience, isn't it? Just remember that you and I and people of our class do far more volunteer work than any other group does."

"It's always volunteer work, though, isn't it? I wonder if we should do some involuntary work. The kind where you can't back out when the going gets tough or when you have another engagement."

She smiled at him. "All right, dear. What did Mr. Callahan and that Donetti person want you to do?"

He took a deep breath. "They want me to run for District Attorney in the next election and for Mayor four years later."

The smile balanced delicately on her lips. "How ridiculous," she said lightly.

"That's what I told them. But they wouldn't accept it. They had all kinds of arguments."

"Of course they would."

"I ended up saying I wanted to talk to you and that I'd give them my answer by tomorrow morning."

"That was very tactful of you, Tony."

Taking a deep breath wasn't enough. What he needed was an iron lung. "I wasn't being tactful," he said. "I needed time to decide."

That knocked the smile off her lips. She stared at him as if he had showed up for dinner with a beard and dirty nails. "Oh, Tony," she said reprovingly. "Time to decide! The whole idea is impossible and you know it."

"It's not as impossible as you think. They both believe I could win and they have some good arguments. Let me tell you how they worked it out, and why they think I ought to run." He gave her all the background, and said, "So it's not ridiculous or impossible at all, don't you see?"

She had listened quietly, with no sound except a light clicking of her fingernails on the Duncan Phyfe table. "Tony darling," she said, "my remark had nothing to do with whether or not you could win. I'm willing to admit you'd be a strong candidate. But that doesn't enter into it. Nor do the reasons people might have for wanting you to run. The thing is impossible because it simply doesn't fit into our way of life."

"We've got something pretty fine here, have we?"

"Oh really, Tony! Ten generations of breeding and culture back of it, and you're going to question the way we live? Would you even for a moment consider trading this for politics? Begging the lowest type of people to vote for you? Letting your name be dragged in the mud? Moving into the city with all its dirt and noise and crime? Oh my dear, can you see me campaigning for you on street corners!" She laughed pleasantly, and rose from the table. "I'm going to round up the children and get them started for bed. I've been reading them a chapter of *Swiss Family Robinson* the last few nights. So I have to start them for bed a little earlier than usual."

She smiled at him and went out of the room, a slim straight goddess, at home in her temple and very sure of herself. He sighed, and got up and went into the living room. It was a very pleasant way of life, of course. Neat and hygienic. Insulated against rude noises. A lovely wife and two swell kids and a blue-chip career and the respect of everybody. Grace had strong arguments on her side. The trouble was that she hadn't argued with him. She had coolly taken the decision out of his hands. He was going to talk to her some more about it.

He finished the *Evening Bulletin* and riffled through a few magazines. It was odd that Grace was taking so long with the kids, even with reading them *The Swiss Family Robinson*. Apparently she considered the Robinsons a proper family for them to know. Perhaps the Robinsons were acceptable because they were the original settlers on that island of theirs. First families, you know, even if they did live in a cave. The first families of Philadelphia lived in caves along the Delaware, during their first winter as settlers. So a cave was a perfectly good address, provided that it was far enough back in history. Where the hell was she?

He went upstairs and looked in at the boys. Grace wasn't there and the kids were asleep, with *The Swiss Family Robinson* lying on the table open to a picture of someone shooting a bear. Bears were dirty smelly things and deserved to be shot, especially when they tried to push their way into the caves of the best people.

He walked down the hallway and saw light showing under the door of Grace's dressing room. He rapped on the door and called, and she told him to come in. She was sitting at the dressing table with her back to him. She had been brushing her hair, and as he entered she turned off the light on the table. He wondered if his eyes had tricked him in that second before the light went out. She had changed from the dress she wore at dinner into a black chiffon negligee. But, during the moment the table light had been on, it looked as if she had changed more than her dress. The light had probed through the chiffon and glinted on the ivory curve of shoulders and the slim taut waist and the roundness of a breast.

Now that the light was off, he couldn't tell whether or not it had been imagination. Probably it was, though. She had always been rather prudish about her body and never flaunted it in the nude.

He wasn't imagining the black chiffon negligee, however. He had given it to her several years ago. She had worn it once or twice, and then it hadn't appeared again. Later he found out that she considered black chiffon lingerie a bit vulgar. But here she was wearing it tonight.

"Tony," she said, in an oddly husky voice, "I was going to call you in a few minutes."

"Were you?"

"I wasn't fair to you when we were talking at dinner. I realized that afterward. I just brushed it all aside, didn't I?"

He was right behind her now, staring down. The lighting was dim and he still couldn't be sure what he was seeing. But it looked as though there was nothing on her body but the faint shadow of the chiffon. "You were a little rough," he said. His hands touched her gleaming hair and traced the curve of her neck and moved out slowly across her shoulders. His fingers tingled. There was nothing under the chiffon.

"You deserve better than that from me," she said, trembling under his hands. "I think you deserve more than you've had all along. Do you remember giving me this negligee?"

His fingers dug into her shoulders. "Don't pull a tease on me."

She got up quickly, and turned and moved close to him. "Listen," she said tensely, "you know I'd never give up everything and tag along with you into politics. You know that, don't you? It would mean a separation, Tony. I'd stay here and keep the boys, and you'd have to go your way alone. But I'm not going to let that happen. I'm going to keep you. Do you understand?"

"I'm not sure I do. If you want me to think clearly you'd better put some more clothes on."

"Tony, can't you stop thinking for at least a few minutes?"

He ran his hands outward along her shoulders. The chiffon whispered away from his hands and bared her shoulders and slid down her arms and body like a shadow flitting through moonlight. He didn't want his emotions to get out of control but it was not easy to keep them in line. Her body was lovely, and it had never been offered to him before tonight in this way, as if she wanted to give it.

"Do you like me this way?" she whispered. "Is this the way a woman gets her man? Because I'm going to keep you here, Tony, no matter what I have to do."

He gathered her into his arms. She was no longer a cool goddess who permitted certain rites to be celebrated over her body at traditional times of the year. This was a slim white animal that leaped at him in the dimness of the room, writhing and clawing and biting, fighting both against him and on his side. It was a mad business. You could think of it as ten generations of breeding and culture going down the drain. Or you could think of it as ten generations of tough-minded people fighting for the things they had always fought to possess. Or you could stop thinking entirely and let yourself sink into a purple darkness.

When it was all over he got up slowly and painfully and dressed himself, conscious of her lying on the bed watching him with wide questioning eyes.

"Tony," she whispered at last, "something happened to me tonight that never happened before."

"Yes?" he said. "What was that?" His voice sounded like a noise coming from a very old phonograph.

"Tony, after seven years of being married, would it be silly for me to fall in love with you?"

He didn't answer.

"It makes a difference, doesn't it, Tony? You couldn't leave me now, could you?"

He walked to the bed and bent to kiss her. It was strange to find her lips so soft and warm and yielding. He pulled the sheet up over her. "Yes, it makes a difference," he said. "It makes it just that much harder to decide. I'm going downstairs and think it over."

Behind him, as he closed the door to the room, he heard the weeping start.

20

HE CAME DOWNSTAIRS slowly from the bedroom, with the pulse of blood hammering inside his skull like a rivet gun. He had always trained himself, however, not to let things that hurt him show on the outside. So he kept a smile on his face as he went into the library. He lowered himself into the desk chair with a sigh of relief. A man felt better at his own desk. It was like a fort protecting you from a strange and sometimes hostile world. If you were fighting another man, it was always a mistake to carry the attack into his office. Get him into yours, in front of your desk, where he wouldn't feel sure of himself.

But this time his opponent was not a man. It was a woman, and women felt just as much at home fighting a man across a desk as across a bed.

The pounding in his head made him dizzy, and for a moment his thoughts whirled in every direction like autumn leaves in a gale. He had to work hard to sweep them back into neat piles. His name was Anthony Judson Lawrence and he was forty-two years old. He had come into the library to make a decision. He had made a number of important decisions in his life, and judging by the results he had made them carefully and well. But this one would be the most important of all.

When you were a lawyer you did not make snap decisions. You looked up the law and the precedents that bore on the case. He would do that now before trying his case and reaching a decision. There were ninety-nine years of precedents which had to be studied. He had been building his whole life on them, and adding new ones to the record. He unlocked a drawer of the desk and took out a photograph in an old German silver frame.

There they were, the three wonderful and rather frightening women who had created many of those precedents. His great-grandmother and grandmother were standing like sentries behind a chair. His mother was seated on it with a baby on her lap. For a family picture it was unusual because no one was looking at the camera. The three women were staring at the baby, who was looking up with wide eyes as if asking what they wanted of him. The baby's name was Anthony Judson Lawrence.

As he studied the photograph now he could feel the blood of the three women pulsing through his body and their ideas marching through his head. It was queer to feel all that so vividly and yet to know so little about the women in the picture. He knew what their hopes and beliefs had been. But he didn't know why they had clung to certain hopes and followed certain beliefs. It was like reading a judge's decision, and knowing you ought to abide by it, without having a chance to look at the testimony that came before the decision. He wished he could have read the testimony of their lives, because it would have helped him now.

However, he could read the testimony of his own life. A dozen times he had been faced by the need to make an important decision. What he had done, each time, had been to a great extent decided for him by the lives and hopes and beliefs of the three women in the photograph. So he could learn something about them, and about himself, by going to the record of those decisions.

He took each one out of its filing place in his mind and examined it carefully. This was no time to keep things hidden, so he even dug out all the details of the first decision. He had been seven years old and his hero was Uncle Mike. His mother wanted to get rid of Uncle Mike, and wasn't strong enough to do it by herself, and asked him to pretend that he didn't like the man he thought was wonderful. He knew now why he had tried so hard to forget that decision, because it was just as raw and throbbing a hurt as it had ever been. He examined it and put it aside, without digging into the question of why his mother had wanted things that way. Her reasons were private property and he was not going to trespass.

After that decision came a long line of them, some hard to make, some rather easy, some painful to remember, some that made him feel fairly good. What made each of them important was that a different decision could have changed the course of his life. He put them in question form and paraded them slowly through his mind and examined the moral problem that each contained:

Should a teen-age kid sell out his gang to help his mother?

Should a boy who is unhappy at school try once more to make a go of it, just to please his family?

Should you give up a chance to star in football because the coach says it will help the team?

Which Salutatory are you going to give—the brilliant and radical one, or the dull safe one?

Should you ask a girl to put off marrying you and having the babies she wants badly, because you don't think it's right to let somebody else support you?

Will you let passion outweigh the rules of conduct and lead you into an affair with a married woman?

Will you stick your neck out for a general who doesn't mean a thing personally to you, merely because he's doing a good job and needs to be helped out of a jam?

Will you toss away your first deep friendship with another man so that you can go on helping that same general?

Are you willing, because you want to get ahead fast, to try to steal a big client from another lawyer, when you know that the slightest mistake will wreck all your chances for the career you want?

Will you agree to defend a bum named Chet Gwynne, although that too may wreck your career?

Will you carry your defense of Gwynne to the absolute limit, and put your own class of society on trial?

Well, he had made a decision in all those cases, except the last one. He had managed to find a side exit and avoid making that decision. But apparently you could not keep on dodging a decision forever. Because right now, tonight, that decision which he had avoided making was back again, in only slightly different form. Will a man who has everything he has struggled to win pick a different way of life? It might not be so hard to decide, except that he had just won a final thing which he had wanted. Grace was falling in love with him.

When you came right down to it, however, was he really facing a different way of life in the career Mike Callahan and Louis Donetti had mapped out for him? Or would it be the same way of life he had always followed? Would it be like an old familiar house in which merely a little of the furniture had been changed? And would staying with Grace be like tearing down the house and keeping the furniture?

Now that he had thought things over, it turned out that he didn't have to make a decision after all. It had been pieced together for him over the long slow years by many people. The decision was there waiting for him, already made. He had been carefully trained and you could count on him to do the predictable thing.

He lifted the telephone and dialed a number. After a minute's wait, the growl of Mike Callahan rumbled across the wires. "Yeah?" Mike said. "Yeah?"

"This is Tony."

"Yeah, I knew when I picked up the phone."

"I'm with you, Mike."

There was a rather long silence.

Anthony said, "Did you hear me?"

"Yeah," Mike said, a bit more hoarsely than usual. "I heard you. I was just thinking, it kinda makes things worth while."

"What does it make worth while?"

"Oh, just a personal matter. All right, Tony, thanks for calling. Louis and I will drop in on you tomorrow. Good night."

"Good night," Anthony said, and slowly hung up the phone.

A light footstep sounded at the doorway, and Grace came in. She wore a heavy dressing gown fastened tightly up around her throat, and above it her face looked pale. "I heard your telephone call," she said. "I've been sitting outside the door for two hours, waiting for you to make it. I knew you were going to make it, and what you were going to say."

"You know me fairly well, don't you?"

She walked to the window and parted the curtains and stared out. "You can see the glow of the city from here, can't you?" she said. "It's not the sort of view most people think of, when they talk of the lights of a city. They're thinking about diamonds on black velvet. All you can see from here is just a big dirty glow, made up of tiny particles of dust and fog that pick up the shine of electricity and the glare of neon tubes. It's hard to believe that anybody can have a love affair with a city. And yet some people do."

He didn't know what was in her mind, so he didn't answer.

She turned and snapped the curtains shut behind her. "Where will we live?" she said. "Are there still some good addresses left in town, Tony?"

He smiled and got up and walked toward her. Perhaps she hadn't really had to make a decision, either. Perhaps it had been waiting for her, pieced together over the years by many people. You could count on her, also, to do the predictable thing.

—The End—

MORE GREAT FICTION AND NONFICTION
FROM PLEXUS PUBLISHING, INC.

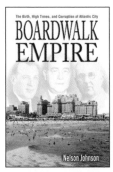

BOARDWALK EMPIRE
The Birth, High Times, and Corruption of Atlantic City
By Nelson Johnson

"This is the best book I've read on Atlantic City ... extremely well researched and documented ... reads like a novel."
—Robert Peterson, *Egg Harbor News*

Atlantic City's popularity rose in the early 20th century and peaked during Prohibition. For 70 years, it was controlled by a partnership comprised of local politicians and racketeers, including Enoch "Nucky" Johnson—the second of three bosses to head the political machine that dominated city politics and society. In *Boardwalk Empire*, Atlantic City springs to life in all its garish splendor. Author Nelson Johnson traces "AC" from its birth as a quiet seaside health resort, through the notorious backroom politics and power struggles, to the city's rebirth as an entertainment and gambling mecca where anything goes.

Softbound/ISBN 0-937548-49-9/$18.95

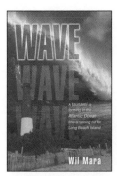

WAVE
A novel by Wil Mara

As this exciting thriller opens, it's a beautiful spring morning on Long Beach Island. High overhead, aboard a 747 bound for the U.S. capital, a terrorist's plot has gone awry. The plane nosedives into the Atlantic and a nuclear device detonates, creating a massive undersea landslide. Within minutes, a tsunami is born and a series of formidable waves begins moving toward the Jersey shore. The people of LBI are sitting ducks, with only one bridge to the mainland and less than three hours to evacuate.

Hardbound/ISBN 0-937548-56-1/$22.95

KATE AYLESFORD
OR, THE HEIRESS OF SWEETWATER
A novel by Charles J. Peterson
With a new Foreword by Robert Bateman

"Plot twists, colorful characters, timely observations, lyrical descriptions of the Pine Barrens, and ... an unusually strong and well-educated female protagonist."—Robert Bateman, from the Foreword to the new edition

The legendary historical romance, *Kate Aylesford: A Story of Refugees*, by Charles J. Peterson, first appeared in 1855, was reissued in 1873 as *The Heiress of Sweetwater*, and spent the entire 20th century out of print. As readable today as when Peterson first penned it, *Kate Aylesford* features a memorable cast of characters, an imaginative plot, and a compelling mix of romance, adventure, and history. Plexus Publishing is pleased to return this remarkable novel to print.

Hardbound/ISBN 0-937548-46-4/$22.95

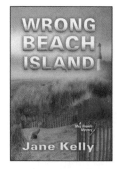

WRONG BEACH ISLAND
A novel by Jane Kelly

When the body of millionaire Dallas Spenser washes up on Long Beach Island with a bullet in its back, it derails Meg Daniels's plans for a romantic sailing trip. As Meg gets involved in the unraveling mystery, she soon learns that Spenser had more skeletons than his Loveladies mansion had closets. The ensuing adventure twists and turns like a boardwalk roller coaster and involves Meg with an unforgettable cast of characters.

From the beaches of Holgate and Beach Haven at the southern end of LBI to the grand homes of Loveladies and the famed Barnegat Light at the north, author Jane Kelly delivers an irresistible blend of mystery and humor in *Wrong Beach Island*—her third and most deftly written novel. Meg Daniels, Kelly's reluctant heroine, may be the funniest and most original sleuth ever to kill time at the Jersey shore.

Hardbound/ISBN 0-937548-47-2/$22.95
Softbound/ISBN 0-937548-59-6/$14.95

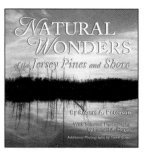

NATURAL WONDERS OF THE JERSEY PINES AND SHORE
By Robert A. Peterson with selected photographs by Michael A. Hogan

Additional photographs by Steve Greer

"In capturing the beauty and uniqueness of southern New Jersey, Natural Wonders makes it clear why so many people have worked so hard to save its treasure of nature and human history. This extraordinary book will inspire readers to cherish the Pine Barrens and coastal estuaries anew."—Carleton Montgomery, Executive Director, Pinelands Preservation Alliance

In this exquisite book, 57 short yet informative chapters by the late Robert Peterson celebrate a range of "natural wonders" associated with the Pine Barrens and coastal ecosystems of southern New Jersey. The diverse topics covered include flora, fauna, forces of nature, and geological formations—from birds, mammals, and mollusks, to bays, tides, trees, wildflowers, and much more. More than 200 stunning full-color photos by award-winning photographers Michael Hogan and Steve Greer bring Peterson's delightful vignettes to life. For South Jersey aficionados—young and old alike—this is a book to treasure.

Hardbound/ISBN 0-937548-48-0/$49.95

DOWN BARNEGAT BAY
A Nor'easter Midnight Reader
By Robert Jahn

Down Barnegat Bay is an illustrated maritime history of the Jersey shore's Age of Sail. Originally published in 1980, this fully revised Ocean County Sesquicentennial Edition features more than 177 sepia illustrations, including 75 new images and nine maps. Jahn's engaging tribute to the region brims with first-person accounts of the people, events, and places that have come together to shape Barnegat Bay's unique place in American history.

Hardbound/ISBN 0-937548-42-1/$39.95

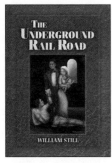

THE UNDERGROUND RAIL ROAD

By William Still

"The Underground Rail Road *is a masterpiece ... a powerful and triumphant work that demands our attention.*" —Bill Cosby

Originally published in 1872 and out of print for many years, this landmark book presents firsthand accounts of slaves escaping north via the human support network known as the Underground Railroad. The narratives were painstakingly documented by William Still (1821–1902), a son of emancipated slaves who helped guide untold numbers of fugitives to safety in the mid-19th century. Based in Philadelphia, he corresponded with, interviewed, and recorded the stories of hundreds of fugitives at great personal risk. The 2005 edition features the complete 1872 text, including more than 200 slave narratives, 60+ black and white illustrations, hundreds of letters and newspaper clippings, and biographical sketches of abolitionists and other contributors to the cause of freedom. By turns heartbreaking, horrifying, and inspiring, *The Underground Rail Road* is a remarkable reading experience.

Hardbound/ISBN 0-937548-55-3/$49.50

GATEWAY TO AMERICA
World Trade Center Memorial Edition

By Gordon Bishop
Photographs by Jerzy Koss

Based on the acclaimed PBS documentary, *Gateway to America* is both a comprehensive guidebook and history. It covers the historic New York/New Jersey triangle that was the window for America's immigration wave in the 19th and 20th centuries. In addition to commemorating the World Trade Center, the book explores Ellis Island, The Statue of Liberty, and six other Gateway landmarks including Liberty State Park, Governors Island, Battery City Park, South Street Seaport, Newport, and the Gateway National Recreational Area. A must for history buffs and visitors to the area alike.

Softbound/ISBN 0-937548-44-8/$19.95

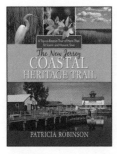

THE NEW JERSEY COASTAL HERITAGE TRAIL
A Top-to-Bottom Tour of More than 50 Scenic and Historic Sites

By Patricia Robinson

"*This comprehensive guide will surely be a treasured resource for those who hope to discover—or rediscover—all that New Jersey has to offer.*"
—Thomas J. Kean, from the Foreword

Patricia Robinson (*Wonderwalks*) brings together all the information you'll need to explore and enjoy the New Jersey Coastal Heritage Trail. From Perth Amboy Harbor in the northeast to Fort Mott State Park in the southwest, this 275-mile stretch of Jersey coast links more than 50 natural and historic destinations. Whether you plan to visit one or all of them, this well-organized, fully-illustrated guide makes it fun and easy. It includes a description of each site along with driving directions, contact data, history, trivia, and more, plus seasonal lists of flora and fauna you may encounter, over 100 full-color photographs, and recommendations of the best sites for bird-watching, biking, camping, dining, hiking, paddling, picnicking, and many other outdoor activities.

Softbound/ISBN 0-937548-58-8/$19.95

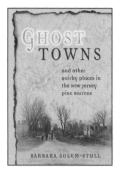

GHOST TOWNS AND OTHER QUIRKY PLACES IN THE NEW JERSEY PINE BARRENS

By Barbara Solem-Stull

The Pine Barrens of New Jersey contain more ghost towns, some say, than the entire American west. Author Barbara Solem-Stull tells the story of the towns that rose up around the iron furnaces, glass factories, paper mills, cranberry farms, and brickmaking establishments of the 18th, 19th, and early 20th centuries. With easy-to-use maps and over 100 photographs and illustrations, the book provides driving directions and self-guided walking tours of many of the Pine Barrens' intriguing historic sites and ruins.

Softbound/ISBN 0-937548-60-X/$19.95

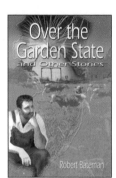

OVER THE GARDEN STATE AND OTHER STORIES

By Robert Bateman

Novelist Bateman (*Pinelands, Whitman's Tomb*) offers six new stories set in his native Southern New Jersey. While providing plenty of authentic local color in his portrayal of small-town and farm life, the bustle of the Jersey shore with its boardwalks, and the solitude and otherworldliness of the famous Pine Barrens, Bateman's sensitively portrayed protagonists are the stars here. The title story tells of an Italian prisoner of war laboring on a South Jersey farm circa 1944. There, he finds danger and dreams, friendship and romance—and, ultimately, more fireworks than he could have wished for.

Hardbound/ISBN 0-937548-40-5/$22.95

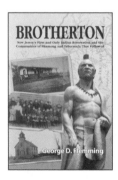

BROTHERTON

New Jersey's First and Only Indian Reservation and the Communities of Shamong and Tabernacle That Followed

By George D. Flemming; Foreword by Budd Wilson

In *Brotherton*, author George D. Flemming presents the history of the Brotherton Indian reservation (1758–1802)—the only Indian reservation ever established in the state of New Jersey—and the communities that followed. Following the exodus of the Brotherton Lenapes from the reservation, white settlements and industries began to dominate the area. Flemming chronicles the early churches and schools, hotels and taverns, forges, furnaces, mills, and notable citizens of "Old Shamong."

Hardbound/ISBN 0-937548-61-8/$34.95
Softbound/ISBN 0-937548-57-X/$24.95

To order or for a catalog: 609-654-6500, Fax Order Service: 609-654-4309

Plexus Publishing, Inc.

143 Old Marlton Pike • Medford • NJ 08055
E-mail: info@plexuspublishing.com
www.plexuspublishing.com